Books by Pamela L. Todd

Beautiful Sinners

Secrets, Lies & Vegas
Secrets, Lies & Imperfections
Secrets, Lies & Revelations

Single Titles

Now You See Me
When You're

I0607506

Secrets, Lies & Revelations

ISBN # 978-1-78686-151-1

©Copyright Pamela L. Todd 2017

Cover Art by Posh Gosh ©Copyright 2017

Interior text design by Claire Siemaszkiewicz

Totally Bound Publishing

Published in 2017 by Totally Bound Publishing, Think Tank, Ruston Way, Lincoln, LN6 7FL, United Kingdom.

Beautiful Sinners

SECRETS, LIES & REVELATIONS

PAMELA L. TODD

Dedication

Well, here it is, Mrs. Stewart! Thank you for all your
support, your love and warmth.
You're a fantastic neighbor, and an even better friend.
Now go find the character you so generously donated
your name to!
A special nod must be given to my super special cousin,
Susan. I am so grateful for all your encouragement and
your enthusiasm. I've left a surprise for you amongst the
pages.
And for Nick, the best friend a girl could ask for.
Here's to all the parties we had, and still enjoying them in
our nineties.

Chapter One

As always, the food at Per Se was out of this world. The restaurant drew in a different class of clientele, a certain pedigree who only wanted the best. Situated in Midtown, it was elegant and intimate without being overly pretentious — crisp white linens, sparkling hardwood floors and wide, clear windows that showed off stellar views of Central Park and Columbus Circle. Tonight was a beautiful night, the city flung out before us like a perfect, twinkly Van Gogh painting.

I felt like a million bucks in my vintage Dior black cocktail dress. The deep V neckline flattered my modest chest, the fitted waist and back criss-cross straps gave it a sexy edge without being overt. And the front pleat that made the material swish when I walked was just for fun. The man sitting across from me looked like he dined in this kind of restaurant every night of his life. Which, incidentally, he pretty much did.

Marcus Tate was a thirty-two-year-old investment banker for a leading firm in the city. He was the youngest broker to have scored top figures for his clients, resulting in a hefty pay packet for himself and an arrogance that came from building yourself up and *knowing* you were the shit. That, and he was hung like a boss. His face was nice to look at, too.

We'd met a few months ago at the Met and had hit it off after discovering our mutual hatred for the tourists that crowded all the best displays. Tonight marked our five-month anniversary and I couldn't help but wonder what the rest of the evening would bring. Marcus was the kind of guy who liked to throw his money around. So far in our romance he'd spoiled me rotten, whisking me away for long weekends, buying me jewelry and *shoes*. Marcus was, without a doubt, my ultimate Prince Charming.

Once our table was cleared after dessert, Marcus shifted in his seat. He finished the rest of his wine in one gulp. "I had a specific reason for inviting you here tonight," Marcus said as he met my eye.

"Our anniversary wasn't enough?" I asked, giving him a playful smile.

Marcus blinked. His face took on a rosy hue and he nodded. "Our anniversary. Of course." He blew out a breath and shifted in his chair again.

Man, he's nervous tonight. Oh, God. Marcus was never nervous. Like, ever. So it stood to reason that whatever he was trying to say was a doozy. *Oh my God... Was he—was Marcus about to propose?*

"Hayley, these last few months have flown by. It feels like I've hardly blinked and yet here we are, five months in. You're fun and energetic, and I love that fire you have inside you."

Remember every second of this—don't you dare forget!

"It's time I got serious. I'm facing a promising career and my responsibilities are only going to increase. I'm not a stupid kid anymore and it's time I stopped acting like it. Which is why I'm breaking up with you."

I gasped and pressed a hand to my chest, my eyes filling. A girlish laugh lodged in my throat and—wait a second, did he say *break up*? Marcus was breaking up with me?

"I really care for you, Hayley, but we were never going to be serious. And it's time that I was. I can't dick around for another few years—I need to settle down." Marcus gave me a kind smile that made me want to punch him in the throat. "And you're not the kind of girl who settles down."

"I'm sorry, I just want to check something since my brain and my ears seem to be arguing with each other—you want to break up with me because you want to settle down...

just not with someone like me?" I asked. This couldn't be happening. Marcus was perfect for me, in that lukewarm, affectionate kind of way. He was the epitome of everything I had ever wanted for myself...and now he was ending it?

"Yes, exactly."

"What the *fuck*?" I exclaimed, louder than I'd intended. A few curious stares were sent our way and I guessed this was the exact reason I wasn't the kind to settle down with. "Are you seriously breaking up with me on our five-month anniversary?"

Marcus tapped his fingers on the table. "Come on, that isn't even a real thing."

"Of course it is!" I huffed. "What, so, are first kiss anniversaries not a real thing either? Or the one-month anniversary of the first time we slept together? Because I seem to remember how enthusiastically you enjoyed that one."

All humor drained from Marcus' face. "Hayley—"

"For chrissake, Marcus, my dad was the mayor of New Haven! My mom's family comes from old railroad money. I'm not a goddamn nobody." I drew in a quick breath and clenched my hands into fists to stop them shaking. Christ, had I really just said that? What an idiot. It was totally true, though—my family was extremely well respected back home. We had a comfortable life that I—most of the time, anyway—didn't take for granted. It allowed me to do pretty much whatever I wanted here in the city.

"It's not about status," Marcus said, lifting his hand in a bid to get me to lower my voice. "Hell, your background is half the reason—" He stopped himself mid-sentence.

A surprising calmness settled in my blood as I pinned him with my stare. "Half the reason you what, Marcus?"

He shook his head and seemed to decide against finishing the sentence. "You're not a serious girl, Hayley. How many nights out a week do you have? Half the time you aren't even home before dawn. I'm sorry, but I left that behind in my twenties."

Our waiter approached the table with his hands clasped behind his back. "Can I get you anything else this evening?"

Marcus opened his mouth to answer, but I beat him to the punch. "Actually, yes, we'll take the Barbaresco. The 2011 Gaja, I think, will do nicely."

"Of course. Glass or the bottle?"

I winked at Marcus. "Oh, the bottle, please. We are celebrating, after all."

The waiter nodded. "May I ask what the occasion is?"

"It's a double actually — our five-month anniversary, and also our breakup." I wrinkled my nose in a 'how cute is that' sort of way.

He glanced between Marcus and me for a second. "Coming right up."

Wise man.

Once the waiter was out of earshot, Marcus' polite smile fell and he shot me a hard glare. "A four-hundred-dollar bottle of wine? Really?"

I shrugged and flashed him a carefree, happy, not-the-type-to-settle-down grin. "Call it a parting gift."

And so we sat in tense silence while I drank most of that damn bottle. It was too dry for my taste, not something I'd usually choose. But it was the principle of the matter. Marcus settled the bill and walked me out of the restaurant with his hand on the small of my back.

"I hope you find what you're looking for, Marcus," I said, pulling my phone out of my purse.

"You too, Hayley," Marcus said quietly before slipping away. To avoid another scene, no doubt.

Giving him a jaunty salute, I dialed Eve's number and looked down the street for a cab with its light on.

"Hey, girl," Eve said as she answered, a blast of club music behind her. "Aren't you out on the super romantic not-really-an-anniversary dinner with Marcus?"

I snorted. Whatever. Five months totally qualified for an anniversary. "Yeah, during which he dumped me. In the middle of Per Se."

Eve gasped. "Are you kidding?"

"Nope. Where are you guys tonight? I so need my girls."

I just wished my main girl was here. But no. She was living it up in Vegas with the love of her life.

Eve giggled. "We're at Industry. Are you coming out?"

A cab pulled up at the curb in front of me and I paused with my hand on the door. "The gay bar in Hell's Kitchen?"

"One and the same. Get your ass down here, girl. See you in a few." Eve disconnected the call before I could even argue.

Not that I wanted to.

What was the one thing that was sure to cheer a girl up after getting her ass dumped by the guy who was so *not* her Prince Charming? Dancing the night away with ridiculously hot men who wanted nothing more than to compliment her fabulous vintage dress.

Hot guys. No pressure. I was so there.

* * * *

Industry was one of the hottest gay bars in the city. I'd been once before—Marley and I had ended up there one night, drunk off our asses on cocktails, and had had a blast. I think. It was mostly a blur, as was the photographic evidence.

The sidewalk bustled outside Industry as I stepped out of the cab. The music inside the bar poured onto the street. The sidewalk was crowded with bodies—people smoking, people laughing and enjoying the night. Inside, the place was packed and I pushed my way through, trying to find Beth and Eve. It shouldn't have been hard—there was probably only a handful of women in the bar. Men, men, fit, hot men as far as the eye could...

Stop. Focus.

Beth and Eve. If I were a man-loving, energetic ball of fun looking to have a good time, where would I be?

Right where *I* would be—in the middle of a man-sandwich

on the dance floor.

Sure enough, I spotted Eve's short blonde hair and Beth's long, curly brunette locks among the chiseled pecs and sweaty torsos. They bumped and grinded with the best of them. Beth saw me first as I made my way toward them. Her face lit up and she reached out to grab my hand and tug me into the middle of their huddle.

Eve threw her arms around my shoulders, screaming something I couldn't quite make out. I hugged her back and laughed at how excited she and Beth were.

"Why have we never been here before?" Beth asked with a giggle.

A tall, ripped dude with a shaved head strutted past us in a pair of jeans that left nothing to the imagination. "I have no idea," I said, my eyes glued to his ass.

"Girl, that dress is hot," Eve said, shaking her hips to the music. "Where'd you find that one?"

Beth held up a hand before I could answer. "When will you learn? I don't want to hear about how she rifled through some dead old lady's closet."

I threw my head back with a laugh. "My God, you make it sound so seedy! It is what I was hired for, you know. I don't just stalk the obits and go knocking on their door."

We danced for the next few songs, loving the attention we got from guys who actually wanted to dance with us and loving even more that we didn't have to worry about unwanted hands.

By the end of the third song, I was a hot mess. I signaled to the girls that I was going to the bar and they nodded. It took some time to push my way through the throng of bodies. I found a prime spot of bar real estate and prepared myself for a hefty wait.

My usual feminine wiles wouldn't work in my favor here.

Yes, it being a gay bar, I expected good-looking guys to be served faster than me. But fifteen minutes was a joke. The diva behind the bar was getting a seriously crappy tip. When the guy beside me—who had just appeared only seconds ago—got served, I huffed and popped a hip, fully intent on running my mouth.

"Whatever you're about to say, I advise you—don't."

At the sound of the masculine voice with the deep New York accent, I turned to the body on the other side of me.

And Holy Hot Guy, Batman.

Was it Superhero night or something? Because I was pretty sure Thor was in front of me right now. Looking at me with clear, pale blue eyes and a quirky, amused smile on full, luscious lips. He was tall—clearing six foot and then some, with dirty blond hair that was styled back off his face. And Jesus Christ, was he built. Broad, muscular shoulders, strong, thick arms and a narrow waist. His thighs strained against the denim of his jeans and I'd bet my favorite pair of Manolos that I could grate cheese on the abs hidden beneath the crisp white shirt that accentuated his golden tan.

His smile widened and I was surprised he didn't hand me a napkin to wipe the drool I was sure had gathered on my chin.

"I'm sorry, what?" I asked, trying to shake away the hot-guy fog that clouded my brain and cognitive functions.

Hot Guy jerked his head toward the bartender. "That one doesn't take kindly to threats. Or angry women."

I cut a glance to the bartender, who was still actively not looking in my direction. So much so that he had completely overlooked the freaking God beside me. Ha. Served him right.

"What are you drinking?" the guy asked me. "I'll order for you. Turn around and pretend you don't know me."

A laugh bubbled in my throat. "I *don't* know you. For all I know you could be a predator."

He grinned. "And if I were, I'd pick my venues a little differently, don't you think?"

Well, he had a point. Any man looking to stalk innocent women wouldn't do it in a gay bar, for chrissakes. I smiled at him. "Thanks. I'll take a cosmo." I reached into my purse for some cash but he stopped me with a hand on my arm.

"I got it. Now turn around and put that cute little pissed-off frown back on," he said with a wink.

I did as I was told and the second my back was turned, a sharp whistle sounded from behind me. The bitchy bartender glared in my direction, but his face soon smoothed over when he saw who was actually doing the whistling.

The bartender didn't spare a glance my way as he sauntered toward us. He leaned an elbow on the bar and drank up my gallant hero with his eyes. "What can I get you?"

"Cosmo and a Heineken. And whatever you're drinking."

Well. That just took him down a notch or two in my estimations. He clearly had terrible taste in men, if his type was bartender on a power trip.

They bantered back and forth for a minute and when my best friend had our drinks he picked them up and gave me an imperceptible nod to follow him. And like the grownup I was, I resisted the urge to stick my tongue out at the bartender before I left.

I followed him through the bar, made easier by the fact that he cut a clear path through the bodies with his huge frame. He took a seat on a low couch and patted the spot beside him. No one else paid us a speck of attention as I squeezed in next to him. It was a good thing I was small—he took up more room than the average person.

He handed me the cocktail, his fingers brushing mine as I accepted it. "So. What's your name and what brings you here tonight?"

I laughed at his candor. "I'm Hayley. And my charming boyfriend dumped me over dinner, so I called my girlfriends. They were already here having a girls' night out, so I joined them. You?"

He blinked. "You got dumped? What the hell for? He has seen you, right? I mean, he's not blind or anything?"

Man, he was sweet. Gorgeous, sweet and considerate enough to look out for a stranger at a bar. Why were all the best ones gay? "Nope, not blind. Just serious about his future," I said, rolling my eyes. "And apparently, I'm not the kind of girl you get serious about."

"What a jackass." He raked me over with a gaze that left me feeling naked and well and truly sized up. When his eyes met mine again, they were as serious as Marcus claimed I wasn't. "An absolute, clueless jackass."

Seriously — why were all the best ones gay? "So, are you ever going to tell me your name?"

His smile widened, flashing straight, white teeth. Man, he had a gorgeous smile. "Colton. Colton Deluca." He shrugged one shoulder. "Just Colt is fine. And I'm here with my friend. These kind of places make him nervous, so I'm here for moral support."

Add extra sweet and thoughtful to the list of reasons why I wished he were straight. "That's sweet of you."

Colt's smile turned modest. "He'd do the same for me. So, tell me about yourself, Hayley…"

"St. Clair," I supplied. "Do you come here often?"

He leaned a fraction closer, his delicious, masculine cologne teasing my senses as I drowned in his piercing gaze. "Are you hitting on me?"

A blush warmed my cheeks. *Jeez, I'm such an idiot.* "No — God no, could you imagine?" I let out a nervous laugh and shifted away from him, turning my head so I could swallow half my cocktail in one without him noticing and giving him the impression I had a drinking problem along with a *thinking* problem.

I tipped my head back to drain the rest of my glass. Colt startled me by prying it out of my hand when I was done. He rose from his seat and touched my shoulder, a wide, friendly smile stretching across his gorgeous face. "Relax, St. Clair. I've got you."

Colt pushed his way through the crowd, heading for the bar again. I watched his backside, marveling at how I'd suddenly become an ass woman. He glanced over his shoulder, grinning when he caught me staring. A full-body blush tore through me and I lowered my gaze.

He turned back around when the bartender approached him in record time.

"Who's the beefcake?"

I almost jumped a foot in the air as Beth and Eve dropped themselves onto the couch beside me. Releasing a long breath, I smiled at the uncanny sixth sense my two friends had when it came to a hot guy in their vicinity. "Colton Deluca. He saved me at the bar when I couldn't get served."

Eve snorted, disgruntled. "Only downside of partying here. My boobs don't work."

Beth nodded sympathetically. "Why did we even decide to come here?"

At that moment, three ripped, beautiful guys with sharp haircuts walked past the table.

"That's why," Eve murmured. "This place is amazing. It's like being at an all-you-can-eat buffet and knowing you can eat whatever you want with no risk of calories."

"Or heartbreak, in our case," I said.

Beth squeezed my knee. "Sweetie, he's an ass. We never liked him anyway."

This made me sit up straighter. "What? You said last Tuesday that you thought he was perfect for me."

Beth scrunched her face up. "Because that's what you say to friends."

Wrong…that's what you say to casual acquaintances. You tell friends the truth. Man, I miss my girl.

"Are you bumming out my new friend?"

We all twisted around as Colt reclaimed his seat beside me. He handed me my fresh cocktail and winked before turning his sharp gaze to Beth and Eve.

"We were talking about her most recent ex, so, yeah. Sort of," Beth said with a wide grin.

One of Eve's favorite songs came on and she grabbed Beth's hand. "You coming, Hayles?"

I glanced at Colt and shook my head. "I'm going to miss this one out."

14

Neither of them argued, and they stormed the dance floor once again.

"Are you okay?" Colt asked quietly.

Giving my head a quick shake to shed my sudden drop in mood, I smiled my fullest, even if it didn't feel completely genuine. "I'm fine. Just a little sting."

Colt nodded in understanding. "Tomorrow it will feel better."

"Nothing a night with my favorite man and a bottle of wine...maybe some raw cookie dough, too, won't cure."

"And who is your favorite man?"

"Warren Beatty."

Colt blinked. "Warren Beatty?"

I lifted one eyebrow. "Is there something wrong with Warren Beatty?"

"Is he even still alive?"

Unable to hold back my huff, I folded my arms. "Of course he is. I like his movies, what's wrong with that?"

"Nothing, nothing," Colt said. He sipped his beer, his lips curving into a smile.

Sighing, I waved my hand at him. "Make fun of me, it's fine. I'm used to it."

Colt's lips twitched. "Can't imagine why."

"I like old movies."

"So I can tell." Colt rubbed his jaw. "Okay, what I'm about to tell you is confidential. Do you understand?"

I nodded, completely curious about what he could have to say.

"I don't admit this to anyone, but I'm feeling the need to even things up between us." He leaned a degree closer and the gentle tease of his enticing aftershave wreaked havoc on my nervous system. "I like Disney movies."

"What?" I asked.

Colt shook his head. "Actually, make that love Disney movies. Mostly animated, but I have a soft spot for the likes of *Eight Below* and *Homeward Bound*."

For a second, I couldn't even process what he had told

me. Was he messing with me? This man...this *man* man—a man so much more of a man than I had ever really seen before—liked the softest brand of movies ever made? "Are you joking?"

He smiled. "Wish I were. Sadly, my Netflix recommendations can attest to my taste in movies."

A startled laugh bubbled in my throat. "Oh my God...you're totally serious, aren't you?"

"I could take you home with me to prove it, if you'd like." Colt nudged me with his shoulder. "We could have a sleepover and watch all the movies from your childhood."

I wrinkled my nose. "Thanks, but I'll pass. There is nothing more depressing than a Disney flick."

"What? You think Disney is depressing?"

"Of course!" I cried. "A parent dies, a kid gets lost, a robot is alone on Earth...they're all the same."

He perused me with those clear, blue eyes. He gave his head a soft shake, as if he had been disappointed. "Woman, you have no idea. Do you even watch them to the end?"

"No," I admitted as I shifted uncomfortably in my seat.

"Then maybe you need a re-education," Colt murmured.

My cheeks warmed from the flush of attention that came from the keen gaze of an attractive man, and I had to remind myself both where I was and, more importantly, where *he* was. This Disney debate was not a come on...granted, in a different situation it would have been weird then, too.

"Besides, let me ask you this—you like Warren Beatty?" Colt grinned. "What's your favorite movie?"

Well, damn.

Colt's smile widened. "Tell me."

I took a breath and resigned myself to my fate. "*Bonnie and Clyde.*"

"And that isn't depressing?"

"It's romantic!"

"It's flawed bullshit. There is nothing romantic about being shot to death by the police after ripping off a bunch of banks." Colt shook his head and took a drink from his beer bottle. "Besides, Bonnie only ran off with Clyde because she was bored."

"She did not," I protested. "She ran away with him because she finally met someone who spoke to her soul, who—you know what? I'm so not doing this."

Colt's eyebrows shot up. "Doing what?"

"Everyone makes fun of me for liking old movies and being a romantic at heart. I really don't feel like having someone else tell me how stupid I am." I finished my cocktail in one and set the empty glass down on the table in front of me.

"Hayley, we're having a debate about movies. No more, no less." A soft smile touched Colt's lips. "Actually, that's not true. I'm taking your mind off of other stuff. Right?"

I blinked. He was right. For the first time that night, Marcus wasn't present in my thoughts. Not even his shadow.

Colt's smile widened. "Told you."

Man, this guy was amazing. What a goddamn waste that I couldn't have him. But whatever. Life was full of unfairness. At least tonight I could enjoy him however he let himself be enjoyed. *Wow, way to sound creepy, Hayley.* I laughed under my breath. "Want to do some shots with me?"

He nodded. "Sure. Then after that, how about you dance with the best-looking guy in here?"

I giggled. Like I was ten years old again. "Absolutely."

Colt accepted the money I insisted on giving him for the next round, and he returned shortly with another beer for him, a cosmo for me and a couple of shots. I didn't ask what they were, and I would bet any money that they were a lethal cocktail of high percentage alcohol the bar had concocted.

The minute our drinks were finished, Colt grasped my hand and pulled me to my feet. He led us through the crowd to the dance floor and glanced at me over his shoulder, a half-grin pulling at his lips.

Music pulsed through me, fast and hard. We were surrounded by a mass of sweaty, writhing bodies as the crowd took on an almost animalistic tribal dance. Colt cleared a space with his large frame. With a hand on my hip, he drew me into his body and — Oh holy hell…the man could move.

Not to buy into a crappy stereotype or anything, but Colt had moves like I'd never seen before. For a big guy, he had a kind of grace, similar to the muscular litheness of a lion. Colt moved his hips and I was hypnotized. My head swam with him, every nerve ending hyperaware of every inch of Colt.

And if I hadn't met him in a gay bar, I'd be taking him home with me tonight.

I caught sight of Beth and Eve, who both grinned and nodded their appreciation of Colt and his undisputed hotness. My friends weren't the only ones who stared. Countless eyes were on us but I couldn't bring myself to care.

Colt lowered his head so he could murmur in my ear. "Do you see how many people are staring at you right now?" His breath was warm and sent a shiver down my spine.

"Yeah. They're out for my blood because I'm monopolizing the best-looking guy in here," I said, parroting his earlier words.

He laughed low in his throat and I felt it rumble in his chest. "Maybe. But I'll protect you, don't worry."

"You'd better. These guys would eat me alive."

Colt chuckled again. He tugged me closer to him, wrapping his arm around my lower back. "You're tiny."

I felt small and petite and absolutely feminine in his presence. Colt crowded me with his body in a way that made me dizzy. It wasn't surprising that he found me tiny. I doubted I was his regular body-type of choice. "You're huge."

"I like you, St. Clair," Colt commented. "I'm really glad my friend is such a wimp."

"Me too," I said, peering up into his clear blue eyes. "Thanks to him, my night went from sucking ass to pretty decent."

He pulled back a little, frowning as though he were offended. "Pretty decent? That's all I am to you?"

I pretended. "Maybe."

For another few hours I lost myself in Colt's company. He was attentive and focused all his attention on me. We danced and drank and I forgot all about why I was in a crappy mood to begin with.

Beth and Eve left. Whether they'd gone home, or to another bar, I had no idea.

"Just you and me, St. Clair," Colt said as he placed his empty beer bottle on the table.

"Another drink?" I asked.

He shook his head softly. "I've hit my limit. Any more and I'll go from cheerfully drunk to crying outside in my underwear."

A laugh bubbled in my throat. "Why does that make me want to buy you another?"

"Because you're a sadist?" he asked, chuckling. "Come on, St. Clair. I'll get you a cab."

I wanted to argue, to come up with some other reason for us to stay. But when I rose to my feet I swayed and would have done a spectacular face-plant had Colt not had a firm grip of my elbow. "Yeah, okay. But I'll warn you — my limit was around three shots ago."

The crisp night air hit me square in the face when we stepped outside. The city was still alive with bustle and noise, proving once again that it didn't sleep. At the edge of the curb, Colt held his hand out to flag down a cab.

He curled an arm around my waist to keep me close to him and I appreciated the anchor. As well as the masculine scent of him. The large bulk of his frame. Screw it — I appreciated everything.

Colt had given me the best night I'd had since Marley had uprooted her life here in Manhattan and crossed the country to Vegas. And I didn't want it to end. At all.

"Hey, Colt?"

He swung his cool, pale blue eyes to meet my gaze.

My heart stuttered and I prepared myself for rejection, but I didn't care. I had to ask. "Come home with me?"

Chapter Two

Colt ignored my protests and paid the cab driver when we arrived at my place in SoHo. We stumbled out of the cab and into my building, to find that the elevator was busted — again — and we had to climb the stairs.

I'd bet Everest wasn't as challenging.

Especially in my heels.

At long last we reached my floor and I flung open the door after negotiating my locks.

Colt turned in a slow circle in the middle of my living room, scanning all the little quirks that made up my apartment. "I like your style, St. Clair. All your styles. Except — what the hell is that? An egg?"

I huffed and crossed the room to my pride and joy. "No. It's a sixties swivel chair. It took me forever to find a genuine one of these. I reupholstered it myself." I stroked my hand over the soft white velvet lining and smiled. It had been Marley's favorite when she visited.

Colt tugged on the end of my hair. "I'm messing with you. It's cool. Sort of."

"I have eclectic taste."

"I can tell."

Mostly, I decorated my apartment in whatever I liked... regardless whether it matched any of my other stuff or not. At the minute I had gorgeous Indian silks in different shades of orange hanging from the main wall, twinkly lights strung around the ceiling and an enormous framed noir movie poster from the fifties that I had never heard of propped against another wall.

My TV set was old but I barely used it, preferring to

stream on my laptop. There was a battered trunk in lieu of a coffee table in front of my even more beat-up orange couch. There were haphazard piles of books and DVDs around the room and most surfaces were littered with photo frames.

"Who's this?" Colt asked, picking up one frame.

It held a photo of me and Marley, grinning like idiots during some night out early in our friendship. When I'd met Marley, it had been like meeting my other half. I adored that girl and missed her like crazy.

"That," I said, leaning my head on his arm as I peered at the photo, "is my best girl, Marley."

"Where was she tonight?"

"She's at home with her ridiculously hot husband-to-be in Vegas, the wench. I want her back." I giggled and nudged him in the side. "Feel like a trip to Vegas to commit a little kidnapping?"

"I'll pass," Colt replied dryly.

"Damn. And there I was thinking this was the start of a beautiful friendship."

"Sorry to disappoint." Colt replaced the picture and turned to face me. "Can I get a water, please?"

"Sure thing."

Colt followed me into the tiny kitchen and watched as I retrieved two bottles of water from the fridge. He picked up two mismatched plates off the side and turned them in his hands. "You really don't like conformity, do you?"

I plucked them out of his hands and put them back in their place. "Nope."

Back in the living room, Colt sprawled across the couch, absolutely dwarfing it with his big body. I curled up beside him and he draped an arm along the back, idly tracing lines on my shoulder. "This couch is amazing."

"Tell me about it. I found it at an estate sale and couldn't leave it behind."

"An estate sale? Is that how you find all your furniture?"

I poked him in the ribs and sat up straighter. "No. Okay — I'll tell you what I do, but you have swear not to tease me.

Or think I'm seriously weird."

Colt grinned. "I make no such promise."

"Fine." I released a breath. "I sort of...source vintage clothes. From dead people."

"You what?" Colt asked, his eyebrows shooting up into his hairline.

"I work at this vintage boutique a few blocks away, and my main job is to find the clothes to sell. Estate sales have the most amazing finds and I have a good eye." This was usually the point where people either got creeped out or teased me mercilessly.

Instead, Colt nodded. "Find what you're good at and own it."

It took a moment for me to form a reply. I swallowed hard, meeting Colt's intense gaze. "No one has ever said that to me before. You're kind of awesome."

Colt flashed me a skeptical look. "How long have you spent with me now, St. Clair? And you're just now realizing this?"

With a quiet laugh I pushed his shoulder. About a fraction of a millimeter. The guy was as immovable as a brick wall. "No way. I've suspected since the minute I met you. And, because you're you, I can tell you that. I'm not usually so quick to inflate the already bloated male ego."

"I'll take that compliment and run with it."

"You should." I relaxed against him again and Colt brought his arm down to curve around my shoulders. He reached to pluck my heels off, letting them drop with a clatter to the floor. Colt caught my calves and draped my legs over his lap. I sank into the space under his arm, so content I could have purred. "I bet you're an amazing spooner."

Colt's chest rumbled with laughter. "No one has ever said that to *me* before."

I smiled and pressed my face into his side. "Sorry. You're just so big. Like a giant teddy bear. With muscles I could bounce quarters off."

He snorted. "Your thought process is unbelievable. I'm going to keep you, St. Clair."

"Good."

"Are you feeling better? Not bummed out over the jackass ex anymore?" Colt moved his fingers over my bare knee, making me shiver and break out in goosebumps.

"I'll be fine. But I already sort of miss having a boyfriend. You know, someone to curl up with at the end of the night. Someone to talk to. Someone to kiss."

"I have a hard time believing that you'll be alone for long."

I shrugged. "I have a type and it's not easy to find. What about you — is there someone waiting for you to come home right now?"

A wry smile pulled at the corner of his lips. "I wouldn't be here if there was."

So not only was he charming, smart, funny and spectacularly awesome — he was considerate, too. There wasn't some poor man waiting for Colt to crawl into bed beside him. Mold himself to his body and slide his hand —

Wow, okay. Don't go there, Hayley. The last thing I needed was to start fantasizing about Colt with another guy as equally hot and huge as him. I'd probably attack the poor bastard.

But in all seriousness, I'd bet that Colt was an amazing boyfriend. His cheeky nature would keep him playful, and that mouth... I'd bet he knew how to use that mouth.

"What are you thinking?" Colt asked as he teased my hair with his fingers.

I touched his bottom lip and ran my finger across the silky feel. "That you're a phenomenally good kisser."

Colt chuckled, his breath stirring my hair. "It looks like you're giving it some serious consideration."

"Oh, I am." I let out a breath and flopped my head against his shoulder, all at once miserable and exhausted. "It's so not fair. The girls were wrong, it's not like being at an all-you-can-eat buffet and the calories don't count. It's like being at an all-you-can-eat-buffet and not being allowed a single crumb."

"I have no idea what that means," Colt said drolly.

"It means that I want to know if you're a good kisser, because, I doubt you'd be good. Good isn't a strong enough word. I think you'd be incredible. I'd bet you could give me the best damn kiss of my life. But I'm not going to be a creeper and ask, because, hello, weird, right?"

Colt's long, calloused fingers cupped my chin. He tilted my face up so I had no choice but to look at him. "St. Clair, if you want me to kiss you, I have no problem kissing you."

I blinked. He didn't? But...why? A straight guy wouldn't kiss a gay man because he asked for it. Would he? I couldn't do this—I couldn't entertain accepting a knee-buckling kiss from Colt because he felt sorry for me. It would probably be horrific for him.

"Okay, wherever your thoughts are going, stop them now." Colt smiled and stroked my cheek. "You're gorgeous. If you want me to kiss you, then hell yes, I will kiss you. If it's just to take the sting out of that asshole dumping you, I guess I'm okay with that. And I sort of feel privileged that I'm the guy who is making you feel better. And maybe I'm curious if you are as good a kisser as I think you are. So, St. Clair. Do you want me to kiss you?"

His speech left me breathless. I wanted to grab his face with both hands, slam my mouth over his and never, ever come up for air. Colt slid his arm around my waist and tugged me closer to him. He pressed his thumb to my lip and it took all my self-control not to dart my tongue out to taste him.

"Yes," I whispered.

"Good answer," he mumbled.

Colt lowered his head and swept his mouth over mine, just once. He was hot to the touch, his lips burning in a way that made me crave the heat of them again and again. He pressed another soft kiss, then another, to my waiting, willing mouth.

A noise I wasn't aware I could make clawed its way up my throat. I wrapped my fingers around Colt's thick wrist and squeezed, trying to convey some message that... Even I wasn't sure of what.

He kissed me harder, the pressure making my head spin. I gasped and Colt slid his tongue inside, teasing my own.

And oh my ever loving God... The man was a demon with a set of lips, sent down—or was it up?—to lure and entrap his prey. I was hooked on him.

Colt groaned and tugged on my legs, pulling me onto his lap. I parted my knees so I could straddle his hips, aching to get closer to him. I shoved my tongue into his mouth, making him take me the way I had taken him.

His fingers bit into my hips where he held me flush against him. I'd probably have a tiny bruise or two the next day, but I didn't care. It would be proof, and a reminder, of this unbelievable kiss.

I thrust my hands into Colt's soft hair and tugged on it as I kissed him harder, faster. Colt growled low in his throat, a purely masculine noise that left me physically hurting for him.

Colt shifted his hips, his thick erection straining through his jeans. It was instinctual for me to rock against it, igniting an inferno of heat at my core.

Wait...what?

He was aroused?

Like, seriously aroused?

How could I have...?

Okay, not to think too highly of myself, but was it possible that I was turning Colt? Or at the very least, letting him know there were different varieties of flavors to be enjoyed? A bisexual Colt was too much to hope for...or was it? It wasn't like being bi was unheard of. I had friends who were bi, who figured life was too short for just one kind of loving.

Colt slid his hands up my back, his fingers grazing over the zipper of my dress. "Jesus, St. Clair, you're driving me crazy."

"I know what you mean," I mumbled. I kissed him again, fast and hard, and tried to clear the fog from my head. "I'm going to kick myself for breaking this spell we've got going on, but I have to ask — is this a curiosity thing for you, or are you genuinely feeling this?"

Colt lifted his hips, his erection straining his jeans. "Does that feel like curiosity to you?"

I smiled and dropped a small, quick kiss to his mouth. "No. But I have to make sure. Jesus, I have never been so grateful that someone is bisexual before."

He pulled back, his forehead creasing and a look of confusion on his face. "I'm not bi."

My heart sank. "You're not? But how can you really want this — want me — when you're gay?"

Colt's eyebrows shot up. "Whoa...what? I'm not gay."

"What are you talking about? Of course you are."

"Nope. Pretty sure I'd have figured it out by now."

I scrambled off Colt's lap and jerkily got to my feet. "What the hell?"

Colt stood and held his hands up as though to show me he wasn't a threat. "I don't get what's going on here. Are you pissed because I'm not gay?"

For a second I was the polar opposite of pissed. I was freaking ecstatic. But then the whole night settled around me like a cloak of deception. And I wasn't pissed. I was super pissed. "Of course I'm pissed! You — you let me think you were gay."

He lifted his eyebrows. "And the hours and hours of flirting was me letting you think this?"

"All my gay friends flirt with me," I cried.

Colt made a strangled noise in his throat. "Christ, St. Clair, I was working my ass off with you. How could you seriously think that was just gay flirting?"

"Oh, I don't know, maybe because I met you in a gay bar?"

"Oh, that same one I met you in, you mean? So tell me, how long have you been a gay man?"

I rolled my eyes and tried not to stomp my foot like a petulant child. "That's not the same! Everyone knows girls like to blow off steam in gay bars. You had to have known I would think that you were gay."

"Maybe at first," he admitted quietly. His shoulders slumped and he took a single step toward me. "But I told you I was there for my friend — who is gay, by the way — for moral support. Doesn't make me gay, makes me a good friend. I flirted all goddamn night with you. Because I like you, not because I'm some creepy gay dude who likes to trick women. I came home with you because you asked me to. Call me a jerk, but I had hoped it was for a night of crazy sex, not to get the third degree over my sexuality."

I shook my head, my mind spinning. Was he telling the truth? It was entirely possible that he was. But that little voice in the back of my head kept nagging that he should have told me hours ago. Shouldn't have let me think what I had. "Can you leave, please? I'm suddenly really tired."

Colt was in front of me before I could blink. "No. You're pissed at me, I get it. But, come on, St. Clair. Let's laugh about this. Let's kiss again, because I was right. You're amazing."

Something in my chest pinched. I so badly wanted to do what he asked — simply forget about it and laugh at the misunderstanding. But my pride had already taken a hit tonight and this one somehow felt all the more damaging. I stepped out of reach. "No. Make all the excuses that you want, but I'm not buying them. Now, again, please get out."

He opened his mouth as if he was going to argue his case again. But instead he gave a quick nod and strode toward my door. At the last moment, he turned around to pin me with a sharp gaze. "I'll see you, St. Clair. I swear to you that I'll get this right. Somehow."

And with that, he left.

I stood in the middle of my apartment, which suddenly seemed so big and empty without him in it, and swiped away the single traitorous tear that slid down my cheek.

Chapter Three

Sleep eluded me. I tossed and turned for hours, replaying every exchange I'd had with Colt, searching for some kind of clue that he really had thought it was obvious he was straight. But I found none. Maybe that was his game. He went to gay bars and masqueraded as a gay man to lure in women. Then, once their defenses were down, he swooped in with a panty-dropping kiss and they would be so relieved that he was actually straight, they wouldn't care that he had lied and coerced.

Sounded like a lot of work to me, but hey, some guys were into that sort of thing.

In a lot of ways, Colt's actions hurt a hell of a lot more than Marcus'.

And now here I was — single, miserable and without a date the week before my best friend's wedding.

I had planned on showing Marcus off to Blake and Marley, and acting all smug and happy with him. I'd wanted her to see me happy and together, like she was. Instead, now I would show up dumped and stupid once again.

But I took it on the chin like any single girl and hit the clubs most nights with Beth and Eve. I partied hard and slept till dinnertime. I went to work to organize the clothes when I woke up then I went out to start all over again.

It probably wasn't the greatest idea I'd ever had, since I ended up sleeping clean through my alarm and missed my flight to Las Vegas. I managed to find another seat on the next flight out of JFK before I called Marley to tell her I'd screwed up.

She didn't chew me a new one, so either she was getting

enough hot sex with her hot almost-husband that she didn't care, or she was waiting to see me in person to let me have it.

Knowing my luck, it would be the latter.

I dozed on the plane and hoped it would be enough to get rid of my monstrous hangover.

It wasn't.

The moment I was clear of the plane, I ran into the ladies' room to change into my gorgeous one-of-a-kind dress made by my so-talented-it-hurt designer friend, Joey Falcone. He lived in his mom's basement in a narrow house in Queens, but I swear to God, he would be a household name someday. He'd designed the dress especially for Marley's wedding, and it was seriously a work of art. On its hanger, it appeared to be typical sleeveless tea dress. But once I had it on, it skimmed my every curve because it was made for my body. And the fabric was vintage, from the sixties, with little blue and yellow birds and pink flowers.

Pairing it with an amazing set of Jimmy Choos, I had a kickass outfit.

And no date.

Story of my life.

I hauled ass outside to get a cab and somehow managed to apply my makeup without making myself look like a student at a clown college.

Finally, the cab pulled up outside Blake's monstrosity of his own creation, and after shoving a wad of bills at the driver, I rushed into the house.

"Hello? Anyone home? Or am I so late I missed the entire thing?" I called as I pushed open the front door.

"Hayley? We're in the kitchen!" Marley said, her voice almost getting lost in the wide, lofty halls.

There was definitely something to be said about marrying well.

Except that was totally unfair. There were no two people on this earth who deserved each other like Blake and Marley did. After a torrid affair that I had only been *moderately* jealous of at the time, they'd still had a whole ton of crap to work through before they could finally be together. If anyone knew the importance of marrying for the right reasons, it was Marley.

Once upon a time, Marley had been engaged to the biggest asshole I had ever met. All because she felt like she owed him. It had taken an affair of his own, a tangled web of lies and Blake himself to make Marley open her eyes and realize selling herself to slavery was no way to live her life.

I made my way through the house to the kitchen, where I was greeted by Gayle, Marley's mom, Natasha, a mutual friend of Blake and Marley's, and the woman of the hour herself. They sat at the huge island in their bathrobes, sipping champagne and orange juice — and not their first, if the two empty bottles of Bollinger were anything to go by.

In their bathrobes.

I shot Marley a withering look. "You told me the wrong time again, didn't you?"

Marley smothered a laugh with her hand as she rose from her stool. She rounded the island and wrapped her arms around my shoulders. "I'm sorry. But it worked, didn't it?"

Two point five seconds. That was all I could stay mad at her for. I sighed and hugged her back, breathing in the familiar smell of her perfume. Not to be creepy, but, man, I'd missed this chick.

Marley released me and caught my hand, tugging me over to the island. She pulled out a stool beside hers and Gayle started pouring me a cocktail.

"Was your flight okay, Hayley?" Gayle asked as she handed me the flute.

I nodded and finished the drink in three long swallows. "I sleep like a baby on planes."

Marley snorted a laugh. "A baby? I had no idea babies were capable of snoring like a bulldozer."

With a huff, I tapped her hand. "So this is what I came all the way to Vegas for?"

Softening, Marley wrapped an arm around my shoulders.

"I'm sorry, you know I love you, Hayley."

Aw. "I love you too, Marley."

"But you do snore."

* * * *

The morning was spent in a fog of hairspray, cosmetic fragrance and champagne. The other three women readied themselves in Marley's bedroom, and I helped, since I'd already made myself as gorgeous as was possible in the cab ride from the airport. Hairdressers and makeup technicians flitted around each woman, transforming them into beauties.

It was a small affair — Blake and Marley weren't big on flash, and only their closest friends and family were coming to witness their wedding. Which was a damn shame because weddings were prime opportunities to meet new... acquaintances.

Although Marley had mentioned that Blake had a younger brother who was twenty-five, from what I had heard he was a good-time-guy and wasn't interested in anything serious. Pity. I could do worse than land myself a Hamilton.

But still, if he looked anything like his brother, who was to say having a good time was such a bad thing? I was here for the weekend. That was it. And hey — if anyone deserved some meaningless fun, it was me.

Finally, it was time for Marley to slip on her dress.

I'd been over the moon, crazy kind of happy, when Marley had asked me to source her wedding dress. It had taken me months of searching, and finally, in a tiny, out of the way boutique in the West Village, I had found it. A fifties tea-length princess dress, with three layers of chiffon, a liner and an underskirt to give the skirt some volume. It had a ruched bust to give the illusion that Marley had a bigger set of boobs than she really did, and a laced waistband enhanced with tiny rhinestones.

I'd had Joey alter it so it fitted Marley to perfection, and he'd added a few little touches here and there to take it from gorgeous to absolutely breathtaking.

She had cried when I'd sent it to her.

We four piled into Natasha's car and headed to the Marebello, where the wedding would take place in the gardens.

Natasha and Gayle headed inside while Marley and I hung back for a second.

"Are you nervous?" I asked her.

She smiled and shook her head. "Not in the least. I'm—" She blew out a breath. "I want him forever and even that doesn't sound like long enough. This is just like making it official, you know?"

I nodded. "I'm so proud of you."

Marley wrapped her arms around my shoulders. "It'll happen for you, Hayley, I know it. Out there is a guy who will see what I see."

"A five-foot-four blonde with expensive taste in shoes?"

She laughed and let me go. "A knockout with a heart of gold who would do anything for anyone."

"Yeah, I like your description better," I grinned. I peered around the corner to check out where Marley was getting married.

The gardens were pretty spectacular anyway, but somehow they were even more special now. The place burst with color, erupting from every corner with outstanding displays. A large archway in the center dominated the space, with bright summer flowers wrapping around the structure.

Blake stood under it with their minister, the guests fanning out in a V. And wow... Okay, if that was the other Hamilton... Holy hell, he was hot. Easily as tall as Blake, he had the same wide shoulders and lean build, too. Dark, messy hair but, unlike Blake's relaxed smile, Seth wore no expression at all. As though he wished he were somewhere else entirely.

Well. Maybe I would just have to get a few drinks in him

and we could take our minds off what was bothering us both. Because, wow. Seriously. I could lose a few hours of my life to a man like that.

Blake spotted me and shot me a pointed look. I smiled and waved before turning back to Marley. "I think your almost-husband is getting impatient."

She laughed. "Well, get out there, then."

I kissed her cheek and stepped into the gardens. I took my spot and flashed Blake a wink. He grinned and turned back to face the entry, waiting for our girl.

When she appeared, barefoot and smiling as if she had never been happier — which she probably hadn't — my heart soared for her.

Tears welled in my eyes as Blake and Marley exchanged their vows. They only had eyes for each other, and the love they shared filled the space around them.

I wanted what she had.

I wanted someone to look at me the way Blake looked at Marley.

I wanted someone to want me the way he wanted her.

My chest tightened and my heart physically hurt.

I was so, so happy for her. And I'm not too proud to admit, a little jealous, too.

With the ceremony over, and champagne reception complete, we headed to one of the smaller restaurants in the Marebello that Blake's dad had shut down for the night. I guess that was the kind of power that came with owning the hotel — among quite a few others.

We were served another round of champagne and I took it as the perfect time to make my toast that Marley had totally forbidden but knew I'd do anyway.

I chimed a fork against my champagne glass and rose to my feet. "Hi, everyone," I started with a wide smile. The whole table turned to look at me and I was hit with a stab of nerves. "I'm Hayley, Marley's best friend…and unofficial maid of honor, since she refused to put a label on it."

Dropping my gaze to Marley, I grinned at her eye roll.

"Nice, Hayley. Real subtle. Are you ever going to forgive me for not having bridesmaids?"

Absolutely not. I was still kind of pissed I hadn't gotten a revolting, garish and unflattering monstrosity of a bridesmaid gown. It was like the best friend rite of passage or something. I grinned. "What's to forgive? I'm totally your maid of honor... I just don't think you know it yet. And since I'm the maid of honor, it's my job to make a toast." Looking at Seth, I said, "Seth, you're next, by the way. You're the only logical best man."

Seth glanced at Blake, who shrugged. He dropped his eyes to his plate again. When I'd arrived at the wedding, I'd expected to see the younger Hamilton brother beside the older at the altar. Instead, Blake had stood alone as he'd waited for Marley. Seth had stood so far apart from the rest of the guests he'd practically been in another state. There was a tension about him that was palpable, his eyebrows drawn into a perpetual frown.

I let out a breath and pushed Seth out of my head for the moment. I looked down at Marley, who didn't seem at all surprised at my ambush toast tactic. "You've been my best friend for a few years now. In that time, I've gotten to know a lot of sides to you. I've known you during the worst times in your life, during drunken nights with the girls and through less-than-desirable relationships. And today, my dearest friend, I'm seeing a brand new side — the happiest I have ever seen you.

"Blake, I can't even begin to thank you for making my friend so happy. She's a different woman with you, a better woman. I have never seen a couple so in love, so contented, so glowing, just from being around each other. I have no doubt in my mind that this is it for you two. You're done. You've gotten your happy ending. And I couldn't be prouder that you shared this day with me." Marley reached up and clutched my hand, squeezing tight so I understood what she wanted to say without her uttering a word. I swiped at a tear threatening to fall. With a laugh, I looked out across the rest of the table. "So if you will all join me in toasting the beautiful Mr. and Mrs. Hamilton."

Everyone lifted their glasses and cheered the bride and groom. Man, my best friend was a *wife*... How weird was that? I took my seat and Marley leaned over to kiss my cheek.

"Thank you," she whispered.

I winked.

Across the table, Seth rose to his feet. He cleared his throat before speaking. "I always thought people who stuck around to work on problems and make amends were idiots. Why bother with something broken when you can go out and find something new? Then I saw Blake and Marley together and I realized it was because I'd never had anything worth fixing before.

"Recently, Blake and Marley were gracious enough to open their home to me. In my time with them, I've had my eyes opened and my expectations—along with my preconceived notions—changed. I've learned that even if you're lucky enough to find that one person you were absolutely meant to be with, real life can still fuck it up.

"Problems are problems and everyone has them. Every relationship has them, including the great ones. I always thought when, and if, you find your soul mate, that's it. The hard work is over. You don't need to do any more work.

"I couldn't have been more wrong. I think the greater the love, the harder the work, because you have something greater to lose. Real life isn't a fairy tale, and it is in thinking this that people don't bother working out their problems, thinking they'll solve themselves.

"But just because you work at something, doesn't mean it's a chore. Take the time to remember why you fell in love in the first place. Take the time to remember, out of all the billions of people in the world, why it was that one person who stole your heart.

"Thanks to Blake and Marley, I don't believe in fairy tales. I believe in something better. I believe in something real."

Seth's speech was met with dead silence.

I couldn't stop staring at him. It seemed no one at the table had expected that sort of depth to come out of a man like Seth Hamilton. From what Marley had told me, he was a party guy, lived his life to the fullest and enjoyed all it had to offer. In a lot of ways, he was me. Except with a dick.

Seth then handed Blake a wad of papers, telling him that Blake and Marley's wedding gift was that he was moving out. Seth's smile seemed genuine, giving the distinct impression that he was as laid-back as everyone made out he was.

But the second the attention drifted from him, Seth's easy smile slipped and he put that indifferent mask back on.

* * * *

My efforts to engage Seth in conversation were shunned at every turn. He was dismissive without being rude, vague without being deliberate. Gayle chewed my ear off and as much as I loved her, I'd about hit my limit on French patisseries. How different could they all be, anyway? I needed to make headway with the only semi-interesting person in the room.

After the meal, Seth took down everyone's drink orders and went to the bar at the rear of the dining room. His father excused himself a few moments later and followed him. It was the only time I'd met Blake and Seth's parents, and I had to admit—Anthony Hamilton scared the shit out of me. He had clearly given his sons his height and good looks, but apparently they got all their charm from their mother.

No one else seemed to notice the charged exchange between Seth and his dad. Blake and Marley were wrapped up in their private little rose-tinted bubble. Gayle and Henry were discussing the differences between Vegas and New York and everyone else was too busy enjoying the free-flowing champagne.

When I glanced back at Seth, his face had shut down. He

pulled on a sardonic smile that was more feral than a rabid dog and leaned against the bar. Anthony Hamilton radiated tension and held his body so rigidly I was surprised he didn't snap in two.

Without further thought, I rose from my chair and approached the men.

"Hi," I said as I reached them. "I thought I would come and lend you guys a hand."

Seth and his dad turned to face me, both blinking as though they had forgotten anyone else was even in the room with them.

At a loss for how to proceed, I smiled and prayed it looked genuine rather than maniacal. Seth nodded and turned back to the bartender, who loaded drinks onto a tray.

Anthony flashed a tight smile. "Well, it looks like you two have things under control. I'd better go and rescue Marley from your mother. She's been gushing over her dress for the last twenty minutes." Anthony tapped the bar with his knuckles and headed back to the table.

With Seth and I left alone, I gave him a moment to see if he would come out of his shell now his scary dad wasn't around.

Nope.

I'd be waiting all night for him to start chatting. Guess it was all up to me, then.

"I know a loaded conversation when I see one, and the look on your face made me feel seriously bad for you. Everything okay?" I asked, moving to the other side of him so that he could turn his back to the rest of the party. If he wanted to talk, he should be able to do it without an audience. I'd bet good money his dad was watching his every move.

Seth glanced down at me. "Nothing unexpected," he said eventually.

I snorted a highly unladylike laugh. "Someone has parental issues."

He narrowed his eyes. "Someone should mind their own

business."

"Someone should be thankful someone didn't, or someone would still be dealing with the hostility that just left the area." I folded my arms across my chest and shot him a pointed look. Didn't he get that I was only trying to help?

A moment after my convoluted reasoning, he laughed. "Sorry. I guess a thank you is in order."

Something in me softened. I shrugged. "Don't worry about it. Besides, I have an ulterior motive."

"Such as?"

I dropped my arms and took a step closer to him. *Wow, he's tall.* And so much more physically imposing now that I was up close. I liked it. A lot. Almost as much as when I'd first seen— *Nope, not going there.* "You're the only other person here I even remotely want to talk to. Marley's swooning and Blake's not moving an inch from her side. I love Marley's mom, but if I have to hear one more story about a cute café somewhere in Europe, my ears will bleed because I've stabbed myself in the head." I laughed, a little shocked at my honesty. "I figured if I did you a solid, you'd do me one back and engage me in somewhat youthful conversation."

Seth's gaze seared into mine. Something about that look made me think that he saw more than he let on—that he was exceptionally good at reading people. I felt stripped and exposed. And not in an unpleasant way.

He scanned me, taking in all my features. I knew I was attractive. *Let him look.*

I could lose myself in someone like Seth. Spend a meaningless night with him and forget about all the drama back home. Seth would be brutally honest about what he wanted and I wouldn't have any doubts that it meant more than it actually did. Seth would be simple. I needed simple. I...needed to be needed.

And somewhere deep down, I think he did, too.

Seth blew out a breath and lowered his gaze, as though all his energy had drained away. The mask he'd worn all day was finally cracking and letting me see what was really underneath. "I'm not exactly great company right now."

I could only stare…for way longer than was socially polite. Whatever was going on with him was bad. He was hurting in ways I knew nothing about. A random hook-up at his brother's wedding was the last thing on his mind.

"Fine," I said when I realized I had done nothing but eyeball the poor guy for close to a solid minute. "Then let's get drunk and bitch about the people in our lives."

The bartender placed the tray of drinks in front of him. After a moment, Seth turned to flash a hesitant smile my way. "I may be getting more thankful for your rescue."

I laughed. "That's because I'm awesome."

I motioned for him to follow me and helped him serve the drinks to the others. When we got to Henry, I placed his Scotch in front of him and beamed my most winning smile. "Henry, Seth and I just got talking and we've discovered our mutual love of punk rock music. Would you mind trading seats with me? I'm dying to know his thoughts on modern releases compared to eighties British."

Henry glanced between Seth and me before smiling and rising from his chair. "Not at all, it's all yours."

"Thank you," I said, claiming the seat beside Seth.

Seth angled his chair toward mine as he sat. "Where the hell did that come from?"

I smiled. "I think pretty good on my feet, don't I?"

He snorted a laugh. "Seems that way."

"So," I said, settling back into my chair with my cocktail. "Tell me all about yourself."

* * * *

The wedding party was long forgotten.

Seth and I had vacated the table hours ago and sat by ourselves at the bar. I had no idea what time it was, only that people had started leaving. Seth was like a kindred spirit. He got my weird sense of humor and loved partying almost as much as I did. The hours had flown by and I had no desire to find them.

He had been telling me about this sick club in Spain that was open for days and days at a time, making partying a full-time occupation, when Marley touched my shoulder.

"Hey," I said, drawing her in so I could loop my arm around her neck. "I missed you, where've you been?"

Marley laughed, the sound smothered by my hair. "With my husband. Some maid of honor you are—I haven't seen you for hours."

I let go of her to pat Seth on the knee. "I've been getting to know your brother-in-law. He's super nice, isn't he?"

"Yeah, he is. So. How many drinks has my super nice brother-in-law gotten you?"

"A few. A lot. I don't know. Why?"

"Because I think it's time to go to bed."

I stuck my tongue out at her. "Man, married people really are old and boring."

"You'll thank me when you don't have to fly home with a monster hangover in the morning."

That was an excellent point. "I think you're right."

"Do you want me to walk you to your room?"

I glanced over Marley's shoulder to see Blake waiting for her. I looked back at my friend and smiled. "No, you go home with that gorgeous husband of yours. I'll be fine."

Marley chewed her lip as though uncertain. "Do you have your key card?"

I reached for my bag on the bar top and searched through it for the aforementioned item. "Yup. Come on, I'll walk you out."

She nodded and crossed the room to Blake.

Turning back to Seth, I smiled and was hit by a strange stabbing of guilt. A huge part of me didn't want to leave him there alone. "Thanks for making my night. You're just as awesome as me, it turns out."

Seth chuckled under his breath. "Yeah, I'm great."

Before I could overthink it, I slid off my stool and wrapped my arms around Seth as much as I was able. He was taller than me and still sitting. It was sort of—okay, make that *really*—awkward. "Bye, Seth."

"Bye, Hayley."

With nothing else to say, I let him go and followed Blake and Marley out of the restaurant. The remaining wedding party, sans Seth, also came to see the happy couple off. They hugged each of us in turn, thanking us for coming. Then they were laughing and practically running out of the door.

Horn dogs.

Then it was just me.

Releasing a sudden melancholic sigh, I turned to head for the elevators. I was staying at the Marebello to give the newlyweds some privacy on their first night of wedded bliss. I had no desire to witness—or be anywhere near the vicinity of—Blake and Marley getting their freak on.

"Hayley."

I twisted around at the sound of my name and saw Seth standing a way off, hands shoved into his pockets and a world of sadness on his face.

"I'm so lame it's unbelievable, but do you want to come home with me?"

I was hit with the memory of Seth showing Blake his wedding gift to him—the papers for his house. As far as I had been aware, Seth still lived with Blake and Marley, and they'd obviously had no idea he'd gone and bought himself a house. So he hadn't officially moved in yet.

I guessed he had planned to spend his first night there tonight. After his recent heartbreak, maybe he couldn't face it alone.

I didn't blame him.

There was nothing worse than feeling like the only sad person in the world and going home to an empty apartment with nothing but a box of Lucky Charms to cheer me up.

"Of course I will."

We caught a cab and Seth remained pretty quiet during the journey. It was short, maybe fifteen minutes. The cab let us out in front of a nice-looking house with a curving walkway to the door.

Seth searched his pockets for his keys and eventually came up with them. He unlocked the door and let me in first.

"Wow," I said once in the entryway. "Nice place."

And it was. Big without being flashy, wealthy without showing off and homey without being a mess. Seth shut the front door and started down the hall. He motioned me into a room.

It was a spacious living room with a gigantic squishy couch and — holy mackerel — the biggest TV I had ever seen. I kicked off my heels and sank onto the couch.

Seth returned a moment later carrying a bottle of tequila and two glasses. He sat beside me and poured us each a drink.

He toasted me before throwing back the drink in one shot.

Okay. Maybe I would be flying home with a monster hangover after all.

Seth refilled his glass and motioned for me to pick up mine. "Come on, don't make me drink alone."

"Wouldn't dream of it," I murmured as I reached for my glass. Instead of gulping it down in one, I sipped slowly, letting my throat get used to the liquor first. Tequila had never been my drink of choice. "Any reason for knocking them back like the world is ending?"

"Nope," Seth answered bluntly. He sat back and let out a world-weary sigh. He clutched his glass and stared into the liquid as though it would magically produce the answers he needed.

"Seth, I'm going home tomorrow. You don't have to bullshit me. If you want someone to talk to, I can be that person for you."

He didn't lift his eyes from his drink.

"Okay, I'll start then." I sipped again and tucked my legs underneath me. "I got dumped by my boyfriend. To make myself feel better after getting my ass kicked to the curb—

again—I met my friends at a gay bar. I met this absolutely gorgeous guy. Seriously gorgeous. He looked like freaking Thor. Except with shorter hair and a better sense of humor."

I sighed as image after image of Colt flashed in my mind. The sheer size of him, bulky and huge in a way that made me feel so utterly feminine. How demanding his mouth had been, yet he had held me as though I was something precious he didn't want to break.

"He cheered me up and took my mind off my asshole ex. We flirted, I guess. You know how it is in gay bars."

"Actually, I don't," Seth said, his lips curling into a sad sort of smile.

I rolled my eyes and smacked him in the arm. "Well, for me and my friends, gay bars usually mean dancing with hot men who don't try to grope us and some light, friendly flirting. And this guy... He was just so nice. And hot. But really nice. He made me feel good, I guess. Less like a loser who had just been dumped. Again. I invited him back to my apartment because I was having such a good time with him. Somehow we got to talking about kissing and I said I bet that he was a good kisser. Next thing you know, our mouths are going at it like the world will end tomorrow. And holy crap, the guy can kiss.

"Next thing I know he's telling me he's not gay and we must have got our wires crossed or something." I shook my head, my eyes stinging with mortification all over again. "He used a ruse to get me to let my guard down. And I fell for it, like a gullible idiot."

"Sounds like an asshole," Seth mumbled. "And pretty shady."

"You're telling me."

There was a loaded pause. I tipped the rest of the tequila down my throat to try to numb the stabbing pain in my chest.

"Think of it like he did you a favor. Better to find out he was a dick now than a few months down the line when you'd fallen for him."

I hadn't thought of it like that. Maybe he had a point.

"My girlfriend dumped me." Seth rolled his glass between his hands. "Her poisonous friend hit on me and after I told her to fuck off, she told Cass *I* had hit on *her*. And she believed the bitch. She was meant to be here today. She texted me last fucking night to say she wasn't coming." Seth shook his head. "I shouldn't have even been surprised. I sort of knew I would do something to fuck it up eventually."

I frowned as I processed his words. "But you didn't fuck up. She did, by not believing you."

Seth shook his head. "Don't blame her, it isn't her fault. I have a history... A less than squeaky-clean reputation."

He was telling me. Marley had mentioned he had a voracious appetite when it came to women. But that didn't matter. His girlfriend should have believed him. "It's her who has the problem, Seth. Who cares if you've slept with a ton of people? If you were committed to her, that should have told her everything she needed to know."

"No, you don't get it. I was a major asshole. I blew every chance I had with her and I sure as shit didn't deserve the last one she gave me. This is on me. No one else."

Man, he had it bad. Even though he was the one who'd had the raw deal, he was still defending his girl. "I hope she comes around, Seth. I really do. It's painfully obvious how much you care about her. If she has a lick of sense she'll remember that."

He shrugged. Seth sat forward and refilled our glasses. "If she had a lick of sense she never would have gotten involved with a piece of shit like me."

And I thought I had issues. Seth was damaged in a way that no amount of booze, female company or even forgiveness could cure. He had to accept himself first. And accept that he was good enough.

"Jesus, I'm sucking the joy out of the room," Seth said. "Tell me something funny before I go and play in the traffic."

"Um... My boyfriend dumped me on our five-month anniversary." Because that was the funniest thing I could think of.

Seth turned to stare at me. "That's a thing?"

"Yes, it's a thing," I huffed. "What is it with everyone and asking me that?"

"Sorry. I've never celebrated anything, let alone a five-month anniversary. So. You like to celebrate stuff, huh?"

"Yeah. Me and Marley have a first time getting drunk together anniversary. We celebrate every year by recreating it. It's a lot of fun."

Seth cracked a smile. "It sounds like fun."

"That's actually coming up in a few months. I can't wait. I barely get to see my girl since your stupid brother stole her away from me."

He snorted a laugh. "I'll be sure to kick his ass for it next time I see him."

Chapter Four

I woke up feeling considerably better than expected. To start with, I'd matched Seth drink for drink, but when it had become obvious he wasn't stopping until the bottle was empty or he passed out—whichever came first—I'd switched to water.

Turned out he could empty the bottle before he succumbed to an alcohol coma. I hadn't known whether to be impressed or concerned.

Around four a.m., he'd finally stretched out on the couch and fallen asleep. I'd been worried for all of fifteen seconds about leaving him alone in case he choked on his tongue or something, but when he'd started snoring like a freaking foghorn, I'd known he was safe to be left unattended.

After grabbing a few hours of sleep in his guest bedroom, I checked on Seth—who was in the same position as when I'd left him—then headed into the kitchen. Seth's supplies were way more than sparse, but there were coffee and filters at least, and enough to make him a greasy breakfast to help with what would be a killer hangover.

A while later, groans came from the living room and I guessed Seth was awake. And suffering.

I found him sitting up on the couch, cradling his head in his hands.

"Oh good, you're up. You might want to crack a window. It stinks of ass in here."

Seth turned his head as though it about killed him to do so. He stared at me for a solid minute, a baffled frown marring his forehead. He nodded. "Hayley. Marley's friend."

My eyebrows shot up and I let out a startled laugh.

"Wow, really? After last night I'm just Marley's friend?" He must not remember the heart-to-heart we'd had. Or the drunken, angry ramblings he'd let flow out of him for a good few hours. Seth had needed to vent and I had been more than happy to be the person he'd vented to. Lord knew he needed someone to talk to.

But I guess in the cold light of day I was just another girl. The wrong girl. Story of my freaking life.

I turned on my heel and headed back into the kitchen to make his breakfast.

He followed, shuffling his feet as though every step was sheer agony.

Grabbing a bottle of water out of the fridge, I turned and tossed it at him. It hit Seth square in the chest as he made no effort at all to catch it.

A laugh bubbled in my throat. "Really?"

He groaned and bent to pick up the bottle. Seth slid onto a stool at the breakfast bar. "Please put me out of my misery," he mumbled.

"Sorry. Nothing for it but to ride it out."

"Not the hangover," Seth said, still covering his face. "You."

I sat opposite him. "Me what?"

Slowly, Seth lifted his head to peer at me. His eyes, while bloodshot to hell and back, were infinitely worried. "Did we hook up?"

Something in me broke for him then. Despite being crapped on by the person he loved more than anything, he still worried he had somehow done wrong by her. "No, Seth, we didn't hook up," I answered softly. If he had no idea whether we'd slept together or not, he must not remember a damn thing about last night. The guy looked bad enough, so I said, "After the wedding, I really didn't want to just go back to my hotel room, so you said I could come here. We drank—you considerably more than me—then you passed out on the couch. I slept in the guest room."

"Oh, thank Christ," Seth breathed, his face relaxing as

though the weight of the world had been lifted from his shoulders.

"You really love that girl, don't you?"

He took his time, as though considering how best, or how honestly, to answer me. "Sometimes I wish I didn't."

There was something about that painful confession that stirred a pang of longing in my chest. I wasn't sure if I bought into it being better to have loved and lost than never to have loved at all. It sounded like bullshit to me. But... Seth loved her, maybe more than she really deserved.

"Don't talk like that," I said, a weird knot forming in my throat. "If she knows what good thing she had, she'll come around. And if she doesn't...there are other people in this world you can love, Seth."

He blinked at me.

I blinked at him.

Emotion welled in my eyes and I hopped off my stool and whirled away before he could see. I so badly wanted to fix his pain, to somehow make it better. It wasn't fair that this guy had so much love to give and the person he'd chosen to give it to didn't want it. How badly did I want someone to care for me like that?

"I'm going to cook you some breakfast. Don't even think about arguing."

"Yes, ma'am," Seth answered, a touch of amusement in his voice.

I set about making bacon and eggs with a side of toast and refilled his coffee mug every time it hit the halfway mark. Once he had finished, I cleaned everything up in the kitchen. Though I hadn't cured him of his heartbreak, I hoped I had made a small difference somehow. Made his hangover bearable, at least.

"Okay, I'm going to drop in on my best friend before I head back to New York. How naked do you think they'll be?" I asked Seth as I gathered up my things.

He snorted a laugh. "Is that a rhetorical question?"

I sighed. "Maybe I should text first."

49

"I would highly recommend texting first."

Seth walked me out and blinked in the fierce sunlight as though he'd been underground for a decade. Poor guy. I'd hate to have his headache right now.

The cab I had called was waiting for me on the street, ready to take me away from this bizarre night. Seth was the one really hurting, but I sort of felt like he'd helped me, too. He had said maybe it was better to have found out that Colt was an asshole right away and I think I agreed with him.

We were kindred spirits, him and I.

For that one night at least.

With no warning, I threw my arms around Seth's neck and held him as tightly as I could. "Thank you for last night. Things at home...they could be better right now. You're good company...even for a guy on a bender."

Seth's arms came around me, and he sank into the embrace as though he craved human affection as much as I did. "I think the bigger thanks should go to you. You did rescue me from my dad, after all."

I laughed and pulled back. "No trouble. Try to stay positive, okay?"

He nodded. "Sure thing."

My confident smile wobbled. I knew he was only agreeing because it was easier than being real. "I know it's easier said than done."

"It is what it is."

Blowing out a breath, I gave him one last quick hug before darting down the path to the cab. I gave the driver Marley's address and turned to wave to Seth out of the window. He lifted his hand in return and was still in the same spot as I drove off.

* * * *

Are you naked?

I tapped my phone against the palm of my hand as I waited for Marley's reply.

50

Are you outside my window again?

I snorted a laugh. Funny girl.

Close. Front door.

Come around back, I'll be right down.

Heading around the side of the house to the back yard, I tucked my phone into my purse. Bob, Blake and Marley's faithful husky, was sprawled on the patio, bathing in the morning sun. He lifted his head at my approach and yawned.

I scratched his head on my way past him and slipped inside the French door that led into the kitchen. The house was quiet, so at odds with the mayhem of yesterday. I started a pot of coffee and took a seat at the island, thumbing through a magazine as I waited for my best friend to get her clothes on.

Marley appeared a few minutes later, flushed and grinning like a maniac.

I rolled my eyes at her. "You know you don't have to make good on the whole newlyweds thing, right?"

She winked as she poured herself a mug of coffee. "Where's the fun in that?" Marley turned to sit beside me at the island but paused at the last moment. She scanned me up and down. "Why are you wearing your dress from yesterday?"

I glanced down at myself. "What? It's not like it's a ho dress and I'm crawling home with my ass hanging out."

Marley frowned. "No, I mean, why are you wearing it again? Didn't you bring a change of clothes with you?"

"Of course I did. I haven't been back to the hotel yet." At Marley's baffled expression, I remembered that she didn't know where I'd spent the night. "Oh, right. I haven't told you yet. I stayed at Seth's last night."

She blinked. "You stayed with Seth. Last night. At his house. His new house. Holy shit. You screwed my brother-in-law."

I huffed and smacked the back of her hand. "Hello, gutter mouth? I didn't screw him. I slept there and we complained about our shit lives to each other. It was sort of depressing. But totally cathartic."

Marley frowned. "Why is your life shit? Your life is freaking awesome."

There'd been a time when I'd actually wished Marley and I could do some weird role reversal thing. She'd been in this picture-perfect relationship with a high-powered lawyer who'd given her everything she could ever possibly want. Seriously, the clothes alone had been reason enough to marry him.

He'd moved her into his enormous penthouse apartment on the Upper East Side and she hadn't had to work if she hadn't wanted to.

But then she'd looked at my life and wanted what I had — independence, my own place to live, no ties to anyone and total freedom.

Because that Upper East Side penthouse apartment had really been a gilded cage. It had taken a long time in our friendship for me to realize how unhappy she'd been, how miserable Theo had made her.

And I don't think she knew how lonely *I* was.

"OhmyGod." Marley slammed her mug down so hard on the island coffee sloshed over the sides. She scrambled to her feet and ran out of the room. "Blake! Blake, get your ass up!"

"Jesus, Marley, I'm still here for chrissakes," I called after her.

"What? What's wrong?" Blake asked, his voice distant, somewhere in the house.

"Call Seth. Call him right now. I sent— Jesus, I sent Cassidy over to his place."

"So?"

"So I just found out that Hayley *just left* his place."

"Oh. Shit."

"Yeah. Oh shit."

"Why was Hayley there?"

Marley made a strangled noise in her throat. "Blake!"

"All right, I'm calling, I'm calling."

Marley reappeared in the kitchen doorway a moment later, looking pale and anxious. "I did a bad, bad thing."

I sipped my coffee. "Who's Cassidy?"

She let out a breath and crossed the room. Marley slid back onto the stool beside mine. "Cassidy is Seth's...whatever the hell she is now. She's a really sweet girl, and *so* good for him. They're going through something right now and aren't talking."

I snorted my derision. *Sweet girl, my ass.*

"Anyway, she about broke down my front door this morning looking for him. But obviously he wasn't here so I gave her his new address."

Ah. And the plot thickens. "When was this?"

"About an hour ago."

An hour... There was a chance we had missed each other. I shrugged. "She might not have seen me. But then again, she might have. What's the big deal?"

Marley frowned. "Because she would assume that you and Seth hooked up last night."

"Not if he tells her the truth."

She made a face. "Seth sort of has...a colorful reputation. Of the sexual appetite kind. If you had a boyfriend who'd slept with half of Europe and saw some girl coming out of his house in the morning, would *you* believe he hadn't slept with her?"

I'd like to think I would believe the word of my make-believe boyfriend, but the truth was, I was as insecure as the next girl. "I see your point. But like I said, she might not have even seen me. And actually, you know what? I hope she did. Seth told me all about her last night and I think she needs a kick in the ass."

"Hayley, that's..." Marley shook her head. "Don't say stuff like that. You don't know anything about this girl."

"So you're happy about the fact your brand new brother-in-law is heartbroken right now? All because of that girl." I sighed. "Seriously, Marley, Seth is hurting. Bad. And it's all because of her. So do I feel terrible that she might get her feelings hurt over wrongly reading a situation regarding me and Seth? No, I don't."

Marley studied me for a long minute. Finally she released a breath. "Fine, I guess I see your point. But, Jesus, you need to get laid. You're getting cynical."

"Yeah well, that's what happens when you get dumped and conned by a non-gay guy all in the same night," I mumbled.

"What?"

"It's a long story."

She laughed and refilled our coffee mugs. "You'd better get started then. I don't want you missing your flight. Again."

* * * *

Marley was true to her word and made sure I didn't miss my flight this time around. After being up half the night with Seth, all I wanted to do was wriggle down in my seat and catch a few z's.

But no.

The person beside me was a talker.

As in, wouldn't shut the hell up.

I got no sleep and I was cranky as hell by the time the plane landed. The second I got home to my apartment, I stripped down to my T-shirt and panties and crawled into bed, planning on sleeping away the rest of the evening, night and hopefully a good chunk of tomorrow, too.

It felt like only seconds before that I'd lain my head against the soft, squishy pillow when someone hammered on my door, ripping me out of much-needed sleep. Glancing at my lit-up M&M clock, I saw I'd actually been asleep for almost four hours and not the few minutes I'd thought.

Huh. I must have been in one of those completely coma-like sleeps.

The hammering stopped and I let out a contented sigh. Finally, they'd given up.

Nope. It started again.

"NYPD!"

My eyes flew open and suddenly I was wide, wide awake. Why the hell were the cops at my door?

Oh God ohGodohGodohGodohGodohGod...

I scrambled out of bed and rushed to the door, my hand poised above the handle. Wait a minute... For all intents and purposes, I could still be in Vegas right now. I could have missed my flight and therefore wouldn't be aware of the police force outside my door trying to get in.

Hold up... Why was I freaking out? I hadn't done anything wrong.

Unless that bitch cousin from the estate sale a few weeks ago had reported me for vastly underpricing a collection of sixties cocktail dresses.

"Miss, I know you're inside, I can see the shadow of your feet."

I jumped about a mile out of my skin at the voice on the other side of my door, and scooted back a fraction.

"Yeah, perfect, I definitely know you're not home now."

What a wiseass. I huffed and threw open my door. "Police harassment of the public is federal crime, buddy—" My voice caught in my throat and I made a strangled noise of surprise. "What the hell are you doing here?"

Colt smiled, lopsided and—I hated to admit it—freaking gorgeous. He wore dark pants, a blue shirt and a black jacket. My God, he was just as beautiful as I'd made him out to be in my head. Part of me had wondered if I'd exaggerated his hotness. But nope. Here he was, all sexy and shit.

"I came to see you. Can I come in?"

"Wha-how-no!" I spluttered. I folded my arms across my chest. "Did you seriously impersonate a police officer to sneak into my building and lure me out of bed?"

Colt pointed to the police badge clipped onto his belt. "I'm not impersonating anything. I'm a detective for the New York City Police Department."

Okay. I couldn't have predicted that. I shot him a steely glare. "Well, I'm not hiding any bodies, or drugs, and I have an alibi for all weekend, so go find another lead."

"I know you haven't been here all weekend. I've come around every day."

"Then crime must be at an all-time low for you to have so much time on your hands."

Colt's confident smile slipped. He grasped the doorframe. "I'm pretty persistent when it comes to getting what I want. And what I want is to apologize to you, and for you to realize that it's completely heartfelt."

I snorted. "I doubt that. No guy comes knocking on a girl's door at eleven at night to apologize."

"This one does."

I studied Colt, his every feature, every fleck of color in his pale blue eyes. There wasn't an inch of him that made me feel like this was another con, some new game he'd concocted to mess with me and get into my panties. But I couldn't forget how we had first met and his ultimate betrayal of my trust. "Fine. I accept your apology."

"No you don't." Colt took a step forward, filling my doorway with his large frame. "Don't ever lie to me, St. Clair, because I'll know."

"Well, given that this is the last time I ever plan on seeing you, that's just fine and dandy."

He blew out an agitated breath. "Christ—I've said I'm sorry. It was a genuine mistake, I swear to God. I never meant to trick you."

I wanted to hold on to my anger. I wanted to not believe him, but dammit… I did. Which, in my experience, was a very stupid thing to do. Anyway, he was so far removed from my usual type he was practically an alien. I liked ambition, men hungry for a powerful career, not sexy NYPD detectives. "I believe you, Colt. It doesn't make me any less pissed at you, but I believe you."

"Good. Because I want to take you out. On a real date, where you don't think that I'm gay for most of it."

A startled laugh rose in my throat. "You have to be kidding. Why the hell would I go out with you?"

"Because we've got something here, and you can't deny it."

Cocky jackass. "There's nothing here."

"So prove it. Go out with me and prove we've got nothing."

He was trying to reverse psychology me, I could smell it. "No."

"Why?"

"I don't want to?"

"Was that a question or an answer?" He grinned.

"God, you piss me off." I thrust my hands on my hips and opened my mouth, fully prepared to tell him off. But he dipped his gaze and when he lifted it again, it was so heated I felt scorched all the way down to my toes. "What?"

"You really should be more careful in checking out your outfit before answering the door. Not everyone will be an upstanding officer of the law like me."

I glanced down at my naked legs, skimpy lace panties and the pale pink T-shirt that also bordered on skimpy. No bra meant visible nipples and no way to hide the fact that he not only irritated me, he aroused the hell out of me as well.

My cheeks warmed and I swallowed. No one had ever looked at me with such intensity before. Not even my high school boyfriend the first time we'd rounded second base. Warmth pooled in my core and I was hit with a fierce stab of need.

Colt blew out a breath and took a step back. He shook his head. "Go back to bed, St. Clair, before you drag me there then hate me for it."

I opened my mouth—whether to argue or, as he said, drag him to my bed, I had no idea.

He looked back up at me, flashing his gorgeous smile

again. "I'll see you around, beautiful. Count on it."

I couldn't peel my eyes off Colt as he sauntered down the hallway with all the swagger of a genuine sex god. His firm behind made my mouth water, the strong lines of his back and shoulders stirring something animalistic in me. He stepped inside the elevator, meeting my gaze as the doors slid shut.

With a gasp I stepped back and slammed my door closed, fastening every lock in place. I couldn't rule out the possibility of chasing after him.

Jesus, what the hell did that guy do to me?

I slowly made my way back to bed, wider awake than ever.

Chapter Five

It was a beautiful sunny morning — okay, technically it was closer to afternoon than morning, but whatever — on the island of Manhattan. I was rocking a white felted jersey pleat skirt and yellow sleeveless blouse, paired with a cute set of Irregular Choice shoe boots covered in white lace. I picked up my usual coffee order from the little place on the corner before heading a few blocks over to the boutique.

A bell chimed as I opened the door, and the hinges creaked as badly as ever. I really needed to remember to get some oil for them. Or whatever they needed to stop screeching like an angry cat.

"Hello? Anyone home?" I called, closing the door behind me.

"In here, Hayley," Fiona called from the rear of the store.

I pushed past the racks of clothes and slipped behind the counter. I poked my head around to peer into the storage room slash office slash break room. Fiona sat cross-legged on the floor, writing some price tags.

Sighing, I stepped into the room and snatched them from her. "We've talked about this."

"I know," she said, snatching them right back. "And I don't care. Whose name is above the door?"

"Technically, no one's. Unless you've changed your name to 'Back in Time'."

Fiona poked out her tongue.

"Can I at least take a look at what you're giving away this time?" I asked, waving my hand at the garment bags on the rail in front of her.

She nodded and gestured for me to go ahead.

I unzipped one to find a stunning Dolce and Gabbana evening dress in the most gorgeous midnight blue fabric. "This is from the Clydesdale estate I was at last week. I told you to leave it all alone until I got around to it."

"Well, they'd be back here for a few years if I waited for you." Fiona grinned. "I'm saving you a job, that's all."

"You'll put me out of a job when your business goes belly-up because you've given all your stuff away for next to nothing. How much were you selling this one for?" I plucked the price tag out of her hands again. "Twenty-five bucks. Are you serious right now? This dress is worth a few thousand at least!"

Fiona made a disgruntled noise. "That's ridiculous. No one should pay that amount of money for a silly old dress."

I laughed. "Fi, this is why you hired me — so I could find the gems that keep your business afloat. This dress is one of my best finds this year. And people do pay that amount for dresses. It was only a few weeks ago that that Upper East Side princess paid five grand for the Valentino, remember?"

She sighed and rose to her feet. "Yes, yes, I know. You've done more for the boutique in the last three years than I have in the last thirty. But maybe we should have a sale day or something, so ordinary people who aren't dripping in diamonds can afford some beautiful things."

Handing her her usual black-as-coal coffee, I kissed her weathered cheek. "I think that's a great idea. Just not the Dolce, okay? It would break my heart to see some brat wearing it to her prom."

Fiona poked me in the chest. "You need to unthaw that black heart of yours, missy."

"And you need to toughen yours up."

"We'll agree to disagree."

"We always do."

I adored Fiona. I'd worked for her for three years now and she kept me on my toes. For a woman in her late sixties, she was still as feisty and opinionated as ever, and was way too generous for her own good. She was an enigma in a fast-paced and unforgiving city like New York. But she was like the beating heart of the block.

She put out bowls of cat food in the alley for all the strays — and didn't pay a blind bit of notice when I told her it would only attract the rats — and when she'd found out Mr. Greenberg down the street had been having trouble with his small grocery business, she'd started buying all her food from him. Everyone who met Fiona loved her. She wasn't shy about coming forward and giving me a good kick in the pants when I needed it, but she was the first person to lend a listening ear.

I'd been walking home after an insane party in Tribeca followed by an after-party that would turn your hair white when I'd found Back in Time. At first I'd thought it was a quirky movie memorabilia store, but when I'd seen Fiona dress a window mannequin in a one-of-a-kind Stella McCartney, I'd known it was my kind of place. Part genuine vintage boutique, part vintage-inspired new stuff and, most recently, thanks to me, high-end designer gear looking for its forever home.

I'd spent hours there that first morning, browsing all the delights and wonders Fiona had for sale. I'd had my arms loaded down with designer gems at knock-off prices, but I hadn't been able to go through with it. I'd told Fiona exactly how much money she was losing out on and she'd hired me on the spot. I hadn't been working at the time — hadn't even been looking, really. But me, Fiona and Back in Time were pretty well suited to each other.

I didn't work regular hours. Instead Fiona was more than happy for me to go out and do my thing and bring her in new stock, which she would then sell at — usually — the prices I recommended. And every now and then I'd hang out in the boutique and style the place up a little. Today I planned on dressing the window in a fun summer display with the cute little playsuit and a few bikinis we had in stock. Which were new — just vintage-designed. Because otherwise...gross.

"Hayley, I'm running out for some lunch. What are you in the mood for?" Fiona asked as she slid a huge pair of Jackie-O sunglasses onto her nose.

"Ooh, you know what I'd kill for? One of those sandwiches from that place over by that store."

Fiona made an agreeing sound. "Done. The works?"

"Hell freaking yes."

She laughed. "I'll be back in a few. Be careful on that ladder while I'm gone."

"Yes, ma'am."

Fiona swatted my bare leg on her way out of the door. "Ma'am, my ass."

I waved to her out of the window as she disappeared down the street, strutting her stuff better than some twenty year olds I knew. Man, I hoped I was that cool when I was in my sixties.

Shifting my weight on the rung of the ladder I was currently standing precariously on, I reached higher to try to pin the stupid thread the stupid seagull dangled from to the ceiling.

A sudden knock on the window made me yelp and wobble. I grabbed the ladder and squeezed my eyes shut as it rocked ominously on the floor. *Please don't die, please don't die...*

Risking opening one eye, I confirmed I was still on the ladder, still upright and thankfully, still alive. I let out sigh of total relief and turned to see who had tapped on the window.

Colt stood on the street, cringing. "Sorry. Did I frighten you?" he called.

"Only in the literal sense." I glared at him. My stomach flipped and once again his raw attractiveness set me on edge. It had been over a month since the night he'd shown up at my apartment and clearly it hadn't dulled my reaction to him. But reaction or not, he was still a manipulative liar.

Or so I kept telling myself.

He pushed open the door and stepped inside the boutique.

"So this is the place you were telling me about? I can see why you like it."

"Yeah, that's great, Colt. What do you want? I'm busy here."

"I can see that. What the hell are you doing with that seagull?"

I huffed out an irritated sigh. "I'm creating a fun beach scene."

"Actually, I think you're failing at creating a fun beach scene because you're two feet too short."

Stepping up another rung on the ladder, I ground my teeth as the whole thing wobbled again. Christ, this goddamn seagull would be the death of me. "I'm fine."

"I could help you. All you have to do is ask me nicely."

I snorted a laugh. "Oh, I'll be sure to put a cherry on top."

Colt chuckled. "Now you're talking."

Was he flirting with me? Again? Jesus, this guy had me running in circles. "What are you doing here, Colt? I'm pretty sure this is just a mannequin, not a dead body. No need for the cops."

"I was in the neighborhood and a beautiful woman in a store window caught my attention."

"I've told those strippers to keep the blinds closed. It's very distracting for the average pedestrian."

"Will you let me help you, St. Clair?" Colt asked after a tense moment of silence. "I'm terrified you're going to break your neck up there."

"I'm fine, I've got it." I wasn't fine. I didn't have it. And there was the very real possibility that I would fall and break my neck. But there was no way in hell I would ask for his help.

The bell above the door chimed as Fiona came back into the boutique carrying a white paper bag and a holder of drinks. "Oh, hello. Look, Hayley, a customer."

"This isn't a customer, Fi. This is one of New York's finest. Apparently we have something to do with a police investigation," I said drolly.

"What?" Fiona asked, her eyes darting between me and Colt.

Colt sighed and extended his hand for her to shake. "Detective Colton Deluca. I'm a friend of St. Clair's, here. I had no idea she was such a comedian."

Fiona giggled. "She has a very dry sense of humor. It's a pleasure to meet you, Detective. And I must say, I had no idea Hayley had such attractive friends."

God. "It's time to kick you out, Colt. We're about to have lunch," I said.

"Are you busy, Colton? Would you like to join us? It would be wonderful to break bread with one of the fine officers who keeps our city safe." Fiona held up the takeout bag. "I had a feeling I would need an extra, so there's a sandwich going spare."

The woman had ESP, I was sure of it. "Fiona, he doesn't want to have lunch with us."

"What are you talking about? I'd love to have lunch with you two ladies." Colt winked at me before turning to Fiona. "And I wouldn't dream of turning down a sandwich from Fabricio's."

Fiona smiled. "Well, that's settled then. Hayley, flip the sign and I'll get the camp chairs." She headed to the back of the boutique where we kept the modest furniture. Fiona was a firm believer in an honest-to-goodness lunch break and would lock up shop to enjoy it.

Colt looked back at me with a smug grin. "I like your boss."

With a sigh, I started down the ladder. Colt caught my elbow and helped me with the last few rungs. My skin burned under his touch. "She attracts people to her. Everyone loves Fiona. She's good people."

He didn't let me go right away and instead took a discreet step closer. "I know I was pretty cocky a minute ago, but are you cool with me being here?"

I studied him, his unflinching blue eyes keen on mine. Was he playing a new angle, or was he really being contrite?

I narrowed my eyes. "Would it make a difference?"

Colt's lips twitched. "Nope. I can't wait to have lunch with you."

"God, you're a cocky asshole."

"I think you're learning to like it."

"I think I'll be seeing a lot more of your colleagues when I finally snap and kill you."

* * * *

Colt spent the full lunch hour with Fiona and me. He charmed her into girlish giggles and earned a soft spot in her heart after he finished hanging the stupid seagulls for me. And, okay, even though it irritated me to no end, it kind of warmed me to him, too.

Once he left, I got the third degree from Fiona. Who was he? Where had I met him? Why were we not dating? Why had I said no when he'd asked me out repeatedly throughout lunch? Was I soft in the head for letting a beefcake like that slip through my fingers?

Like Marley, Fiona didn't exactly approve of my boyfriend choices. She thought I was looking for love in all the wrong places and in all the wrong people. But she didn't get it. None of them did.

My phone buzzed that afternoon with a text from Beth.

Hey bitch – drinks at Alibi tonight?

Ugh. I was so over the Meatpacking District. It wasn't the same as it used to be since it had gone all commercialized. But I guess it was better than nothing.

Sure thing. 9?

See you then.

* * * *

Beth and Eve loved Alibi. They lived in the neighborhood and always found someone they knew to flirt with and buy them drinks. I'd never had any luck with men in the Meatpacking District. A few dates that hadn't come to anything, but that was it.

Still, it didn't mean a girl shouldn't put in the effort. I chose a magenta Alexander McQueen one-shouldered dress that clung to my curves and a pair of black velvet Kurt Geiger pumps with jeweled backs.

When I arrived, Beth and Eve were already there and had a table in the back. Eve spotted me first and waved me over.

"Finally!" she cried. "I thought you'd never get here."

"You're just in time, Hayles," Beth said. "The cutest group of guys came in a few minutes ago."

I followed her pointing finger to a group of guys in fierce suits. Attractive enough, but the way they scanned every woman in the place suggested they were only looking to score.

"Where've you been all day?" Eve asked me.

"I was at the boutique."

"Aw, how is Fi?"

"Good, you know Fiona."

"I need to come see her soon."

"She'd love that." Fiona adored my friends. She liked their fun, voracious outlook on life and especially loved that every day was a party to them. They in turn loved that Fiona had quirky clothes that she sold at ridiculous prices.

Even a couple of trust fund brats could appreciate a good bargain.

"That guy came by today."

Beth raised her eyebrows. "The non-gay guy from Industry?"

"One and the same," I confirmed with a nod.

"Huh. He has balls of steel."

"Tell me about it. And I have a feeling they're persistent balls, too."

"Babe, that guy was *hot*. Why don't you just...try him

66

out for a night? Who cares if you hate him? You don't have to see him again. And, you know, that's probably all he's looking for anyway."

I blinked at Eve. What a romantic my friend was. "Because I'm not interested in a random hook-up, least of all with a guy who lied to me for an entire night."

She shrugged. "I'm just saying, you have no real interest in him. There's no risk of getting hurt. May as well use him for something while you can."

"Yeah, what if you get to your death bed and you regret not sleeping with more unbelievably hot guys?" Beth asked, her eyebrows up in her hairline.

"Somehow I don't think that will be on my list of regrets." I laughed at my friends. "I'm going to get a drink, you guys want?"

They nodded their assent.

I left their table and headed for the bar, squeezing myself into an empty space.

"A woman as beautiful as you should not have to buy her own drinks."

I turned the direction of the masculine voice. A tall, good-looking guy in a sharp gray suit leaned one arm on the bar. He turned on a mega-watt smile that I knew would earn him his fair share of phone numbers.

"Oh? I don't see anyone else around here offering to pay for them," I said, cocking a hip and turning on my own flirty smile—the one that had earned *me* my fair share of phone numbers.

"Then maybe I should be more direct." His smile widened. "Can I buy you a drink?"

I scanned his handsome face then down his three-piece suit that fit him too well to be anything other than tailored. He was every inch my perfect type. "Sure."

The bartender stopped in front of me. "What can I get you?"

The guy shifted closer. "I'll take a Bud, and whatever my new friend here is having."

"Cosmo, thanks," I said.

The bartender nodded and turned to get our drinks.

"Thank you. I'm Hayley, by the way."

"Spencer."

"It's a pleasure to meet you, Spencer."

"The pleasure is all mine, Hayley."

Our drinks were served and we moved down the bar a little to escape the thick crowd.

"So what brings you out tonight?" Spencer asked as he sipped his beer.

"Nothing special—just a few drinks with my girlfriends. You?"

"The same. Though I only intended staying out for one— I've got a crazy early morning tomorrow."

"Only intended?" I smiled. "Does that mean you could be persuaded to stay longer?"

"I could. If the right person was persuading me."

And suddenly, my night was looking up.

It turned out that Spencer lived in the neighborhood, worked on Wall Street and drove a Ferrari. Just for fun, of course. He had his Porsche as a little runaround. He stayed for more than one and drew out the other two drinks to last a few hours.

Before he left, we arranged a date for that weekend and he promised to call.

The longer I spent with Spencer, the clearer it became that he was exactly my type. Good job, flattering, attractive and, yeah, wealthy.

Either my luck was changing in the Meatpacking District, or Alexander McQueen was my fairy godmother.

Chapter Six

Spencer picked me up on Saturday night at seven on the nose. He arrived wearing another beautiful tailored suit and smelling divine with his cologne. We went to Kurumazushi in Midtown, with Spencer ever the gentleman by holding the door and pulling out my chair. Old-fashioned manners were a must for me and he had them down.

"Have you been here before?" Spencer asked as we sat.

"Oh yeah, a bunch of times. My friend Marley and I used to come here all the time."

"Then you know how good the food is. I like a woman with good taste," he said, smiling.

"I'm nothing if not known for my spectacular taste. Are you glad to be done with work for the week?"

Spencer shrugged. "It's not exactly a nine-till-five gig. Guaranteed I'll have a hundred emails when I check my phone."

"That's the good thing about fashion, I guess. I can fit it into my life, not the other way around." Wasn't that the truth. I loved that my job didn't interfere in the slightest with my social life. I'm not sure which would win if I had to choose one or the other.

"Yeah, it's good to have a hobby. I haven't had the time for one for years."

A *hobby?*

"Have sir and madam had a chance to look over the menu?" the waiter asked as he arrived at our table.

"Yes," Spencer said. He plucked the menu out of my hand and held it out along with his own to the waiter. "We'll both take the Omakase Course, and I think a bottle of Riesling will do nicely as well."

I blinked at him in surprise. Well, it was better he had a take-charge attitude than a simpering, unconfident attitude.

Over dinner, Spencer told me what it was like to work for a prominent trading company and I tried to get a word in edgewise. We shared a cab home and Spencer got out with me at my building.

"I had fun tonight," he said. "We should do it again."

For some reason, Colt's face flashed in my mind. "I'd love to," I said, forcing the image away. Stupid Colt, ruining everything.

"Great," Spencer said with a grin. "I'll call you." He stepped forward and pressed a dry kiss to my lips. Spencer flashed one last smile before climbing back into the waiting cab.

I was sort of surprised—and therefore subsequently impressed—that he hadn't offered to walk me to my door. The classic hint to getting invited in then not leaving. Maybe Spencer was one of the last true gentlemen.

* * * *

I fell into a whirlwind romance with Spencer. He called me the very next morning after our dinner at Kurumazushi and invited me out for brunch. We ended up spending the day together and he invited me back to his über-trendy apartment in the Meatpacking District. It was as though chrome and glass had gotten together and had a shiny, sharp-edged baby.

It reminded me a lot of Marley's old apartment with Theo—high-end appliances that looked as though they had never been used, absolutely no personal touches—unless the TV counted—and a glossy, polished interior that meant I was sort of afraid to touch anything in case I left grubby fingermarks.

Spencer never made a move that weekend, keeping up his gentlemanly ways. Since then, he had taken me out for late suppers and drinks at Alibi, where we'd met, and on a couple of lunch dates. It was hard to fit much in around his hectic schedule, but that was the beauty of my totally non-hectic one — I was virtually always free.

"So," Spencer said as he walked me to my door after another dinner together. This time it had been at Jean Georges with tableside service. I had to admit, my wardrobe was thrilled with all the places Spencer took me to. Tonight, my little black Marc Jacobs had had a ball. "Are you positive I can't steal you away from your plans tomorrow night?"

I twisted my key in the lock and peered over my shoulder at Spencer. "Sorry, no can do. I haven't seen my girl in almost three months."

Spencer sighed. "And here I was thinking new boyfriend trumped old friend."

A laugh bubbled out of me. "Trust me, no boyfriend will ever trump my friends." I pushed my front door open and turned to look at him. "Wait a minute — boyfriend?"

He grinned and stepped inside. "Hayley, I've spent all my free time with you over the last month. What else would I be?"

In all honesty, I had no idea. It usually took a blow job and regular sex for a guy to even hint at being my boyfriend.

"And if I wasn't your boyfriend, would I have gotten you this?" Spencer reached into his breast pocket and pulled out a red leather jewelry box with a gold inscription.

Holy crap…is this happening?

Spencer opened the box to reveal a pair of platinum studs with a diamond in the center of each. The light bounced off the diamonds, casting sparkles that made my breath catch.

"Spencer, I can't accept these."

"Of course you can," he said simply, as though any other alternative was ludicrous. "I would have gotten you a pendant, but I've noticed you mostly only wear that one."

I touched the vintage locket at my throat. He was right — I rarely wore anything but.

"Try them on," he said, holding out the box to me.

I carefully took the Cartier studs from their box and slid them into my earlobes.

Spencer smiled. He pushed my hair away and tilted my face up to meet his. "Beautiful," he murmured, brushing his lips once over mine. "Almost as beautiful as the woman wearing them."

"Thank you," I whispered.

"Anything for you." Spencer kissed me again, harder, demanding.

I let him pull down my zipper and stepped out of my heels and dress as the material fell in a pool at my feet.

Spencer shrugged out of his suit jacket and loosened at his tie. "Bedroom?"

"Back there," I breathed.

Anticipation curled in my belly. Until now, Spencer had been respectful and attentive, but now he was bold and daring. He broke our kiss and caught my hand, tugging me in the direction of my bedroom. Spencer ushered me onto the bed and quickly shed the rest of his clothes.

I fumbled in my nightstand for a condom. He ripped the packet open then slid it on. We fell back onto my bed in a tangle of limbs. Spencer pulled my panties down. I kicked them away.

He slammed his mouth over mine and nudged my knees apart. With one quick push, he shoved inside. I gasped in surprise and at the lick of pain... I hadn't exactly been ready for him.

Spencer groaned and thrust in again, harder and faster. I tried to catch my breath, tried to keep pace with him and somewhat coordinate our movements.

He was done before I was fully aware of what was happening.

Spencer panted in my ear, collapsing on top of me with his full weight so I could barely breathe. After a long moment, he twisted his head to kiss my cheek then rolled away. He sat up on the edge of the bed and discarded the condom in the wastepaper basket.

"You're amazing," he said, rubbing a hand across his forehead.

"Um... So were you."

"Can I grab a shower? I don't want to stink out my suit."

I sat up and inconspicuously maneuvered a blanket over my naked body. "Oh, you're leaving?" *Already?*

Spencer's lips twisted into a smile. "Babe, I can't sleep anywhere but my own bed. Next time we'll go to my place, okay?" He crawled toward me and planted a heavy kiss on my mouth. "Though I can't guarantee I'll get any more sleep there, either, if you're with me."

I forced a smile and Spencer got up and left the room. Soon after later the shower started.

Flopping back against my pillows, I screwed my eyes shut. It wasn't fair. He was the whole package...except for sex. Was he nervous? Had he had a rough week and hard and fast sex was the only way he could blow off steam? Only, I'd had hard and fast sex before. And it had been hot. This was more like...jacking off with a body instead of a hand.

Unfortunately Spencer was a clear example of Hot Guy Syndrome—so attractive he'd never had to be good in bed to get laid.

* * * *

Saturday dragged. All day long I glanced at the clock, until I was positive the damn thing was running backward. Marley had flown into town yesterday but was spending time with her mom first. She was due to arrive sometime this evening, and we were planning on ordering in food and just hanging out.

I couldn't wait.

It was around six-thirty-seven when my buzzer finally sounded. I tripped over the edge of a rug and almost face-planted the floor in my haste to get to it. My toe smarted as I hit the intercom button.

"Marley?"

"Hey! I'm here," her voice came through the crackly speaker.

I pushed the button for her to open the door. "Hurry up!"

After unlocking my door, I hurried down the hall to meet her at the elevator. The moment it slid open, I threw my arms around her.

"Hi," she said with a laugh. "Miss me?"

"Man, you have no idea." I caught the handle of her suitcase and pulled it down the hall. "I made your room up. And I got bagels for breakfast tomorrow."

Marley laughed again. "Are you trying to make sure I don't leave?"

I glanced at her over my shoulder. "Maybe."

After depositing her suitcase in the room she had once briefly lived in, we sank onto the couch, both of us rushing to tell the other all about what we'd missed in the last few months.

"So... How's it going with the new guy?" Marley asked, tapping her foot against mine.

"Well, we finally slept together."

"And?" Her eyes widened.

"It was... Nice."

Marley pulled a face. "Nice? Sex with him was *nice*?"

Actually, sex with him had been awful, but no way in hell was I about to say *that*. "Yeah. Nothing earth-shattering, but you know. It was nice. You should see his body. He treats it like a temple. Nothing but the best."

Marley nodded. She looked like she had more to say but was somewhat reluctant.

I rolled my eyes and nudged her. "Come on, you know you can say it. Lord knows I gave you a few home truths when you were with Theo."

She blew out a breath. "Okay, fine. Shouldn't you want more than nice? The first time with Blake... I'd never felt anything like it. And I don't think it's just about being good in bed. I think it's about the connection, too."

"But what if he's my soul mate and I tossed him for one bad sexual experience? Who knows — maybe last night was a fluke. You should see him, M, he's goddamn beautiful with a body to drool over."

"Maybe he has Hot Guy—"

I held up a hand to stop her. "Do not say Syndrome." Because if she said it out loud it would confirm what I already knew.

Marley mimed zipping her lips. "Shutting up."

"So how's your delicious brother-in-law?"

"He's good. Really good." Marley smiled. "He and Cassidy made up."

I pulled a face. "I give it a week."

Marley laughed. "It's been months. Seriously, I think this is it for them. You should see them together, Hayley. Seth's happy — like, me and Blake happy. And he's really stepped up lately. Did I tell you about his bar?"

"No, what bar?"

"He's opening this insane multi-level bar, and it should be ready in another few weeks. It's going to be amazing, seriously. He's got Henry totally running scared. The big boys in Vegas have no idea what is about to hit them."

I couldn't help but smile. "You sound really proud of him."

"I am," she agreed. "And you know, I think you and Cassidy would really get along if you gave her a chance."

"Ugh. I'll pass, thanks. You forget that I'm the one who saw Seth without his mask on. *I* saw how much she fucked him up."

"Hayley, she's making up for it. He's forgiven her. Don't you think you could, too?"

Folding my arms, I glared at a spot on the floor. "I don't think she deserves it."

Marley laughed. "Jeez, you're a hard ass. Is it all the bad sex making you cranky?"

I snapped my head around to glare at her. "It wasn't bad, it was—"

She held up her hand. "Nice, I remember. Actually, I have something to show you that will take your mind right off bad—I mean, nice—sex." She rooted around in her purse at her feet and pulled out an envelope. She slipped it open and withdrew a photograph. Marley handed it to me and on some level I already knew what it was before turning it over.

There, in black and white, was a sonogram. I looked from the picture to Marley and back again. "Jesus, are you serious?"

"No," Marley said, plucking it out of my hands. "I'm messing with you. Of course I'm serious!"

"Hey, give that back! That is my little niece or nephew and I want to see."

Marley smiled and held it back to me. "All you can see is the yolk sac right now. You'll see more later."

I took it, staring at the best picture I'd ever seen. Swiveling around, I lay down and rested my head in her lap, holding the sonogram up so I could still see it. "How is it this is a good-looking kid already, when it sort of doesn't even look like anything except a blob yet?"

"Hamilton DNA. Has to be."

"How far along are you?"

"Just five weeks."

I peered up at her with a wide grin. "Newlywed sex hasn't faded yet?"

Marley laughed. "Not yet."

"So…I'm guessing our anniversary is canceled this year?" I asked, pretending to pout.

"The one where you try to kill me by alcohol poisoning?" Marley laughed. "Yeah, H, it's cancelled this year."

"Fine," I huffed. I flashed her a wicked grin. "Just wait till next year. I'll make up for it."

"I'm terrified for my liver."

"You should be." I lifted the sonogram picture, staring at the little life that currently grew inside my best friend. My eyes stung. I was so freaking happy for my girl. "Wow, M.

I don't even know what to say right now."

"I thought for sure you'd have plenty to say," she said quietly.

I sat up and twisted around to face her. "What does that mean?"

Marley shrugged. "I just figured you'd think it was fast or something. We're still young, plenty of partying left in us both."

I pinched her cheeks. "But that's why God invented nannies."

"Oh, my God, you did not just say that." Marley laughed as she batted my hands away.

"Seriously, I'm so happy for you guys. You're growing up, Marley."

"Had to happen sometime."

"Not to me," I said, sighing dreamily. "I'll be the female version of Peter Pan forever."

Marley scanned me, her big brown eyes cutting through my bullshit. "Are you happy, Hayley?"

I opened my mouth to toss a carefree comment back, but it caught in my throat. Of course I was happy. I had my beautiful apartment, I had a job I loved. I had my friends... granted, the best one lived so far away now. That had always been enough.

For as long as I could remember, I had chased a dream. But now, looking at how insanely happy Marley was as she and Blake embarked on this new chapter together, could I call what I felt every day *happy*?

I forced a smile on my face. "As a clam."

"At a clambake, maybe," Marley murmured, whacking me with a pillow. "Now, are you going to feed me, or what? This little bean has given me one hell of an appetite."

We ordered a ton of Chinese food and spent the rest of the night talking and laughing. It reminded me all the more why I loved that girl, and I hated that I didn't get to see more of her.

The night slipped away and I was loath to see it end.

Marley disappeared into her room — I would always think of it as her room — sometime after midnight, despite my pleas for her to stay up a little longer.

I lay in my bed, replaying Marley's question over and over.

Am I happy?

* * * *

The following afternoon we met Beth and Eve for lunch in Midtown, spending hours laughing. The girls were just as thrilled as I was to hear Marley's news, and immediately asked what they were planning on calling the baby and whether they were hoping for a girl or a boy.

Marley had already told me they would be happy with either, just as long as the baby was healthy. And as for names, she wasn't budging. We would find out at the birth, she said.

We left Beth and Eve around three and hit Fifth Avenue to do some serious shopping. Marley had to drag me away from every baby section, saying it was too soon to buy anything.

Once I'd done some damage to my credit card, Marley and I decided to make a pit stop at Caffébene. We found a table and I left Marley and our bags so I could go to the counter.

I joined the line and hoped it wouldn't be long. Marley looked famished and I had to wonder just what in the hell that baby was doing to her already. I scanned the display of treats and tried to decide what to get her. She had said she didn't want anything, but I'd bet my ass a chunk of that chocolate fudge cake would make her day.

"I like a girl who enjoys her desserts. What are you going for?"

A shiver crept up my spine at the voice, at the nearness — so close his breath tickled my ear. I bit down on the inside of my cheek so hard I was surprised I didn't draw blood.

I glanced over my shoulder, and Colt wore a shit-eating grin, like he knew exactly what kind of reactions he could draw out of me.

"And here I was having a good day."

He chuckled and shifted even closer. "Pleasure as always, St. Clair."

"My ass," I mumbled. "What are you even doing here? Aren't my tax dollars meant to be ensuring you catch all the bad guys roaming the city or something?"

"It's called a break, sweetheart. It's against the law to deny them."

I rolled my eyes and concentrated on anything but him.

Warm fingers curled around my elbow, sending sparks up my entire arm. "Would you let me buy you a coffee, St. Clair?"

Swallowing the lump that rose in my throat, I shook my head. Whether to answer him or to clear the fog, I wasn't sure. "No. I'm treating my girlfriend."

"One of the friends you were with the night I met you?"

"No, Marley," I answered before I could stop myself.

"*The* Marley? The one you told me all about? Is she visiting with you?"

The line moved forward and I was saved from answering as I gave my order to the barista. I headed to the end of the counter and bounced on the balls of my feet, praying they would make my complex coffee order in record time. Colt struck me as the black filter type.

The barista hustled, and before long she set two steaming mugs beside the two slabs of chocolate fudge cake on a tray. Just as I reached for it, a takeout container joined my order, and the tray was lifted from the counter.

Colt winked. "Show me the way, sweetheart."

"God, you are irritating. Has anyone ever told you that?" I asked, stomping in the direction of Marley and our table.

"Nope. But I have a feeling that you will. Often."

I didn't need to see his face to know he was wearing that wide, gorgeous—I mean, stupid—grin. Arriving back at the table, I folded my arms beneath my chest. "Sorry," I said to Marley.

"For what?" she asked, frowning.

"Hey, you must be Marley. I've heard a lot about you, and it's great to finally meet you."

"That," I answered, hitching my thumb over my shoulder at the six-foot-four hunk of blond muscle.

Marley glanced between me and Colt, her lips twitching with amusement. "And you must be Colt. I've heard a lot about *you*."

Colt slid the tray onto the table and took one of the available chairs. "I'll bet." He flashed Marley another dazzling smile. Jeez, at this rate he was going to use up all his charm on my best friend.

"She's married. And pregnant. Stop hitting on her." I scowled at him as I sat across from Marley.

"I'm pretty sure he wasn't hitting on me," Marley said, a puzzled look on her face.

"Yeah, St. Clair, I wasn't hitting her." Colt leaned closer to me. "I mean, we aren't even in a gay bar."

Marley smothered a laugh with her hand. She cleared her throat and at least tried to appear contrite. "Sorry. Sorry. Not funny."

Colt leaned his elbow on the table and rested his cheek against his fist. "So, Marley, what's it going to take for you to convince your friend here to go out with me?"

"Excuse me, I have a boyfriend," I said, indignant.

Colt swiveled around to face me, his eyebrows up around his hairline. "Since when?"

His reaction startled me, and a twinge of guilt pinched at my heart. Was Spencer even really my boyfriend? I'd bet Marley didn't think so, especially after I'd told her how bad the sex had been. "Since a month ago."

Colt nodded, seeming to consider my answer. "What do you see in him?" he enquired, as though he knew anything about Spencer.

His question made me bristle and I wasn't altogether sure

why. "Spencer treats me like a princess."

Colt flopped back in his chair, those pale blue eyes of his never leaving mine. "Well, how long?"

"How long until what?" I asked warily.

A smile pulled at one corner of his lips. "Until you figure out he's a poor replacement for the guy you really want— me."

"Oh my— You're just— Goddammit, Colt, you drive me bananas," I cried.

His smile turned into a grin. "Then I guess my work here is done." He turned to face Marley. "I'm so glad I met you. But work on your friend, okay?"

"Sure thing," Marley agreed.

"Marley!"

"What?" She widened her eyes. "I haven't even met the other guy and already I like this one better."

"Traitor," I mumbled.

"I'll see you around, St. Clair," Colt said, flashing me a wink as he rose. "You too, Marley." He picked up his coffee and left the café, but not before looking back to see if I was watching.

Which I totally was.

Dammit.

"I really like him," Marley said.

"You go date him then." I folded my arms and huffed like a pouty six year old.

Chapter Seven

In the two weeks since Marley's visit, I'd only seen Spencer once for a lunch date. He'd been super busy and, if I was totally honest, I was a little relieved. I probably would have been avoiding him anyway. After talking with Marley, I couldn't deny that there was something missing. A big something.

And there was nothing bigger than an orgasm.

I was scared to sleep with him again. Scared Marley would be proved right and I would have to confront the fact that Spencer wasn't the prince I had waited my whole life for.

But I couldn't delay the inevitable, and when Spencer called and invited me out to dinner, I had no reason to say no.

He picked me up at seven-thirty sharp and took me to another sushi place, this time in the Meatpacking District.

"So," Spencer said as we left the restaurant. "Can I convince you to have a drink with me at my place?"

That was a blatant code for sex if I ever heard one. I peered up at him, at his exquisite, handsome face. He couldn't have been that bad. Surely I'd exaggerated it, because there was no way in hell a guy as hot as Spencer had been that bad.

I smiled and slipped my hand into his. "Sure. No convincing needed."

Spencer grinned as he led me in the direction of his apartment. With his free hand, he reached out to touch my earlobe. "These look beautiful on you. You wear diamonds well."

I'd worn the Cartier earrings especially for Spencer. Men like him didn't buy gifts for them to be worn for someone else. "Honey, if there's one look I can pull off — it's diamonds."

"I don't know. I liked the look you had shortly after I gave them to you," he murmured, before dipping his head to kiss my jaw.

Something in my belly twisted unpleasantly at his words. Women all over the world thanked men for their generosity by giving them sex, so why, when Spencer insinuated that that was exactly what I'd done, did it make me feel cheap?

We turned onto a quiet street, away from the bustle of the rest of the neighborhood. Only a few other people were in sight, a strange occurrence for any part of the city.

"Your street is quiet," I said.

"This isn't my street — I live a few blocks over. It's quicker to cut through here, though." Spencer smiled. "You're not scared, are you?"

I laughed. "Should I be?"

Spencer let go of my hand to slip his arm around my waist. "I don't think you should be afraid of anything when I'm with you. Or didn't you notice the cut of my muscles the other night?"

"Of course," I said, playfully rolling my eyes. "I couldn't drag my eyes away."

Spencer slowed us to a stop. He cupped my cheek with his hand before leaning in and pressing a kiss to my mouth. "I should hope so."

He parted my lips with his tongue. I clung to his shoulders, waiting for the butterflies or the sparks. Waiting to feel something. Anything.

Spencer pulled back, his eyes heated. "Let's get back to my place."

I smiled weakly.

He turned around to all but haul me back to his apartment, but Spencer stopped short. I bumped into his side. Looking up at him in question, I followed his stare to the guy in front of us.

Holding a gun.

He wore a dark hoodie that shielded the top portion of his face. In a disjointed sort of way, I noticed the poor quality of his clothes, the grime in his fingernails and the twitchy way he held the gun.

Jesus Christ.

"Hey, man, we don't want any trouble—" Spencer started.

"Shut up," the guy spat. "Wallet. Watch. Anything else you got."

Spencer seemed frozen to the spot. What the hell was he doing? Was he stupid? *Christ, Spencer, give him your wallet!*

I unsnapped my purse and hastily pulled out my wallet. My motion seemed to startle Spencer and he jerked away from me. He didn't even spare a glance my way as he turned...and ran.

He left me. He actually left me.

My eyes widened with both shock and fear as I dragged my gaze back to the gun-wielding maniac. He took a step closer and swung the gun to point it at my chest.

I held out my wallet with shaking hands. "Just take it, please."

The guy shook his head, as though as confused and thrown as I was at Spencer's sudden departure. He scanned me from head to toe, maybe sizing me up to see what else he could get now his victim pool had shrunk. "No—I want your purse and everything in it."

"Okay, no problem." My heart pounded. I had never been more aware of every part of my being as I was in that moment. Blood coursed through my veins and my ears whined with some high-pitched noise. I dropped my wallet back into my purse and held it out for him, keeping my movements slow and smooth.

He yanked the purse from me and I almost expected him to run off.

But my luck wasn't that good.

"Jewelry too. Hurry the fuck up."

The bracelets I wore were cheap costume pieces I'd bought from Fiona, and relatively worthless. But I slid them from my wrists anyway. Next came the Cartier earrings from Spencer, and I didn't even flinch when I dropped them into my open purse in the thief's hand.

He waved the gun at me and inched closer. "Don't try to fuck with me! Necklace too."

I squeezed my eyes shut. "Please, it isn't worth anything, I swear."

"I said *now*," he grunted through clenched teeth. Another step closer put him too near. The gun was less than an inch from my chest.

A single tear rolled down my face.

He let out a groan of impatience, wrapped his dirty hand around the chain of my locket and snapped it right off my neck. "Now give me your fucking jacket and shoes."

I numbly stepped out of my Jimmy Choo pumps and slid the Stella McCartney jacket from my shoulders. He snatched the jacket from me, bent to pick up my beautiful shoes then ran. Dipping into a nearby alley, the thief was gone in the blink of an eye.

Now that I was cold and shoeless in the Meatpacking District, a shiver crept up my spine. I touched the empty space at my throat and already mourned the loss of what was worthless to anyone else, but completely irreplaceable to me.

* * * *

The police precinct was quiet save for the hum of the water cooler next to me. From somewhere beyond the foyer I could dimly hear catcalls and drunken shouts of people waiting to be processed. The desk sergeant hadn't looked my way for a solid thirty minutes, and I was beginning to think he hoped I would just disappear and save him the trouble of helping me.

After I'd come to my senses and realized I was probably catching any number of diseases by standing barefoot on a New York City sidewalk, I'd hightailed it to the nearest police precinct I'd been able to find. I'd given my statement to a nice officer who'd opened up a case for me, but even I knew that it probably wouldn't go anywhere.

Because I'd been left penniless thanks to my friendly neighborhood mugger, I had no way of getting home without walking, but the cop had told me to sit tight and a patrolman would gladly give me a ride as soon as one was available.

But apparently every patrol car in the city was currently responding to calls.

So here I was—hanging out with a cranky desk sergeant who probably didn't like the idea of one of his patrolmen being taken away for a civilian favor.

All I wanted to do was shower, lock my doors and disappear into my bed for a week. I pulled my feet up and hugged my knees, resting my cheek on them.

The desk sergeant coughed and when I glanced at him, he gave my feet a pointed look.

Oh. Right. Gross street feet. I wouldn't want them on my furniture either. With a sigh, I dropped my feet back to the ground.

I smoothed an invisible crease out of my dress when a door swung open. It took one single heartbeat for me to realize it was Colt. For once, the sight of Colt didn't antagonize me. Instead, a sort of comfort warmed me somewhere deep inside. He was familiar and strong and… I was so relieved to see him

He tapped on the front desk. "Take it easy, McCloud. Tell Frank I'll call by next week." Colt glanced at me on his way to the door, doing a double-take before veering my way.

"St. Clair?" Colt stepped in front of me. Gone were his playful smirk and flirty eyes. In their place were a creased forehead and drawn-together eyebrows. His blue eyes scanned every inch of me, quick and calculating. Cop face. I'd wondered what Colt's would look like. "What happened?" he asked, crouching in front of me.

"Mugging, Meatpacking District," Desk Sergeant

86

McCloud supplied. "Currently awaiting an available patrol car to get a ride home."

I resisted the urge to stick my tongue out at him. It wouldn't be a good idea to provoke the person who would determine whether I got a ride or walked home to SoHo in bare feet.

Colt gritted his teeth. "How long has she been waiting here?" he asked over his shoulder.

McCloud glared at Colt. "It's a busy night."

Colt swung his gaze back to me, his eyes softening. "You've got two choices—I can give you a ride home myself, right now, or I can sit here and wait with you until someone is free."

The thought of spending one more minute in that precinct was enough to make my skin crawl. I needed to be home. I managed a meek smile and nodded at Colt. He offered me his hand and without a further thought, I took it. Colt guided me outside to where a sleek black Hyundai Tucson was parked. He opened the passenger door for me before jogging around to the driver's seat.

I fastened my seatbelt, marveling at how neat and clean his car was.

Colt eased into the traffic, one hand on the steering wheel, the other rubbing the scruff on his jaw.

I cleared my throat. "Is that your precinct?" I asked, more to fill the silence than anything else.

"No," Colt answered, his voice gruff. "I'm based out of eighty-fourth. I was just visiting a buddy tonight. He wanted my help on a case he's stumped with. H-how long were you in there?"

I shrugged and stared out of the window at the buildings we passed, the streetlights washing over me. "I'm not a sure. A couple of hours, at least."

"Probably just missed you," Colt said quietly, as though he was bothered by this. I wasn't sure why. It wasn't like it would have changed what had happened. He couldn't make my night suck any less this time.

"Hey, can I borrow your phone, please?" I asked after a few minutes.

Colt reached into his jacket pocket and pulled out his cell phone. He handed it over to me.

"Thanks. I need to call a locksmith. I'm seriously hoping they don't take all night."

"The guy took everything you had?"

"From my purse to my freaking shoes," I murmured, tapping in the number for information.

"Did you have ID in your purse? With your address?"

I paused with my finger poised above the screen. "Yes."

Colt blew out a breath. "Then I can't take you home, St. Clair. I'm not saying this guy would be smart enough — or maybe stupid enough — to try to get into your home, but he could. He's got your keys, your address. Where do you want to go?"

My breath caught in my throat. I hadn't even considered that the creep would know exactly where I lived. That he could be there *right this second*, pawing through my stuff and taking even more of my things.

"Where can I take you?"

Really... I had no idea. Beth and Eve would probably be out partying somewhere and wouldn't be home. I didn't know their numbers off by heart so I couldn't call them. Did I have anyone I could call? I would call Marley in a heartbeat...if she were here.

"Help me out, St. Clair," Colt said eventually. "I can't take you home." He sighed when I still didn't answer him. "Look — you've got two options here again. Tell me a safe place I can take you. Or you can come to my place and in the morning we'll call a locksmith and I'll install new security for you."

God, I'd been such a bitch to this guy. Granted, he'd sort of deserved it. But still — here he was. It was dumb luck we'd stumbled on each other. Right place at the right time and all that. Despite how I might have acted in the past, tonight Colt had saved me.

"I, um, I don't have anyone to call," I said quietly.

"Then I guess you're coming home with me," he replied.

Colt got the car turned around and headed south, toward the Brooklyn Bridge. We drove into Brooklyn and through to Williamsburg, where Colt finally pulled up along a tree-lined street in front of a two-story brownstone. I'd never really thought about where Colt called home before—but this would have been the polar opposite of my expectations.

I'd figured he'd have a tiny one-bed apartment someplace close to work, a haven to rest his head before going back to solving crime. But this... This was a home if I ever saw one.

Colt ushered me up the stoop and unlocked the front door. We stepped inside a large, open entryway. A wide, curving staircase led upstairs and beyond that, toward the rear of the house, there was a gleaming kitchen. He moved into a room to the right of the entryway. Colt flicked on a lamp, which cast a low, comforting glow across a huge puffy couch, solid wood coffee table and massive flat screen mounted on the wall.

He turned to face me, his gaze traveling down the length of my body and back up again. "Are you cold?"

The chill hadn't left me. It had become more of a bone-weary ache that nothing but time could cure. I nodded.

Colt jerked his head. "Come on."

I followed him back out of the room and up the stairs. He opened one of the closed doors to reveal a large bathroom with a deep tub and separate shower with rain showerhead. I'd always wondered what it felt like to take a shower with one of those bad boys.

Colt crouched in front of the tub and started the hot water. He opened a bottle of bath cream, and soon the room filled with spicy steam. It smelled like Colt himself—clean, masculine and utterly delicious.

He left the room and returned with a large green towel, which he hung on the rail by the tub. Colt shut off the water once it was full and turned to face me. "Take all the time you need. I'll go put a pot on, get some food for you."

I nodded and glanced down at my legs and my dirty feet. I must look awful. I was filthy — no wonder he wanted me to take a bath. I'd probably left gross footprints throughout his house.

Colt took a step back and my heart galloped in response. I opened my mouth to ask for something, though what, I had no idea.

He stopped, his eyebrows pinching together. "St. Clair?"

A hard lump lodged in my throat.

Colt nodded, his features smoothing out. "Get in the tub. I'll be right outside." He left the bathroom and closed the door softly behind him. A moment later I heard him settle on the floor outside and rest his back against the door.

I stripped out of my clothes as fast as I could and all but jumped into the bathtub. I bit my lip as my feet stung, and I figured I probably had a few cuts. Sinking into the water, I lay back until it reached my chin.

"Do muggers ever get caught?" I asked sometime later, my voice echoing around the room.

"Sometimes. Not often," he answered eventually, as though he had been deciding how honest he should be.

"What about the things they steal? Are they ever found?"

"Sometimes," he said again. "It depends what it is, I guess. Phones, never. Jewelry, sometimes. A few low-rent pawnshops will take things without proof of purchase. More often than not, the stuff is sold on the street."

I blew out a breath. The hopes of seeing my things again was like hoping for snow in July.

"What did he take?"

"Everything. He took everything," I said, my voice breaking.

"I'm sorry," Colt said, low and quiet.

"It's just stuff, Colt. It doesn't matter." I let out a humorless laugh. "I bet Spencer wishes he hadn't wasted his money on the Cartier earrings."

Colt snorted a laugh. "Your boyfriend bought you Cartier earrings?"

I let his question hang in the air a moment. I knew Colt would have wondered why I hadn't called Spencer. "He's not my boyfriend anymore."

There was a long moment before Colt spoke again. "I would say I was sorry to hear that, but it would be a total lie."

A real laugh bubbled in my throat. Colt—the eternal optimist. Or opportunist. I couldn't decide.

I dipped under the water, submerging my entire body as though I could rinse away the horrors of the night. I borrowed some of Colt's body wash from the side of the tub and used it to wash my hair. The water was beginning to cool when I finally rose and wrapped the huge green towel around my body.

Colt was leaning against the wall opposite the bathroom when I emerged. He held a pair of sweats and a flannel shirt in his hands, which he offered to me. I ducked back into the bathroom to pull them on.

"Are you kidding me with the sweats? You realize you're about four feet taller than me?"

Colt chuckled. "Just put them on, St. Clair, and stop griping. I'm sorry I don't have Prada pajamas for you to wear."

I huffed and threw open the door. "Wow, tell me what you really think about me. I'm not some pampered little prima donna, you know."

"I know," Colt agreed. "You're a woman who likes high-end clothes. Not a thing wrong with that." He took a step closer to me and reached out to roll up the shirt cuffs. "If I'd known you were going to be coming by for a sleepover I'd have gotten something more appropriate for you."

I couldn't tell if he was being serious or not. Either way, I wouldn't have traded wearing his shirt for anything.

"Come on," Colt said. "We'll get that coffee. Decaf okay?"

"Perfect," I said, following him down the stairs.

Colt headed into the kitchen, a wide-open space that was both homey and modern. Cream marble covered the worktops and aged hardwood flooring was underfoot. A breakfast bar split the room in half, the kitchen in one section and a family area in another. There was a worn-out couch against one wall, a coffee table in the center and another flat screen on the wall opposite. French doors led out to what I assumed was the back yard. Shades covered the glass, blocking the darkness of the night.

"How do you like it?" Colt asked, as he started making the coffee.

"Plenty of cream and a crap-ton of sugar," I answered, sliding onto one of the stools at the breakfast bar.

Colt was silent as he moved around the kitchen.

I chewed on my bottom lip until I could stand the silence no longer. "I like your house."

He peered at me over his shoulder, one corner of his lips tilting up. "Thanks. Does that mean you'll visit me, then?"

I couldn't help but smile back. "You never quit, do you?"

"Not when I'm trying to get what I want."

My cheeks warmed at his statement and, for once, I didn't mind his flirting. It was oddly comforting, that this—us, Colt's chasing of me—was still something constant in my world.

"So. What were you doing wandering around the Meatpacking District alone? On your way to meet the boyfriend who is no longer in the picture?" Colt asked as he poured coffee into two mugs.

"Um, no. I wasn't alone."

He paused with the cream for a second before adding it to my coffee. Colt turned to face me and folded his arms. "He was with you? Why wasn't he at the precinct filing a report for his mugging?"

"Because he wasn't mugged." I lifted my eyes to meet Colt's, wishing he hadn't mentioned Spencer in the first place. Having to admit what I was about to was entirely too humiliating for my liking. "Spencer took off the second he saw the gun."

For a long moment, Colt did nothing. He was still and

silent. Then his jaw clenched and he took one step toward me. "You're telling me that fucker *left you alone* with a guy waving a gun in your face?"

I nodded once, dropping my eyes to my fingernails. I should really make an appointment to get them done again. I was bored with navy blue.

"Jesus fucking Christ," Colt muttered.

"He was afraid, Colt. You can't blame him for that." Except I did. I totally, totally did.

He snorted. "And you weren't afraid? You'd better hope we never run into that worthless piece of shit, I swear to God."

I suspected Colt was angrier with Spencer than he was the mugger.

Colt released a heavy breath and placed his hands either side of mine. He hung his head, his arms rigid with tension.

"I'm okay, Colt," I said quietly. "I'm fine, and...it was just stuff."

He lifted his head and pinned me with those clear blue eyes. "You're lying."

A shock went through me. Was Colt more perceptive than he let on? I'd been trying to act relaxed about the whole thing, as if by pretending I could convince myself as well as Colt that I really was fine. "You're right," I said, slapping on a smile. "Those shoes were like my babies. I freaking loved them."

He shook his head and leaned down, resting his forearms on the bar. "You don't have to bullshit me, St. Clair. He took something important to you. What was it?"

"My-my locket." My throat thickened again and I tried to swallow the raw emotion climbing to get out. Without thinking, I touched the empty space where it used to lie, heavy and reassuring.

Colt's eyes dipped to my hand. "The old-fashioned piece? I remember it."

"You do?" I asked, my eyes widening with surprise.

He nodded. "I noticed it the night we met. I liked it—it

93

was different. And you sort of fidget with it when I annoy you."

A startled laugh rose in my throat. "What?"

Colt smirked. "Yeah. You'd tug on it as though you'd dick-punch me if you didn't."

I couldn't stop the smile from spreading across my face. "I had no idea."

His expression sobered. "I'm real sorry, St. Clair."

Lifting one shoulder, I tried to maintain my nonchalance, but it was faker than a cheap Fendi. "It is what it is, I guess."

He stared me down, not buying what I was selling for one flat second. Colt stood and rounded the breakfast bar. He took my hand and gently pulled me to my feet. Colt looped his arms around my waist, drawing me into his big body. He held me, firm and sure, yet it felt like he was holding back. As though he was scared of crushing me.

I rested my cheek against his chest and the thrum of his heart helped to work a calm through my body. I let out a shaky breath and all the carefully squashed emotion threatened to bubble to the surface.

Colt slid one hand up my back to thread his fingers through my damp hair. "I'm sorry, St. Clair."

"Thank you," I whispered.

* * * *

Colt and I took our coffees into the living room. He turned on the TV and started a movie. As the big fairy tale castle came on screen, I shot Colt a withering look.

"What?" He grinned. "I told you I'd give you a re-education."

"Haven't I been through enough tonight?" I asked, curling up in the corner of the couch.

"Hey, this is one of the best movies Disney has ever made. I guarantee this one will change your mind about them," Colt said as he settled in beside me. He threw his arm over the back of the couch and I had to refrain from burrowing into the space his body made.

"Yeah, we'll see," I mumbled.

Okay.

So the ice queen totally changed my opinion on animated musicals. Within five minutes I was riveted and I knew I would be singing the songs for the next week, at least.

It was late when the movie ended. It was over too soon — and not just because I'd been enjoying it.

Colt shifted to the edge of the couch. He scrubbed a hand over his face. "Are you tired?"

No, I wasn't tired. I was exhausted. And by the rough quality of his voice, so was Colt. I didn't want to go to bed. I didn't want the silence of the night to settle around me like a bad dream that was sure to find me anyway. I didn't... I didn't want to be alone.

"Come on," Colt said as he rose from the couch. He offered me his hand and I accepted it, sliding my palm against his and feeling the rough calluses.

Everything about Colt was different from what I liked — what I usually looked for in a man. But tonight, he was everything I needed. Colt led me upstairs and pushed open a door.

The bedroom had to be the master. It was large and a huge bed dominated the space. An armchair took up one corner, and a shirt was draped over it. The room was basic and simple and was filled with Colt.

"You'll be fine in here. If you need anything, I'll be right downstairs, okay?"

I nodded. "Thank you, Colt. For everything."

"It's nothing." He flashed a quick smile before squeezing my shoulder on his way out of the room.

And I was alone.

In Colt's bedroom.

I stood in the center of the room for a solid minute before I mentally shook myself, peeled off the sweatpants and crawled into the bed.

Colt's bed.

Colt's scent enveloped me like a lover's embrace as I pulled the sheets up to my chin. Tonight could not have ended any more differently than I'd imagined. For most of the day I had wondered whether I was doing the right thing in moving forward with Spencer. I couldn't ignore that he didn't create a storm of butterflies in my belly or make my toes curl in bed. But he was good to me. Treated me the way I'd always wanted to be treated.

Until a lunatic had pulled a gun on us and he'd fled the scene quicker than I could blink. Muscles did not make for bravery, it seemed.

Colt would never have run.

The thought sent a chill up my spine. Colt never would have left me alone. Hell, Colt probably would have gotten the gun off the creep and perp-walked him to the nearest precinct. Or beat the living daylights out of him. Either way, I would still have my locket.

I curled up into a ball on my side, my hand pressed against my bare throat. Out of all the meaningless crap I owned, why, *why* did that have to be taken from me?

Chapter Eight

Despite Colt's bed being super big and comfortable, I tossed and turned for hours. In the end I gave up and padded quietly down to the kitchen. The house was silent, save for the hum of the refrigerator. I poured myself a glass of juice from the fridge and tiptoed down the hall to the living room.

When Colt had said he would be downstairs, I had thought there was a guest bedroom. Instead I found him sprawled out on the enormous couch, the TV muted, the flickering of the screen casting shadows over his exquisite sleeping face.

I curled up on the couch near his feet and tugged the ends of my shirt over my thighs. Colt's shirt was the shit. I wondered if he would let me keep it. The worn flannel was soft and warm and I'd sleep in it every night until the damn thing fell apart.

The night I'd met Colt, I'd known he was the most attractive guy I had ever laid eyes on. I'd drunk in glances of him in greedy slurps. But since then, my annoyance at him hadn't allowed me to fully appreciate how handsome he was. I'd avoided looking at him for too long. Probably because if I didn't, that face of his would hypnotize me into forgetting what he'd done to piss me off so badly in the first place.

But now I had the opportunity to stare at him all I wanted, without fear of embarrassment or anything else. Colt's face was relaxed and peaceful in a way that I'd never seen before. He was often playful and jovial, but Colt always carried an air of seriousness about him. Some deep-rooted cautiousness that came from knowing exactly how evil the world was. That had to affect a person, and Colt would be no different. But rather than let it turn him into something cold and hard, I had a feeling it would make Colt fiercely protective of those he cared about.

I was attracted to every single thing about Colt. His strong jaw, covered in a layer of scruff, his lips that I ached to kiss again. His pale blue eyes that seemed to see right through me and stared at me...

Wait.

Are staring at me.

Colt pushed up onto his elbow and pressed his fingers into his eyes. "What time is it?" he asked, his voice low and gruff.

"Um, I'm not sure," I said, my heart thumping at having been caught openly staring at him while he'd slept, like a total freaky creeper. "Sometime after three, I think."

Colt blew out a breath. He swung his legs off the couch and sat up, our bodies only inches apart. "Couldn't sleep?" His eyes bored into me, past the party girl to the raw person inside.

I shook my head.

"You look exhausted, St. Clair. You need to rest." Colt rubbed a hand over his hair. "Do you want me to come lie down with you?"

"Would you mind?" I asked, feeling like the world's biggest loser.

"Of course I wouldn't mind. Come on, get your ass upstairs."

When we stood, Colt draped his heavy arm around my shoulders. I fit perfectly against his side, as though someone had designed our bodies to fit like jigsaw pieces.

In his bedroom, Colt stripped out of his jeans and T-shirt, letting them fall to the floor. I had been poised to climb back into bed, but the sight of Colt in only a pair of boxer briefs froze me to the spot.

Holy crow, he was beautiful. Actually, completely,

beautiful.

His body was every bit as cut and carved as I'd imagined it would be. Strong, muscled shoulders led to a broad chest with pecs to die for, down to washboard abs and into a tapered waist. Well-defined arms with biceps that could throw me around his bed with ease...

Okay.

Stop staring.

Anytime now, Hayley.

Oh, what the hell. Something that gorgeous was meant to be stared at.

"As much as I'm enjoying you looking at me like that, I'm about three seconds from passing out. Can we go to bed, please?" Colt asked as he threw back the sheets.

My cheeks scorched. "Uh, yeah. Sure. Why not?" *God.*

We both slid into the bed, a good foot of distance between us.

Even though Colt was with me, and so close I could reach out and touch him, the same problem still existed. Every time I closed my eyes, all I saw was the gun in my face, and I was gripped with the same fear as when Spencer had turned, ran and left me all alone.

"Colt?" I whispered. "Would you hold me?"

There was a pause after I'd spoken. So long I thought he must be asleep already and hadn't heard me. But then the sheets rustled and Colt pressed his front to my back, his big body curling against mine. He brought one arm around me to hold me more firmly to him. And yes, he was a great spooner.

I sank into his warmth, letting the strength of him calm my anxious heart.

And because he was holding me like he would never let a single thing happen to me, I fell asleep.

* * * *

The first thing I was aware of was how hot I was. Toasty-warm and so relaxed I was practically boneless. The second thing I was aware of was *why* I was so warm and relaxed.

Colt was wrapped around me like a blanket. One of his legs was pushed between mine, his knee dangerously close to the apex of my thighs. His head was nestled into the crook of my neck and he gripped my side with one large hand. Most of his body was draped over mine. And honestly…I sort of liked it. I felt soft and feminine, small and delicate… yet at the same time, wanted. As though at any second he would roll me on top of him and make good use of the impressive erection currently pressing against my hip.

He murmured something in his sleep and tugged me closer to him. Without thinking, I brought my hand up to his hair and ran my fingers through the soft strands. Whatever product he used to style the blond locks was more or less gone, leaving his hair silky and natural.

Colt groaned, stretching his long body. "Man, a guy could get used to waking up like this."

I laughed. "I'll bet."

He nuzzled my throat. "You smell good."

You feel good. "Is this the part where you ask me to get naked to thank you for coming to my rescue last night?" I asked, teasing.

Colt pulled away from me, pushing up onto his elbow to peer down at me. I instantly missed the warmth. A frown creased his forehead. "No. Because I'm not an asshole." The frown smoothed out and his trademark half-smile appeared. "But if you *want* to get naked, I won't object."

I shoved at his chest. "You're all heart, Colt, seriously."

"That's what they tell me," he said with a grin before climbing out of the bed. "Get your butt downstairs. I'll make you breakfast." Colt picked up the T-shirt he had discarded the night before and pulled it over his head on the way out of the room.

I blew out a breath. I'd just spent the night with Colt.

And I wanted to do it again.

With a whole lot less clothing.

That thought scared me way more than the mugger had last night.

I made my way downstairs in just the shirt. Colt's sweats were ridiculously big on me and I didn't have the energy to keep yanking them up every two minutes. In the kitchen, Colt was busy whisking something in a bowl.

"Omelet okay?" he asked, not looking up from his task.

"Perfect," I answered, surprised. When he'd said he would make me breakfast, I'd assumed he'd meant toast and OJ.

"Coffee's in the pot," he said, jerking his head to the coffee maker.

I rounded the breakfast bar and set about making us a cup of coffee each. I retreated to a stool with my mug, watching Colt work his kitchen like a boss. There was something seriously sexy about a guy who could cook... and was willing to cook for me.

"So, I was thinking we'd stop by this security place I know of on our way back to your apartment. I want new locks fitted, an alarm and maybe even a security camera. What do you think?"

I blinked. "I think you've obviously given this some thought."

"Your safety isn't something I'm willing to compromise." Colt finished with the omelets and slid one onto a plate. He placed it in front of me. "So?"

"I think it sounds like a good idea," I said, picking up my knife and fork.

"Good. I've already called a locksmith. He's going to meet us at your apartment in a few hours."

Once we finished breakfast, Colt ran out to try to find me a pair of shoes. He returned twenty minutes later with a pair of black ballet flats, in the correct size, and I gave him points for going at all—even if he had played it safe with the style. I wore one of his hoodies over my dress and, despite our best efforts, I still looked like a chick doing the walk of shame.

I didn't really care. After last night... There were other things to care about.

Colt drove us to a home security store on the way out of Brooklyn. He talked shop with the owner and I hung back like a naïve girl who had no idea what the boys were talking about. Mostly because... I had no idea what they were talking about.

We left with an alarm system, extra locks and a deadbolt, a security camera and a stun-gun disguised as a pretty pink perfume bottle. Whether it was because he was a cop and therefore knew exactly what some people were capable of, or he was simply concerned about my safety, it was clear Colt wasn't taking any chances.

Colt carried the bag with all my shiny new security stuff upstairs to my apartment. The locksmith hadn't arrived yet, so we sat on the floor in the hallway to wait for him.

"Do you do this a lot?" I asked, reaching for the huge bag of potato chips we'd bought in case we were in for a long wait.

"What?"

"Play security guard for helpless women."

Colt flashed a crooked smile. "Not half as often as I'd bet you're thinking."

I shrugged. "Even if it really is half, the number is still a high one."

He sighed and rested his head on the wall behind him. Colt didn't look at me when he next spoke, though that smile was still in place. "St. Clair, you have a really skewed perception of me. Maybe one day you'll give me half a chance to prove myself."

Despite his words, Colt already was proving himself to me. Every moment I spent with him showed me that he wasn't the cocky, man-whore seducer who lowered a woman's guard to get what he wanted. Okay, so he was still totally cocky, but deep down, I think there was something...solid about Colt.

"Maybe," I said, my lips pulling into a smile.

Colt snatched the bag of chips from my grasp. "Maybe," he mimicked. "Woman, are you ever *not* going to bust my balls?"

I giggled. "I doubt it."

He mumbled something that I didn't quite catch.

Just as I was about to ask him to have the nerve to repeat it so I could hear him, the sound of someone coming our way echoed down the hallway. I turned to see a guy carrying a toolbox.

"This must be our guy," Colt said, rising to his feet. He held out a hand and hauled me up.

"You Colton Deluca?" the guy asked as he approached us.

"Yeah, that's me."

Once inside, the guys talked...lock stuff and security and I rooted around in my bedroom for an old cell phone. Colt had grabbed me a new prepaid SIM while he had been out buying my shoes. Eventually I found a dinosaur in my vanity drawer and I plugged it in to charge. While I waited for it to get some life, I changed out of last night's clothes into a pair of shorts and a Goo Goo Dolls concert tank that was a little big on me.

The phone flickered to life, letting out a cheerful tinkling noise. I punched in the number for the store and listened to the ring as I waited for Fiona to find the damn cordless.

"Hello, Back in Time, where can I take you today?" Fiona answered.

I giggled. "That never gets old, seriously."

"Hayley!" Fiona cried. "How are you, my darling girl?"

I sighed. "To be honest, I've seen better days." I gave Fiona a brief rundown of the events, my heart pinching when she took a sharp breath. For a woman as loving and caring as Fiona, it physically hurt her when someone she cared about was harmed or had a rough break. She was a sensitive soul.

"I'm okay," I assured her. "It was just stuff, Fi. Totally replaceable." Except that one piece I would never see again. I squeezed my eyes shut as I touched the empty space at my throat again.

"Even so, you're allowed to be sad. But, I have to ask, because I'm dying to know... How are we feeling about the young man who gallantly came to your rescue?"

I glanced toward my open bedroom door. Colt could be anywhere. At the front door where I'd left him...or in the kitchen and therefore within earshot. "We're feeling grateful."

"And...?"

"And what?" I asked with a laugh.

Fiona huffed. "Come on, don't act clueless. You know I like the boy. Your opinion of him has to have changed."

Only Fiona could refer to Colt as a boy. He was as far removed from a boy as someone could be. There was nothing boyish about Colt. Nothing at all. Not his cut muscles or strong shoulders or that huge... *Okay. Not going there.*

"Yeah, my opinion has changed. But I have a type. And he isn't it."

"You and your type," Fiona mumbled. "Hasn't it occurred to you that if you stopped looking so hard for what it is you *think* you should want, then the thing you *really* want would find you?"

I laughed again. "I'm not even going to pretend like I know what that means."

"Fine, don't listen to me and my sage advice. You were going to come into the store today — are you calling to say you won't make it? Because if you aren't, I'm telling you not to come in. You have enough to deal with right now."

Man, this woman was amazing. "Thanks, Fi. I'll make the sale next weekend though, okay?"

"Sweetheart, I would understand if you didn't. Don't come down here until after the sale at least."

"Only if you promise not to price anything until I'm back?"

"I'll...try."

"Sure you will." I giggled. "Take care, Fi. I'll see you

soon."

"You too, dear girl. Give my love to the handsome young man."

"Bye."

I left the phone on my nightstand to continue charging and headed back out to see what Colt and the locksmith were up to. After looking, I still didn't really know what they were up to. So I sat on the couch with my legs folded under me to skim the latest *In Style*, even though I'd already devoured it from cover to cover.

Sometime later the locksmith left and Colt fitted the extra locks we'd bought, then hooked up the camera in the hallway so it pointed at my door.

"Okay, ready to see how this bad boy works?"

"I'm guessing...dinner and drinks then heavy petting?" I asked, tossing the magazine onto the couch and rising to my feet.

Colt slowly turned from where he stood in my tiny kitchen, separated from the living room by a counter. He really dominated the space. My apartment was on the cozy side, but with him taking up more room than the average person, it shrunk even further.

I didn't mind. I liked that he filled my apartment. It felt... safe with him there.

"You know," Colt said when I joined him in the kitchen. He took one step closer, crowding me with his body. "You really play with fire when you say things like that to me."

I rolled my eyes as though his nearness, and his words, didn't affect me at all. "Of course I am. Because someone making a joke is really code for *jump my bones.*"

Colt smiled, slow and sure. "No, because when you say things like that to me, you aren't joking. You're flirting. And if I knew you were ready, I'd flirt back. Don't you remember what happened the last time we flirted?"

I glanced to the couch where I'd kissed him as if he were my last chance to breathe. A warm flush swept through my body at the memory of his lips on mine, the feel of him beneath my fingertips, the ghost of his tongue pillaging my mouth.

The last time we'd flirted, it had ended up with him giving me the best damn kiss of my life. "You tricked me last time." I swallowed.

Colt dropped his head and shook it softly. When he lifted it again, his pale blue eyes pierced mine. "I didn't trick you. You misunderstood me. And I swear to God, there will be no misunderstanding next time around."

Next time. The words sent a thrill up my spine. But did I want a next time? Colt was everything I *didn't* want when it came to the type of guy I wanted to be with.

He moved away from me slowly, as though it was hard for him to do so. "Come look at this. Let me show you how it works."

When he turned away, I squeezed my eyes shut and gave myself a mental kick in the pants to get my crap together. I joined Colt at the counter and watched as he tapped on the tablet he'd brought from his house.

He opened an app, and right there on the screen was my apartment door, with views of the hallway, too. "Anyone comes knocking you're not expecting, open this up and you'll see exactly who is on the other side of the door. And if it's someone you don't know and don't feel right opening your door to, call the cops. Or call me. Got it?"

"Got it," I said with a firm nod. I had to admit, it was pretty cool.

"I've set it up so the camera starts recording the instant it detects movement. You can get notifications to your phone when it picks up movement, and you can view the recordings on your phone when you're out. But it also has a live feed, if you just want to check out your hallway."

"Wow, you're like a total security nerd."

Colt peered at me. "Yeah. I'm like a total security nerd. What's so wrong with having someone take care of you, St. Clair?"

His words made me start. All my life, the idea of a man

taking care of me hadn't meant hooking up a security camera outside my door or fitting locks. It had involved spoiling me rotten, surprising me with a new dress or a pair of expensive earrings. It had involved romantic dinners in high-end restaurants where they didn't print the prices on the menu and being whisked away for minibreaks to Italy.

I forced a laugh. "Something tells me you don't want the job of taking care of me. I'm high maintenance, or hadn't you noticed?"

"I noticed," Colt said, not taking his eyes from me for a second. "Something tells me you wouldn't know how to handle a real man who wants you for you."

"What is that supposed to mean?" I asked, bristling.

"It means you refused to even consider going on a date with me—a guy who has proven a few times now that I'm interested in you. That I want to get to know you, and yeah, kiss you again because, before"—he gestured to that stupid couch that held a perfect and awful memory of him—"that was the best goddamn kiss of my life, and forgive me for wanting a hell of a lot more of them. You're feisty and pig-headed and...and a royal pain in my ass, but I *like* you, St. Clair. But will you give me a chance? No. You want to go out with rich fucks who will buy you diamond earrings and leave you alone with a mugger."

I was too stunned to respond. Too stunned to move.

He was right, of course. He had my number down and for the first time in my life, I felt ashamed by it. I'd always thought I was simply aiming high, not wanting to settle for second best. But maybe all the things I wanted weren't aiming high. Maybe the things Colt could offer weren't second best. Maybe—*no*.

No. I knew what I wanted and there was no shame in that.

Colt was...just a hot guy with muscles that made me drool and clouded my better judgment.

And who was really good at home security.

"But then again, that asshole never tricked you into thinking he was gay, so who the hell am I to talk, right?"

Colt asked, snapping me out of my reverie. He nudged me and flashed a perfect crooked smile.

I rolled my eyes, grateful for the reprieve. "Totally."

"Okay, time to start the phone calls. I'll make a pot of coffee, you get all the information you need." Colt turned and started preparing the coffee machine.

Ugh. This was the part I had been dreading. But I did as I was told and hunted out the paperwork I needed.

I spent hours on the phone cancelling credit cards, ordering replacements and arranging for a new phone. I'd have to go down to the DMV for a new license and I was so not looking forward to that trip. I'd put it off for another day.

"Man, am I glad that is over," I said, replacing the phone in its cradle.

"You did good. You can start moving forward from here," Colt said, picking up our empty coffee mugs and taking them into the kitchen.

"So, you know those low-rent pawnshops you mentioned last night? Could you maybe give me the addresses? I might hit them up, see if anything has been pawned."

Colt didn't turn around for a long second. When he did, his face was sober. "They aren't the sort of places I'd be happy for you to go to. They aren't in the sort of neighborhoods I'd want you in. And, if I'm being totally honest...if your jewelry really wasn't worth much, the creep probably just tossed it."

My eyes burned. I turned to the stack of magazines in front of the couch and started tidying the pile. "Right. Of course. It was stupid to even ask."

"It wasn't stupid, St. Clair. There's nothing wrong with hope. I'm sorry this is happening to you."

"It is what it is," I said with a shrug.

"Want to fool around for a while to take your mind off it?"

A startled laugh burst out of me. I clamped a hand over my mouth and turned to look at him. He leaned against the counter, his feet crossed at the ankles and his arms folded. Colt's eyes were full of mirth and his lips twitched with amusement.

"Man, you never miss a beat, do you?"

Colt snorted. He pushed off the counter and dropped down on the other end of the couch from me. "I never miss an opportunity. There's a difference."

"I really like you," I said. "Against my better judgment, maybe, but I like you."

He sighed and rested his head on the back of the couch. "Why do I feel a *but* coming on?"

"Maybe because there is one. I really like you, but we'll only ever be friends."

Colt twisted his head to look at me. "Do you honestly believe that?"

"Yes, I do."

He grinned. "Keep telling yourself that, St. Clair. Maybe one day you'll start *really* believing it."

I huffed and nudged him with my foot. "Jeez, you're annoying."

Colt caught my foot and pulled it onto his lap. "That's what they tell me."

"So I figure you've earned yourself a lunch. Do you feel like going out or ordering in?"

"Sweetheart, when it comes to you, the answer would be stay in — always. Why would you think I want to share you?" Colt sighed. "But I need to take a rain check this time around."

"Blowing me off for another chick?" I asked, teasing.

"What else?" Colt rolled his eyes. "I don't want to wreck this chance and never have you ask me out again. So how about I make a counter offer? Instead of you taking me out, how about you let me take you somewhere? Lunch tomorrow."

"Sure."

He grinned. "It's a date."

"It is not," I laughed.

"Is too."
"Is not."
"Is *too*."
"Is *not*."

Chapter Nine

Once Colt had left, I had nothing better to do with my time than haul ass down to the DMV and wait for hours in line to get a replacement license. Not that I did much driving in the city, but I figured it was better to have than not. I spent the rest of my night watching Disney movies on Netflix.

It was around eleven when I crawled into bed and stared at the ceiling for well over an hour. The events from the last few days spun around and around in my mind in a never-ending loop. The mugger's face, along with Spencer's and Colt's, flashed again and again and there was a piece of me that wished I was spending another night in the safety of Colt's big bed, in his arms.

I reached for my cell phone and dialed a number I knew by heart. She answered a hell of a lot faster than Fiona had.

"Hello?" Marley asked.

"Hey, it's me," I said, snuggling farther down in my bed.

"Hayley? What number are you calling from?"

"A temporary one. Do you want the long or short version?"

"Both," Marley said with a laugh.

"I got mugged last night and the asshole took everything. I bought a prepaid SIM for my old phone."

"Okay," Marley said after a pause. "Maybe you should start again with the long version now."

"I was out with Spencer and we were heading back to his place when a mugger pulled a gun on us. Spencer freaked and took off—can you believe it? So there I was in the Meatpacking District all by myself with a freak with a gun, who stole everything from my wallet to my freaking shoes. Once he bolted with all my stuff, I hauled my ass to the nearest police precinct to file a report. I was waiting for a ride home when Colt showed up."

I let out a long breath, instantly back at that quiet precinct. The relief I'd felt when I'd seen Colt had been palpable. "He took me home with him. My keys and everything had been in my purse, along with my ID. Colt... He was worried the creep would be greedy enough to try to break into my apartment so I went with him to his place in Brooklyn. Oh, man, you should have seen it. This big brownstone. And it was nice inside. Like, really nice. A home, you know? This morning we went to a security store and Colt bought a bunch of stuff, extra locks, a stun gun and even a security camera. He arranged for my locks to be changed and hooked up the camera and everything. Colt, he was— Jesus, Marley, he stepped up."

"Christ," Marley whispered. "Jesus Christ. Are you okay?"

"I'm fine. Short a few bucks, but fine."

"You must have been so scared."

I snorted a laugh. "Yeah, I was scared. But...okay, if I tell you something, do you swear not to throw it in my face later when the hero worship wears off?"

"No," Marley said then giggled. "Not at all. Because when it wears off is probably when you need to hear it again."

"Fine," I sighed. "Colt stepped up. And he dragged me up, too. If he hadn't showed, I probably would be a frightened, cowering mess right now. But he sort of— Colt, he saved me, Marley."

"That's because he's a good guy. And because he cares about you."

"I like him, I do. But just as friends. I'm not going to avoid him anymore. In fact, we're having lunch tomorrow."

"Man, Hayley, you're really telling yourself that you only like him as a friend?"

"You sound like Colt, you traitor." I yawned. "Anyway,

why'd you answer? Isn't my little niece or nephew supposed to turn you narcoleptic or something?"

Marley laughed. "Something like that. But the three-hour nap I had this afternoon really refreshed me."

"Jeez...you're allowed to have three-hour naps when you're pregnant? Where do I sign up?"

"You do realize you could have all the sleep in the world if you would cut back on the partying, and shopping, and eating out, and all the other stuff you do when you could be sleeping?"

"Yeah, but when I'm lying on my deathbed, I'm not going to be thinking about that awesome early night I had, am I?"

"Good point."

"So tell me all about the little person you're cooking. Can you feel them yet?"

"Little flutters. Soft, like I'm excited about something." Marley laughed. "Does that sound weird?"

"Sort of," I admitted. "Are you showing?"

"No, not yet. Don't worry, when it's time for the shower I'll be huge and you can make fun of me all you want then."

"Ooh, I can't wait for the shower! I am going to spoil you rotten and invent weird, baby-themed games. And get one of those diaper cake things. When are you having it?"

"Not for a few months. You have been told how long these pregnancies are, right?"

"I can't remember. Maybe I skipped health class that day."

"I wouldn't be surprised, Hayley."

"Have I told you lately how proud I am of you?"

"Only almost every day."

"Well, I am."

"I know." She laughed quietly. "So what are you wearing tomorrow?"

"I'm not sure. Maybe my blue lace DVF?"

"Ooh, killer. Isn't it a little formal for a lunch?"

"If he's taking me somewhere I can't wear a DVF, then I'm not sure I want to go."

Marley snorted. "Of course not, Hayley."

* * * *

Dressed in my prettiest DVF dress, dark blue lace with a short skater skirt, scalloped edges and cute little capped sleeves, combined with some nude heels, I felt flirty and feminine. Which maybe wasn't the best idea, I thought as I waited for Colt to pick me up. I was messing around on the tablet he'd left me until I got around to buying one of my own, and clicked on the app that would let me view what the camera was seeing.

A few minutes later, a form headed down the hallway and my heart picked up speed in response. *Colt.*

I watched, and heard, him tap on my door. Padding over, I glanced at the image of him on the tablet screen again. He wore a white T-shirt and faded jeans, completely nondescript and yet completely delectable.

I bit my lip. "I'm not sure if I should open my door. The camera is picking up a shady-looking dude."

Colt turned to face the camera and flashed a cocky smile. "Quit pretending that you weren't watching for me on that thing."

Well, damn, he had me there.

I threw open the door, a flush of pleasure coursing through me at Colt's blatant appraisal.

"If I had told you to dress casual, would it have made a difference?"

"Nope," I answered.

"I didn't think so." Colt shook his head. "Come on, St. Clair, I'm starving."

We made our way out of my building and into Colt's car, which was parked in a rare spot right outside.

"Where are we going?" I asked.

"Call it a surprise," Colt said and grinned. And no matter how many times I asked, he wouldn't budge and tell me.

We drove over the bridge into Williamsburg again and I

turned to Colt. "Are you taking me to your place for lunch? I can't tell if I should be offended or impressed at your determination."

A laugh rumbled in Colt's chest. "Relax, St. Clair. I'm not taking you to my place. We're going somewhere different."

"Where? I don't think I've been to any restaurants in Brooklyn."

He scoffed. "Of course a Manhattan princess like you hasn't eaten in Brooklyn. Are you afraid we serve dog or something?"

"Man, you're huffy." I rolled my eyes. "And what's so wrong with being a princess?"

Colt slid a sideways glance at me. "Aside from the obvious?"

I frowned. "What obvious?"

"Princesses are generally simpering idiots waiting for a man to come rescue them."

"Coming from the man who watches Disney, which is generally full of those simpering princesses, that's a touch ironic."

Colt snorted a laugh. "Okay, I'll give you that. I'm sorry, but I figured a modern woman like you would be all for equality among the sexes."

"I am. But I still want a man to treat me like one."

"A princess?"

I nodded.

"Why?"

"Why not?" I asked. "Maybe it makes me spoiled, or less of a feminist, whatever. Some women like tall guys, lean guys, buff guys—I like guys who will treat me like a princess."

"Again, why? What is it that you want—presents? Meaningless, thoughtless gifts that shows the guy knows nothing about you?"

"No," I said after a long moment. "I want to be the center of someone's attention. I want to be surprised by them, yeah, maybe with gifts, because I want to know they were thinking of me. I want to be whisked away to fancy restaurants and on trips. I want to be someone's everything — that they can't help but want to show it to me." Dropping my eyes to my lap, I smoothed a hand over my skirt. "And it might be nice to have someone save me every once in a while." *Just like you did.*

Marley loved my independence. So did I, to a certain point. But what would it be like to not have to make all the decisions? To come home to someone cooking for me, to not lie in bed alone every night, to have someone to lean on?

Colt didn't respond right away. There was quiet in the car, save for the sound of the engine and the tires on the road. He scrubbed his hand over his jaw. "Do you want to know what I think?"

"I think you're going to tell me anyway," I said, folding my arms and turning to stare out of my window.

He chuckled. "I think you shouldn't want a man who will treat you like a princess. I think you should want a man who will treat you like a woman. Because anyone can pander or suck up someone's ass. It takes a real man to treat a woman right. To make her feel loved and cherished. Adored. Wanted. *Safe.* A princess is something wholly untouchable and a worthless dream. A woman is something to revere."

My breath lodged in my throat. I couldn't have responded if I wanted to.

Was he right? Colt was an entirely different breed of man from the ones I was used to. So foreign I wasn't even sure if I spoke the same language as him.

His speech left me feeling like I didn't fit within my skin. I snuck a sideways glance at him. For all intents and purposes, Colt was relaxed, his hands loosely gripping the steering wheel as he stared out at the road in front.

But I thought I knew better. Whatever had moved him to speak to me like that…it had shaken him as much to say as it had for me to hear.

We traveled the rest of the way in silence and, true to his

word, we didn't end up at Colt's place. We were, however, on another residential street.

"Where is this place we're eating?" I asked as I climbed out of the car.

"I don't think you'll have heard of it. What with your fear of crossing a body of water to another borough and all," Colt said as he rounded the car and joined me on the sidewalk.

"It wasn't like I made a conscious decision not to come to Brooklyn—to eat out or otherwise. The opportunity just never came up." I paused, remembering one past experience when I had, in fact, come to Brooklyn. "I've partied here before, though. It was this awesome rave in a warehouse that went on for two days before the cops shut it down."

"I guess you get points for that." Colt opened a gate and jogged up the stoop to a red-tiled house. He turned back to face me when he realized I hadn't followed. "Are you coming or what?"

I slowly made my way up the stoop, wearing a confused frown. "Why do I have the feeling you've totally tricked me into something I wouldn't have agreed to?"

"Maybe because if I'd told you, you never would have agreed to come," Colt answered with his charismatic smile. He opened the front door and motioned for me to follow.

"Who is that now?" a male voice shouted from inside the house.

"It's me," Colt called back.

"Who in the hell is me?"

Colt snorted a laugh. "Are you going deaf as well as senile now?"

A young girl, maybe seventeen, popped her head into the hall. She glared at Colt. "Do you have to get him all riled up? He's only just calmed down after Uncle Sal kicked his ass at checkers." The girl glanced at me and straightened. "Who are you?"

"This is Hayley St. Clair. She's a friend of mine. Hayley, this is my sister, Tess." Colt turned his back on the girl and faced me with a grimace. "I'm really sorry. But it should only last a few minutes."

"What will?" I asked.

"Mom! Colt brought a girl home!" Tess yelled, disappearing.

My eyes widened. "I'm going to regret this, aren't I?"

I got my answer within half a second.

"He what?"

"Who is she?"

"Is she his girlfriend?"

"Where are they?"

Colt laughed under his breath. He caught my hand and tugged me down the hall. "Trust me, it's better to get it over with." Colt led me into a family room where two older men sat with a board game between them on a small card table at the rear of the room. A girl older than Tess was curled in an armchair near the TV. My presence, it seemed, didn't matter a smidge to her.

"Well, turn around, let me get a look at you."

I jumped about a foot out of my skin at the voice behind me. I whirled around to see a petite, smiling woman. Standing about my height, it was obvious from the clear blue eyes to the blonde hair — even though hers was peppered with gray — that she was Colt's mother.

"Now I know you're not this joker's girlfriend. You're far too good-looking for him."

A surprised laugh bubbled up in me. I cut a glance toward Colt. "I like her."

"You laugh at her jokes. She'll like you," he teased. Colt stepped forward and bent to kiss his mother's cheek. "I stole St. Clair for lunch. You don't mind an extra person, do you?"

"What's one more?" she smiled. "I'm Jessie. And I assume you have a first name to accompany the second my son insists on calling you by?"

"Yeah, Hayley," I said. "Thank you for having me."

"Pleasure is all mine, Hayley," Jessie said.

"Hey, what do we look like over here? Garden gnomes? No one feel like introducing us?"

Jessie smiled. She gestured to the two older men. "Meet Grandpa Joe and Uncle Sal. Cantankerous old bats for the most part, but we like having them around. And the zombie in front of the TV is Sophie."

I stifled a laugh and raised my hand in greeting.

"You're right, Jessie girl," Uncle Sal said. "That girl is far too pretty for Colton."

"Man, I come home to see you old fools and all I get is attitude." Colt shook his head, the smile he wore taking any sting from his words. He turned back to his mother. "Is Faith here yet?"

Jessie nodded. "She's in the kitchen helping with the brownies for dessert."

Colt loosely clasped my elbow and drew me a touch closer to him. "I should probably give you a heads up—"

Something barreled into my side, knocking me away from Colt.

A tiny girl leaped into his embrace, wrapping her thin arms around his neck. "Daddy!"

Wait a minute... *Daddy?*

Colt met my eyes over the top of her dark head. "St. Clair, meet Faith. My daughter."

The girl turned and peered at me, her eyes so much like her father's and grandmother's. We observed each other for a moment, both of us a new addition to each other's worlds.

"Faith, this is my friend Hayley."

"She's pretty," Faith said quietly, her inquisitive blue eyes never leaving mine.

"She is," Colt confirmed.

"Do you like brownies?" she asked me.

"I—" I cleared my throat and tried again. "Yes, I do."

"Good, because I'm making some with Nana J and they're super yummy. I'll make sure you get a big one." Faith wriggled in her father's arms until he released his hold on her. She dropped and hit the ground running.

119

Jessie sighed. "I'd better supervise whatever carnage that girl is inflicting on my poor kitchen." She touched Colt's arm and leaned in to kiss his cheek. "It's good to have you home."

Once she'd left to follow Faith, Colt rubbed the back of his neck. He flashed me an innocent, boyish look. "On a scale from one to ten, how freaked are you?"

"A solid seven-point-five," I answered honestly.

He nodded. "I'll take that as a win. I thought for sure it would be off the charts."

"Why didn't you tell me?" I asked quietly.

Colt opened his mouth to respond, but his sister brushed past us on her way into the room. He glanced at her and the other girl by the TV. "Later."

I nodded my understanding.

"Hey, pretty girl, you any good at seven-card stud?" Uncle Sal called from across the room.

"You're meant to be playing Monopoly," Sophie said from her spot in the chair, never dragging her eyes from the TV. "Mom took the deck away when you both got too competitive."

"Girl, you think we don't have a spare or two stashed away?" Grandpa Joe looked at me. "Well? Are you in?"

"Grandpa Joe, she doesn't want to play poker with you." Colt's tone was exasperated, but the amused quirk of his lips said he wasn't serious.

"I've never played seven-card stud, but my Texas hold 'em is passable," I said.

Grandpa Joe and Uncle Sal exchanged a look before turning to me with wide grins. I guess that meant I was in their game.

So my poker was more than rusty, but after getting hustled by the two old coots over a few hands, I stepped up and managed to hold my own. Colt watched with amusement from the couch and whooped when I finally won a hand.

"Lunch is—" Jessie started as she entered the living room. She folded her arms and glared at Grandpa Joe and Uncle

Sal. "What are you two doing?"

"Regretting asking this one to play," Uncle Sal griped as he tossed down his hand.

Jessie sighed. "Dining room, please. Lunch is ready."

I followed Colt down the hall and into the dining room, where Faith was carefully laying down cutlery at each place setting.

Colt ruffled her hair. "Good girl, helping Nana J."

Faith looked up and smiled. "She said I got an extra brownie if I helped."

"Of course she did," Colt said, rolling his eyes.

Jessie patted Colt's arm on her way past him. "Bribery. How do you think I got you to do anything when you were little?"

I snorted a laugh. "I am so glad I came."

"Oh, honey, that's nothing," Jessie said, flashing me a wink. "I've got plenty of stories for you that will embarrass the life out of Colton."

"Can't wait," I giggled.

Colt pulled a seat out for me and dropped into the one beside it. "You are enjoying this way too much."

"I like stories about Daddy," Faith said, scrambling into the seat on Colt's other side. She peered around him to me. "The ones Nana J tells are funny."

"I'll bet."

Colt blew out a breath. "I think *I'll* be the one to regret you coming here."

It turned out the stories Jessie told were relatively tame. Maybe she was worried she would scare me off, or Colt would never bring me back if she embarrassed him too much. But the ones she did tell were enjoyable enough — childish pranks and mischievous behavior.

Colt's family was a big one. He had an older brother, Josh, who was serving overseas in the military. Jessie had a huge portrait of him in his dress uniform and I got the impression none of his family could have been prouder.

There was also another sister, two years Colt's junior,

Sara, who was visiting with her in-laws with her husband and their three children. Then it was Sophie and Tess.

Grandpa Joe and Uncle Sal lived in a separate annex over the garage. They were a tight-knit group and I couldn't help but envy their dynamic. That lunch, full of vibrant characters, conversations layered on top of one another, so much laughter and cheer, was so different from the meals I'd grown up with.

When Colt excused himself to use the bathroom before lunch, Faith hopped seats and stared at me with the inquisitive nature only a child could get away with.

"I'm six," she stated.

I lifted my eyebrows. "Sweet."

"How old are you?"

"Faith, don't be rude," Jessie chided.

"How come it's rude? Everyone is some kind of old," Faith argued.

Jessie smiled at me. "She's got us there."

"She sure does," I agreed. "I'm twenty-six. Twenty-seven in a few weeks."

Faith's face lit up. "Are you having a party? I want a party for my birthday with pancakes and a bouncy house."

I couldn't help but laugh. "That sounds awesome. I never had pancakes *or* a bouncy house at my birthday parties."

"Why don't you have one this time, then? Grownups get whatever they want for their birthday."

Man, I loved this kid's logic. "My friends are throwing me a different kind of party. Maybe next time."

"Can I come? You can come to my party." Faith looked up at me with her big, pale blue eyes. I'd bet anything she got her own way more often than not thanks to those bad boys.

"I would love to have you, but you have to be a few years older before they'll let you in." I smiled at her. "But the year I have a bouncy house, you'll be the first person I invite."

Faith grinned.

When Colt returned, Faith refused to relinquish her chair. She'd conjured a tub of rainbow bands and was weaving me a pretty cool bracelet. Her little fingers worked the hook and loom so fast they almost blurred, and I had no idea how she did it.

"Daddy," Faith said, her voice garbled from a mouthful of brownie. "Don't you think Hayley looks like my Barbie doll?"

Colt coughed and placed his piece of brownie on his plate. "I...can't answer that question, sweetheart. There's no way for me to win or dig my way out of that one."

"Okay. But don't you think she does? *I* think she does. She's so pretty. I like her dress. And her blonde hair. Don't you, Daddy?"

"I think Daddy likes everything about Hayley," Jessie said, rescuing Colt from an impossible question.

"Well, what does Hayley like about Daddy?" Faith asked, inconspicuously sliding Colt's plate toward herself.

Grandpa Joe snorted. "Honey, we're *all* trying to figure that one out."

Oh yeah, I was so glad I'd come.

* * * *

"What, no inquisition?" Colt asked after we'd been driving for a few minutes in silence.

Hugging the Tupperware full of leftovers that Jessie had insisted I take with me, I thought about how to answer. "I think you have your reasons for not telling me about Faith, and really, you don't need to tell me. We're...friends, Colt. You don't owe me any explanations."

"Is it wrong that I want to explain anyway?" he asked quietly, rubbing a hand over his jaw. "I was married, before. To Faith's mother, Susan. We married young, barely into our twenties. Faith...she wasn't planned, but I have loved that girl since she was barely a grain of rice in the sonogram picture. Things with her mother hadn't been going well. I tried to keep us together, but Susan left anyway. It was a few weeks later that she discovered she was pregnant.

"By the time Faith was born, it was over with us. Now we make it work. She splits her time between our houses, and loves to hang out with Nana J. She stays there a lot. We try to split custody straight down the middle, but with my job it isn't always possible. So she goes to my mom's, or she stays with Susan and I see her a different weekend. Susan remarried two years ago. Faith loves Kent, her step-father, and I have to admit he's a great guy. And he's awesome with my daughter. We all get along, and I eat with them often."

"It sounds like you guys have a good set-up," I said. And I meant it. The little girl I'd met today was not starved for love, despite her parents not being together anymore.

Colt glanced at me. "Are you wondering why I didn't mention Faith to you before?"

I shrugged. "Maybe a little."

"Maybe it was a dick move on my part, but the night we met, we were in a club. You were hot, we were flirting. I didn't want to scare you off by telling you right off the bat I had a kid." Colt chuckled low in his throat. "Then again, maybe if I had, it would have saved a whole lot of confusion."

"Yeah, you're probably right," I agreed.

"After that, I guess there just didn't seem like a right time."

"It's not an easy thing to slip into conversation." Releasing a long breath, I leaned my elbow on the door and twisted the colorful band Faith had made me around my wrist. She said it meant we would be friends forever. I sort of hoped she was right. "She's amazing, Colt." I smiled, thinking of Faith's sweet and curious face. "A real character."

"She is," he said softly, as though pleased I thought so, too. He cleared his throat. "I don't allow temporary people into my daughter's life. You say we're friends now? Good. Friends stick around."

"So now you're glad we're friends?" Something knotted in my chest. It was odd to hear him call me his friend...even though I'd told him that was all we would ever be.

Colt seemed to think about my question. "I'm glad you're around. However you want to label it."

Chapter Ten

The backroom of Back in Time was filled with boxes I'd brought with me from an estate sale on the Upper East Side. This time it wasn't being held because of a death, rather a purging. A model turned socialite had been dumped by her wealthy older husband in favor of someone younger. She was getting rid of everything that reminded her of him and it turned out a lot of stuff did that.

One of a kind Valentinos, custom-made Elie Saabs and racks upon racks of Gucci and Dolce and Dior…oh my. I blew my entire budget—something I'd never done before, not even close. I came away with enough clothes and accessories to keep Fiona in stock for more than a year. The items had been couriered over the day before, and I was still trying to organize everything. I opened another box and sighed at the beautiful dresses before me.

"Hayley? I think this customer is looking for you," Fiona called.

"I'll be a second!" I closed the box again and tried to negotiate my way around all the others to safely make it out. Out in the front of the store, Fiona stood with Colt and Faith. Faith was fascinated with the collection of costume jewelry and ran her fingers over the sparkling jewels.

"Hey, what brings you two down here?" I asked, unable to keep the grin from spreading across my face. It had been almost two weeks since I'd seen them at Jessie's, thanks to our conflicting schedules. And now that he was right in front of me, I realized how much I'd missed Colt.

"Daddy said you had pretty things here," Faith said, not taking her eyes from a mermaid pendant.

I smiled. "We do."

Colt cleared his throat and stepped forward with two takeout coffees. "We brought these, fuel for the workers."

"Marry this man," Fiona said, picking one up and removing the lid to inhale the scent. "If you don't, I will."

"Daddy can't marry you, you're too old." Faith cocked her head and gazed at me. "But it would be nice if he married you. He likes you. And so does Uncle Sal. He said you have a sweet bottom."

"Jesus Christ," Colt muttered. "Faith, sweetheart, Nana J told you not to repeat that."

Faith frowned. "But you said it was true."

Colt's cheeks flushed. "I know I did, but it isn't polite to say so."

"Why?"

"Because...because it will embarrass Hayley."

Faith looked at me. "She doesn't look embarrassed."

"Actually, I think your father is the one who is embarrassed. Why don't you come and see the seashell bracelet I have?" Fiona led the girl to a nearby stand with baskets of bracelets.

Colt sighed and took a step closer to me. He scrubbed a hand over his jaw. "Sorry."

"Don't be." Jeez, they made for one heck of a two-man show. "I know I have a sweet bottom."

He snorted. "I am never going to live that down."

"Never ever."

"You were a big hit. Ma keeps asking when I'm bringing you back around." Colt smiled, crooked and perfect.

A laugh rose in my throat. "Is this your new game now? Lure me in with your family?"

He grinned wider. "Is it working?"

A little, I admitted to myself.

Colt straightened, as if he had heard my thought. Instead of pressing his point, he said, "We have someplace to be. I just wanted to drop these coffees in to you."

"How did you even know I'd be here?"

"I called Fiona a few days ago and asked when you were next going to be here. It just so happened to coincide with my days with Faith, and she wanted to see you, too."

Something in my chest tightened at his admission. For all he had seemed to accept that I was calling this… whatever it was between us…a friendship, Colt was still actively pursuing me. And despite my determination that friendship was all there would ever be…I sort of liked it.

"You're very thorough," I said eventually.

Colt laughed, low and sexy, hitting me right where it counted. "Yeah, St. Clair, I'm thorough."

Fiona and Faith rejoined us at the counter and Faith immediately reached for the mermaid pendant.

Colt dropped his hand to her shoulder. "Come on, baby, we need to let Hayley and Fiona get on with their work."

Faith smiled up at her father. "I like it here."

"Well, you have excellent taste," Fiona said, lifting the mermaid pendant from its hook. "And I can't think of anyone better to take care of this."

Faith's eyes lit up as she accepted the pendant from Fiona. "Really?"

"Oh, you don't—" Colt started.

Fiona waved his protests away. "It's been here for months. Your girl is the only person to ever appreciate it."

His face softened. "Thank you. Faith, what do you say?"

"It's *so* pretty."

Colt sighed. "Apart from that."

Faith looked up at Fiona and clasped the necklace to her chest. "Thank you."

"What are you two doing with the rest of your day?" I asked them.

"Daddy's taking me to the museum with the dinosaurs."

"Oh cool. I love museums." Wasn't that the truth. On the rare occasions I had time on my hands, or wanted to clear my head, I always hit up one of the many museums this fine city had.

"Yeah? Which is your favorite?" Faith asked, hopping up

and down on the spot as though this was the most exciting thing she had ever learned about someone.

"Um... Probably MoMA. I like the paintings. Especially *Starry Night*. Do you know that one?"

Faith wrinkled her nose as she searched her memory. "I don't know. Do I, Daddy?"

"Yeah, baby. The blue one with the bright yellow stars, remember?"

"Oh yeah." Faith grinned at me. "That one is pretty."

"It is," I agreed.

"Is it your birthday soon? Am I old enough to come to your party yet?" Faith asked.

"No, not yet. Sorry," I said, smiling.

She scowled at me. "That's not fair."

"I'll save you some cake to make it up to you, okay?"

Faith brightened at this news. "Okay." She slipped her new pendant over her head and perused the sparkly mermaid.

Colt leaned his forearms on the counter, completely invading my space.

I could have moved back. I didn't.

"So, aren't *I* going to get an invite to this party of yours?"

A frown creased my forehead. In total honesty, it had never occurred to me to invite Colt to my party. Even though I'd met him in a club, Colt struck me as the homebody type. The kind of man who preferred to relax with a cold beer and a football game rather than in a busy, sweaty nightclub.

"Do you *want* to come?" I asked.

He grinned. "Do I want to celebrate your birthday with you? Is that a serious question?"

A smile pulled at my lips. "I didn't think it would be your scene."

Colt shook his head as though I was the most frustrating thing in his world. Which said a lot when he had a six year old who took after his own stubborn personality. "Just send me details, okay?"

I rolled my eyes. "Jeez, you're bossy."

"That's what I always say," Faith said as she peered up at me.

Colt sighed and took Faith's hand. "Come on, before you really make St. Clair not like me."

"I think she likes you lots," Faith said. "Don't you?"

He looked at me with a cocky smile. "Of course, baby. She likes me so much she doesn't even realize how much she does."

I shooed them toward the door. "Okay, out with you both, before I have to call the cops."

Faith let out a high-pitched giggle at this and tugged on Colt's hand.

"Bye, you guys," I said when we reached the door.

Faith waved and Colt nodded once, watching me until the last second. I stared at their retreating figures through the window in the door, squeezing my hands into fists to keep from bolting after them and asking if I could tag along.

Fiona came up behind me and patted my shoulder. "You're in so much trouble, girl."

"I am?" I wondered quietly, even though I didn't need to. I was totally in so, so much trouble.

"Yep." Fiona laughed. "But the very best kind."

* * * *

I'd been looking forward to my birthday party since... well, last year's birthday party. Henry, Marley's boss, pulled some strings and got me a killer section at Provocateur in the Meatpacking District. He owned one of the hottest PR firms in the city. While he had recently moved to the hotel business in Vegas, Henry had someone manage his New York firm while he was out west. But Henry's name still had a lot of weight behind it, especially on the social scene.

The guest list for my party was huge. I knew just about everybody there was to know and then some. The night was set to be spectacular.

Beth and Eve giggled in my living room as I sat on the edge

of my bed to slip on my shoes. Man, they were gorgeous. And an early birthday present to myself. Gianvito Rossi courts with a sleek panel design. The body of the shoe was clear plastic and was framed by a sharp white pointed toe and a black heel.

Standing to look in my full-length mirror, I smoothed down my outfit — a stunning Antonio Berardi asymmetrical number. It was so beautiful it was practically a work of art. It was a tailored midi pencil dress with classic monochromatic stripes. It was sexy with its off-the-shoulder touch and the peplum fold at the waist. The bodice was accentuated by contrast striped panels, giving it a sharp edge that emboldened me.

I stepped out of my bedroom to the gasps and shrieks of Beth and Eve.

"Hayley, you look *amazing!*" Beth said as she threw her arms around me.

"Totally worthy of this!" Eve popped the cork on a bottle of Bollinger and poured three flutes of the champagne. "All right, I think a toast is in order."

I laughed and pressed a hand to my cheek. "You'll embarrass me."

"That's what friends are for." Beth giggled and rested her head on my shoulder. She, along with Eve, lifted their glasses in the air.

"To Hayley. I hope all your birthday wishes come true."

"I bet one of them involves a sexy-ass cop," Beth said.

My cheeks burned. "Of course not." *Liar*, a secret, quiet voice inside me whispered. I finished my drink. "Come on, let's get to the party. I have a burning desire to dance until my feet bleed."

Eve threw her champagne down her throat. "I second that."

We caught a cab to Provocateur, the driver kind enough to turn the radio up and not kick us out when we sang along to a Beyoncé track. The line for the club was around the block when we spilled out of the cab. We headed straight for the doormen and a flutter of excited butterflies took flight in my belly.

A huge, beefy stud in a suit dipped to kiss my cheek. "There's the birthday girl."

"Hi, Jeff. How's Cindy?" I asked, hugging him as best I could, given he was at least a foot and a half taller than I was.

"She's good, how about you?"

I grinned. "Ready to get in there."

Jeff smiled and unclipped the rope, letting me, Beth and Eve past. "Have a great night, girls."

We headed through the entrance, past the café and into the club. Simone, our hostess, greeted us and led us to our own area. Thirty or so people were already present, dancing around the booths. A few saw me and raised their glasses in greeting.

"Everything is set up. Bottle service as agreed and we have your guest list, so don't worry about gatecrashers. Can I get you anything right now?" Simone asked me.

I shook my head. "This is all fabulous, thank you."

"People have been bringing gifts and I've been storing them in the cloakroom for safekeeping. And you still want the cake around midnight?"

"Yeah, thanks so much for taking care of all this."

Simone smiled and touched my arm. "That's what I'm here for."

Beth, Eve and I slipped into the roped-off area and within seconds I was in the middle of a swarm of friends and well-wishers.

Tonight was set to be spectacular.

* * * *

The problem with being the birthday girl, I discovered, was that everyone wanted to talk to me. I'd been at my party for an hour and I hadn't had the chance to dance even once. I'd no sooner moved on from one person than another

132

would fill the space. Parties were for partying, not talking, but these guys definitely hadn't gotten the memo.

Finn, a hot DJ I'd had a long-standing flirty friendship with, pulled me into a tight embrace. "This party has been the talk of the town for months."

I nodded. "I can hardly believe it's here already. I've looked forward to it for months."

"Drink?" he asked, signaling to one of the girls working in our area. She smiled and started mixing my usual cocktail.

When she handed it to me, I sipped it slowly. I'd already lost count of how many I'd had and the night was still young. If I kept it up, the party of the year would be nothing but a haze. With me passed out in a booth.

"Thank you," I said to the girl and smiling at Finn. "When's your next gig? It feels like forever since I've seen you mix it up."

Finn smiled, a lazy, predatory grin. "I'm up at Ecstasy next month. But I keep telling you I've no problem giving you a private show at my loft any time you want."

"I haven't forgotten, Finn."

He lifted both his eyebrows. "Then what's the problem?"

I swatted his arm. This was a conversation we'd had countless times. "I like you too much to have sex with you."

Finn huffed out a breath. "Story of my life."

"I find that hard to believe," I said. My attention was pulled from Finn to a large frame cutting its way through the crowd toward us.

He came.

Colt approached us, an amused quirk to his lips. "St. Clair."

"Colt."

He slid a glance toward Finn. "Who's your friend?"

My mind went blank. All I could focus on was Colt. My heart seemed to thump his name. *Colt. Colt Colt.* "Um... He's, um..."

Finn made a noise of displeasure in his throat. "Finn. The friend is Finn. Who are you?"

Colt's smile widened. "Who am I, St. Clair?"

I couldn't stop my responding smile. "I don't know. Who are you?"

He swore quietly and curled his fingers around my elbow, his grip firm but gentle. "Excuse us," he told Finn, "I need to speak with the lady."

"How did you get in?" I asked Colt as he led me to a more secluded section. "Did you flash your badge?"

Colt turned his body so he leaned against the back of a booth. "You know I was on the list. Top of it, in fact."

I giggled. "Jeez, you're full of it."

His smile softened. "Are you having a good party?"

"The best." *Now you're here.*

Colt glanced over my shoulder. "I won't keep you long. I know how popular you'll be tonight."

My own smile faltered. "Oh."

"I only came over to deliver your gift."

"Colt, you didn't have to give me anything. Don't you think you've done enough for me lately?" I asked him. If I lived to be a hundred and fifty-seven, I could never work off the debt I seemed to have accumulated with Colt. He kept on giving with me. From quite literally coming to my rescue, to inviting me into his home, his family. He gave me more than I think he even realized.

"I thought this was what you wanted — to be treated like a princess." Colt gestured to Simone, who passed us with her arms full of gift bags. My friends were generous and liked to throw their money around. Most of us could afford to and it showed.

Something pinched in my gut. I didn't want *stuff* from Colt. I wanted all the things he could give me that no one else could. He made a security system feel like a fairy tale castle.

"Besides," Colt said, a lazy grin spreading across his plump lips, "I have a feeling my gift will earn me major points with you."

I laughed. "What makes you so sure?"

He lifted one shoulder in a shrug. "A feeling."

A pair of cool hands covered my eyes and a familiar perfume teased my senses.

It can't be...

"Guess who?"

My breath lodged in my throat, a well of emotion rising. I spun around and threw myself at my best girl, hugging her harder than I probably should have.

Marley chuckled in my ear. "Happy to see me?"

"What are you doing here?" I whispered, too afraid to speak any louder in case in my voice broke.

"Your boy called and talked me into it."

When Marley had last been in town, she'd told me she wouldn't come to the party. She wasn't in the mood for being in a crowded club when she was pregnant, and Provocateur wasn't known for being quiet and laid-back. She had even stopped working the club doors back home.

I'd been disappointed for sure when she'd told me, but of course I'd understood. It was just one of the many ways Marley was now further away from me. She was settled and so in love, and now there was another person to steal her attention — her kid.

And I still partied most nights.

The closest I'd come to commitment lately was to a jumbo pack of M&Ms.

I squeezed her tighter for another second before releasing her. She took a tiny step back and Blake tucked her into his side. Of course he'd come. They were a package deal these days.

I hugged him next. "Thank you for bringing my girl."

He laughed. "She was yours first. It was only fair."

Tipping my head back to laugh, I felt like finally things were okay, that they were *going* to be okay.

A familiar song started playing and Beth and Eve rushed to our sides. The three of us grabbed Marley and pulled her to a vacant spot on the dance floor. We sang along and danced like no one was watching.

Which was stupid.

Because I distinctly felt a set of eyes on me.

"Look, our men are getting along," Marley said in my ear as we danced to another song.

I glanced over and spotted Blake and Colt chatting in a booth, each man clasping a bottle of beer. Colt and Blake couldn't have been more different if they tried—in looks, personality and background. Colt was fair to Blake's dark, Colt was stacked with muscle, Blake was lean. Colt was a cocky son of a bitch and Blake was more reserved. Colt came from humble roots, worked in the public sector and earned everything he had. Blake came from one of the richest families around and, okay, he was a self-made man now, but it hadn't always been that way.

They were as opposite as night and day. And yet, there they were, both enjoying a beer and laughing as though they'd known each other for years.

"Good sign, don't you think?"

I forced a laugh. "You're seeing things."

Marley clasped my wrist. "Hayley, Colt sent us plane tickets. He picked us up at the airport. Those aren't the actions of a man satisfied with a friendship."

"Why would he do that?" I wondered aloud.

She smiled. "I asked him the same thing. And he said he wanted to get you something amazing for your birthday. The only thing he knew you loved more than shoes was me."

"He's an idiot."

"He's in love with you."

Whatever cocky answer I'd had disappeared in the air as I stared at her. She smiled, confident and smug that she'd reached a conclusion I hadn't even thought of.

Beth mimed that she was going to get a drink, and Eve pulled Marley toward an empty booth so she could chew her ear off about the pregnancy.

The girl was sixteen weeks along now and still didn't even look remotely pregnant.

I looked back to Colt and found his eyes already on me. A jolt went through my body, as though his gaze was electric. Everything felt amplified when he was around. He aggravated me to the point I thought I'd rip my own hair out, but he could also warm me to my bones.

Blake said something to him and Colt released me from his magnetic gaze. I took the opportunity to duck out of the area and have a quick breather in the bathroom.

I clutched the porcelain sink, sucked in a deep, soothing breath and tried to slow my pounding heart. *Get it together, St. Clair.* I was half drunk. I'd just been given the best birthday gift I could ever have asked for. That was it. It wasn't because he was here — looking devilishly gorgeous and hugely male.

Get it together.

I didn't dare splash water on my face because of my makeup, so I settled for a few more deep breaths. Staring at the girl in the mirror, I gave myself a mental shake. This was *my* party, dammit, and I wasn't going to spend it in the freaking bathroom.

My dress was hot.

My shoes were hot.

I. Was. Hot.

Maneuvering my way back through the crowded club to the party area, I couldn't ignore the tingle low in my belly. There were so many people who had come to the party for me. My closest friends included.

And I could only think about getting back to one single person.

Someone stepped into my path, jostling me to the side. A hand reached out to steady me.

"Hey, sorry about that... Hayley?"

Oh, God, I know that voice. I looked up, dread and irritation swirling in my gut. "Spencer."

He grinned. A stupid, shit-eating grin that made me want to dick-punch him. "What, no kiss hello?"

I glared at him, but it made no difference. That grin was

still there. Spencer's eyes were bloodshot and I realized he was drunk off his ass. Which must be the only reason he was speaking to me. I'd thought — or maybe hoped — that if ever confronted with me, Spencer would be far too ashamed to muster a civilized conversation.

It had occurred to me that maybe it was a bad idea having my birthday party in a club in Spencer's neighborhood, but I'd decided a very long time ago to not let the location of an ex ruin my city for me. I mean, hell, if I avoided every neighborhood that an ex of mine lived in, I…would have to move back to Connecticut.

Spencer shuffled closer to me, his eyes trailing down my body. "You're looking good, Hayley."

My skin crawled under his blatant perusal. "Get out of my way, Spencer. I was having a good night until I ran into you."

He laughed and slid his arm around my waist, pulling me against his sweaty body. "I don't remember you being so hard to get. If I recall, you were a done deal at the sight of my black Amex."

"Spencer," I said with a sickly sweet smile. "I recommend that you get your hand off me before you lose it."

Spencer laughed again as though my warning amused him, the asshole. "What are you doing later? Want to come to my place?"

My lips curled into a sneer. "I can't think of a stronger no than *fuck you*."

"Stop fighting. You know you want me again." Spencer gripped my hip so hard I grimaced. "I bet you haven't stopped thinking about the night I banged you."

"Trust me, it was memorable for all the wrong reasons. Now let me — "

Spencer moved his hand up, his fingertips grazing the underside of my breast.

And I saw red.

"Shut the fuck up, Hayley. A greedy bitch like you should be grateful," Spencer growled, lowering his head. His hot breath in my ear made my skin crawl.

I darted my hand up to grab his, covering his fingers with my own.

He laughed quietly. "That's it. Just relax, okay? Come on, we'll get out of here."

Wrapping my hand around his index finger, I tipped my head back and locked gazes with him. "Because of you, something irreplaceable was taken from me. Something a heartless, materialistic and chauvinistic bastard like you could never comprehend. Get the hell off me, right this second, or I swear to God you won't like what happens."

Spencer's lips curled into a sneer. He opened his mouth, but I didn't give him the chance to spew whatever poison was about to come out.

Instead, I jerked my hand, snapping his index finger back the wrong way. It gave the most satisfying pop and his mouth fell into an 'O' of surprise.

Spencer yelped in pain and shoved away from me, bumping into a few other people. They turned to glare at him but otherwise seemed oblivious to the fact that I'd just broken his finger. Which, when I considered how much damage I'd really like to inflict on him, was pretty minor.

A hand curled around my elbow and pulled me back, putting a good few feet of distance between me and Spencer. I twisted around and stared into Colt's eyes, which were pissed. Seriously pissed. Even, I thought, more pissed than I had been when confronted with Spencer.

"What the fuck is going on here?" he demanded.

Oh. Right. He was a cop. And technically I'd just assaulted someone. In front of a lot of potential witnesses. *Whoops.*

"Get that psycho bitch away from me!" Spencer yelled as he cradled his wounded hand.

"St. Clair?" Colt prodded. He clenched his jaw and I knew whatever anger was coursing through him was being carefully contained, but could erupt at any second with one wrong move. Sort of like a landmine.

I folded my arms below my chest and turned to glare

at Spencer. "I told him, several times, to let me go and he didn't. I gave him fair warning he wouldn't like what would happen if he didn't get his slimy paws off my boob."

"Oh, please, I've felt a hell of a lot more than your boob — and it wasn't covered with a stupid fucking dress," Spencer spat out.

Colt held up a hand and took a single step toward Spencer. "I would advise you to shut the hell up, right this second."

Could it be that I'd misunderstood? Was Colt angry with Spencer, not with me? Maybe he'd seen more of the exchange than just me snapping Spencer's finger like a lollipop stick.

I stepped forward and touched Colt's arm, which was straining below the soft fabric of his dark shirt. "Colt? Let's just go back to the party."

Colt finally released Spencer from his death stare and swung his piercing eyes back to me. He scanned me from head to toe, as though searching for some invisible injury.

"I'm fine, can we just go, please?"

He slid his arm around my waist, holding me closer to him.

My breath caught in my throat and I pressed my palm against his chest.

"You sure you're okay?"

I nodded, unable to break his stare.

He squeezed my waist. "Let's go. Before I do something really stupid."

"Yeah, take that crazy bitch out of here before I call the fucking cops," Spencer called after us.

Colt paused and turned his body slightly, standing off against Spencer whilst simultaneously keeping me from him. "What?"

Spencer shuffled forward and I turned to see him glare at me with hateful eyes. "She assaulted me — I could see that she gets charged." He sneered and flung his hand out toward me. "I wouldn't waste your time on this kind of girl. You'll be the idiot who buys her Cartier earrings like I did.

140

I bet those got hawked the second I was out of the picture, right, Hayley? I wouldn't expect any less from trash like you."

Colt visibly stiffened as Spencer's words sank in. He turned his head in my direction. "This is him, isn't it?"

It was pointless lying. Colt already knew. He didn't need me to confirm anything.

He looked back at Spencer and took a few quick, menacing steps toward him. "You listen to me very carefully, you little shit," Colt hissed.

I rushed over to him, wrapping my hands around his biceps. I tried to tug him away, but he was as immovable as a thousand-year-old oak tree.

"You ever come within breathing space of this girl and I will put you in the ground. Do you understand me?"

Spencer's lips curled in disgust. "You're welcome to her. Trust me on this, buddy, all she'll get you is a large credit card bill and bad sex."

At his side, Colt's hand curled into a fist.

"Colt, ignore him. He's drunk and an asshole," I pleaded. The last thing I wanted was Colt's temper to come to a head and for him to knock Spencer on his stupid ass. If Spencer ever found out he was a cop, it could lead to some unpleasantness for Colt.

"Nah, leave him be, Hayley. Because if your new boyfriend here takes a swing at me, I can call the cops on both your asses."

"Spencer, you really need to learn to shut the hell up," I groaned.

Colt curled his hand around mine and gently pried me off his arm. He took a single step toward Spencer, which put him right in his face. When he spoke, it was with eerie calmness. "I'll say this one time only, so listen very carefully to me. You are a worthless, spineless, pitiful excuse for a man. You, a grown man, left a woman alone with a mugger because you're nothing more than a chicken-shit momma's boy. And when a woman tells you to leave her be, you back the fuck off immediately. You don't? That, in my opinion, means she can do whatever the hell she wants to your pathetic ass to get you away from her.

"You want to call the cops on her for breaking your finger? Go ahead. You'll be calling me, because I *am* a cop. And I'll see to it that you pay for harassing her, for abandoning her. You so much as point a finger in my direction and I'll see to it you're charged with assaulting an officer of the law. I'll find a cozy little cell with a *friendly* roommate, if you get what I mean." Colt smiled. "Now again, since you didn't seem to listen last time. Stay the fuck away from Hayley, or I will personally put you in the ground. Do you understand me now?"

Very slowly, Spencer nodded.

"Great. Now be a good little boy and run along home. But be sure to carry pepper spray. I hear this is a rough neighborhood."

Spencer didn't hesitate for a second. He rushed past us, giving me a wide berth in the process.

I counted to five once Spencer was gone.

Colt didn't turn to face me.

Releasing a long breath, I moved to stand in front of him. I covered his fist and wiggled until I was able to thread my fingers with his. "I'm sorry."

Colt frowned. "Why are you sorry?"

"Spencer. Causing you unnecessary trouble."

"You think I'm —" Colt huffed out a breath. "Do you think I'm pissed at *you*?"

I shrugged. "Maybe. I don't know. You came here to party, not defend an idiot like me."

"St. Clair, I came here for *you*." Colt shifted closer to me. "Whether that means watching you dance with your friends, being the one to dance with you or defend you from dickless assholes — I'm here for *you*."

I let go of Colt's hand. Standing on my tiptoes, I looped my arms around his neck and held him as tightly as I could. "You're sort of amazing. Thank you."

Colt chuckled and dipped his head to the crook of my neck, his strong arms coming around my waist. "All part of my master plan to win you over."

I laughed and pulled away from him. "Come on, I want to dance."

"Yes, ma'am."

Colt let me lead him back to the party, where it seemed no one had even noticed our absence, let alone the little altercation with Spencer. I dragged him into the center of the other dancers. He kept his arm around me as we danced, never letting me get far from him, despite the speed of the music.

I glanced to the side, to where Marley was dancing with Blake. She smiled up at him and he looked at her as though they were the only two people in the room. Like they were in their own impenetrable bubble. I leaned my head against Colt's shoulder and wondered if that was what people thought when they looked at us.

Chapter Eleven

My entire world was spinning.

I was fairly certain I was lying on a bed, but it felt more like a tilt-a-whirl going so fast that any second I would be launched into space. No, not just space. Outer space. Or maybe to some unknown galaxy beyond.

Chatter drifted in behind my closed door and I forced myself to sit up. Kicking the blankets away, I saw that I was wearing my favorite set of pajamas — an old Knicks jersey and black satin girl boxers.

Okay. So I was dressed. That was a good sign. It meant I hadn't had sex last night. And the other side of my bed appeared unslept in. Another good sign.

Especially since all I could really remember from last night was Colt.

Laughing with Colt.

Drinking with Colt.

Dancing with Colt and hanging off him as though he was a lifeline.

Someone laughed out in my apartment — a girlish, female laugh.

Yet another good sign.

"Okay, just do it, Hayley. Rip off the Band-Aid." I sighed and swung my legs out of bed. As I stood, I swayed on the spot for a second. "Whoa." When the dizziness subsided, I shuffled to my bedroom door and stepped out.

"The beast awakes!" Eve cackled.

I squinted from the bright sunlight streaming through the living room window and held a hand up to shield my eyes. "Ha."

"How's the hangover?" Marley asked from the swivel chair.

I mumbled something incoherent and nudged Beth until she moved over on the couch. Slumping down, I laid my head on Beth's lap and sprawled out on the rest of the couch.

"Here, drink this," Eve said as she handed me a cold bottle of water from the fridge.

I accepted the bottle and held it against my eyes. "Ooh, that's good. Great. Better than sex, even."

Marley snorted a laugh.

Shooting my finger out to point at her, I said, "Don't you say a word."

"Are you hungry?" Beth asked, smoothing my hair with her fingertips.

"Not in the least," I groaned. "What time is it, anyway?"

"A little after noon," she answered.

I pushed myself up so I could sip the bottled water. "Did you all stay here with me last night?"

Beth and Marley exchanged a look.

"You don't remember?" Marley asked.

The last thing I remembered from last night was doing shots with Eve while I'd made Colt hold my purse. "I don't even remember getting my cake. I had cake, right?"

Beth laughed quietly. "Yeah, Hayley, you had your cake. But no, none of us stayed here. Colt did."

"Colt?" I bolted fully upright and crossed my legs under me. "Colt stayed here?"

Marley laughed. "Actually, you all but begged him to take you to his place, since you said his bed was nicer than yours. But you passed out in the cab and he brought you here instead."

"Oh, God," I moaned, covering my face with my hands. "I'm an idiot."

Beth nodded. "You said it."

I stuck my tongue out at her. "And you, who call yourselves my friends! How could you let me embarrass myself like that?"

"Hey," Eve said, holding up her hands in defense. "You think we didn't try?"

"You were hell-bent on spending the night with him," Marley said softly. "You said he made the perfect big spoon."

"Fuck my life," I muttered.

"Don't be embarrassed," Beth said, tapping my knee. "We all got the impression he was more than happy to be your big spoon. He sort of... Hell, he adores you, Hayley."

I glanced around at the sincere faces of my friends. There was no teasing, no mirth in their expressions. I had no idea what to do with the feelings tumbling around inside me. It felt as though I was on the precipice of a huge rollercoaster drop. Adrenaline, excitement, anticipation—I was a smoothie of emotions.

"So... Where is he?" I asked.

"He called and asked if we would come hang out. He and Blake headed to the club about an hour ago to get all your stuff." Marley smiled. "I think they have a bromance going on."

My eyebrows shot up. "Really?"

"Oh yeah."

The door buzzer sounded and Eve got up to answer it.

"The boys are back," she said, unlocking the door and left it ajar.

A few minutes later, Colt and Blake burst through the door, laden down with wrapped presents and gift bags.

"That's a lot of shit," Beth murmured. She shoved my shoulder. "How the hell do you know so many people?"

"Didn't you know? I'm a social butterfly," I answered.

Colt carefully placed the things he was carrying in a heap on the floor in front of the couch. He pinned me with a glare. "Your super is getting a visit from a building inspector about getting that elevator serviced."

I looked at all the things Blake and Colt had brought in and cringed. "It's not working again?"

"No, it is, we just thought it would be fun to carry all this crap up the stairs," Blake said, shooting me a look as he dipped to kiss Marley.

Colt patted Blake's shoulder. "Come on. One more run should do it."

"There's more?" I asked, incredulous.

"Yeah. Someone put a pot on!" he called on his way out of the apartment.

"Man, he's got some muscles," Eve said, sitting on my other side on the couch.

"Right?" I asked, a laugh rising in my throat.

"Why aren't you sleeping with him, again?" Beth asked.

"Yeah, Hayley," Marley said, a smiling tugging at her lips. "Why aren't you sleeping with the hot cop who's seriously into you?"

I tossed a pillow at her. "Shut up."

She laughed and caught the pillow, hugging it to her chest.

I rose from my spot on the couch and padded barefoot into the kitchen to start a pot of coffee. I hoisted myself up on the counter and pulled a bag of M&Ms out of the cupboard behind my head.

"Healthy breakfast, Hayley?" Marley asked.

I poured a few onto the palm of my hand before shaking the bag at her. "Don't even try to tell me that thing in your belly makes you eat only healthy crap."

She laughed. "Not in the least. Last week all I wanted to eat were orange popsicles. Blake had to practically force carbs and protein into me."

Blake and Colt returned a few minutes later, Blake carrying a few more gift bags and Colt straining under the weight of my birthday cake. A perfect four-tiered creation of different designer shoeboxes, with pretty pink and purple decoration — stripes, polka dots and flowers — topped with a cute pair of Manolo Blahnik sandals.

It was a thing of beauty.

Colt slid the cake onto the counter and leaned beside me.

He snagged the bag of M&Ms and pulled out a handful. "Don't you want real food?"

"Nope. Junk only." I tossed a few of the colorful candies into my mouth. "It's so unfair kids are the only ones who get to go trick-or-treating. I love candy."

"I'm taking Faith this year. Do you want to come with us?"

"Trick-or-treating?" I asked, unable to stop the smile from spreading across my face.

Colt nodded.

"No way, absolutely not!" Eve cried. "We have that amazing Halloween party to go to, remember?"

I did remember. I'd been looking forward to it for months. But now, faced with a choice I would have laughed at before meeting Colt, the party had suddenly lost its sparkle. "It's not until late. I can be done in time."

"Don't worry, St. Clair. I'll make sure you get to your party in time," Colt said, smiling. He studied my Knicks jersey. "You're a Knicks fan? I never would have guessed."

I snatched my bag of M&Ms back. "Why? Because I'm a girl?"

Colt laughed. "No. Because you look more at home in a department store or a nightclub than the Garden."

Sucking the colored dye off my fingers, I poked him in his strong, firm biceps with my other hand. "I'll have you know I'm a huge Knicks fan. Just because I wore a Prada cocktail dress and Jimmy Choo heels to the last game makes me less of a fan than a jean-and-Chucks-wearing guy like you?"

He grinned. "I guess not. There's a game tonight. You want to go?"

"Hey," Blake called from the living room. "You gave that spare ticket to me."

Colt shot him a lazy glare. "And if the situation were reversed and your girl wanted to go, you'd still take me?"

"Fine," Blake huffed. He turned to Marley. "I guess I'm free to take you to a show tonight after all."

Marley scowled at him. "So I'm your second choice.

Nice." But she couldn't even pretend to be mad at him for two minutes. She giggled and he kissed her.

"Are you going to wear these shorts to the game?" Colt asked me, teasing the edge of the boxers, his finger making my thigh break out in goosebumps. "Because if you do, not a damn person will be watching the game."

I swatted his hand away. "You're deluded."

"I'm observant." Colt scooted me along the counter so he could reach the pot. "Are you having one?"

I nodded.

"Blake, coffee?" Colt asked.

"Sure, thanks."

"Aw, you have a new boyfriend," I teased Colt with a smile.

He pinned me with a look. "I thought we'd covered how not gay I was?"

A cocky retort formed in my mouth, but it never made it out.

Colt leaned closer to me, his hands on my hips, his face an inch away from mine. "Or do I need to kiss you again to prove it?"

Oh, sweet baby Jesus. It took all my self-control not to grab his face and assault his mouth. Maybe it was his reminder of the kiss we'd shared, but it was suddenly blasting my mind in perfect Technicolor wonder. 1080 HD, in fact.

"Holy hell, Hayley, if you don't kiss the life out of him, I will!" Beth called.

"You're out of luck, Beth," Eve said as she turned to smile at me and Colt. "He's only got eyes for our girl over there."

My cheeks heated and I risked a peek at Colt. He stared at me with his piercing blue eyes that held so much warmth.

Colt grinned at me. "At least someone is starting to get it."

* * * *

I couldn't wipe the smile off my face as I followed Colt

to our seats. Everything about the experience was familiar. The smell of the food, the air, the noise that echoed around the stadium as thousands of fans piled in.

To show Colt I could pull off another look besides 'young hot clubber', I'd dressed down in a pair of ballet flats and a modest navy blue jersey dress. I'd tied my long hair up in a messy bun and wore next to no makeup. It was as close to casual as I knew how to get, and I felt almost naked being out in public like this.

"Do you come a lot?" I asked Colt as we shuffled along the row to get to our seats.

"Not as often as I'd like." He sat down and took my vat of popcorn from me so I could plop down in my own seat. "You?"

"Hardly ever these days." I let out a huff of air. "My dad used to bring me all the time. It was sort of our thing. We lived in New Haven, and I would get so excited when he'd bring me to the city."

"Couldn't wait to grow up and make it home?" Colt asked softly.

"Something like that."

"He doesn't still come to games with you?"

My chest pinched. "No, he and Mother were killed when I was thirteen."

Colt sighed. "Oh, shit, St. Clair. I'm sorry."

I shrugged, used to the reaction. "It was a long time ago."

"That doesn't matter." He shifted closer. "Look at me."

As I lifted my eyes to his, my breath caught in my throat.

"I'm really sorry, St. Clair." Everything about Colt was sincere. His tone, his words, his eyes — which didn't hold the usual pity. Instead they were sad, as though he was sad for me. That I'd had to go through something like that. "I think I would have liked your parents."

"And why would you think that?"

"Because they made you. Like it or not, we're all representatives of our parents and our environments."

"I think you're right. After all, I've met Grandpa Joe and

Uncle Sal," I said, unable to stop my grin.

Colt tipped his head back and laughed, a rich, full-bodied sound. "I should defend myself, but I think you've got me."

"Told you." I plucked my huge tub of popcorn off his lap and lifted a handful of kernels.

"So, can I ask what happened? Is that okay?" Colt asked as he helped himself to my popcorn, despite the fact that he had a tray of nachos.

I nodded. "Car accident. It wasn't anyone's fault, which, back then, sort of made it worse. There was no one to blame. No drunk driver, no mechanical failure. Just a tight corner taken a tiny bit too fast. I had to live with my grandparents. My mother had been their only child and they weren't exactly nurturing."

"You didn't like living with them?"

"Do you know why I like your family so much, Colt?" I asked him. "Because they're so different from the family I grew up with."

He chuckled and settled back in his seat. "Don't go getting all wistful on me. They're noisy. And *nosey*. They're in my pocket as much as possible and bug the hell out of me. Our house was full to bursting when I was growing up. One bathroom between seven people."

"But all that stuff that drives you nuts? I would have killed for a taste of that." My grandparent's house was cold and formal. A far cry from the warmth of Jessie's home. "I grew up in a gated community, in a six-bedroom house. I wasn't allowed to have posters on the walls, or even a purple bedspread."

"That explains a lot about your current décor." Colt smiled.

I nudged him with my elbow. "I'm just trying to say that you're lucky. Really lucky."

"I know I am, St. Clair. They do drive me nuts, but I wouldn't have any of them any other way. And I meant what I said. I'm damn sorry I never got to meet your parents."

"What about your dad?" I asked softly. It had occurred to me that he hadn't been present when Colt had taken me to his mother's house for lunch and that there had been someone missing. But I hadn't felt comfortable asking then.

"You picked up on that, huh?" Colt's smile faltered. "He was a patrolman for thirty years—never wanted to move up, never had any interest in becoming a detective or a sergeant. One night he answered a call to a domestic disturbance in Queens. The guy was loaded on meth and took a shot at Dad."

"Jesus," I whispered.

"He survived, but the shot left him with a mangled hip that meant he couldn't be a cop anymore. At least, the kind that he wanted to be. They wanted him to take a desk job, but that isn't Dad. He was built to walk the beat, you know?" Colt ran his hand over his jaw. "So rather than spend the rest of his career behind a desk, he chose to help select the next generation of police officer. He's an instructor at an academy and he guest lectures around the country, offers himself as a consultant, that sort of thing."

"Is he happy?" I asked.

Colt considered my question before lifting one shoulder in a shrug. "I think he's as happy as he knows how to be. He needs to be useful, he needs to make a difference. You know?"

"But I'm guessing all that usefulness takes him away from his family a lot."

"You got it," Colt said wryly. "I haven't seen him for a few months. He's been working out of Chicago."

"And your mom doesn't mind?"

"If she does she's never told me. Mom supports everyone's choices, regardless of how they affect her."

"She's an amazing woman," I murmured.

Colt grinned. "She kind of likes you, too."

I reached over and stole a nacho from Colt's tray. "That's because I'm awesome."

He snorted a laugh. "And because you're so modest."

Shortly after that the game began, and Colt and I fell into easy silence. Colt, I discovered, was a tense basketball fan. He sat on the edge of his seat for the most part, his fists interlocked and his elbows on his knees. He shouted his disagreement and cheered when the Knicks gained momentum.

By the time half time came around, I thought Colt would have aged ten years from stress.

"I'm going to get us a beer," I said, tapping Colt's knee.

"No, I'll go," he protested.

"Colt, I'm more than capable of going to the bar. Just chill, okay?" I laughed.

The line was huge when I got to the bar, not surprisingly. I didn't mind the wait. I only hoped that Colt used the downtime to take a breath and relax. But I sort of liked that he cared so much. He was a true fan and got involved with the game. What was the point of going to these sort of things and just sitting there, feeling nothing and looking as bored as if you were watching paint dry?

I'd take Colt and all his feelings any day.

Colt was slouched in his seat when I returned, his phone loosely clasped in his hand, completely ignoring the dancers performing at the half time show.

"Hot girls dancing don't do it for you?"

He peered up from his phone, a half-smile tugging at a corner of his mouth. "Nope. Sassy blondes all the way for me."

"Ha," I said, handing him a beer. "Checking your Facebook?"

Colt smiled fully and tossed his phone onto my lap. "It's Susan and Kent's anniversary so Faith is sleeping over at my mom's tonight. She and Tess are taking selfies and messing around with a face swap app."

I pressed the home button on Colt's phone and it awakened to a picture of Faith and Uncle Sal. With their faces switched around. It was the creepiest — and funniest — thing I had ever seen in my entire life. "Oh, my God!"

"Right?" Colt said. "They've sent me like twenty pictures like this. And, trust me, you don't want to see the one of Grandpa Joe making a sexy face."

"Actually, I do."

Colt made no objection when I went to his gallery and started going through his pictures. By the time I reached the end of the ones Tess had sent, I could barely breathe for laughing. Fat tears rolled down my face and my stomach ached.

"Do I get to go through your photos?" Colt asked when I regained composure and gave him his phone back.

"Sure," I said, pulling my phone out of my purse and handing it over. "But it's totally boring compared to yours."

And it was. Mostly of nights out with the girls, and a ton I'd clearly taken the night before at my party that I had no recollection of. Most of which were of Marley, Colt and my shoes.

"You like pictures," Colt murmured, flicking through them all. "Especially of the people in your life."

"I love pictures. Here, let's take one," I said as I snatched the phone back. I held it at arm's length above us and twisted to lean into Colt. He draped his arm over my shoulders and smiled up at the phone's camera.

"Do me a favor and text that to me," Colt said.

"Sure."

On the court, the dancers finished their routine and left the floor. A moment later, a cover of *Kiss the Girl* blasted over the speakers.

I turned to Colt with a smile. "This is your kind of music, right? Is *The Little Mermaid* one of your favorites?"

Colt leaned back in his chair and flashed a lazy smile. "Of course. But this song is perfect for that." He pointed to the huge screen suspended from the ceiling.

I followed his finger and my cheerful smile fell flat when I realized what was going on. A goddamn kiss cam.

There were thousands of people here. No way would they choose Colt and me. No *way*. The odds alone were— Nope.

There we were.

"What's the matter, St. Clair?" Colt asked, sitting forward in his seat. "Chicken?"

It was a kiss cam at a basketball game. Not a freaking kiss on an altar. It didn't mean a thing. Not. A. Thing. No one I knew—I hoped—would be watching. No one I knew had to find out. A peck, that was all it would be. Nothing more, nothing less.

So why, as Colt leaned a fraction closer to me, did my heart start galloping? My breath caught in my throat when he cupped the back of my neck and drew me the rest of the way to him. Colt pressed his lips over mine and I was right back to the night we met.

This kiss was chaste in comparison—neither of us even had our mouths open. But oh, sweet baby Jesus, it hit me everywhere it counted. I wanted to grab the back of his head, assault his mouth and never come up for air.

It was over in seconds. But Colt kept his forehead to mine for another few beats before pulling away and flopping back in his seat. "One of these days, St. Clair... One of these days I'm not going to need an excuse, or beg permission, to do that."

I made a noise in the back of my throat. Denial, refusal, I had no idea. It was completely incoherent, whatever it was.

Colt chuckled and handed me his beer. "Here—I think you need this more than I do."

* * * *

After the game, we caught a cab back to my place. Yet again, the elevator wasn't working, so we headed up the stairs.

"This has been the best birthday ever," I said as we stepped out on my floor.

"Wait a minute—*today* was your actual birthday?" Colt asked. "Why did you have your party yesterday?"

"Who wants to have a birthday party on a Sunday night?"

I asked. "It's why I wanted my cake to be brought out at midnight."

"You should have told me."

I unlocked my door and Colt followed me inside. "Why?"

"I don't know," Colt said, closing the door. "But I'm sure you could have done something more exciting than go to a basketball game with me."

Leaning my hip against the back of the couch, I smiled at Colt. Man, he was gorgeous. All tall and blond and... hunky. My cheeks warmed and I couldn't stop the soft, girlish laugh that rose in my throat. "I had a blast today. I love going to basketball games. You made me remember that and I should—no, I *will*—go more often."

"Good. I'm glad," Colt said softly. "Did you have fun last night?"

"From what I can remember," I admitted. "I especially loved my surprise present."

Colt smiled. "Yeah?"

"Best gift I ever got. Bar none." I padded into the kitchen and opened the box that housed my cake. "Do you want to take the top tier for Faith? I think she'd like the shoes."

"She'd love the shoes. Don't you want it, though?" Colt asked.

"There's plenty of cake to go around. Whatever is left tomorrow I'll take to the homeless shelter near the store. I do every year." I glanced up and paused at the look on Colt's face. "What?"

He shook his head and offered a soft smile. "Nothing. I just realized that you will never stop surprising me, St. Clair."

I grinned. "I'm a multi-faceted diamond. Do you want a drink?"

"Boring as it is, I should get going."

"Oh," I said, surprised. And somewhat disappointed. "Sure. Let me just box up some cake for you."

Colt was quiet while I worked in the kitchen, and headed for the door once I'd handed him the smaller box of cake.

"Hey, Colt?" I asked as he stepped out into the hallway. "Do you — do you think you became a cop to honor your dad somehow?"

A frown creased his forehead. "Why do you ask?"

I shrugged and dropped my gaze to my shoes. "I was just thinking about the choices that we make and whether they reflect our parents and what they would want for us. Sometimes I think that's what all my choices have been about."

"I think when parents are taken too early, what they would want for their child would weigh heavily on them and deeply affect the choices they make. But more than anything, your parents would want *you* to be happy, St. Clair. Not do things you think would make them happy."

"Really?" I asked, worrying my thumb between my teeth.

Colt smiled and reached out to take my hand. "Really. And I didn't become a cop to honor my dad. Or to carry on where he left off. I became a cop because it was what *I* wanted to do. I wanted to make a difference because *I* wanted to, not because he did."

"Thank you, Colt."

"No worries." He stepped forward and pulled me into his arms. "Thank you for sharing your birthday with me."

"Thank you for putting up with me last night," I said, trying my damn hardest not to burrow into his embrace and stay there forever.

Colt chuckled. "You're a charming drunk. I'd take care of you more often, if you'd let me."

Everyone who knew me knew that I wanted a man to treat me like a princess. A man who could take care of me and spoil me and give me the life my parents thought I deserved. But I had no idea how to let a man like Colt take care of me.

Because with every breath he took, Colt would take care of me in all the ways my usual type of guy wouldn't even think of.

And I didn't know how to let him.

So instead of overthinking it, I melted into his body, wrapped my arms around his neck and tried not to imagine a time when he wouldn't be here to hold me like this. Which had to happen someday. When a woman not as screwed up as me knew a good thing when it was right in front of her and snapped him up in a heartbeat.

"Are you sure you don't want to stay for a drink?" I asked quietly, my belly a flutter of nerves. What was I doing? Because it sure as hell wasn't asking Colt to stay for a drink.

Colt released his hold on me and shifted back an inch. He studied me, his eyes hot and knowing. He tipped my chin up and gently ran his thumb over my bottom lip.

"You're playing with fire right now, asking me that. Especially after I was reminded how good your mouth feels under mine."

His words scorched a searing trail through my body. I was torn between putting sizeable distance between us so I could regain some of my faculties...and pulling him back into my apartment and feasting on his body.

Colt chuckled and lowered his hand. "We'll have that drink. Not tonight, but I don't think it will be much longer now."

I frowned as he stepped away. "What does that mean?"

"It means you're almost ready to wake up and see what's going on here." He grinned. "It's a good thing I'm patient, St. Clair. I'll call you about Halloween."

Then he was gone, disappearing into the stairwell. I closed my door and leaned on it, my heart banging against my ribcage. Somewhere in my head I was thankful that Colt had walked away. I wasn't sure, if the roles had been reversed, that I would have had the strength to do so.

Maybe Colt was right.

Maybe I was almost awake.

Chapter Twelve

There was one good thing about riding the subway to Brooklyn dressed like an animated character — it was Halloween, so plenty of other people were dressed up, too. Although I was the only one who was carrying a plastic baggie full of water.

Aside from when he'd stopped in at the store again with another surprise coffee for me and Fiona, I hadn't seen Colt in the three weeks since my birthday. We'd spoken on the phone a few times, leaving me holding my phone with a stupid, girlish grin when his name lit up the screen.

Anticipation unfurled in my belly as I headed for his place. And not just because of all the free candy I hoped I was in for. I'd...missed him. And Faith. One of the times Colt had called me, Faith had been with him and she had snatched the phone from her daddy and chewed my ear off for half an hour about how amazing the cake had been.

She was a cool kid.

Colt's neighborhood teemed with trick-or-treaters. Tiny vampires, werewolves and...Justin Beiber? *Whatever floats your boat, kid.* They roamed the streets like candy-hungry zombies looking for their next meal, banging on doors and begging for treats.

A gang of miniature witches crashed into me and I almost dropped my baggie. They laughed — or cackled — and ran up the stoop to their next house. Smiling at their enthusiasm, I hurried down the street to Colt's house.

Part of me was still surprised he'd asked me to spend Halloween with him and Faith. I'd thought he might have wanted to spend it just the two of them, since he rarely got time with her himself. I guess that was the downside of having a huge, involved family.

But whatever his reasons, I was glad he'd asked me. I loved Halloween. The chance to dress up and be someone else for a night…or several. This was actually my third Halloween event this holiday already. And I had another lined up for later. No one did Halloween like New York, and man, did she like to party.

I checked my wig in a car mirror before skipping up Colt's stoop. Two jack-o-lanterns grinned maniacally at me from their spot by the front door. One was clearly the art of a six year old, the other a man-child of thirty-five. Pressing the doorbell, I glanced down at my outfit, smoothing out my skirt.

The front door swung open and… *Oh. Holy. Hell.*

Colt was dressed like Thor.

Like, legit, he was Thor. From the body armor to the hammer…and the devilishly hot hair.

He grinned at my blatant perusal and if I didn't know better, I'd say he knew just how tingly my body was at the sight of him.

"That's very unfair of you," I said, somewhat reluctantly stepping inside.

Colt took the tiniest of steps back to let me in, but not enough that I couldn't avoid brushing against him on my way past. He wore typical Thor garb, with forearm cuffs, detailed body armor and pants tight enough that they molded to his strong thighs but were still sexy. His long red cape reached the floor past his heavy boots. He didn't wear a wig, like some guys would have. Instead he'd styled his own hair so it appeared longer, almost chin-length.

He chuckled and closed the front door. Colt stalked toward me like I was his prey. My heart hammered. "I'm not looking to fight fair, St. Clair. I'm going to take every advantage I've got."

"Go… Point your sexy somewhere else. Please." I darted away from him. "Where's Faith?"

"Getting ready. Speaking of which—who the hell are you supposed to be?" Colt invaded my space again and plucked at the hem of my purple sweater. "If you were going for a schoolgirl vibe, you sort of overshot it."

I rolled my eyes and batted his hand away. "I'm not a schoolgirl. Well, actually, I guess I am— No. I'm not a schoolgirl."

"Daddy? Is Hayley here yet? I need some help." Faith's voice drifted down to us from somewhere upstairs.

"Yeah, I'm here, Faith," I called up to her.

A moment later she clattered her way downstairs. Colt and I met her in the living room, where she stood in what could only be described as a cat costume. From, like, three years ago. It didn't fit—at all—and threatened to burst at the seams.

Tears filled the little girl's eyes as she peered up at us. "Daddy got the wrong one."

Colt's eyes widened. "I guess I did, I'm sorry, baby."

"We can fix this, don't worry." I crouched in front of Faith. "Why don't we go look in your closet and see what we can find? I'm sure I can make something for you."

Faith sniffed and nodded once. She glanced at my own costume. "Who are you supposed to be, anyway?"

I huffed and rose to full height. "Why does no one get this? I thought it was genius. Okay, let me know if this clears it up." I lifted my plastic baggie full of water and shook it with considerable force. "Fishy! Wake up!"

The little plastic fish inside the baggie bobbed pathetically in the water before flopping onto its side. Faith pulled her gaze from the baggie and she scanned me from head to toe—my red wig in high pigtails, fake braces, purple sweater, plaid skirt and my knee-high white socks.

Faith's lip wobbled.

Oh, shit. Maybe this had been a bad idea.

She ran sobbing from the room.

I whirled around to Colt, who wore a look of horror on his face.

He, too, looked down at my costume and back up again. He let out an involuntary snort of laughter. "Shit, you're Darla, aren't you?"

"I thought it would be funny."

"Not to the six year old who can't understand why she kills fish."

Oh, God. *OhGodohGodohGodohGod.* "Okay, I can fix this. You go calm her down, and, Christ, tell her I'm sorry."

Colt frowned. "But—"

I turned and rushed down the hall.

"Hey, St. Clair, you don't have to leave—"

"I'm sorry! Just... Tell her I'm so sorry." I threw open the front door and rushed down the stoop.

A little band of werewolves scattered in my wake as I hurried down the street. The costume store I'd passed on my way still had its lights on and if I had any luck on my side, it would have what I needed.

Bolting inside, I almost careened into a guy with a set of keys in his hands.

"Oh, hey, sorry, but I'm just about to lock up for the night," he said.

I grasped his forearm. "Five minutes—please."

He perused me for a long moment before nodding and moving to the side, letting me farther into the store. "Can I help you find something?"

"Wings?"

"Over here." He pointed to a large wall display with dozens of different varieties of wings. I chose a huge, delicate and intricately designed pair and handed them to the guy.

"Um...what kid costumes have you got left?"

He lifted a solitary eyebrow.

"Right, duh, stupid question. Okay, let me see what I've got." I dropped to the floor and pulled open my purse to rifle through the contents. A green party dress, killer shoes, eyeliner, perfume, sewing kit, wallet, phone...that was about it. With a sigh, I rocked back on my heels.

I pulled the stupid red wig off my head and stared at it, as though it would somehow give me an answer to this problem.

"Oh, hey, I get it! You're Darla from *Finding Nemo*, right?"

"Yup."

"Nice."

I scanned the store before landing on a short smock top. Probably intended for an adult, but on a kid it would be more like a dress. I jumped to my feet and darted across the store for the top then threw it on top of the set of wings the guy had placed at the counter. "Do you have Santa hats? Crazy glue? Scissors?"

"Yes," he said, eyebrows pulling together at my bizarre request. He picked up one, then another when he caught my headshake.

When he'd brought the items back and rung them through the till, I chopped the pompoms off the two Santa hats and glued them onto the toes of my sparkly green shoes.

"Awesome. Do you mind if I get changed real quick?" I picked up the wings and headed into the changing area before he could even answer me. I pulled off the stupid Darla costume and shoved my body into my tiny green sequined cocktail dress. Entirely too short for trick-or-treating, but entirely appropriate for the party I had been intending on going to with the girls later. But whatever. This was a crisis and the disapproving moms could suck it.

I rolled my long blonde hair into a bun on top of my head and rushed back out into the store. The guy's eyes almost rolled into the back of his head at the sight of me, so I figured I looked damned better than before.

"Thanks so much, you've totally saved my life." I hopped on one foot as I pulled my heels on before grabbing all my stuff and darting out the door.

This time it was the older kids, the ones a few years past trick-or-treating age, that stopped and stared. Them and the dads.

I bolted up Colt's stoop and pounded on his door.

163

It took longer than before for him to answer and I bounced on the balls of my feet, praying I hadn't been so long that they'd left without me.

Thor opened the door and I was knocked speechless all over again. Holy hell, he was hot.

Colt blinked and dragged his gaze over me from top to toe and back again. "Jesus Christ," he mumbled.

"Is Faith okay? Have I scarred her for life?" I asked, worrying my bottom lip between my teeth.

"No, but stop doing that or I won't be held accountable for my actions." Colt reached forward to catch my hand and tugged me inside his house. "Fuck me, St. Clair, where the hell did you go?"

"The costume store on the corner."

Colt's eyebrows shot up. "And they had this costume left on Halloween?"

"What? No, the dress and shoes are mine, I already had them with me. I just bought the wings. And a few things to make Faith a costume. If she'll let me."

His face softened, his eyes losing a little of their raw sexual heat. "Of course she will, St. Clair. Come on." Colt took my hand again, holding it loosely in his large palm, and guided me upstairs. "So you just happened to have that dress with you, huh?"

For some reason, a shot of guilt tore through me. Colt himself had said we would be done in plenty of time for me to make the party. Why, then, with him taking me up to see his upset daughter, in his big house that I felt so welcome in, did I feel like a selfish creep for planning on leaving them?

My cheeks warmed. "A girl has to be prepared for all eventualities."

A smile touched his lips. "It's cool, I know you have other places to be. I wouldn't expect anything less from a party girl like you."

We reached the top of the stairs and Colt led me to a closed door down the hallway. He tapped lightly. "Faith? Baby, Hayley's back. She's changed her costume, and says she can help with yours."

He pushed the door open to reveal Faith sitting cross-legged on her small bed, her elbows on her knees and her chin resting in her palms. The sight of her made my heart hurt.

I scooted past Thor — I mean Colt — and crouched in front of Faith. "Hey, I'm really sorry about before. I thought it would be funny. Pretty stupid, huh?"

Faith peered up at me with her huge blue eyes, so like her daddy's, and nodded once. She glanced behind me at Colt. "Daddy said you don't know much about Disney. That's really weird."

I laughed. "Well, your daddy would probably tell you that I'm really weird. But I do know one Disney movie really well — in fact, it's one of my favorites. Do you want to know what it is?"

Faith nodded.

"*The Nightmare Before Christmas*."

Her eyes lit up. "I love that one!"

"You do? Well, that's fantastic, because I brought some stuff to help make you your very own *Nightmare Before Christmas* costume."

Faith scrambled to her feet and all but shoved her father out of the room. "Go away, I want it to be a surprise!"

Colt stuttered his protests but relented. He winked before Faith slammed the door shut, almost taking off his nose.

I laughed again. "Okay, I need you to find the most hideously disgusting dress you own that I can chop up into little pieces."

Faith giggled and opened her closet, immediately choosing a plaid dress with weird puffy sleeves and A-line skirt. I could see why she hated it. I let Faith — carefully — cut some squares out of the dress while I stitched them onto the smock to create a patchwork dress.

Once she had it on, I drew some stitches onto her arms, legs and face and placed my Darla wig on her head, covering her thick dark hair. She bounded down the stairs and into the living room where Colt waited for us.

"Daddy! I'm Sally!"

Colt grinned at Faith. "You are. I like it, baby. Are you happy?"

Faith nodded and turned to me, looping her thin arms around my waist. "Thank you, Hayley. And I like you so much better as Tinkerbell."

"Me too, kid." Colt gave a wide grin.

I stuck my tongue out at him.

"Come on, let's go or all the good candy will be gone," Faith said. She slipped her hand into mine and pulled me toward the front door.

Colt caught my eye again, another small, intimate smile at play on his lips.

"What?" I asked.

He shook his head. After locking up the house, he draped his arm around my bare shoulders. "Aren't you a popular fairy?"

"Everybody loves Tinkerbell," I said, peering up at him.

Colt dipped his head so his lips touched the shell of my ear. "No one more than me right now."

A shiver crept up my spine at his closeness. I wanted—

Get it together, St. Clair.

He smiled as though he knew exactly what I'd been thinking... Or been about to think. The man was too intuitive for his own good.

Faith tugged on my hand again and we headed up the stoop of our first stop.

We made an absolute killing that night. Especially the houses where the dads handed out the candy. Faith's little trick-or-treat bag was soon full to bursting and Colt had to run into a grocery store to buy a few more.

Faith kept us out for hours, walking up and down entire neighborhoods. We must have been a sight to see—Sally, Tinkerbell and Thor walking down the street. I had way more fun than I thought I would and I felt a bloom of pride when Faith opened her bag to show me what she'd received.

But even the most hardcore of trick-or-treaters couldn't last all night, and it soon became clear that Faith was beat.

"Come on, baby, let's head home," Colt said.

"But I'm not done yet." Faith pouted.

"Look at Hayley's shoes — they have to be killing her."

I snorted a laugh. "You're kidding, right? I was practically raised in heels. These bad boys are good to go all night." At Colt's pointed look, I pretended to wince and limp. "Uh, I mean, ouch, actually, they totally pinch."

Faith rolled her eyes. "Da-ad."

Colt grinned. "Home, Faith. And you can eat three pieces of candy before bed."

She huffed. "Make it four and a movie and we have a deal."

He laughed. "You're an extortionist!"

"I'm an opportunist."

"Yeah, you've been around your mother too long."

A laugh bubbled up in me. "I really like this kid."

Faith beamed at this and slipped her hand into mine once again.

Back at Colt's place, Faith sat cross-legged on the floor and tipped out her loot into one big pile. She sorted through it, pulling out all the pumpkin Snickers bars. "Daddy, can we watch *The Nightmare Before Christmas*, please?"

"Sure, go grab the DVD. I'm going to call Hayley a cab."

Faith twisted around and peered up at us. "Why? I thought you liked this movie?"

My stomach twisted. I was a little surprised that Colt was dismissing me so fast. I'd thought for sure he would try to sweet-talk me into staying longer. Which was his usual MO.

Colt crouched in front of Faith. "You see how pretty Hayley looks? She's going to a party. She can't waste a dress like that on just us."

"Why not?" Faith asked, peering up at me with her huge eyes, making me feel like the biggest asshole on the planet. "Don't you want to watch a movie with me and Daddy?"

Jesus H. C., this kid should go into politics when she's bigger. Or sales. Whatever her occupation, if it involved getting people to do what she wanted, then she would absolutely kick ass. I smiled, but I knew it wouldn't look sure or confident. "Sweetheart, I would love to watch a movie with you. But I'm not sure I'm invited."

Faith grinned and leaped to her feet. She jumped up and down on the spot. "You're invited, you're invited! I'll go get the movie!" Faith ran out of the room and clattered upstairs.

Colt rose slowly from his crouch and crossed the room to where I stood. He simply perused me for a long, heavy moment. Finally, he said, "She'll be asleep within twenty minutes, I guarantee it. Do you want me to call you a cab for then?"

That feeling in my gut curled tighter and for the first time since I'd met Colt, I felt in the way. A nuisance. "You want me to go?"

He blinked, surprise flitting across his handsome face. "No, why would you think that?"

I fidgeted with the hem of my short dress, which seemed to be shrinking the longer I wore it. Or maybe that was just how Colt made me feel — as though I was practically naked in front of him. "You're all but shoving me out the door."

Colt took a single long stride closer. "I'm just trying to give you an easy out. Trust me, I know how well my daughter can work the guilt angle."

The last thing I wanted was an easy out. My friends and I had looked forward to this party for months, but now, here with Colt and Faith, it was the last place in the world I wanted to go. I wanted… I wanted to stay with them. For as long as they'd let me.

Shaking my head, I said, "I don't want an out. I'd like to stay with you guys. If I'm welcome, I mean. I don't want to impose. You probably want the rest of your night just the two of you, right?"

"St. Clair, Faith adores you. She'd never speak to me

again if I tossed you out because I wanted her all to myself. My kid doesn't starve for my attention, even though we don't get a huge amount of time just us two." Colt closed the remaining distance between us. He dropped his large, warm hand onto my shoulder then moved it up to cup my neck. "And for the record, you are always welcome here. Always."

All I could do was stare at him.

Something passed between us that I couldn't articulate, let alone process. I shifted forward, leaning my body toward his, letting his heat draw me in like a spell I didn't want to break.

I reached up to cover his hand with mine, my eyes fluttering closed.

"St. Clair," Colt said in a low, gravelly voice that was so primal I about melted. "You're playing with fire. Don't expect me to back off."

My heart banged against my ribcage. Every nerve ending in my body was alive and aware of him. I wanted to kiss him again, to prove to myself once and for all that it wasn't just as good as I remembered—it was better. This time I wouldn't stop with a kiss. I would keep going until I knew every inch of his body and what it could do...what it could make me feel.

"I found it!"

Faith's sudden announcement had me springing away from Colt as if I'd been prodded with an electric pole.

Colt made a noise in his throat and swallowed hard as he put more distance between us.

Faith skipped into the room, waving the DVD case above her head like a flag of victory. She dropped onto the floor in front of the entertainment center and started to set up the movie.

Colt cleared his throat. "Are you hungry?"

It was an innocent enough question—yet it felt loaded with possibility. Or risk. Or opportunity. I considered my answer, before going with the most honest one. "Starved."

He stared hard at me, seemingly conflicted with what he wanted to — or could, with Faith in earshot — say. Eventually, he blew out a breath and reached for the cordless phone on the end table. "Playing with fire, St. Clair," he mumbled as he dialed.

Colt ordered dinner at a Chinese place, asking for enough food to feed an army. He replaced the phone and moved over to Faith. "Come on, baby, go get dressed for bed then you can watch the movie."

"But I want to keep my costume on."

He shook his head. "PJs, now."

Faith sighed like it was the biggest inconvenience of her life. Damn pajamas. Finally, she lifted her arms and flashed Colt the cutest smile I'd ever seen. "Carry me up? Please, Daddy?"

Colt rolled his eyes but leaned down to swoop his daughter into his arms. He tossed her tiny body over his shoulder, her shrieks of delight filling the room. "We'll be right back."

When they left, I took the opportunity of being alone in Colt's living room to, well, give in to my curiosity, I guess. Last time I'd been here, Colt and I had mostly stuck to the kitchen.

Like a typical guy, he didn't have much by way of decoration. What he did have was an abundance of photographs, like me. There were dozens of shots of Faith, documenting her progress through life. She was there as a chubby baby with a drooling smile, a mischievous toddler holding an upturned houseplant by its roots. Her and Colt at so many family activities. At the beach, Coney Island and the park. And his whole family around Jessie's dinner table, Grandpa Joe with his head tipped back and laughing at something Uncle Sal said next to him.

Something in my chest tightened — a pinch of jealousy coupled with a hint of longing.

"Hey, St. Clair," Colt called from upstairs.

I shook myself out of the sudden melancholy and headed

to the foot of the stairs. Colt leaned over the bannister and tossed a wad of fabric that hit me square in the face.

"Get changed, or I won't be held accountable for my actions." His head disappeared and I unfurled the clothing he'd tossed. Another one of his old shirts, the material of the flannel worn and faded but so, so soft. It had felt like heaven the last time I'd worn one, and I couldn't help but smile that I was wearing another one.

I ducked into the downstairs bathroom to wiggle out of my dress. Pulling Colt's shirt over my head, it fell to just above my knees. I turned my face into the collar, catching a hint of pure unadulterated Colt.

Crap, I'm in trouble...

Forcing myself out of the bathroom, I went back to the living room to find Colt and Faith had come downstairs. Colt was sprawled on the couch while Faith lay on her belly in front of her hefty pile of candy, both changed out of their alter ego costumes. Colt wore soft workout pants and a T-shirt while Faith looked super cozy in her pink fluffy onesie.

"Hayley, what's your favorite candy?" Faith asked without looking up.

"Um, I love Laffy Taffy. And M&Ms. I don't eat much candy anymore."

"Grownups are so weird," she mumbled as she searched through her pile. Faith rose up on her knees and held up a handful of miniature Laffy Taffy and a few fun-sized bags of M&Ms.

I accepted them and ruffled her wig-free hair with my spare hand. "Thanks, sweetheart."

She flopped back onto the floor and hit Play on the remote beside her, starting the movie.

Smiling, I turned to make my way to the couch but froze at the expression on Colt's face. "What?" I asked, baffled at his look of disbelief. Glancing down at myself, I confirmed that I hadn't missed any buttons and wasn't actually flashing anything.

He shook his head and sat up straighter. "I'm an idiot. Why the hell did I think that was a safer alternative for me?"

"Daddy, don't swear," Faith said past a mouthful of candy.

"Sorry, baby." Colt patted the cushion beside him. "Sit your a—apple bottom down, St. Clair."

I snorted a laugh and sat beside him, curling my legs underneath me. "Nice save."

"Thanks. Now cover up." He dropped a thick fleece blanket on my lap.

Rolling my eyes, I did as I was told.

For once.

The food came shortly after, and we ate out of the cartons on the couch. Faith couldn't be persuaded to have any, preferring to tuck into her candy loot.

Once we were done, Faith rose from her spot on the floor and came over to us on the couch. She dumped a small pile of pumpkin Snickers onto Colt's lap before wedging herself between us.

With a huff, Faith pushed her hair out of her face only for it to flop back into exactly the same place a moment later.

"Do you want me to braid it for you?" I asked her. I reached into my bag, which was in front of the couch, and found a hair tie. Faith turned around so she had her back to me and I could reach her long hair better.

She sat quietly, as patient as a saint as I worked her hair.

When I was done, she whipped around to kiss my cheek before wriggling down and resting her head on Colt's lap and her feet on mine. A second later, soft snores blew past her lips.

"She really likes you," Colt said in a low whisper.

"I really like her. She's amazing, Colt. Seriously."

He stared at me as if there was more he wanted to say. He shook his head after a moment. "I can't believe you pulled that Halloween costume out of the bag tonight. They just had that patchwork dress left?"

"What? Oh, no, I bought the shirt and Faith gave me an

old dress she didn't like and we chopped it up to stitch squares on."

Colt lifted his eyebrows. "Which dress?"

I pulled a face. "This God-awful plaid thing. It was seriously hideous. You have terrible taste in little girl dresses, Colton Deluca."

There was a pause, a moment where Colt didn't move. Didn't even blink. Then his lips twitched and he tipped his head back, his entire body shaking with silent laughter.

"What? Am I missing something here?"

Colt dug the heels of his hands into his eyes and it was a full minute later before he had regained some composure. "Nothing. Nothing at all, St. Clair. But you've made my daughter the happiest girl in the world."

"Why does that feel like a double entendre?"

He grinned. "I'll tell you someday."

I pulled a face at him and tried to stretch out a little without disturbing Faith. The couch pillows were super soft and squishy as I laid my head down, warm and tired.

"Falling asleep on me, St. Clair?" Colt asked, his voice quiet and a hundred miles away.

"No," I said, not sure if my eyes were open. "I'll call a cab once the movie finishes."

He chuckled. "Yeah, right. I thought you were a party girl. It's not even nine yet."

I felt like I hadn't slept for a week. Which was actually sort of accurate. With all the parties, my usual nights of drinks and dinner with the girls and squeezing in work somewhere in between, I'd had to forgo luxuries like sleep.

I'm not sure if I answered him. I might have. Then again, it could just have been mumbled nonsense.

* * * *

I woke with sudden awareness that I didn't know where I was. The pillow under my head, while soft, wasn't mine. It smelled masculine and fresh. The blanket was warm and snuggly, and wrapped around me like a burrito. Hyped-up music played and there were sounds of life somewhere close by.

Stretching out, I was reluctant to move from my cozy bed. But…I wasn't in my bed.

At the sound of girlish laughter, it finally hit me where I was.

Colt's.

I'd had a sleepover at Colt's. Again.

Thankfully, I'd slept on the couch, alone.

I scrubbed the remnants of sleep out of my eyes and got up out of my makeshift bed. Faith's obnoxious kids' show blared from the TV in the kitchen. She sat on a high stool, shoveling Lucky Charms into her mouth, never looking away from the TV.

Coffee was in the pot so I poured myself a mug, drinking it black. "Morning. Where's your daddy?"

"In the shower. Can I have some juice, please?"

"Sure thing." I grabbed a glass from the cabinet and took out some fresh OJ from the fridge.

Colt's cell blared to life on the breakfast bar and Faith reached for it, sliding her finger across the screen and lifting it to her ear. "Hi, Mommy."

Shit. Susan. Please don't tell her I'm here, Faith.

"No, he's in the shower. Hayley, can I have my juice now?"

Ah, Christ… "Sorry, sorry," I mumbled, setting the glass down in front of her.

Faith smiled her thanks. "Yeah, Hayley slept over."

On the couch! Tell her I slept on the couch!

"When are you coming to get me? I can't wait to tell you all about my Halloween! I didn't dress up as a cat, Daddy got the wrong size, but Hayley made me a super cool Sally costume." Faith glanced at me with a conspiratorial twinkle in her eyes. "She cut up my gross party dress to make it."

Party dress? I'm too young for this kind of stress.

Colt appeared in the kitchen doorway, a towel hanging

low on his hips.

I'm having a stroke. I'm having an actual stroke.

He plucked his phone out of Faith's grasp and held it to his ear. "Morning, Susan."

Water droplets clung to the ends of his hair, dripping down his strong back to the dimples above his hips. *God, those dimples are sexy.*

"Yeah, noon is fine. Okay, see you then." Colt hung up and placed his phone back on the breakfast bar. His eyebrows drew together when he turned to look at me. "What's wrong?"

"I cut up her party dress?"

Colt's lips twitched. He turned to Faith. "You told your mother Hayley cut up your party dress?"

"Maybe," Faith said slowly.

He sighed and shook his head. "Go brush your teeth, please."

Faith hopped down from her stool and smiled at me on her way past — her unintentional partner in crime.

"I cut up her party dress?" I repeated.

His eyes were full of mirth as he nodded. "That God-awful dress, as you called it last night, is the one she's supposed to wear tonight for her grandmother's birthday party."

"I'm sorry, what?" There had to be a mistake. I had to have misheard. No way had I been conned so hard by a six year old.

"Susan bought it for her, but she hates it. Who wouldn't? But yeah, it's for her other grandmother's birthday party. Guess you saved her the humiliation."

I'd never met Colt's ex-wife, Susan, and I had a feeling I didn't ever want to now, either. "But — That — She — I was coerced!"

Colt snorted a laugh. "I hear you. Don't worry about it, seriously."

I pressed a hand to my belly. "God. I'm getting an ulcer, I'm sure of it."

He squeezed my shoulder. He leaned around me for a

coffee mug and poured himself some from the pot. "St. Clair, Susan and I are perfectly aware how calculating our kid is. When you meet her, just ask her about the time Faith convinced her that her kindergarten teacher had died to get out of going to school that day. Imagine Susan's surprise when Mrs. Parson made a full recovery—from her death—the following day."

I clamped a hand over my mouth and swallowed a burst of laughter. "No way. Are you serious?"

"As Mrs. Parson's fake heart attack."

"Oh, my God... I don't know whether to be impressed or terrified."

"Welcome to my life."

I liked it. I liked his life. A lot, it turned out. I liked his big, crazy family and his evil—or genius—child. I liked...*him*.

"St. Clair?"

Squeezing my eyes shut for a second to try to clear my head, I forced a smile then met his gaze. Colt's stare seemed to cut right through me, past all the outer layers the rest of the world saw, to get right to the inner workings of me.

Colt took a step closer, reaching out to place his hand on the counter behind me. He crowded me in with his big body. He completely overwhelmed me, made me crave something I couldn't vocalize.

"You're doing it again," Colt said, his voice low and rough.

"Doing what?" I asked, my own voice thick.

"Playing with fire."

He'd said it to me so many times I should have been used to it, but the truth was, I wasn't. I didn't think I would ever be. But this time was different. He wasn't teasing me, or even flirting. He was warning me that I was toeing a very fine line. But I wasn't even sure where that line was anymore.

"I don't want to get burned," I whispered, my pulse hammering.

Colt leaned an inch closer, bringing his other hand up

to cup my jaw. He stroked his thumb over my cheek and dipped his head, his forehead a fraction away from mine. "I could never hurt you, St. Clair. Never."

I swallowed. My head swam. I felt like I was drowning and had no idea which way was up — only that he was my air. Every day he was making me forget why this was a bad idea. He made me want to jump into this thing with both feet and say to hell with consequences.

"I can't think when you don't have any clothes on."

"So stop thinking."

The heavy sound of six-year-old feet clattering down the stairs saved me from answering. I had no idea how I would have responded, or reacted, if Faith hadn't made it impossible.

Colt stepped away from me and adjusted his towel. "I'd better go get dressed."

I nodded.

Faith came back into the kitchen dressed in a pair of hot-pink leggings and a shirt with a picture of a cat on it. Her French braid had survived the night and she had added a sparkly headband to it. The kid had individuality — it would do her well in later years.

Colt made to ruffle Faith's hair but she ducked out of the way at the last second. "*Da-ad*! You'll ruin my hair."

He rolled his eyes. "Sorry, baby. I'll be right back, okay? I'm going to throw some clothes on."

Faith nodded as she climbed back onto her stool to carry on watching the show that looked like it had been made by crack addicts.

Colt flashed me a wink on his way out of the room.

Lord, I need to get out of here.

"I'm going to take off, I have some stuff to do so I'd... Yeah, I'd better go and take care of... That. Stuff." *Smooth, St. Clair. Real smooth.*

Colt ducked back into the kitchen. "Right now?"

"When are you coming back?" Faith asked, not pulling her eyes from the TV.

"Um, I'm not sure. But you have fun at your grandma's party, okay?"

I edged past Colt and headed down the hall into the living room so I could get my dress from the night before. It wouldn't be the first time I'd gone home in broad daylight wearing my party clothes.

"If you give me five minutes I can take you. Faith likes driving into the city."

"No, it's fine. I'll be fine."

"Let me call you a cab at least."

I turned around with my hands full of stuff, my heart lodging in my throat at the look of confused hurt on Colt's face. "The subway is quicker. Seriously, I'll be fine. I'll see you later, okay?"

Without waiting for a reply, I darted into the bathroom to quickly change back into my dress. I fixed my hair so I didn't look like a total whore and shoved my feet into my shoes.

Beyond the closed bathroom door, the only sound to be heard was Faith's show. I could hope that meant Colt was upstairs getting dressed and I could slip out unnoticed.

Nope.

I stepped outside and walked smack into his hard, naked chest. The sneak had waited for me. Quietly.

He lifted an eyebrow. "Hoping to run out when I wasn't looking?"

My cheeks flushed. "Maybe."

"Why?"

I shrugged and tried to move around him but he refused to budge his big, firm body. *Stupid muscles.* "Please, Colt? I really do have to go."

"What's going on, St. Clair?" he asked, reaching out to grasp my hip and tug me closer.

I couldn't have resisted if I'd wanted to. I shook my head and placed my hand on his chest—whether to lean in, or push him away, I wasn't sure. Closing my eyes for a second, I focused on the rise and fall of his chest beneath my hand, the constant, rhythmic thump of his heart. Colt was real and solid, somehow *more* than anyone else I had ever met.

He invaded my thoughts and my desires.

He was everywhere.

"Are you still running?" Colt asked, his voice low and gravelly.

"No," I whispered.

Colt's lips curled into a smile that was more resigned than anything else. "Yes, you are. But you're getting slower." He dipped his head to kiss my cheek, lingering a moment longer than needed.

When he pulled back, it took all my self-control not to grab that towel and yank him back to me, to hell with the right choice and the fact his daughter was in the other room.

Colt chuckled and retreated a few paces. "Yeah, you're getting slower all right. Take it easy, St. Clair." He turned and took the stairs two at a time.

Shaking my head to get rid of the lust-filled stupor, I stumbled to the front door. "Bye, Faith," I called, wrapping my hand around the door handle.

"Oh, hey, what are you doing tomorrow night?" Colt shouted down from the landing.

I headed back to the foot of the stairs and peered up at him. There was a birthday party for a DJ I knew at one of the clubs me and the girls always hit up. It was the most talked-about party of the year, and I'd been looking forward to it for months. I had the best dress picked out—a totally sexy Armani number that hugged me everywhere it should. "Nothing."

Colt grinned. "Come have dinner with me? Ma is putting on her usual feast, and she's been asking when I'm bringing you back around."

His smile was infectious and my own widened. "Done. I'm there."

"Great. I'll pick you up, okay? Six? You remember how long these things go on for."

Did I ever. Colt's family turned mealtimes into a ritualistic act. It brought them closer together through the simple act of eating and talking. A world away from what dinner had been like for me growing up — awkward, tense silence with the only sound coming from our silverware against the china. "Six is perfect. I'll see you then."

* * * *

The second I was home, I stripped out of my green party dress and kicked off my heels. I pressed Play on the answering machine as I passed it and darted into my closest, which had long ago reached bursting point.

"Hi, darling," my grandmother's voice drifted into the room from the machine. "I'm just calling to remind you that our reservations are for twelve-thirty at the Carlyle. See you soon."

"Awesome," I muttered as I rooted around for something to wear. Eventually I went with a forties-inspired navy floral fishtail tea dress and a pair of navy pumps. After tugging a brush through my hair, I negotiated it into a style that looked way more complicated than it actually was — two French braids either side of my head and rolling them into a wreath at the back.

I freshened up my makeup, then I was straight back out of the door.

Sometimes, on days like this, I had to wonder why I bothered with an apartment. Surely a storage unit would suit my needs just as well, seeing as I was never in the damn thing.

Luck was on my side and there was an abundance of cabs when I hit the street. I threw myself in one and slammed the door closed. "Bergdorf's, please." I pulled my cell out of my purse, found the number I was looking for and hit call.

"Hayley, *bella*, long time no speak!" My amazing friend Paulo answered after a few rings.

"Paulo! I'm on way to you right now — please tell me you're free," I said, pressing a hand to my forehead.

He made a disgruntled noise in the back of his throat. "I wish. Mrs. Size Eight who insists she's Mrs. Size Two will arrive at any moment. Why, what's the matter?"

I groaned. "I need a dress, like, *now*, and I need your help."

Paulo laughed. "Why do you need my help? I've been trying to poach you for years to work here—you'd make a fortune in commissions."

"It's not a dress for me, it's for a little girl. I've never bought a tiny dress before, what if I don't even get the right size?"

"Breathe, Hayley, breathe. Okay, head for the kid section and I'll get away from Mrs. Size Eight as soon as I can."

My relief escaped me in a sigh. "Great, thank you."

I could barely sit still. I tapped my foot, fidgeted in my seat and almost smacked my head off the window a few times, trying to gauge how much farther the store was. Time was of the essence, and I was running out of it.

When the cab finally stopped, I tossed a wad of bills at the cabbie before spilling out of the cab and into the store.

True to his word, Paulo met me after a few minutes. I was pacing in front of the clothes, trying—and failing—to think what would work best for Faith.

"Ah, *ciao, tesoro mio*," Paulo said, clutching my arms and kissing both my cheeks.

"I'm so glad you're here," I said on a breath. Man, I loved Paulo. Hot as hell and gay as they come, he was a New York girl's wet dream. Paulo loved to share his employee discount and often sent me and the girls samples of clothes Bergdorf's would be carrying. We were great advertising—we were at all the best clubs and restaurants, after all. It was a win-win relationship. He was a genuinely great guy and I adored him.

"Who are you looking for?"

"A little girl, Faith. I totally wrecked the dress she's supposed to wear tonight." I told Paulo the costume story, and his loud, belly-clutching laugh reverberated across the entire floor.

"How old is she?" Paulo asked once he had regained composure.

"Six."

"Then I'd go with one of these." He waved his hand toward a selection of small dresses, and it was then that I saw it.

A Zoë black and white sleeveless pointe dress with black lace on a white bodice, and slivers of matching white lace on the black skirt. Faith would look amazing in it with her dark hair. "This is it. Do you have shoes to match?"

Paulo arched a single, perfect eyebrow and led me to the shoes. I picked out a pair of Gucci suede sandals and, because I couldn't help myself, a tiny matching purse.

"I have a new dress in that you would look fabulous in, darling, why don't you try it on before you leave?" Paulo asked as I gathered my small haul for Faith.

"I wish I could, but I have, like, no time left today. I need to get these to Brooklyn then back to the Upper East Side for lunch with my grandparents." I heaved out a breath. "I just hope I miss Faith's mother. She'll probably skin me alive for this mess."

Paulo chuckled. "Don't be so hard on yourself, *bella*. Everyone makes mistakes."

"And apparently I make epic ones," I mumbled, handing my credit card over to the clerk.

Paulo shook his head and shooed the clerk out of the way. "You can have this on my discount," he said, running the transaction through. "And I'll throw in a fifty percent discount card for the mother, too, to sweeten her up for you."

"Paulo, you're the best, seriously." I accepted the bags he handed over and kissed his cheeks. "I'll come see you again when I have more time—we'll break that sales record we made last spring!"

Paulo laughed. "You'd better! Now go and make that little girl look like a princess."

I all but ran out of the store and into another cab. I was in no mood for the subway and I could only hope traffic was on my side.

In the end, I made it back to Colt's a little after noon. I ran up to his front door and knocked so hard I thought I'd bruise my knuckles.

Faith opened the door, her little face lighting up when she saw me. "Hayley! You're back!" Faith rushed out to wrap her thin arms around me, then tugged me inside the house. "Have you been shopping? Can I see?"

"Um, in just a minute, okay. Where's your dad?"

"We made cookies after you left, come try one."

"That sounds great, but where's your dad?"

Faith hauled me into the kitchen and pointed at Colt, who sat at the breakfast bar, his large hand wrapped around a cup of coffee.

"In here with Mommy."

Mommy...? Ah, shit.

Faith frowned. "Where'd Mommy go?"

"Bathroom," Colt said as he rose from his stool. He smiled, making his way over to me. "Can't keep away, huh?"

If she was in the bathroom, I had a tiny sliver of opportunity to make it out of there alive. I thrust the Bergdorf's bags at Colt. "This is a replacement—but only if you guys are cool with it, no pressure, and I don't want to presume anything... God. Okay, I have to go."

Colt's eyebrows shot up and he refused to accept the bags. "Christ, St. Clair, where's the fire?"

I groaned in frustration and shook the bags. "I have somewhere to be, will you please just take these?"

"As someone who spent years getting pissed at this idiot, let me spare you some time and energy. The bigger the rush you're in, or the more irritated you get, he'll just dig his heels in even harder." The woman who entered the kitchen gave me a wry look as she sat on a stool at the breakfast bar. She was tall and lithe, as gorgeous as a model and an apparent natural beauty, as it didn't look like she wore a scrap of makeup. Her straight dark hair hung down her back, and her brown eyes were just stunning.

Colt's ex was a goddamn knockout.

"Mommy, Hayley went shopping," Faith said, tugging on my hand. "Do you want a cookie now?"

I had no clue what to do or what to say. Would they notice if I just turned and high-tailed it out of there? Maybe. Okay, definitely. I cleared my throat and tried to smile at Susan. "Hi."

Her lips twitched as she raised her coffee cup to take a sip. "Hi. Are you okay?"

"I like your dress. But I think you're prettier as Tinkerbell," Faith said, looking up at me with a huge grin.

Susan coughed a laugh. "Yeah, I heard you had to come up with an emergency costume."

I cringed. "Not my finest hour. Um... Or the one where I chopped up Faith's dress."

She waved her hand. "Jeez, don't worry about that. That dress was hideous. Her grandmother picked it out months ago for her and insisted I buy it for tonight."

My eyebrows shot up. "You didn't like it either?"

Susan frowned as she stared at me in bafflement. "That disgusting thing? Of course not. You did us all a favor, seriously."

My breath left me in a rush. "My God, I felt awful about it."

Colt chuckled and pressed a hand to the small of my back. He guided me farther into the room. "Take a seat, St. Clair. I'll get you a coffee—you look like you need it."

"Oh, no, I really can't stay. I only came to bring this," I said, lifting the bags and setting them on the breakfast bar. I faced Susan. "I got this as a replacement, but if you don't need it, you can do whatever you want with it. Exchange it for something else, whatever. No problem."

Susan rose from the stool. "Oh, you sweet thing, you didn't have to do that. Faith, sweetie, come see what Hayley got you."

Faith scrambled up onto the stool beside her mother. "For me?" She dug into those bags like it was Christmas and gasped and oohed over every item. "Oh my gosh, these are so pretty!"

"They are," Susan agreed. She smiled at me. "Thank you, Hayley. You've made my little girl's day."

A flush of pleasure warmed my cheeks. "No worries. My friend works at Bergdorf's so he got me a pretty good deal. And he also gave me this." I pulled the discount card out of my pocket and slid it across the bar to Susan. "You can use it against anything. It was just to apologize. I really do feel awful."

"Seriously, there is nothing to feel bad about."

"So you're going to give that back, Susan?" Colt asked, his lips twitching in amusement.

She snorted a laugh. "Absolutely not."

"Okay, now I really do have to go. Have fun at your party, Faith," I said, tugging the end of her hair on my way past. I smiled at Susan. "Lovely to meet you."

"You too. Are you going to be at Jessie's tomorrow?" Susan asked.

Faith gasped. "You're going to Nana J's?"

"Yeah, she'll be there," Colt said as he came up behind me.

"Good, we can talk more then," Susan said. She nudged Faith. "What do you say to Hayley for your new things?"

"Thank you!" she exclaimed as she peered inside her new purse.

"You're welcome, I'm glad you like them. Bye, everyone," I said.

Colt pressed his hand to my lower back again and kept close beside me as we headed to the front door. "That was totally unexpected."

"Like I said, I feel terrible."

"She loves them. You're incredible, St. Clair." Colt cleared his throat. "Are you absolutely sure you have to be somewhere?"

I nodded, ignoring the twist in my gut when I wished more than anything I was wrong. I checked my watch. "I'm late. Actually, I'm *really* late."

Colt blew out a breath. "Guess I'll have to wait until tomorrow, then."

"I guess you will," I agreed.

"You know," Colt said as I opened the door and started down the stoop. "One of these days, you'll stop running out of here like this."

"Oh yeah? What makes you so sure?" I asked, looking at him over my shoulder and smiling.

"Hope." Colt grinned. "I keep hoping one of these days you won't want to leave at all."

When he said things like that, he made me forget why we were such a bad idea. When he said things like that I wanted to march right back up those steps, slam the door closed and demand that he never let me leave ever again.

"Bye, Colt."

"Take it easy, St. Clair."

Chapter Thirteen

The Carlyle was one of New York's finest old hotels. Situated on the Upper East Side, it stretched high into the skyline, its pointed tip beautifully crafted. Every time I visited – which was usually whenever my grandparents were in town – I was awed by its classic elegance and stunning architecture. The sound of my heels echoed around the lobby as I made my way across the marble floor.

The hostess smiled at me at the entrance to the dining room. "Do you have a reservation?"

"I'm with Mr. Bartlett," I said, cringing at how late I was. I peered around her, trying to spot my grandparents so I could gauge how pissed they were. There was no sign of them in the art deco styled restaurant.

"Of course, follow me, please."

I trailed the hostess across the restaurant to a square table where my grandparents were seated. Soft piano music played, helping to create a light atmosphere.

My grandfather spotted me first. He smiled and rose from his seat to kiss my cheek. "Hayley."

"Hi, I'm so sorry I'm late," I said, bending to hug my grandmother. "Traffic… You know?"

"Yes," she said with a simple smile. "And deciding what to wear also, I'm guessing?"

"Well, you know me," I said as I sank into my chair.

"We've already ordered. I hope you're in the mood for foie gras and a Niçoise salad," Grandfather said.

"Absolutely." I forced a smile. It wasn't because I was late that he had ordered for me. It was something they did all the time. Because they knew best, right?

The food came shortly after and we fell quiet. My grandparents didn't think it was polite to talk over food, and preferred to slowly eat in perfect silence. It was a far cry from a meal at Jessie's house, which couldn't have been quiet if the entire table of people were bound and gagged.

I found it just as awkward now as I had every day for six years.

"So, Hayley," Grandmother said when the plates had been cleared and coffee served. "How are things with you?"

"Just fine. I've been busy with the store, lately."

The downward turn of my grandmother's lips was so slight anyone else would have missed it. But I'd been seeing it since I was thirteen, and it was as obvious as a foghorn. She didn't approve of my job and made no secret of it. It wasn't becoming for someone like me, according to her.

A boutique on Madison Avenue that served champagne to its shoppers would have been a little more to her taste.

"Oh, you will never guess who we ran into last week at the gala," Grandmother said, brightening slightly.

"Who?" I asked, hoping my interest seemed believable.

"Alexander Yates."

I almost dropped my coffee cup. "My ex-boyfriend?"

"He's moving to the city, isn't that wonderful?" Grandmother smiled. "I gave him your number, he's very excited to see you."

"You...gave him my number?" Hearing from my ex ranked as far down on my list of things I'd rather not do as it could get. That wasn't fair. There was nothing wrong with Alex, not really. We'd broken up when he'd gone to Princeton for college and I'd gone nowhere. He had wanted to do his stint in college then follow his dad into the family business and I'd wanted to escape New Haven and party my ass off in the city.

Alex, last I'd heard, was the financial manager for the company his great-grandfather had birthed. They bought smaller businesses in trouble for a low price, fixed them up then sold them on for a hefty profit. It had to be a lucrative business. The Yates family had an estate in New Haven, a penthouse in Manhattan, a cottage in the Hamptons, a chalet in Vale and a few properties dotted around Europe.

Grandmother placed her coffee cup down and pinned me with a look I was very, very familiar with. "Is there something wrong? Do you have a reason for not wanting to see Alexander? From what I remember, he was very fond of you."

And that right there was the key to the problem. Alex and I had been *fond* of each other. There'd been no heat. We had been lukewarm at best. It hadn't hurt when we'd broken up. It hadn't even stung.

"I just don't think we will have much to talk about these days. A lot of time has passed since we last saw each other," I said.

"Exactly. A lot of time has passed. So you will have *plenty* to talk about." Grandmother smiled and Grandfather signaled the waiter for the check, thereby ending the conversation.

* * * *

Seeing my grandparents always put me in a funky mood. They got under my skin and even now that I was twenty-seven, their stiff and cold natures made me want to rebel. Paint my hair pink and stay out all night.

Instead, I headed down to Back in Time to check in with Fiona. When I stepped inside, I couldn't help but smile seeing my boss wearing a huge floral hat, with actual fake flowers bursting from its great height, and her Jackie-O sunglasses.

The sight of her, quirks and all, lifted the bulk of the heavy, oppressing dark cloud that shadowed me after every interaction with my grandparents. Fiona was pure, unadulterated sunlight and I adored her. "Do I even want to know?" I asked, a laugh rising in my throat.

"I found it at a yard sale last week—what do you think?"

Fiona twirled on the spot and held out her arms.

"Fabulous, darling," I drawled.

"What's going on here? What's wrong with your face?" She waved her hand at my expression.

I groaned and slumped down on the stool behind the register. "I just came from a totally awkward and agonizing lunch with my grandparents."

"Yikes. Well, in that case, I think it must be wine o'clock! I haven't had a customer in an hour, let's shut up shop early." Fiona crossed the store to the door, flipped the sign to closed and turned the lock.

Fiona always kept an emergency stash of wine in the back and had consoled me over a bad breakup more than once. And listened to me bitch about my grandparents...oh, a thousand times.

"What did they do this time?" Fiona poured us two mugs full of wine.

"They're setting me up with my ex. My high school ex."

"And you have no interest in being set up?"

"Nope."

"Why? You liked him enough to date him when you were younger." Fiona almost always played devil's advocate. She wasn't the kind of person who would jump on my side and slate my grandparents—she got to the bottom of my thought process and offered advice even if I didn't want to hear it.

I blew out a breath and cradled my wine mug between my hands. "I've known Alex forever. Like, *forever*, forever. Our moms were best friends so we spent a lot of time together when we were little. Then, when we were bigger, it was a natural progression."

"And it has nothing to do with the fact that a certain detective is making his presence permanent around you these days?" She smiled over the rim of her mug.

"Fiona!" I cried. "Colt and I are friends."

She waved my objection away. "When are you going to get a new party line?"

"When everyone stops bugging me about it," I said, tapping my shoe against hers. "Come on, this is really depressing. Can we talk about something else?"

"Actually, we can *do* something else." Fiona finished her wine and set the mug down. She rose from her stool and headed into the back, returning a few moments later with the books for the store. "I need to go over the figures for this month. You can help me."

"Fiona, I didn't come all the way down to my job to…you know, *work*."

She chuckled and hauled me to my feet. "Stop your belly-aching. This will distract you."

"Fine, fine," I sighed.

And so for the next few hours I went over the accounts with Fiona, helping her with the balance and writing checks for the few bills the store ran up. Fiona had never asked for my help with the office side of things before, but she was right. It was a great distraction.

My head was still full of numbers when I got home. I opened the fridge and peered inside at the meager contents. *Bleugh.* But I did have bread and peanut butter, so it looked like I was having sandwiches for dinner.

I'd just sat down on the couch to eat my dinner of champions when my cell phone rang.

Colt's name flashed across the screen.

A smile stretched my lips. "Hey."

"Hey, gorgeous. What's happening?"

"Hi. Nothing, I just got home. I'm about to have dinner."

"Oh yeah, what are you having?"

I took a bite of my sandwich. "Peanut butter sandwich," I said, my voice garbled by the food.

Colt chuckled and the sound reverberated through my entire body. "Nice. Faith would approve."

"Ha. What are you having? Four course gourmet meal?"

"I'm about to start cooking — stir-fry chicken."

"Oh, yum. That sounds way better than a lousy sandwich."

"You could always get your butt in a cab and come

join me." Colt's voice was low and smooth, like melted chocolate. It was entirely addictive, and sent a shiver down my spine.

In my head, I was already out of the door. "You're seeing me tomorrow. Isn't that soon enough?"

"St. Clair." Colt blew out a breath. "You could walk through my door in the next three seconds and it wouldn't be soon enough."

"You're going to get sick of me," I warned.

"Not if I live to be a thousand."

"Yeah, yeah. Go cook your dinner. You're totally putting me off mine."

Colt laughed. "Fine. I'll see you tomorrow."

"Bye, Colt."

We hung up and I squeezed my phone, telling myself it was stupid and pointless to toss my sandwich in the trash and catch a cab to Brooklyn.

* * * *

I helped Susan and Jessie clear the dinner table. The boys were still laughing over Uncle Sal's joke. The man was a natural storyteller and wove such intricate tales I couldn't help but be drawn in.

The whole place was a bustle of noise and activity, just like last time. Faith sat on Grandpa Joe's lap as she colored, and Colt was in the middle of the men, holding his own against all the other big personalities. His sisters hadn't peeled their eyes off their phones for hours and even Tess hadn't looked up long enough to chat with me like she had before.

Susan rinsed the dishes off as I loaded the dishwasher, and Jessie made a pot of coffee for all the guys and carried in a plate full of slices of cake for everyone.

"I still can't believe he didn't tell me it was his birthday," I said when Jessie had left the room.

"He's not big on fuss. And he probably didn't want to

scare you off by inviting you to a birthday dinner with his insane family." Susan smiled before her face took on a more serious look.

I'd really enjoyed getting to know her that night. She was a world of difference from how I'd expected her to be. And it seemed like she and Colt had a great relationship — friendly, amicable...without being so friendly it would make me paranoid.

Wait — since when was there a cause for me to be paranoid?

Susan had been more than friendly with me, so why did my stomach now drop like she was about to say something I wouldn't like?

"You and Colt seem to be getting close," Susan commented.

Is this the part where she warns me off her ex? "Yeah, he's a good friend."

"Just a friend?"

I paused before answering. "We're not sleeping together, if that's what you're asking."

Susan smiled. "I was absolutely not asking that. It just seems that, as an outsider looking in, you guys are... I don't know. If someone didn't know any better, they'd think you two had been together for a while. There's a lot more than friendship there, Hayley."

I shook my head. "I swear, we're really only friends."

"Maybe he's only your friend. But haven't you wondered if that's all you are to him? Because I can guarantee you it isn't."

Of course I wasn't just a friend to Colt. He had made it clear since the moment we met that he wanted much, much more from me. Actually, make that from the moment I'd found out he wasn't gay.

"I like you, Hayley," Susan said quietly. "I really do. You're amazing with my daughter and *she* really likes you. And every single person in that room knows how Colt feels about you. You're a sweet girl. Funny, caring, attentive. *I* like you," Susan repeated. She sighed. "But this is the part where I warn you that if you hurt any of them, I will hurt you back. None of them deserve it. Least of all Colt."

I tried to speak but no sound came out. A hard lump lodged in my throat. I swallowed, trying to force it away. "I would never intentionally hurt any of them." I met her gaze. "Least of all Colt."

"And that right there is the problem." Susan smiled, a small, sad, barely even there smile. "Intentionally or not, playing this game is going to hurt him. He'll kill me for telling you this, but Colt hasn't been in a relationship since our divorce."

"*What*?" I exclaimed. "But you got divorced...what, more than six years ago?"

Susan nodded. "When I was pregnant with Faith. It about killed his family. But we both knew it wasn't working, and a kid wasn't going to change that. If anything, it was kinder to do it before she was born, then she would never know any better. What Colt and I have—it works. We both have our own lives and they overlap with Faith. I have Kent and I couldn't be happier with him. But Colt... He's never gotten involved in a relationship since me. I don't know if it's because he doesn't want to confuse Faith, because at this point all she knows is him on his own and another woman might upset their balance. But it could be—and this has been my opinion for a while now—because he doesn't want to get hurt again. Colt was never the kind of guy who would get divorced. He would have stayed with me forever, even if he was miserable. He believes in marriage and spending your life with the same person. I just wasn't the person for him." Susan glanced at me. "I strongly believe that *you* are. And if you don't believe that...then I think that would just about kill him."

"I don't know what to say," I whispered, my eyes stinging.

Susan smiled, the action finally warm. "Just be careful. And considerate. If you don't see yourself being anything more than a flirt with him, then do all of them a favor and disappear now, before real damage is done."

My head swam with her words. A single tear slid down

194

my cheek and I swiped it away before she could see it.

Susan dried her hands. She touched my arm. "Go freshen up in the bathroom upstairs. I'll cover for you for a few minutes."

I nodded and tried to smile.

"I meant what I said. I *do* like you, Hayley."

"Isn't that weird? Aren't you supposed to hate me?"

She laughed. "Haven't you figured out by now that this family is nothing but unconventional?"

"I'm starting to." I slipped out of the kitchen and hurried upstairs before I ran into anyone. Instead of ducking into the bathroom, I hid in one of the bedrooms. Any number of people could want to use the bathroom and I figured a quiet sanctuary would be safer.

Except... I was pretty sure this was Colt's old room.

The navy blue walls matched the dark bedspread draped across the bed in the center of the room, and a poster of the Giants circa...sometime or another was tacked up above the headboard. A collection of photos pinned to a noticeboard above a modest desk showed Colt as a teenager. He'd been just as good-looking then, the hint of what he would be as a man already showing on his happy, carefree face.

A framed photo of a police academy graduating class rested on top of the desk. I picked it up, scanning the faces for the most familiar. There he was, standing tall and proud in the back row, his expression as serious as I knew he took his job.

"If you wanted an excuse to sneak into my room I would have been more than happy to give you one, St. Clair."

I whirled around at the sound of Colt's voice. He closed the door behind him and leaned against the dresser. He studied me, once again seeing more than I would have liked.

"What's going on?" he asked, pushing off the dresser to join me at his desk.

Forcing a smile, I held up the picture. "Having a laugh at your old photos. You were sort of hot, Colt. What the hell happened?"

"Ha." He plucked the frame out of my hand. "Ma likes to keep these things up. Why in here, I have no idea. I didn't even live at home when I was in the academy."

"She's proud of you. There's nothing wrong with that."

Colt was silent for a long moment. "What's really going on, St. Clair? Are you feeling overwhelmed being here? My family... I know they're a lot to take in."

"No." I frowned. "They're great, seriously. You're really lucky, Colt."

"I forget sometimes," he said softly. "I forget that not everyone has this."

Did Colt really get how lucky he was? He might have been annoyed by his family while growing up and the lack of peace or privacy, but he had never experienced a tense and awkward family dinner like I had. There was always someone there, always a cacophony of noise in his house. I used to go home to silence.

Colt caught my hand and tugged me to stand in front of him. He pushed some of my hair away from my face and tilted my chin, forcing me to meet his eyes. "They'd never turn you away. This place is yours, too. For however long you want it."

Something in me broke. I so badly wanted to sink into his embrace, to accept what he'd been trying to give me for so long. I wanted to be welcomed into his loud, crazy family where his mom knew how I liked my coffee and remembered that I hated carrots.

What made my throat close up was that I knew I already had all those things. I only had to reach out and claim them. Every day my reasons for not doing so were further and further away from logical thought.

"I don't know what's going on with you right now," Colt said, his voice rough and gravelly. "But I've got you."

I nodded and tried to smile again. "I'm sorry. I'm ruining your birthday, aren't I?"

Colt shook his head and cupped my jaw. "Nothing could

be further from the truth. I'm only disappointed you haven't given me a birthday kiss yet."

And there he was — the constant opportunist. This time my smile was genuine. "How long have you been waiting to use that line?" I'd bet all night.

His eyebrows shot up. "Who said that was a line? I'm totally serious right now."

I let out a soft breath and decided, for once, to tell him what I was thinking, whether it was a bad idea or not. "I want to kiss you. I just don't know if I should."

"Oh, you absolutely should," Colt said with a grin. He pulled me against his chest and I melted into him. "And because it's my birthday, you have to do what I want."

"What about what I want?"

"It's a good thing they're one and the same, then, huh?"

I lifted my hand and drifted my fingertip across his bottom lip. Just a touch, that was all I wanted. I could get by on just a touch. "My head is a mess, Colt." Was it ever. It had swum all night.

My grandparents would keel over if they witnessed Colt's family dynamic. Unsuitable decorum, my grandmother would say. But God, I didn't care. I loved them and I... I wanted to be one of them.

"So stop thinking."

"It's not that simple."

"Of course it is."

I raised my eyes to meet his gaze. For once he was serious — there was nothing playful or teasing in his voice.

"How about it, St. Clair? Are you ready to give me a birthday kiss?"

Oh, I was ready to give him a birthday *everything*. Moving my finger from his lips, I inched my hand around to cup his strong neck. "Happy birthday, Colt," I murmured. I stood up on my tiptoes to press my lips to his.

I had meant it to be a soft, dry kiss. Something nice, I guess. Nothing memorable. Except there was nothing forgettable about Colt's mouth. Nothing at all. Colt brought his arm around my lower back, holding me flush against him. I let out a breath, unable to move away.

Everything about Colt flooded my senses. He was under my skin and every nerve ending in my body fired with an electrical current he had sparked into life.

He brushed his mouth over mine again, a barely there gesture that set my blood on fire.

"Colt," I whispered.

"I've got you," he promised. "I've got you."

I found his mouth again and the second our lips met it was as though every barrier I'd erected around my heart had come crashing down. I could think of nothing but him, nothing but the sensation of our kiss. Susan's earlier words fell from my mind and all that mattered was that I never wanted him to stop kissing me.

Sliding my tongue inside his mouth awoke some dormant beast inside me. I had never experienced so much passion from a kiss before. Well, only once before.

With Colt.

Colt made a rumbling noise in his chest. He reached down and lifted me by my ass, his firm hand curving over the flesh. I wrapped my legs around his waist, never breaking our kiss.

He walked us to his bed and my back hit the mattress as he gently laid me down. Colt covered me with his large body, supporting his own weight with his forearm. I threw my arms around his neck, pulling him closer. I wanted his weight. I wanted to know what it felt like to experience all of him.

"Jesus, St. Clair," Colt murmured against my lips.

I scraped my teeth over his bottom lip. "Stop talking."

He groaned and slammed his mouth back over mine. I slid my hand under his sweater, under the T-shirt beneath it, until my palm met warm flesh. Colt shivered at my touch and I dragged my fingers down his pecs, his defined abs.

It wasn't enough.

I didn't know if it would ever be enough.

I tugged at his sweater until he let me pull it over his head. His T-shirt swiftly followed and at last he was bared to me. I drifted my hands over his strong shoulders, down his arms that made me feel more protected than a bulletproof vest.

He trailed a hand up my leg and, even though I wore thick tights, he scorched my skin as though there was no barrier between them.

Reaching between our flush bodies, I unsnapped the button on his jeans.

Colt broke our kiss. He rested his forehead against mine, breathing heavily.

"What?" I asked, my heart pounding.

"I could shoot myself for stopping this, but I have to." Colt pulled away from me to sit on the edge of his bed. "I can't hook up with you in my parents' house. As much as I want to, I can't."

Oh. Right. His entire family was downstairs.

Including his mother.

Including his daughter.

Including his ex-wife.

"Wow, do I feel like a giant whore right now."

Colt laughed under his breath. He turned around and hauled me onto his lap. "I've waited a while for this, you know? I'm going to do it right." Colt pressed a kiss to my throat.

I nodded. "Thanks for not making me feel like a giant whore."

He snorted a laugh. "No problem, St. Clair."

We left his room separately, to at least give the appearance we hadn't been fooling around. But when I entered the dining room a minute after Colt, Uncle Sal let out a belly-aching laugh.

"For the love of God, boy, what the hell were you doing up there? She's walking fine, so whatever it was, you couldn't have been doing it right."

Oh, sweet baby Jesus... My face burned hotter than hell as Grandpa Joe joined Sal in laughing. And Colt too, the jackass. Though he attempted to swallow his laughter when he caught my mortification.

Colt reached for my hand and tugged me to the empty chair beside him. He draped his arm around my shoulders when I sat. "Sorry."

"Yeah, you will be," I mumbled, shooting him a glare.

Jessie whipped Uncle Sal with her dishtowel. "You, stop embarrassing the girl. And you," she said, turning her towel to Grandpa Joe. "Stop encouraging him. And you," she said, turning to Colt. "Listen to your uncle. Whatever you were doing, it wasn't long enough."

F.M.L.

"What were you doing?" Faith asked, leaning her elbows on the table. "Was it a poop? Sometimes mine takes a while to come out."

"Yeah, Faith. It was a poop," I said, agreeing with her. Hell, it was better than the alternative, which was trying to think up a convincing lie that the girl would buy.

"Okay. But why did you need Daddy to help you?"

I should really start thinking things through more.

* * * *

Colt drove me back to SoHo later that night. After I'd finally gotten Faith off the topic of me pooping and her daddy helping me, we'd gone into the den for board games. Colt and his sisters had gotten into a heated game of Monopoly and I'd watched them with a smile.

If I'd met Colt in high school, I would have been on him like glue. He was my dream boyfriend—genuine and sincere whilst being teasing and playful. Not to mention smoking hot. And he had the perfect family. I would have spent every afternoon at his house, entertaining his sisters and eating with his family before sneaking up for hot make-out sessions with Colt in his bedroom.

But we'd met as adults and my views on relationships and love were so skewed I didn't know which way was up anymore.

Colt stopped the car outside my building and I unfastened my seatbelt. I wanted to ask him to come up, so much so that the words formed on my tongue.

"I don't think I should," Colt said, before I could even ask the question.

I lifted my eyebrows. "Aren't you presumptuous?"

He faced me and grinned. "Am I wrong?"

Cocky bastard. "No."

Colt scrubbed a hand over his face. "I want to come up with you, St. Clair. I really do. I just don't think it's a good idea tonight."

"Why not?" I frowned.

"Because you were trying to decide whether or not to ask me." Colt flashed a half-smile. "You're still not all in. And that's okay. There's nothing to rush here. We've got all the time in the world. I want to get it right."

My chest tightened at his admission. It was hard to believe that a man as overtly sexual as Colt could be so thoughtful and sweet. He exuded sex appeal from every pore and had a swagger that came from the deep-rooted knowledge that he knew exactly what to do to a woman.

He pretty much had the green light to come home with me tonight. And instead he'd said no in favor of taking things slow and making sure we didn't screw this thing up.

"You're kind of awesome, Colton Deluca."

"I'm glad you're finally realizing it, Hayley St. Clair."

I leaned across the center console to kiss his cheek. "Goodnight, Colt. I hope you got everything you wanted for your birthday. I'm sorry again I didn't get you a gift."

Colt cupped my cheek and drew me back for a longer, more thorough kiss that made my toes curl. "Who said you didn't give me exactly what I wanted?"

If I lived into my hundreds, I would remember the shiver that snaked up my spine at those words. I would remember the way his blue eyes focused on me so intently I might as well have been laid bare in front of him.

I bit my bottom lip. "Are you sure you don't want to come up?"

"Yes, now quit asking me or I'm going to forget why I shouldn't." Colt grinned. "I'll come see you tomorrow night, okay?"

I pulled a face. "I can't tomorrow, I'm having dinner with my friends. The day after?"

"I'm taking Faith to the dentist. Should be fun after the ton of candy she's had since Halloween. She's sleeping over afterward."

"Oh, okay. Just... Let me know when you're free, then?"

Colt nodded. "I will."

"Okay, great. Goodnight, Colt."

"Night, St. Clair."

Chapter Fourteen

I flopped down on my bed after a grueling afternoon spent negotiating a price for a vintage Dior dress. The granddaughter of the lovely woman who had passed away viewed her grandmother's closet as an extension of her inheritance, and wanted me to pay way over worth.

Greedy, greedy, greedy.

My phone rang in my purse and I rooted around inside it without lifting my weary head. Colt had said he would call me tonight. It had been almost two weeks since his birthday and I still hadn't seen him. We had spoken whenever we could, but I wanted — I needed — to see him. "Tell me you're coming over," I answered.

"Um, no… But give me some time and I'll see what I can do," a male voice — not Colt — replied.

I sat bolt upright. "Who is this?"

He chuckled. "Come on, Hayley, are you really telling me you don't recognize my voice?"

Now that he mentioned it, he did sound sort of familiar. But I was so not in the mood for some ex playing games. "I'm going to hang up."

"All right, all right, I'm sorry. It's Alex."

Alex? Alex… Yates? "Alex Yates?"

"So you do remember me."

"Of course I remember you," I said with a soft chuckle. "Well, this is unexpected."

"Your grandparents gave me your number. I don't know if you heard, but I'm living in the city now."

"Yeah, I heard. Putting your stamp on the family business, right?"

Alex laughed. "Yeah, something like that. So, I have it on good authority that my mom is going to try to play matchmaker while I'm home over Christmas this year. But I'd love to get together soon, catch up without having half the country club eavesdropping. How about dinner? Is tomorrow too soon?"

Great... So my grandparents were going to set me up with my ex while I was home for Christmas, and there wasn't a damn thing I could do about it. "Um... Yeah, tomorrow should be fine." My stomach twisted, and something a lot like guilt shot through me. It was just dinner with an old friend... *Right?*

"Great. I'll pick you up at seven."

"Oh, okay." Damn, I'd wanted to meet him someplace. Easier to break away then. "I'm at —"

"I know your address, Hayley," Alex said and chuckled again. "Your grandmother practically drew me a map."

Of course she did. How helpful. "I'll see you tomorrow, then."

"Can't wait."

I ended the call and flopped back against my bed. What on earth had I just let myself in for?

The phone rang again and I let out a yelp of surprise. This time I checked the caller ID on the display before answering. "How's my best girl?"

Marley groaned. "Fat, fatter and the fattest I've ever been."

"You're cooking my niece. It's totally okay to get fat doing that." I doubted that Marley looked anything but a knockout, heavily pregnant or not.

She huffed. "You have no idea the baby is a girl."

"Hey, I want a beautiful little girl I can spoil rotten, take shopping and turn into a clothing guru like me. So don't take that away from me, okay?"

"Yeah, sure thing, Hayley." I could practically hear her rolling her eyes at me.

I laughed. "Aside from your lying mirror telling you that

you're fat, how are you?"

"I'm good. My feet are swollen, my back is shot and I haven't slept longer than forty minutes at a time in more than two weeks, but I'm good. I have some news, actually." Marley cleared her throat. "Are you busy the weekend after next?"

"I could be free for you. And I guarantee I'll need some girl time with my best girl after Christmas in Connecticut."

"Could you be free for Vegas?"

I grinned. "Free for sunshine, heat, shopping and my bestie? I could be."

Marley laughed. "How about party games, presents—not for you—and your bestie?"

"Okay, now you've lost me." Until her words sank in. "Wait, is it your shower? Oh my gosh, I'm there! Are you throwing it for yourself? That's sort of weird."

"Um," Marley said. "No, not exactly. Cassidy is sort of throwing it for me."

"Cassidy? As in *Cassidy*?"

"Cassidy as in Cassidy," Marley confirmed.

I snorted. "Is she trying to kiss ass with the family now?"

"Hayley," Marley said softly. "I get that you feel protective of Seth, but you have to let this go. She's a great girl, and she's crazy about him. Seriously."

"But hating her is so much fun," I complained.

"God, you're a bitch. And you need a life. What's happening with the hot cop?"

"Everything. Nothing. I have no idea. Oh, but get this— do you remember me telling you about my ex Alex? He called me right before you and asked me to dinner."

She laughed. "How did he take the rejection?"

Rejection? "Uh… Pretty well."

"Oh, for God's sake, Hayley, tell me you didn't agree to go on a date with him."

"Okay, I won't tell you. But it's totally not a date. It's just two old friends catching up."

"Two old friends who used to have sex catching up over

a romantic dinner."

I huffed and rolled my eyes. "Now why do you have to take it there?"

"Don't you think Colt will be pissed — and hurt — when he finds out you're meeting your ex?" Marley asked.

"Why? He sees his ex all the time and I don't complain." *Totally, completely different.* And yes. He would be seriously pissed to know I was meeting Alex. Colt was a man's man and, while he wasn't a Neanderthal, or a domineering asshole, I think it would be a respect thing for Colt. He wouldn't disrespect me by making plans with some random ex-girlfriend. But how could I tell him that I would be doing the same thing?

"Oh, my God," Marley said with a disbelieving laugh. "That is not even the same thing and you know it. They have a kid together, and you said yourself they've stayed friends."

I sighed. "I know. You really think he would have a problem with me catching up with Alex?"

Marley paused for a moment before speaking. "I think he would be fine if you told him the truth. What is the truth, Hayley?"

"That I'd never hear the end of it from my grandmother if I blew Alex off. It's one dinner, one time." I swallowed a knot of unease that had lodged in my throat. It didn't matter how much I downplayed it, how much I justified that it meant nothing… I was still, in effect, going on a date with my ex.

"Hayley, I hope you know what you're doing," Marley said softly. "I'd hate to see you ruin this thing with Colt because of something stupid."

"It'll be fine," I said. "It'll be fine." *It has to be fine.*

* * * *

Even though I wasn't supposed to work the next day, I still headed down to Back in Time the minute I was showered and dressed. The last thing I wanted was to rattle around my apartment all day long, worrying myself into a frenzy.

I needed to talk to Colt. I needed to explain things to him, except I had no idea what to say. And the longer I left it, the worse it would be. It was really no big deal, only the way I acted was turning it into one. By worrying, it could give Colt something to worry about.

Fiona was dressing a mannequin in a blood-red Armani dress when I arrived. "Perfect for the holidays, don't you think?"

I nodded. "Absolutely." Christmas was one of my favorite times of the year, especially in New York City. I loved ice skating in Bryant Park, the giant tree in front of the Rockefeller Center and the store windows. I absorbed every smidge of good cheer before going back to Connecticut for two high-anxiety days with my grandparents. Every year we went to the party at their club on Christmas Eve, spent Christmas morning exchanging a few gifts and ate dinner at the same restaurant we always did.

Me and the girls usually celebrated when we all met back in the city, finding one major party after the other, and not stopping until well after New Year's.

Except this year, I was being set up on a blind date with my ex.

Woohoo.

"To what do I owe this unexpected visit?" Fiona asked as she finished with the mannequin. "Not that I mind, it's always great to see you."

"I need to keep myself busy today. And I figured there was no better place than right here with one of my favorite people."

Fiona laughed. "Flattery will get you everywhere, my dear. Well, if it's distraction you want, I have the perfect thing for you. Follow me."

She led me to the back and gestured to the small desk tucked away in the corner. It looked like a filing cabinet had thrown up on it, with paperwork strewn every which way.

"What happened in here?"

"I've been trying to get everything in order, since my filing system has been getting a little haphazard. Everything needs to be re-filed, accounts settled, that sort of thing. Are you up to the challenge?" Fiona asked.

"Absolutely. This is perfect," I said honestly. Hours and hours would pass in a blur and my mind would be taken off everything boy-shaped.

"Good. I'll leave you to it, then," Fiona said with a warm smile.

Hours and hours did indeed pass, but it felt like I barely made any headway. I had no idea how Fiona did it all. She worked in the store six days a week, handled all the books, the accounts, the inventory, everything. She wasn't getting any younger and it had to be taking its toll. Maybe I should step up and help her more.

Fiona would never agree to it if I asked her, so I'd just show up like I had today.

A little before one in the afternoon, Fiona poked her head around the door. "Hayley, you have a visitor, shall I send him back here?"

My stomach fluttered. It had to be Colt. I nodded.

A moment later, his tall frame filled the doorway. "Hey, bad time?" he asked, gesturing to the messy desk.

I shook my head and pushed up from the ancient and super uncomfortable desk chair Fiona refused to replace. "Perfect time. I think my eyes are starting to cross."

Colt leaned in close to my space and studied my eyes. "Nope. They look great, just like always."

A girlish, delighted giggle burst out of me. "Well, I feel better having your seal of approval."

"You always have my seal of approval." Colt smiled and perched on the edge of the desk. "I went by your apartment, but obviously you weren't home, so I took a chance and checked here."

"You really are a good detective," I said, teasing.

"Better believe it. I was hoping you're free tonight."

My stomach twisted. "You were?"

Colt nodded. "I'm going to be in court the rest of the week. One of my cases is finally going to trial, so I won't be around much. I wanted to get together with you before it starts because I won't have much time while it's all going on. Then with Christmas right around the corner, things are going to be crazy busy."

Man, I wished more than anything I'd turned Alex down. So I'd piss off my grandparents — who the hell cared? I was a grown-up, for chrissakes. *I* chose who I dated. *I* chose who I spent my time with. And yet deep down I wasn't brave enough to rock the boat. "I'm sorry," I said quietly, "I'm not free tonight."

Colt reached for my hand and toyed with my fingers. "And I can't persuade you to break your plans?"

"Oh, you absolutely could, and you know it," I said with a laugh. "But I also know that you won't."

"I wish I was more manipulative sometimes. Big night out with the girls?"

"I wish," I murmured. Glancing up at him, I knew I couldn't lie. But, dammit, I wished I didn't have to tell him the truth, either. "I'm... I'm sort of meeting an old friend for dinner."

"Oh yeah?" Colt asked, his eyebrows furrowing together. "Why do you look like you'd rather be doing anything else?"

I blew out a breath and dropped my gaze. "Because I would be. The friend is my ex-boyfriend. Alex. We dated for most of high school and broke up when he left for college. His family and mine have always been close, and he's just moved to the city. My grandparents gave him my number and said it would be a good idea for us to catch up."

Colt was quiet for a few moments. He rubbed the back of his neck. "Okay. I'm getting the impression that you don't want to?"

"It's complicated," I said softly.

"Then explain it to me."

Where did I even begin to explain? How did I go about telling Colt that, even as a grown woman, I was afraid to go against the wishes of my grandparents? "My family... They aren't like yours, Colt. I bet you did a ton of things growing up that pissed your mom off. Or dated someone she didn't approve of. I have never done something my grandparents wouldn't like. If they suggested I dated a certain boy, I did. If they suggested I befriend a certain girl because my grandfather needed the connection with her father, then I did. If they asked my ex to call me, then I have to go."

"What about what you wanted?"

"It wasn't all bad. But for the most part, it was easier just to go along with it." I sat on the edge of the desk beside him. "When I was little, I always remember my parents coaching me before we visited them. They're seriously old-fashioned and believe children shouldn't be seen *or* heard. I was polite, quiet and kept out of the way. So when I went to live with them, I tried to always be like that. I guess it became a habit."

"Sounds like a stifling way to grow up."

I nudged him with my shoulder. "Why do you think I'm so wild as an adult?"

Colt snorted. "Makes sense. So you're having dinner with your ex to keep your grandparents happy?"

"Yes. Alex... He isn't a bad guy. But he wasn't right for me. We outgrew each other. He was so serious, even at eighteen. I can only imagine how stuffy he is now."

He pushed off the desk and moved to stand in front of me. "Alex wasn't right for you. Have you figured out who is?"

I laughed. "No, but it sounds like you have."

"Sweetheart, I knew a long time ago." Colt dipped to press a light kiss to my mouth. "Thank you for telling me all of that."

"Do you think I'm pathetic?" I whispered. "A grown woman who is too afraid to upset a couple of elderly people?"

"Of course not. It makes you respectful of other people." Colt kissed me again. "I should really get back to the station. I'll call you, okay? Have fun with your friend."

"Hey, Colt," I called as he turned to leave. "Does it bother you?"

Colt scratched his jaw as he considered my question. "I'm not thrilled at you having a meal with some other guy. But I'm not about to throw a fit about it. I trust you, St. Clair. And I believe what you've told me, so no, it doesn't bother me."

I smiled.

There really weren't words to describe a man like Colton Deluca.

* * * *

I was a bag of nerves as I waited for Alex to show up. Sitting on the couch, I flipped through a copy of *Vanity Fair*, but I tossed it aside when I'd tried and failed to read the same article three times. I couldn't deny how nervous I was at seeing Alex again. We hadn't parted on bad terms, but it was still awkward to make polite chit-chat with someone — as Marley had put it — I used to get naked with.

Alex had been my first, but I had been too afraid to ask if I was his. I probably was, but I couldn't be sure. He used to go to an über-exclusive summer camp in Europe every year, and I never asked what he'd gotten up to. To some people, the person they lost their virginity to would always hold a special place in their heart. It wasn't the case for me, but it didn't mean I wasn't fond of him. It also didn't mean I was itching to reconnect with him.

My buzzer sounded at five minutes before seven and I about jumped out of my skin, even though I'd been expecting it.

"Hello?" I asked, pressing the intercom button.

"Hayley? It's Alex."

"Hey, I'll be right down."

"No, don't be silly, I said I was picking you up, didn't I? That means from your door."

Right. Of course. Chivalry and old-world manners. "Oh, okay. Let me buzz you in."

When it took Alex longer than three minutes to knock, I figured the elevator was broken. Again. Maybe I *would* let Colt have a strongly worded conversation with my super.

Sometime later, there was a soft tap on my door. I checked my hair and makeup quickly and smoothed down my dress before opening the door. Alex was every bit as handsome as I remembered. Tall and lean, he had lost the boyishness to his physique and was now a well-maintained man. His dark hair was trimmed and neat, his brown eyes as warm as my memory recalled.

He blew out a breath and a wide smile pulled at his mouth. "Wow. Look at you, all grown up."

"Had to happen sometime, but I'm still in denial," I teased. I stepped out into the hallway and closed my door behind me, locking all the locks.

"I guess you aren't going to invite me inside, then?" Alex asked.

"Why, did you want something? A drink, or to use the bathroom?"

"No," he said, and frowned. "I just thought you would have."

"Trust me, there's nothing special about where I live." I had no idea who Alex was anymore. What kind of man he had turned into. I hardly wanted him to report back to his parents, who would then report to my grandparents, how bohemian my place was. They were still pissed I wasn't in the condo on the Upper East Side they had offered to buy for me when I'd moved to the city.

Better to let him think me rude than a hippy.

Alex didn't comment further, and we took the stairs down. He took me to Bemelmans Bar in the Carlyle Hotel, somewhere that had always been a favorite of mine. I'd loved the Madeline books growing up, and I adored the large-scale murals on the walls. The place was old New York, where it wasn't uncommon to see politicians rub shoulders with movie stars, but it didn't only cater to the rich and famous. Anyone was welcome at Bemelmans.

"So. What have you been up to?" Alex asked after we had been served our wine.

"Not as much as you, or so I hear," I said. I doubted he would be impressed at my being on first name basis with most of the bouncers in town.

Alex smiled. "It's been a crazy few years. I finally convinced my dad and grandfather to move the company to New York. We've outgrown Connecticut, and it's time to look to the future. I'm on the board, and I'm working under Dad now, with a view to taking over for him whenever he decides to step down."

"Nice. Last I heard you were the financial manager. That's quite a step up," I said.

He peered at me, seeming to consider my words. "You've been keeping tabs on me. I'm flattered."

I flushed, which probably didn't help my cause. My grandparents bragging about what a put-together young man he was hardly meant I kept tabs on him. But it would be cruel to point it out. "So how are you enjoying the city so far?"

"A lot. It's great to finally get out of New Haven and, I don't know, be a part of something bigger." Alex sipped his drink. "What about you? It seems like you left town and never looked back."

"I guess I did. Back home… It wasn't me anymore. There wasn't anything left for me there."

"What does New York have for you?"

I let out a breathy laugh. "New York has everything for me. If it was possible to be in love with a place, then this city would be my soul mate." My first day in New York, I'd known I had found the love of my life. I'd moved into a tiny studio apartment on the West Side where the noise from the neighbors had shaken my floorboards. It had constantly smelled like curry because of the Indian restaurant down the block, but I hadn't cared. That apartment had represented my freedom, my independence and my life away from the stifling silence I had been accustomed to since my parents had died.

Fast forward eight years, five different apartments, three kickass friends and one amazing job, and I had a pretty spectacular life. Okay, so I wasn't saving lives or anything else worthwhile, but I was happy. And it had taken a long time to get there.

"In that case, I'm free Saturday."

I blinked. What had I missed during my waxing poetic about New York?

Alex's smile widened. "To show me what I'm missing. Because from what I've seen so far, it's a great place to live, especially if you want Chinese at three a.m., but I haven't seen the parts that make you fall in love. So, Saturday?"

My stomach twisted and I forced a smile, hoping it was genuine. "Saturday is good with me."

* * * *

Alex held the cab door for me as I climbed out, and offered his hand.

"Thanks," I said as I slid my hand into his. "So, this has been great—"

Alex startled me by letting out a soft chuckle. "Hayley, save the goodbye for your door. I'm not leaving you on the side of the curb."

"Oh, okay. Um, thanks."

We were quiet in the ride up to my floor, stunned silence on my part that the damn elevator was actually working.

"I would invite you in for a coffee, but I have a really early morning," I said, fidgeting with my keys. We had reached my door and I had a sinking feeling that he would expect an invitation inside.

"That's fine. I understand," Alex said with an easy smile.

"How is ten-thirty for you?"

I blinked. "Ten-thirty for what?"

"On Saturday, for my love-struck tour of the city." He chuckled.

Oh, right. Just tell him you can't make it.

Just tell him that you were wrong, that you're not free.

Tell him about Colt.

"We're still good for then, right?" Alex asked, a small crease forming between his eyebrows.

My grandmother's face flashed by in my mind's eye, a disapproving scowl puckering her thin lips and powdered forehead. Her disappointment in my choosing a cop over a Yates.

"Yeah, of course we're still good," I said, a thick knot forming in my throat. "Well, tonight has been fun, but I really should be calling it a night."

Alex nodded. "Until Saturday, then."

"Until Saturday."

He stared at me for a long moment, something unreadable in his eyes. "You look really good, Hayley."

I watched in a strange, disjointed way, almost as if it were happening in slow motion, as Alex leaned closer to me, placed his hand on my waist and pressed a kiss to the corner of my mouth.

"Goodnight," he said in a gruff voice.

"Night," I whispered, before slipping inside my apartment. I leaned against the closed door and released a long breath. Was Alex getting the wrong idea about us? I should have mentioned Colt... But what would I have said? *Yeah, sure I can show you around the city, but first I have to tell the guy I'm seriously hot for, and who I think could turn into someone special to me, but I'm too chickenshit to really find out?* Alex would look at me like I'd sprouted three heads.

It would be fine—on Saturday, I would just make it clear that I wasn't looking for anything from him, and that we would only ever be friends. Alex would understand. Besides, he probably had a whole line of trust-fund blondes who wanted to be way more than friends with him.

I kicked off my heels and padded into my bedroom. I hadn't been lying when I'd told Alex that I had an early morning. I'd promised Fiona I would spend all day in the store with her again. She must be getting lonely in her old age.

But when I lay down in my bed, sleep was the furthest thing from my mind. I should call Marley and tell her everything that was in my head. Not that I needed to — I could practically predict everything that she would say to me. That was the thing about a true friend. They didn't just tell you what you wanted to hear. In fact, Marley would tell me everything I *didn't* want to hear.

I paused with my thumb over Marley's contact information, but for some reason I found myself scrolling back up to another number.

He answered on the fifth ring.

"Hey, beautiful."

His greeting made a smile spread across my face. Just hearing his low, gravelly voice made my skin break out in goosebumps. "Hi, I hope it's not too late," I said quietly.

"No, in fact your timing couldn't be better. I'm getting a headache from hell reading all my old reports from this case."

"I'm just all kinds of perfect," I said.

Colt chuckled. "You don't have to tell me, I've known for a while. So how was your dinner?"

"It was… It was okay," I said as honestly as I could. "I mean, it felt kind of weird for a while, like I was playing dress-up in my mother's clothes or something. He hasn't really changed, he's just a more grownup version of the guy I used to know."

"But you don't feel like the girl *he* used to know?"

"I couldn't be further from that girl if I tried." I sighed. "He asked me to show him around the city on Saturday."

"Okay," Colt said carefully. "He hasn't ever been here before?"

"No, he has, but I guess I got all poetic about New York and how much I love it, so he asked me to show him why."

"A reasonable request. Who wouldn't want to spend the day with you?"

"I could name a lot of people," I said. *My grandparents for starters.*

"Can I book you for the weekend after? Faith is with her mother, and I'm wide open."

I groaned. "I wish I could, but I'm flying to Vegas for Marley's shower."

"You know, a guy could get his feelings hurt, St. Clair. Choosing all these other people before me…"

"Oh, quit it."

Colt laughed. "Why is it such a surprise to you that I want to spend time with you? I miss you, St. Clair. For real."

"I miss you, too," I murmured.

"You could always jump in a cab. Keep me company while I read my many, many files," Colt said in a seductive voice that was far from fair.

"Don't tempt me," I said. "I have to work all day tomorrow, and, judging by today, I'll be staring at paperwork all day again."

"Fine," Colt sighed. "So, I guess I'll call you when I get some time?"

"Yeah, that'd be great."

"See you soon, St. Clair."

"Goodnight, Colt."

Chapter Fifteen

I bounced on the balls of my feet, impatience almost making me chew on my freshly manicured nails. Where the hell was she? I swear, if her stupid pregnant brain made her forget about me...well, I wouldn't really do anything, but I would never let her forget it — or me — ever again.

A familiar glossy red convertible appeared. A smile spread across my face, but it slowly slid right back off again as the convertible pulled up to a stop alongside me.

Seth Hamilton grinned at me, wide and toothy, from the front seat of Marley's car.

I sighed. "Where is she?"

"She is seven months pregnant and can't see her feet. I don't trust her behind the wheel of the car." Seth's grin widened. "And since my big brother refuses to leave her side, I got the privilege of picking you up."

"Oh please," I said. "You only wanted to drive her car."

Seth laughed and hopped out of the car. "You got me. What can I say — I see an opportunity and I seize it."

"How very Vegas of you," I mused as Seth shoved my bags into the trunk.

"Man, what have you got in here? How long are you here for, anyway?"

"Just a couple of days. What?" I huffed at his look. "I'm here for the shower. You think I would come and not bring stuff for the mommy and the baby?"

"There's stuff, and then there's going overboard. Judging by the weight of your luggage...I'd say you nailed it," Seth said, climbing back into the front seat. "So, you excited?"

"To see my girl? Excited is not the word. I miss her so

much it hurts."

Seth's smile softened. "She misses you, too."

"How's your new empire doing?" I asked, keen to change the subject before I did something totally lame, like cry.

He shot me a crooked grin. "Kicking ass and taking names."

"Good. I'm glad you're doing well."

Seth lifted one shoulder but didn't comment. I remembered from the wedding how self-deprecating he could be, so I guessed it wasn't in his nature to brag or be all cocky because he was doing well. Except, you know, when he was totally being cocky.

"How are things in the big city? Anymore fake gay dudes hitting on you?" he asked me with a wry look.

A laugh rose in my throat. The last time—the only time— that we'd spoken, I'd spilled my guts about how hurt I was over Colt's deception. It was only now that I truly believed that it really was unintentional. "No, no more fake gay dudes. But I don't know if you've heard, but the totally not gay dude and I have been hanging out. He's... He's really something."

Seth flashed me a sidelong glance. "Oh yeah?"

"Yeah," I said, a goofy smile pulling at my mouth as I thought about Colt. "He is so not the guy I first thought he was. Colt's one of the good ones. One of the only truly decent men I've ever met."

"Hey," Seth said, his eyebrows raised. "What about me? You met me and I'm decent. I'm totally fucking decent."

I turned in my seat to give him a pointed look. "From what I can remember, you were too messed up over that chick to let me take you up on your decent-ness."

His cheeks pinked and he grimaced. "Right. Well, small mercies, I guess."

"Small mercies?" I huffed. "What in the hell does that mean?"

"Jesus, I've never caught this much shit from a girl I didn't hook up with," Seth mumbled, looking at me from the corner of his eye.

"Oh, get over yourself." I turned my head away from him. "But yeah, small mercies. You would have totally been a pick-me-up lay."

Seth gasped. "You mean, you would only have been using me for sex? I am not that cheap."

"Shut up, you idiot. Man, how does that girl put up with you?"

He grinned. "Because I proved to her I really am one of the decent ones. All the time. All night, sometimes. All morning, all afternoon...you feel me?"

"Shut up, you idiot," I grumbled again, folding my arms. Like I needed his fantastic sex life rubbed in my face. I was a healthy, red-blooded woman. I liked sex. I loved sex... with the right person. But I had never felt like I needed it until that moment. All I saw was Colt. His hard chest when we'd shared his bed the night of the mugging. His arms, his defined abs. I had a feeling he would make love to me as though I was the most precious thing in the world to him, and at the same time, he made me feel achingly feminine and sensual.

I wanted to have sex with Colt.

I wanted to have a lot of sex with Colt.

All night, all morning, all afternoon.

Always.

And yet, something still held me back. Something I couldn't name, something I couldn't even vocalize. It wasn't that I wasn't ready to take that step with him, that I was afraid it wouldn't mean as much to him as it would to me. I think... I think I was afraid that it would. Because once I gave that part of myself to Colt, I would want him to keep it forever.

Seth and I arrived at Blake and Marley's a little while later. He parked in front of the closed garage and I wasted no time heading around to the back of the house where I knew my girl would be.

And sure enough, there was she was, sprawled on a huge

lounger, sunglasses perched on her nose and a magazine propped on her bent knees. At that angle, she didn't look anything close to pregnant. But when she saw me, she dropped the magazine and pushed to her feet.

Holy Moses... Yeah, she was pregnant all right. The lucky woman looked exactly like my Marley, but with a beach ball stretching out her stomach. "You look like you're doing an excellent job of cooking my little niece or nephew."

I crouched in front of her, ignoring her outstretched arms, and kissed her belly. "Hi, baby," I crooned, laying my hand against the swell of her stomach. "Have you missed me? Oh, poor love, I bet you have."

"Hey, I've missed you," Marley complained.

"Oh, hey, M, I barely saw you there," I said, laughing as I rose to full height. I carefully wrapped my arms around her and got as close as I could to hug her. And I was rewarded with a healthy kick for my efforts. "What the hell was that for? I said hello to you first, ungrateful spawn."

Marley laughed. "Looks like baby is going to be as needy for attention as their Auntie Hayley."

"I am not needy," I huffed. "High maintenance maybe, but not needy."

"Of course not." Marley kissed my cheek and draped her arm over my shoulders. "Are you hungry? Blake's inside making an army of peanut butter and honey sandwiches."

"PB and honey?" I asked, wrinkling my nose as she led me in the direction of the kitchen.

"It grows on you, trust me," Blake called from his spot at the island where he was, in fact, making an army of sandwiches.

"Who are all those for?" I asked.

Blake slid his eyes to his wife. "Do you want to tell her?"

Marley pressed her lips together and shook her head.

"Miss Newly Turned Diva over here," Blake said, pointing his butter knife at Marley, "demanded them for dinner. She said, and I quote, 'I want enough to quiet the beast—no pussy servings'."

I couldn't help the laugh that burst from me. "Are you serious?"

Marley rolled her eyes. "I didn't exactly —"

"You totally exactly," Blake said. He glanced at me. "Apparently I underfed her last night, and the beast, by which I mean our firstborn, took it out on her all night."

"Man, you're unreasonable when you're pregnant."

"It's the hormones. And I'm burning so many calories growing this thing that I'm hungry all the time. I want, like, a twelve-ounce steak for breakfast."

"Tuesday," Blake mouthed at me with a grin.

I smothered my laugh with my hand. "Oh, M, this part won't last forever. And if it's any consolation, you absolutely do not look like you're eating enough to fuel the Giants."

"Yeah, whatever. Don't come crying to me when you're eating everything in sight when you're knocked up." Marley moved to stand beside Blake and helped herself to a sandwich.

Seth rounded the corner then and slowed to a stop. He looked from the sandwiches to Marley. "I'm not even going to ask."

"Wise choice," Blake and I both said.

"I'm heading out, I have to get to the bar. But I'll see you guys tomorrow. I think Cass is coming around ten to set up." Seth lifted his hand and was gone as quickly as he had appeared.

Cassidy. Great. Can't wait for that ho to totally take over the shower that I should be throwing for my best friend.

"Stop with the face," Marley said, gesturing to me.

"What face?" I exclaimed. "There is no face."

"There's a face. Play nice or you won't be invited to the party."

"Listen to her, Hayley. She doesn't make false threats anymore," Blake cautioned.

"Fine, I'll play nice. Whatever."

"Isn't it so much easier when everyone just does what I tell them?" Marley asked. Her cute little giggle almost hid the fact that that was probably the worst sentence I had ever heard her utter.

"Sure is, evil dictator," Blake said, pressing a kiss to his wife's cheek.

"I'm going to go freshen up before I barf. You two are sickening." I winked at them on my way out of the room. Seth, bless his heart, had taken my bags up to the guest room I usually stayed in when I visited. I really shouldn't give him any shit. He was, as he had said, one of the decent ones.

* * * *

The lights of the Strip were flung out before us like neon galaxies. Marley and I lay on one of the giant loungers on the rooftop terrace Blake had built simply because she'd asked him to...even though, when he'd actually built the house, the possibility of a future for them had been as distant as the real stars. We were huddled beneath a huge, soft blanket and sipping sparkling grape juice in lieu of real wine. We had talked for hours, our voices growing hoarse as Marley had filled me in on everything I'd missed during our months of absence. And I told her how I'd barely survived the holiday season with my grandparents.

But right now, this very second, everything was fine. I was with my best girl, and for the time being, I had her all to myself.

"I'd be up here every night if I lived here," I murmured, settling farther down into the lounger. There was a very good chance that I would fall asleep and spend the night out there.

"We are, usually. It's become my favorite place in the whole world."

"Now that's just not fair. Have you seen the whole world?"

Marley laughed. "Fine, it's my favorite place in *my* whole world. Because Blake, this baby... They are my world. I love other things, my friends, my job, you…but they are my world. My whole world."

I rested my head on her shoulder. "I'm so happy for you, M. I really am. Even if I come lower on the list these days."

"I'll be lower on your list, too," she promised. "I'm surprised I'm not already."

"You really won't rest until Colt has me pregnant and barefoot in his kitchen, will you?"

She laughed again. "What do you think I am, a Puritan?"

"Thank God you're not. Blake would not suit a beard like that." I pretended to shudder.

"I hear that," Marley murmured. "Seriously, Hayley… what's going on with Colt? Every time we talk you're always talking about him."

"There isn't really anything going on right now," I said quietly. "Yeah, we're hanging out, and there's definite attraction, but… Oh, I don't know, Marley."

"What's the problem? Why are you holding back?"

"Why do you think I'm the one holding back? For all you know, he could be acting totally aloof and hard to get."

"Is he?" Amusement filled her voice.

"No," I mumbled. "I-I'm scared, okay?"

"Why?" Marley pressed gently.

"Man, I can't even say. It's like when you're a kid and you're convinced that there's something under your bed, just waiting for you to dangle a big juicy foot in front of its face. If it even has a face. It's irrational and unfounded…but very much real. That's what this feels like. I'm so screwed up it's not even funny."

"You'll get there, I know you will. I just… Please don't tell me that this fear has nothing to do with Alex showing back up in your life."

"Alex? Why would it have anything to do with Alex?" I frowned.

Marley paused, as though choosing her answer carefully. "Because it seemed like Colt was slowly, brick by brick, tearing down that big old wall around your heart. And now all of a sudden, you're afraid again. I'm just trying to understand why."

"It's not like I'm trying to choose between Alex and Colt. It's not like that at all."

"Then what is it like?"

"I don't know," I admitted. "Let's not talk about this anymore. Has the little beast whispered whether it's a she-beast or a he-beast to you yet?"

"No it hasn't, and stop changing the subject," Marley scolded.

"Sorry, mom," I said and rolled my eyes.

"I just have one more question. Aside from the dinner, have you seen Alex again?"

An uncomfortable feeling bloomed in my belly. Something not unlike guilt. "We spent the day together last Saturday. He wanted me to show him around the city."

"And did you make plans to meet again?"

"I thought you only had one more question," I grumbled. Marley responded with a hard look.

"No definite ones, but he said he would call me when I got back to the city."

"What does Colt think about all this? Does he know?" Marley held up her hand. "Actually, it doesn't matter. Well, it does, but at the same time it doesn't. I'm not going to lecture you here, Hayley, because God knows I'm in no position to do so. I've made mistakes — big ones — and you were always there to tell me what I needed to hear. So that's what I'm going to do."

Oh, Lord, this would be brutal. I knew it would be. It had to be. Marley had pretty strong feelings about Colt, and the potential for a future there, and equally strong feelings about my usual type of boyfriend…which Alex fit perfectly.

"Don't make choices that affect your life because of someone else. Blake and I wasted so much time, and it breaks my heart that I'll never get that time back. Life is so, so short, Hayley. Every single moment is precious. My mom misses my dad like he took her heart with him when he died. They had a good long life together, but it wasn't even close to long enough. I want that time back with Blake, I want it like I've never wanted anything in my life. I screwed up so badly, and it would kill me to see you make the same mistakes that I did."

Marley sighed and reached for my hand. She threaded our fingers and squeezed. "I love you to death. You're like my sister. And I don't say that lightly. I'm not going to tell you what to do, because ultimately you are the only one who can make the choice. All I will say, is make the choice you can live with. What can you give up? What can you survive letting go?"

A single tear slid down my cheek. I was so blessed to have met this girl.

Sometimes a soulmate isn't a romantic thing. And I don't even think it's an exclusive deal, that you only get just one. A soulmate is someone you connect with on a level that defies explanation. From the moment we'd met, something had just clicked between Marley and me. From that day on, we'd been like birds of a feather. A big old pink flamingo with really cute feathers.

Marley understood me, and accepted me even when I had no idea how she did it. Which was usually when I needed her to the most.

That girl was absolutely, without a shadow of a doubt, my soulmate.

"I love you, beautiful girl."

"I love you too, babe."

* * * *

Cassidy flitted around the room like a demented hummingbird, straightening already straight plates, moving bouquets of balloons only to put them back a moment later and ensuring that no one got close enough to breathe on the enormous stork-shaped cake.

Marley sat on a lounger, idly grazing on peanut brittle,

and I sat at her feet, glaring at the preppy little blonde.

"Cassidy, will you take a break? Everything looks amazing. You don't need to do anything else," Marley said, pushing her sunglasses up to the top of her head.

Cassidy turned to Marley and worried her bottom lip with her teeth. "I just want everything to be perfect for you."

"It already is perfect." Marley kicked me. "Isn't it, Hayley?"

I forced a smile. "Couldn't have done a better job myself." And I hated that that was the truth. *Stupid skanky skank.*

"Are you sure?" Cassidy flushed. She turned to an empty table, decorated with a pristine white tablecloth and a white satin bow. "What about this table? I wanted something big enough to hold all your gifts, but not so big that it looked like you were expecting a ton of stuff, but not small enough that things could fall off if we over-stack it."

Man, she stressed way more than I did. I totally should have been in charge of this shindig.

Marley got to her feet and gripped Cassidy's upper arms. "Cass, everything is perfect. Now come sit down and enjoy the peace and quiet before the masses descend."

Cassidy blew out a breath and nodded. "Okay."

"Great." Marley beamed. "Do you think I can start eating the food?"

We managed to sufficiently distract Marley from the buffet table, ensuring that she wouldn't eat everything before her guests showed up. At a little before two p.m., people started trickling into the house. Blake's and Marley's mothers arrived, chatting animatedly between themselves, a whole bunch of beautifully made-up women that just had to be some of the PR girls Marley had worked with, and a few more people that I didn't know.

Marley greeted everyone warmly, dishing out so many hugs I didn't know how she still had energy. The pile of presents grew and grew, and I wanted to tell Cassidy that she should have got a bigger table.

The back yard was filled with women. Chatter levels rose

and the scent of many mingled perfumes hung in the air. I let Marley enjoy the attention. There was a sharp stab in my gut as I watched her, so at ease amongst the gathering of people who had all come for her. If I thought about it for too long, I would fall into a depressing mood thinking about how Marley and I were now on opposite paths. Her life was so vastly different from mine, I could only hope there was still room for me in it. And almost as if she knew how I felt, Marley's eyes found mine. She flashed me a wink before turning back to the woman she had been talking to.

Then she did something that had all my apprehension disappearing as quickly as it had appeared in the first place.

She scratched her earlobe.

Back in the day, that had been part of our secret language. If we got stuck talking to a guy we were bored to tears with, but didn't want to hurt their feelings by bailing or having a friend come rescue us, we scratched our earlobe. If we were totally repulsed by a guy and wanted an immediate rescue mission, we scratched our nose.

A laugh burst from me, startling a few people close by. I clamped a hand over my mouth and edged away.

We might have different lives, but obviously Marley and I still spoke the same language.

* * * *

Everyone gathered around the table loaded down with presents. The buffet had been eaten, the requited cheesy-ass games had been played and now it was time for gifts.

Because Marley and Blake didn't want to find out the sex of the baby, they got a crap ton of gender-neutral clothes. The poor thing would be in white until it turned fourteen. Good thing I had my eye on more than a dozen cute little outfits in Barney's. All I had to do was find out if the little babe had a penis or not.

As well as clothes, Marley also received bottles, a breast pump, a bassinette and adorable nursery bedding.

Cassidy delighted Marley with two diaper bags — one that looked like a hot designer purse for her to use, and a pretty cool leather satchel for Blake. She'd loaded them with supplies, including travel-sized pots of ointment and packs of butt wipes.

Marley had saved my things for last. I'd wrapped everything in one big parcel, and Marley took her time rooting through the clothes I'd bought for her. All for her. Comfy and flattering dresses for after she'd had the baby, easy shirts to nurse in and a new pair of pajamas from her favorite store in Manhattan.

She rose and wrapped her arms around me. "Thanks, Hayley. But I thought the whole point was to get things for the baby?"

"I did," I said with a smile. "Wait here." I darted inside and down the hall to Blake's home office, where he had slyly told me the night before was where the surprise was hidden. I'd gotten in touch with Blake months ago to ask if it was okay to buy it for them, and for his help to get it sent to their place. He'd then had the job of making sure Marley didn't accidentally see it.

Marley's eyes widened as I pushed the vintage coach pram outside. It was a navy blue handcrafted Silver Cross Balmoral stroller, with oversized wheels, amazing suspension and a shopping crate underneath.

"What did you do?" she asked on a breath. Marley ran her fingers over the hood, her eyes filling with tears. "Oh, Hayley, this is too much."

"Hey, that's my niece or nephew in there. I want them to travel in style." I laughed. "It's totally impractical, I know, but you can use your city-friendly one for everyday stuff, and keep this for... I don't know. I just wanted you to have it."

"Oh, Hayley," Marley said as she threw her arms around me. "Thank you."

"I'd do anything for you, you should know that by now."

She hiccupped. "I do. But this has completely taken my

breath away."

I kissed her cheek and patted her back. "Anything. Always."

Marley pulled back and wiped under her eyes. "Well, show me this thing already."

"Yes, ma'am," I laughed, and proceeded to show her all the functions and fine details.

The shower came to a close a little while after all the gifts had been opened. Blake and Marley had hit the jackpot, and I doubted there was a single other thing they needed now that the good women of Vegas had spoiled them rotten. Marley showed Blake the coach stroller and he ummed and ahhed and made all the appropriate noises, even though I knew he didn't really care.

Men. They never got it.

I gathered some glasses onto a tray and headed inside with them. Cassidy stood in the corner fussing with a dishtowel, tears streaming down her face. Coming to a complete stop, I could only stare at the pretty blonde, whose usual bright eyes were now red and puffy.

"Oh, hey, wow, I'm sorry..." I said, totally at a loss as to how to react. Did she expect me to comfort her? Ignore her? What was the social etiquette for things like this?

Cassidy jumped about a foot out of her skin and whirled around so her back was to me. "Yeah," she croaked. "Something in my eye."

I slid the tray of empty glasses onto the island. "That happens to me sometimes. What was it that got in there?"

Cassidy let out a rueful laugh. "The past. The future. Everything."

Jesus, I had no clue what to say to that. Thankfully I was saved from answering by Seth strolling into the kitchen.

"Is the ovary party over?" he asked, a grin on his handsome face. It soon slipped when he noticed his girlfriend. Seth reached her side in a second and clutched her elbows. "What the hell happened?"

She opened her mouth to answer, but all that came out

was an indecipherable squeak and a rivulet of fresh tears poured from her eyes.

Seth glanced at me and I held my hands up as if to say 'I didn't do it'. He pulled Cassidy into his body and wrapped his arms around her. Cassidy's shoulders shook as she burrowed her face into his chest.

Okay, things had gone from awkward to downright painful. I turned and quietly slipped back outside. I met Marley heading toward the kitchen.

"Um, I'd give it a few before you go in there," I warned, hitching my thumb in the direction of the kitchen.

Her eyebrows furrowed. "Why?"

I took a step closer to her and lowered my voice. "Cassidy is in there, freaking out about something."

Worry filled Marley's eyes and she sidestepped me.

"Don't," I said, stopping her. "Seth's here, he's got her."

Marley released a breath and nodded. "I knew this was too much for her."

"What am I missing?" I asked. I moved to the buffet table and scooped up a handful of pretzels. "The girl not like baby crap or something?"

"*The girl* put her own baby up for adoption when she was fifteen."

I turned back around to Marley. At the hard look on her face, my witty retort slipped right off my tongue. "Jesus, are you for real?"

She nodded and moved to stand beside me. "Seth told me a few weeks ago. He was worried throwing this shower would mess with her head, and it sounds like he was right."

I glanced toward the kitchen door. Today had had to be one of the hardest days of Cassidy's life. I couldn't even begin to imagine how confused and messed up she felt... and yet she had thrown this shower for Marley anyway. Probably knowing that it would hurt.

Dammit, now I was going to have to like her.

Chapter Sixteen

The music pounded, making my pulse match its tempo. My hair clung to my neck and my feet ached from all the dancing. I threw my hands up and shimmied my hips in time to the beat. Someone grabbed my waist and I maneuvered away without turning around.

In front of me, Beth danced with a tall, dark-haired guy who looked like he wanted to devour her whole. There wasn't an inch between them as they moved together, and if her skirt hiked up anymore there was the distinct chance Beth would be going home pregnant.

"Get a room," I called to them.

Beth turned at my voice and stuck her tongue out at me.

I laughed and threw my head back. Man, I loved dancing. I needed to do it more. I loved the way my body felt, the press of the people all around, the heat that made my head swim.

Well, the swimming head could have been down to the cosmos…which I'd had way more of than usual. I'd landed a few hours ago from Vegas and when I'd powered on my phone and seen that both Colt and Alex had tried to call me, I'd hit up my girls and headed out to join them at the club instead.

Eve shoved a fresh cocktail into my hand, most of which sloshed over the rim, coating my fingers. "Dude, this place is awesome tonight. I'm totally going home with someone. I just haven't decided who yet."

I waggled my finger in front of her nose. "Make sure he isn't too hot."

She wrinkled her nose. "Damn hot guy curse. I bet your

cop is more than adequate beneath the sheets."

Another laugh rose in my throat. "I bet he is."

"Then why the hell haven't you tested him out yet?" she asked, looking at me as though I was more alien than E.T.

I blew out a breath, suddenly exhausted. "You know, I can't remember right now." And I was telling the truth. Maybe it was the cocktails, maybe it was the exhaustion, but I couldn't think of a single logical reason as to why I wasn't sleeping with Colt at every single opportunity. I downed what was left of my cocktail. "Go look for your piece of meat—I'm getting another drink."

Eve saluted me as she disappeared into the crowd.

Her question brought things to mind that I had sought to forget, at least for tonight. I wanted to see Colt. I wanted to talk to Colt. I wanted to...*everything* with Colt. So instead of acting on my wilder impulses, I made a beeline for the bar to drown them out.

* * * *

Eve threw her arms around my shoulders and kissed my cheek, her breath alcoholic and fruity from the cocktails. "Tonight was so much fun, you need to come out with us more."

"I know, it was *so* much fun," I said, hugging her back. We swayed on the spot and Eve started to hum a song I didn't recognize. I pulled back and held on to the open cab door for support. "Enjoy your not too hot guy."

Eve glanced at the guy over her shoulder. She faced me again with a giggle. "Hot enough, but not so hot that he'll have the curse. Night, babe."

I waved Eve and her man off, and climbed—okay, fell—into the waiting cab. Beth had left an hour or so earlier, but I'd stayed with Eve until her and her guy had started making like a pair of teenagers at the prom.

Leaving me to go home alone.

I wish I could go to Colt's...

The cab set off and I slumped against the seat, resting my head on the cool glass of the window. I pulled my phone out of my purse and I had to shut one eye to focus on the screen. When I found the number I wanted, I hit call and held the phone to my ear.

Exactly two rings later, he answered. "St. Clair? What's wrong?"

I laughed. "You worry too much, did anyone ever tell you that?"

Colt heaved out a breath. "You called me at four in the morning. Forgive me for reacting."

I giggled again. "Okay, I forgive you."

"St. Clair?"

"Hmm?"

"Are you drunk?"

"No."

"No?"

"No. I'm totally wasted."

Colt sighed again. "Where are you? Do you need me to come get you?"

"I'm in a cab, I'm going home." I sniffed. "There's no one at my home, Colt. It's an alone home. I'm going to be home alone."

"I always had you pegged for a happy drunk. What's happened to my happy girl?"

"She's going home alone," I said quietly. "I wish I was going home to you."

"St. Clair," Colt murmured. "You can't say things like that to me. Especially when you're drunk. You need to say them when you'll remember, and then I'll make sure you never forget."

"I won't forget," I huffed. "Why would I forget?"

"Forget what?"

"Um...I'm not sure."

Colt chuckled, and it didn't sound like a happy noise. "Exactly my point."

"Hey, Colt?"

"Yeah?"

"Will you stay on the phone with me until I get home?"

"I was going to anyway."

I smiled. "You're so sweet. And hot. I bet you don't have the hot guy curse, though."

"Do I even want to know what that is?"

I laughed again, but I wasn't sure if I answered Colt. The soothing movement of the cab was like a lullaby, and if I wasn't careful, I'd be passed out in the back seat before long.

A tapping at my head that wouldn't quit made me frown. "Someone is knocking at my head," I complained.

"St. Clair, open your eyes," Colt said.

They were closed? I pried one open and looked straight at Colt. "Oh, hi," I said, a sleepy smile pulling at my lips. "Are we here already? Why are you outside my apartment?"

"I'm not," Colt said, still holding up his phone to his ear. "You fell asleep. And you're outside my house."

"Why?"

"Apparently you gave this fine driver my address."

"I did?"

Colt sighed and hung up the phone. He opened the cab door and caught me when I half fell out. "Come on, let's get you inside. I'd like to get back to bed sometime before the sun comes up."

I smiled up at him. "Mmm. I like your bed."

"So you keep telling me."

"Maybe one day it'll be *my* bed. Wouldn't that be something?" I asked with a laugh.

"Yeah, St. Clair. It would be."

Colt helped me inside and deposited me on the couch in the living area of his kitchen. He left me there to rummage around in his fridge.

"Hey, do you have any chips? I'm starved."

"No. But I have donuts. And water," Colt said as he returned.

I folded my legs under me and all but snatched the box of

donuts from him. "Oh, my God, they're glazed."

Donut heaven. I was in total donut heaven.

"Aren't you having one?" I mumbled past a mouthful.

"No, it's a little late for sweets for me," Colt said, an amused smile pulling at his lips.

Man, those lips are hot.

Really hot.

Like, so hot they I want to make babies.

Lots and lots of blue-eyed babies.

"Hey." Colt snapped his fingers in front of my face. "Where'd you go?"

A giggle bubbled in my throat. "Bad places."

Colt shook his head. "Come on, you need to sleep this off."

"I'm fine," I huffed.

He stood, took my hand and pulled me to my feet. And if not for that strong arm around my middle, I'd have fallen straight back down again.

"Okay, maybe I'm not so fine," I said, pressing my face into his chest. Wow, he smelled good.

Colt kissed the top of my head and steered me out of the room. "I got you, St. Clair."

"Promise?"

"Always."

Upstairs, Colt gave me another of his shirts to wear to bed. He helped me out of my shoes and didn't even peek when I let my dress fall to the floor. The dude had better restraint than I did.

Colt pulled his T-shirt over his head and slipped between the sheets in his athletic pants. I climbed in after him and he lifted his arm for me to wriggle into the space beneath it. The space that was quickly becoming my favorite place to sleep.

"I'm not tired yet," I said.

He traced lines down my arm and turned his head so his lips pressed against my forehead. "Go to sleep, St. Clair."

"Man, you're bossy," I grumbled. But because he told me

to, a few seconds later I was out cold.

* * * *

When I woke the next — or later that same — morning, I didn't open my eyes right away. Instead, I took stock of what was sure to be a bitching hangover.

Dry mouth – check.

Headache from hell – check.

Gross, sweaty, grimy feeling – check.

Impending vomit – all clear for now.

I eventually opened my eyes when I was sure the room wouldn't spin and make that vomit a resounding check. I was still in the same spot I'd fallen asleep in, curled into Colt's side like a happy, purring cat.

He was still sleeping, his breath blowing softly past his barely parted lips.

Jesus, he was hot. So hot it was almost impossible to look away. I wanted to trace every inch of his face and commit it to memory. I wanted… I wanted to see his face every single day so I didn't have to commit it to memory.

Get out of here, Hayley, before you assault the poor man… or do so something really crazy, like propose. I climbed out of bed and padded into the bathroom. I took a hot shower, scrubbing away the worst of my hangover with Colt's delicious-smelling body wash.

What on earth had I been thinking, calling him last night? Not only that, but giving the cab driver Colt's address instead of my own?

I didn't have to be a genius to figure out what that Freudian slip meant. In my inebriated state, the only place I'd wanted to be was with Colt. Pure and simple. And hadn't he been there for me? Without complaint or question?

When I felt more or less human again, I turned off the shower and wrapped one of his towels around my body. I used his toothbrush to get rid of the funk in my mouth, and I was pretty sure he wouldn't mind.

Colt had flipped onto his front in my absence, his arms hidden beneath the pillow. He cracked open one eye, and a lazy smile spread across his face. "Hey, beautiful."

I couldn't stop the goofy grin. "Hey."

He pushed himself upright and scrubbed the dust out of his eyes. "What are you doing way over there?"

"I was trying to smell like a human again," I said as I slowly stepped toward Colt.

"And do you?"

"Mostly."

"I'll be the judge of that." Colt caught my hand and jerked me over to him. He flipped me onto my back and hovered above me. Colt took my hands in one of his and gently pinned them above my head. With a wicked smile, he lowered his head and brushed my throat with his nose. He drifted across my chest, over my arms, down to where the towel began and had started to come loose.

Just when I thought he would part it and continue scenting me like a hotty-hot bloodhound, he made his way back up to my throat again. "Gorgeous. Just like always."

I laughed and it sounded as nervous as I felt.

Sometimes, being with Colt made me feel so off balance. Any wrong step could send me careening off course. And at other times, he made me feel so grounded and safe, like he was an immovable weight, keeping my feet firmly on the earth. He was a rollercoaster ride I never wanted to get off.

He lifted his head to peer down at me. "How are you feeling?"

My heart pounded. How was I feeling? At least seventy-three different emotions fought for control and I didn't have a clue as to how to decipher any of them. All I knew for sure was that right now, in this moment, I was exactly where I wanted to be. And the way he looked at me...it reminded me of a couple I had felt more than one pinch of jealousy for.

So I answered as honestly as I could. "Revered."

A tiny frown formed between Colt's eyebrows. Then, as understanding filled his gaze, all traces of humor bled from his face. "It's about time."

He dipped his head then and slanted his lips over mine. I released a long pent-up breath, as though I'd been holding it since the last time Colt had kissed me. He cupped my jaw and tilted my head back, giving him better access as he slid his tongue inside my mouth.

My pulse fluttered, erratic and wild. I hitched one leg over his hip, pressing him against me. He was hard in all the places I was soft, and we fit together like we'd been built that way.

Colt slid his hand down my leg, achingly slowly.

"Colt," I whispered against his mouth.

"What? What do you need?" he asked.

"You. All of you."

He made a noise low in his throat, a raw, guttural and purely animalistic noise. Colt glanced over his shoulder. "I don't have time to do this with you right. Jesus, I wish I did."

I frowned. "What do you mean?" And how long did he think he needed? *Holy hell…*

Colt chuckled and pressed a kiss to my throat. "I mean that I need no time restraints. Because when I finally get to be inside you, it isn't going to be over quick." He dipped his hand beneath the towel at my stomach and inched it away, baring me to him. Colt dipped his mouth and captured my nipple. "I'm going to worship every inch of your body. I'm going to do everything I've visualized doing since the night I met you and I'm going to take my sweet time doing them."

My breath hitched as he palmed my breast. The man was going to make me combust.

"You're not going to be able to walk when I'm done with you. That's what I mean, St. Clair."

"But I can't wait that long," I breathed. "Colt, I want you now." And did I ever. I wanted Colt in a way I couldn't even vocalize.

"I can take care of you right now, but it won't be with me inside you." Colt trailed his hand down my body until he cupped me between my legs. He stroked one long finger against my heat and I about came undone with the motion.

"Do you want me to take care of you?" Colt murmured as he kissed me.

I kissed him hard in response, threading my fingers into his hair and all but yanking it out at the roots.

He pushed that finger inside me and I clenched, so tightly wound that I threatened to burst. Colt made a pained sound in his throat and added a second finger, working me into a state of madness. When he ground his palm on my clit, an explosion went off low in my body.

Colt gripped my hip and pumped me harder, faster with his hand. I clutched his shoulders and threw my head back. Colt didn't relent as my orgasm ripped through me, only slowing his movements when the aftershocks began to lessen and I floated back down into my body.

"Jesus Christ," I said, trying to catch my breath.

Colt chuckled and kissed me, long and slow. "I told you. Now do you see why I need more time?"

"Let me know when's good for you, and I'll clear a month."

He laughed again. "You're amazing. Seriously."

"Thanks," I said, patting him on the back. "You were pretty good, too."

"Oh?" Colt asked, arching an eyebrow. "Pretty good? Do I have to remind you that was better than pretty good?"

I shrugged one shoulder. "I guess it couldn't hurt."

"Greedy." Colt kissed my collarbone. "But I really don't have time now. Faith will be here soon."

"Oh, are you spending the day together?"

He nodded and eased off me, lying on his side. He caught my hip and rolled me toward him. "We're going to the Bronx Zoo. She's been dying to go for months."

"I love the zoo. My dad took me to the Central Park Zoo once when I was a kid, but my grandparents hate that sort of thing so I haven't been back."

"St. Clair, do you want to come to the zoo with us?"

My heart sank. "Oh, no, I wasn't angling for an invitation. Forget what I said. Today is your time with Faith."

"Faith would love it if you came. And so would I." Colt took my hand and kissed my knuckles. "Please come to the zoo with us."

"Okay. But only because you asked so nicely."

He leaned forward and pressed a soft kiss to my lips. "Thank you."

Colt really had no idea how much it should be me thanking him.

* * * *

"Can I come up to see your apartment?" Faith asked from the back seat, where she had still to release the death grip on the giant stuffed flamingo Colt had bought her.

I glanced at Colt, unsure how to answer his daughter. I'd planned on saying goodbye to them both in the car and hopping out at the curb, but clearly I hadn't counted on Faith's curiosity raising its sweet little stubborn head. "I think your daddy wants to get you home for dinner."

"I can have dinner with you. Right, Daddy?" Faith asked, turning those big eyes to her father.

"Baby, Hayley doesn't want us crashing her apartment — "

"Hey," I cut him off. "Hayley doesn't mind anything. I'd love to have you guys over for dinner. If you'd like to come, that is."

Colt held my eyes for a long moment. He slid his gaze to Faith, who was bouncing up and down in her booster seat like she was about to pee her pants with excitement. "What do you think, baby? Can we trust her cooking?"

And with the straightest, sincerest face ever, Faith said, "Yeah. I mean, I eat your cooking, so how bad can it be?"

I choked on a laugh. "Oh, man. Faith, you are so my favorite person."

She grinned. "I get that a lot."

If I ever had a kid, I hoped they would be half as cool as Faith Deluca.

Once in my apartment, Faith was like a puppy dog. She poked around, swiveled in a chair and stared at my old TV set like it came from another planet.

"Hayley, your apartment is weird," Faith said from behind the couch, where she sat cross-legged as she flipped through one of my many, many photo albums.

"Thanks. I like weird."

Faith giggled. "Me, too."

I headed into the kitchen and opened a cupboard door. "So it looks like mac and cheese — is that cool with you guys?"

Colt and Faith both murmured their assents.

"Daddy, look at how funny Hayley looks," Faith said with another giggle. If I had to guess, she'd found the album from a few years ago and had stumbled on my *Alice in Wonderland* themed birthday party. I'd dressed up as the Queen of Hearts — complete with a huge monstrosity of a hat I'd made myself.

The cordless phone rang on the end table. I halted my supreme cooking skills and headed over to answer it.

"Hello?" I asked, glancing over at Colt and Faith, who were pretty riveted by whatever pictures they were looking at. A smile pulled at my lips. I liked them in my apartment, in my world. Being a part of my world.

"Hello, Hayley," my grandmother's stiff and formal voice came through the other end. "I've been trying to call you all day."

"Sorry, I've been out." I held up a finger to Colt to let him know I would be a minute. I moved into my bedroom and closed the door behind me before sitting on the edge of my bed.

"Wasting more time at that thrift store?"

Irritation prickled my skin. "Actually today I was wasting time at the zoo. The thrift store is tomorrow."

"Is that really necessary? You're supposed to be an adult." My grandmother sighed, and when she spoke again she had regained whatever composure I'd made her lose with my insolence. "I had lunch with Mrs. Yates this week and she tells me how well you and Alexander are getting along."

"It's been nice catching up," I said carefully. "I'm not sure how much we'll see of each other once he settles in."

"That is why you must be supportive of him. With his new position in his family's company, he needs a good woman to take care of him and his home. And, of course, you will see each other on Saturday."

Saturday? Had I forgotten something?

"At dinner," my grandmother said when it became clear I had no clue what she'd meant. "Surely Alexander mentioned it?"

"No, he hasn't." It could have been why Alex had tried to call me the day before. I really should return his call. My manners were terrible these days.

"Your grandfather and I are coming to the city, and Mrs. Yates suggested we all get together for dinner since she and her husband will be there also. Alexander will pick you up and meet us at the restaurant."

I couldn't help but notice she'd posed none of what she'd said as a question. My attendance was mandatory. "Oh, okay."

Grandmother let out a pinched breath. "Honestly, Hayley, could you please sound a little more grateful? Alexander is a lovely young man. If you had married by now then you wouldn't have to trouble our family friends for dinner dates."

A gasp caught in my throat. *Trouble family friends? For dates? Jesus Christ, is she serious?* "I'm only twenty-seven, I have plenty of time to find someone I want to marry."

In the other room, Colt let out a raucous laugh, swiftly followed by Faith's infectious giggle. I stared at my closed bedroom door and wished I was out there with them, instead of trapped in here with my passive aggressive grandmother.

"*Only* twenty-seven? Your mother was married and pregnant with you by the time she was twenty-*six*."

"Then she was lucky she met Daddy so young and knew he was who she wanted," I said, defiance rising in my tone.

My grandmother harrumphed. "Your mother saw what was best and listened to my advice. She and your father approved of Alexander. She mentioned more than once how she hoped one day the families would be joined in marriage."

She had? "When she did say that?" I asked quietly. "She never said anything to me."

"Of course she didn't, you were too young. You and Alexander have known each other for your entire lives. You can't do better than a Yates. Your grandfather and I will see you and Alexander on Saturday." With that, she hung up without waiting for my goodbye.

I dropped the phone and flopped down on the mattress. Any exchange with my grandmother left me exhausted and drained. She was like an emotional vampire, sucking me dry. But this one... This one in particular left me with nothing but a beating heart and a racing mind.

Chapter Seventeen

The days inched toward Saturday as if I were on death row awaiting my execution. When it arrived, my head was a jumble of knotted thoughts. So I did the one thing that could quiet them—I spent the day at Back in Time organizing the clothes I'd picked up from the latest estate sale. Being amongst the beautiful fabrics, the dresses that held a hundred secrets and had spent glamorous nights at the opera, on romantic cruises and lustful trysts, calmed something in my soul. Clothes were my life. As comforting as a security blanket.

"How long have you worked for me, Hayley?"

Fiona's voice startled me and I spun around. She leaned against the doorway, a concerned look on her face.

"Um, I'm not sure, why?" I said, hanging up the Oscar de la Renta I really wanted to buy for myself.

"Three years, seven months and fifteen days. That's how long you've worked for me."

"Okay." I frowned. "Is this the part where you tell me I don't take the job seriously and you've gotten tired of me?"

Fiona's eyes softened and she took a step toward me. "Oh, sweetheart, of course not. You have worked for me for three years, seven months and fifteen days. Which means you've known me long enough that I thought you could come to me with anything that is bothering you."

"Why do you think something is bothering me?" I asked as I turned back to the rack of clothes.

"Because you came here, even when you're not supposed to be working. I gave you this weekend off, and yet here you are." Fiona smiled and cupped my elbow. "I'm guessing it has something to do with your grandparents, because every time they upset you, you show up here and hide in the dresses. Do you want to talk about what happened?"

I opened my mouth to tell Fiona everything — how inferior I felt, how pressured to settle down with some wealthy man my grandparents approved of... Bonus points if my grandfather already golfed with the father. How I felt torn in a dozen different directions and I could hardly remember which way I wanted to go myself. But, for whatever reason, I clamped my mouth shut and shook my head.

"Okay," Fiona said slowly. "Then how about we talk about something else?"

"Sure." I cleared my throat to dislodge the lump that formed there. "Let me guess — you're trying to figure out how to break it to me that you sold the Roberto Cavalli for a dollar-fifty?"

Fiona tinkled a laugh and moved to sit in the desk chair. "No. I'd leave the country if that happened."

"Oh, I'd find you, don't worry about that."

She laughed again. "I believe you. No...what I wanted to talk to you about was the reason why I've been asking you to handle things behind the scenes of the store lately."

"I figured you'd gotten tired of me playing dress-up and being a professional shopper and wanted me to finally earn my paycheck."

"Hayley, you more than earn every single one of your paychecks. You're probably the only reason I've finally turned a heck of a good profit these last few years. Because of you, my store has become important to people. Because of you, my store is worth something." Fiona smiled. "And because of that, I want to give it to you."

I blinked. Had she just said what I thought she'd just said? "I'm sorry, what?"

Fiona's smile broadened. She rose from her seat at the desk and gestured at all the carefully organized files that had taken me forever to get into order, since Fiona's carefree and hippy lifestyle extended into her filing system. "When

I opened the store, I had no idea it would last this long. I'm thankful every single day that it has…but it's time for me to do something else now. Take that trip to Rome I've said I would for years… Read all the books I buy and never get around to… Go skinny dipping in the Hudson."

I let out a shocked laugh. "God, I hope that last one isn't true. And if it is, make sure you get your shots first."

Fiona laughed. "Okay, maybe I won't do that last one. But all the others for sure."

"I can't believe you want to retire," I said as I softly shook my head.

She waved my statement away. "Retiring is for old people, and I, my dearest chum bucket, am not old. I'm simply moving on to the next chapter in my life." Fiona sighed and gripped the clothes rail with all the new items I'd recently procured. "I love this place — you know how much."

"I do."

"And I know how much you love it." She turned to me with a bittersweet smile. "Which is why you are the only person who I could ever entrust it to."

"Fiona," I whispered as emotion clawed up my throat. "I don't know what to say."

Fiona laughed quietly. "You don't have to say anything. Just think about it, okay? There's no pressure here. If you decide you don't want to, then that's just fine. Just think about it, Hayley." She kissed my cheek and disappeared out of the room.

My God…had that just happened? Had Fiona really just offered to leave her livelihood, her pride and joy…to me?

Excitement bloomed in my belly…and all I wanted to do was call Colt.

* * * *

"You look nervous," Alex commented as we walked into the restaurant.

"I do?" I touched my cheek and realized I was flushed.

"I'm sorry, my grandparents tend to have that effect on me."

"Yeah, I know what you mean. My parents do the same to me." Alex captured my hand in his and gave it a gentle squeeze. "I'll protect you, don't worry."

"Thanks." I laughed. "But I never would have guessed that your parents were the overbearing kind."

"You're kidding, right? I'm the heir to a company that is starting to turn a hefty profit. It's always done exceptionally well, but these days…it's huge. And now it's up to me to step up and carry it forward into a new generation. All the while my grandfather and father are right behind me, watching my every move. And then there's my mother, who's more concerned with my lack of marital intention."

I peered up at Alex and, for the first time since he had come back into my life, I saw him in a completely different light. He was just a young man with a nagging mom and a pressurizing dad, trying to make it through, just like the rest of us. *Just like me.* "Don't you ever want to say screw it, and do what you want?"

Alex smiled. "Of course I do. There are a dozen things I'd rather have majored in than business at college. I'd like to wake up in the morning and not reach for a monkey suit in my closet." He paused and gave our names to the hostess, who then directed us to where Alex's parents and my grandparents were already seated. "Sometimes I'd like to be someone completely different from Alexander Yates."

"So why don't you?" I said urgently. "Why are we doing this to ourselves? We could turn around and walk out of here right now. Go down the street and get a Happy Meal."

"Hayley," Alex said quietly. "I said sometimes. Yeah, I'd like to have a life that wasn't so pressured…but I wouldn't throw away everything I have for anything."

I plastered on a fake smile. "Right. Me neither."

"Well, well, look at you two," Mrs. Yates said with a wide smile as we arrived at the table. She rose and kissed my cheeks before moving on to Alex. "Seeing you two together takes me back years."

"Mom," Alex said, kissing his mother's cheek.

"Hayley, you look lovely," my grandfather said.

"Thank you so much for collecting Hayley, Alexander." Grandmother embraced Alex with as much warmth as she was capable of.

Alex flashed me a wink. "It was no trouble."

We took our seats, and I looked between my grandmother and Mrs. Yates—who both looked like the cats who'd caught the canary.

"Mom, stop being weird," Alex said, reaching for a couple of menus.

"I am not being weird," Mrs. Yates huffed and tapped Alex's hand. "I'm just happy to see the two of you so happy."

"They do make a darling couple," my grandmother agreed.

"You know, Hayley," Mrs. Yates said with a warm smile. "I remember having a conversation with your mother about how when the two of you were all grown up, you would end up married with an army of children. She would be incredibly proud of the woman you have become."

Emotion rose in my throat. Talking about my parents was always hard for me. I'd never fully accepted their death... what thirteen year old could? It wasn't fair that they'd been taken from me, that my life had been dramatically altered and I'd been forced to live with my cold and emotionless grandparents. Someone telling me that my mom would be proud of me...it didn't happen often. There weren't many people around anymore who'd known her. Fewer still who talked about her.

"She'll be even prouder once Hayley is married and she stops wasting her time in that thrift store." Grandmother smiled tightly over the rim of her wine glass. "Wouldn't you agree?"

Mrs. Yates had the decency to look uncomfortable. "It's good to keep busy. These young girls living in the city...

It's very easy to become a party girl and nothing else."

"It's not a thrift store," I said quietly. "It's a vintage boutique and I love it."

The others at the table blinked at me.

Beside me, Alex cleared his throat and curled his hand around mine under the table. "It's good to have hobbies."

I snapped my gaze to him. *Hobbies?* Did he really look at what I did at the store and think it was just a hobby?

"I daresay this time next year you'll be busy enough." Mrs. Yates smiled. "Those who marry into the Yates empire are encouraged to take a hands-on approach to the business. I myself coordinate the charitable side of things and I would be thrilled to have you work alongside me. And of course, when you have children, once they turn thirteen they'll sit in on board meetings and begin to get a feel for their inheritance."

The noise in the restaurant rose to a painful degree. My grandmother smiled and replied to Mrs. Yates, but I had no idea what she said. My whole body felt too tight, too hot. Blood roared in my ears and, oh holy hell, my fight-or-flight instincts were screaming at me to run as fast as my legs could carry me.

It was like seeing my entire life spread out before me like a road map. All the other possibilities, all the other routes were suddenly dead ends with only one remaining.

I could have told my grandparents about the conversation I'd had with Fiona earlier that day. I could have told them that my priority wasn't finding a rich husband who would find me something to do in between popping out babies to carry on his legacy. I could have told them I was falling in love with another man, a man who spoiled me and worshiped me in a completely different way than a wealthy man ever could.

Instead I just sat there and let the conversations wash over me. By the time the first course had been cleared from the table, I was able to fake cheeriness and participate in what everyone else was talking about. I charmed the pants off

Mr. Yates, who told his son to seal the deal before someone beat him to it.

"Shall we have a drink in the parlor?" Mr. Yates asked when the meal finally ended.

"Well, that would be—"

"Actually," I interrupted my grandfather, "I'm not feeling too well. I'm going to head home." I smiled at Mr. and Mrs. Yates, ignoring the daggers from my grandmother. "Thank you for such a lovely evening."

Alex pressed his hand to my lower back. "I'll take you home."

I nodded and flashed him a thin smile.

Mrs. Yates stepped forward and wrapped her thin arms around me. "It was lovely to see you, Hayley. I just wish your mother could see the wonderful young woman you have become."

A knot lodged in my throat. If I didn't get out of that restaurant in three seconds flat, then I'd embarrass my grandparents even more than I already had. "Thank you."

* * * *

"Did that suck as bad for you as it did for me?" Alex asked as we climbed the stairs to my apartment. I was so ready to stop paying rent until the damn elevator was reliable.

"Is that a trick question?"

"Guess not," Alex murmured. "You mind if I come in for a few minutes?"

My pulse shot up. Alex had never asked to come in before. Once I knew he wasn't likely to spill every detail of our time together to his parents, and then my grandparents, I'd relaxed enough to let him into my home. I'd invited him in a few times for coffee, but he'd always left straight after. And he'd never made a move. So why ask now? He either had to use the bathroom...or he was taking his father's advice. "Um, sure."

Alex followed me inside once I'd unlocked the door. I

threw my purse onto an empty chair and kicked off my heels, leaving them where they lay. "Coffee?" I asked him.

"No, I'll get going in a few." Alex perched on the edge of the couch and wrung his hands. "I just wanted to make sure you're okay. Our parents—I mean, my parents and your grandparents—were on top form tonight with the innuendos and the pressuring. And you were so quiet in the cab. So are you? Okay, I mean."

I blew out a breath and sat beside him. "I am okay. My grandparents... I'm so used to it. Honestly, my head is so full with my mom and dad right now. Your mother talking about her sort of threw me for a loop."

"I'm sorry," he murmured.

"No, don't be," I said with a small smile. "Not enough people talk about my parents. It's getting harder to remember the details."

"It must be hard."

"It is."

"Even now?"

"Especially now," I whispered. I wanted more than anything to talk to my mom, to have her stroke my hair and tell me what to do with my life. Or, at the very least, have her around to pick up the pieces when I inevitably screwed up.

"Look, I know we drifted apart these last few years," Alex said, shifting closer to me. "But I'm here for you—whatever you need. I knew your parents, Hayley. Better still, I liked them. If you want someone to talk to who was there...I can be that person for you."

Tears welled up in my eyes. I squeezed them shut until I was sure they wouldn't spill down my cheeks. "Thank you, Alex."

"Like I said," Alex whispered, "whatever you need."

"What I need right now is a drink. Maybe several."

"Then let's go out. Why the hell not, we're young, right?" Alex asked.

"I'd love to, but..." I sighed.

"I bet you have a ton on your mind right now." Alex nodded. "What about tomorrow? Let's go out and get a drink somewhere."

"Oh, um, sure," I said, forcing a smile.

Alex pushed up off the couch. "I'll get out of your way. You must be exhausted after that dinner."

I let out a soft chuckle and followed Alex to the door. "Are you a mind reader now, too?"

"No," he said, turning to face me. "I'm just getting better at speaking Hayley again after all these years."

"It is a very hard dialect to pick up," I teased.

Alex's smile faded and he took a small step closer to me. "I know your grandparents are pushing you toward me, and I can't deny that my parents are doing the same. But putting them all aside, I'm really glad we're back in each other's lives."

And before I could even process the look in his eyes, Alex clasped my cheek, dipped his head...and kissed me.

He smelled like expensive cologne and his lips were warm with just the right amount of pressure. Alex didn't push me to deepen the kiss, he didn't try to part my lips with his tongue. It was a perfect kiss – a gentlemanly kiss.

Alex pulled back, his eyes searching mine. "I've wanted to do that for weeks."

I opened my mouth, but no words would come out. In truth, I had no idea what to say. My head, which had been spinning with dizzying thoughts for hours, suddenly roared with a thousand different things – so loud, I couldn't hear a thing at all.

Alex stroked my cheek then dropped his hand. "I'll leave you to your thoughts. See you tomorrow, okay? I'll pick you up around eight."

Still unable to form a coherent sentence, I merely nodded and tried to smile. I probably looked like I'd escaped from some super-serious psychiatric facility.

He gave me one last smile then ducked out of the door and I was finally alone. Turning around, I headed straight for the kitchen. Inside the fridge was a bottle of wine that was so getting drunk tonight. Every last single drop.

After pouring myself a huge glass, I carried it into my bedroom. I placed it carefully on the floor and reached under the bed for the vintage hat box. The faded floral pattern brought back a hundred memories of sitting on my mom's bed, wearing the hat my great-grandmother had worn to my mom and dad's wedding. It was a huge, garish affair, but Mom had loved that thing. And because she had, so did I. I'd sit in her bed, wearing that ugly thing, and watch her get ready. I'd watch her carefully apply her makeup and meticulously choose the jewelry that would perfectly accompany her outfit. Mom had loved to look amazing for my dad. As the mayor, he'd attended so many dinners, functions, parties and galas that he had barely been home.

Most of the time Mom had gone with him, the other half of their power couple. But sometimes she'd stayed home with me. We'd put on our PJs, climb into her ginormous bed and put on crappy movies.

The reason I loved watching my mom get ready was for the moment Dad would come into the room to see if she was almost done. He would practically freeze to the spot, his eyes focused solely on my mom. A funny, quirky smile would pull at his lips as his eyes would soften and he'd step forward to kiss her. Mom would shriek about her freshly painted lips, but he'd never cared. And I don't think she had, either. Not really.

I'd dissolve into giggles watching them.

Dad would swing his gaze to me then and seize my ankles to drag me toward him so he could tickle me until tears streamed down my cheeks.

"Make sure you marry a man like your daddy, Hayley," Mom would say. "Nuttier than a fruitcake, but with a big old heart."

"No," Dad would say softly. "Marry a man who treats you like a princess. Because you deserve nothing less. Marry a man who will give you the world."

Until I was seven I'd been convinced I would marry my daddy. Could think of no one else worthy of my time. Until I'd realized the whole illegal thing would make that pretty impossible.

Then they'd gone and died, making it impossible anyway.

I lifted the lid off the hatbox and peered at the mess of photographs and keepsakes inside.

After they'd died, my grandmother had taken charge of clearing out their house. Whatever hadn't been sold had been scrapped. She wasn't a woman who believed in sentimental value. When I'd realized just how ruthless she was being, I'd begun to secrete little things away.

Birthday cards with my mom's handwriting. Photographs I'd pulled from their frames. A bottle of Mom's favorite perfume. A pot of Dad's daily shaving cream. The old, heavy key to a drawer in Dad's home office desk that had always been stocked with candy for me.

The hatbox that held my mother's grandmother's hat that she'd worn to their wedding.

It had been the perfect place to hide all my treasures. It was my fault that, once the hat box had started filling up and there'd been no room for the actual hat anymore, my grandmother had found it while I'd been at school and had promptly thrown it in the trash.

It was around that time, at just thirteen years old, that I'd begun counting down the days until I had my freedom from their oppressive household. I'd sworn blind I wouldn't let them dictate my life, that I wouldn't let them scrub away the years of incredible parenting my mom and dad had instilled in me.

And yet, somewhere along the way, I'd misplaced the fierce heart of my thirteen-year-old self. She was rebellious and untamed, but, looking back, it hadn't taken long for the change in households to have an effect on her.

I was barely aware of the tears spilling down my cheeks until one dropped onto the photograph I couldn't seem to stop staring at. I was curled in my mom's lap, my hair in a ridiculous top ponytail, which stuck straight up in the air like an arrow. I grasped her hands as she read me a story, her cheek pressed to my head. I couldn't have been more than four, my hair still wispy and fine, so blonde it was almost translucent.

God, I missed her. I missed them.

All I wanted was for her to hold me again, to tell me what to do.

While it was a joy to hear someone actually mention her, Mrs. Yates talking about my mother had brought about a tumultuous storm in my heart. It physically ached as I pined for both her and my father.

Would she be proud of me, as Mrs. Yates was certain she would be?

Would she be proud of the woman I had become? Who worked in an expensive thrift store, as my grandmother thought, and who partied all night?

Only, that wasn't the woman Mrs. Yates knew. She knew me as the well-behaved child of my youth, who'd listened to my parents because I adored them, and listened to my grandparents because…well, the alternative wouldn't be tolerated.

She knew me as the well-dressed young woman with the perfectly made-up face, who was dating her son.

"Mommy, what do I do?" I whispered. Of course, there was no answer. I'd tried for months after they'd died. I'd talk to them until my grandparents threatened to send me to a shrink as I'd sat in silence, desperately trying to hear their response. I'd bought a Ouija board and spent hours with my fingers pressed to the pointer, uselessly wishing for it to move. Because, how could two devoted, loving parents just disappear? How could they vanish and not utter a word to their only child?

How could they leave her all alone?

* * * *

The wine bottle was empty. The tequila bottle was almost dry. I lay on my bedroom floor and the room spun like a tilt-a-whirl. Photographs scattered around my boneless form and I clutched my mom's perfume bottle to my chest like a blankie.

Wherever they were, I could guarantee that my parents weren't looking down on me with anything even remotely resembling pride. What a wastrel I was. A pathetic, drunk wastrel.

What if I all I knew was how to let people down?

Like my grandparents. Jeez, I practically made that one an Olympic sport.

And my girlfriends. Since Marley had left and Colt had come into my life, how often did I see Beth and Eve? They never complained, but they could hardly be happy about my lack of presence.

I should have worked harder for Fiona. How could I even consider continuing her legacy? The place would burn to the ground within the month.

Had Marley asked Cassidy to throw her baby shower because she thought I was too flaky to pull it off?

Colt... Let's face it, I'd been stringing him along for months.

It wasn't fair. What I was doing to him wasn't fair. Like Susan had said, if I couldn't give myself to Colt the way he wanted, needed and deserved, I should walk away. Get out before someone really got hurt.

Another tear rolled down the side of my face and right into my ear.

My daddy wanted me to marry someone who would treat me like a princess.

Colt had already scoffed at that idea.

I needed to stop being so selfish with people.

I needed to start making better choices.

I needed to start making serious decisions.

My phone was on the floor beside me and I rooted around for it. I had to close one eye to focus on the screen, and once it stopped being a bright, blurry mess, I went to my messages and opened a recent thread.

I need to stop seeing you. I'm sorry. Bye. XOXO

And before I could change my mind, I hit Send.

My heart thudded, dreading what would be a lightning fast reply. Or, worse, a phone call.

But the minutes ticked by and nothing happened. I realized it was after four a.m., and he was probably tucked up in his huge, comfortable bed, completely oblivious to the text I'd just sent him.

I released a long, shaky breath and went to my photo gallery, scrolling through the hundreds of images until I found the right one.

Me, Colt and Madison Square Garden. It was the selfie I'd taken of us on my birthday at the Knicks game. If I'd known then what I knew now, would I have ever taken it? Would I have ever gone?

If I'd known what Colt would come to mean to me, would I have spurred his every advance and never let him in as far as I had?

I'm not sure.

I peeled myself off the floor and crawled into bed fully clothed. Keeping the phone clutched in my hand, I stared at the picture as fat, hot tears ran in rivulets down my face, until, mercifully, I fell asleep.

Chapter Eighteen

A pneumatic drill had taken up residence in my head.

Someone had swapped my tongue for a nasty, gross carpet.

And if I didn't get to the bathroom in three seconds then I was going to puke all over my bed.

I vaulted out of bed and raced down the hall to the bathroom, where I hurled my guts into the toilet.

Holy Moses, what the hell had I eaten?

Clammy and empty, I slumped against the bathtub and caught my breath. Once I was sure I was done puking — and only because it wasn't possible to have a single thing left in my stomach — I slouched back to bed.

My phone lay on top of the duvet, the battery drained. I picked it up to plug in the charger and paused.

The text.

I'd texted Colt last night.

Breaking things off.

Things that had, really, not even had a chance to take off.

I'd barely had a real chance with him…but as everything from the night before came flooding back, maybe that was a good thing. Get out before someone gets hurt. That was what I had to keep reminding myself.

Right.

So instead of charging the phone, I left it on my nightstand, like the coward that I was, and unplugged the landline phone, too, just for good measure.

A while later, I lay on the couch with an icepack over my eyes and the TV on low. I'd reached the stage of my hangover where the headache had eased off and I'd stopped puking and just started feeling like death.

Which was why, when someone knocked on my door, I almost started crying. Then my stomach bottomed out. What if it was Colt?

I shuffled quietly toward the door and leaned as far over as possible to the peephole, cautious of my shadow being seen. But Eve's smiling face was beaming into the peephole.

I breathed out a sigh of relief and unbolted the door for her. "Hey, what's going on?"

"Nothing. Your doorman was giving me shit. Is he new?"

"Oh, yeah, he is." We were all on each other's approved visitors list, and usually had no trouble getting into each other's buildings. But my new doorman seemed to like to give people he hadn't met before a hard time.

"So I'm just here to borrow back my neon-blue Mary Janes. I've got a hot date tonight and they will look killer with my outfit." Eve bypassed me and headed straight for my bedroom. When I caught her up she was rooting around in my closet. "Ooh, can I have this purse, too?"

"Yeah, sure," I said. I flopped down on my bed.

"Something wrong?" Eve asked as she emerged, her arms loaded down with the shoes in question, two purses and a Hermès scarf.

"Apart from the hangover from hell, nothing at all," I murmured, throwing my arm over my face.

Eve huffed. "You partied and didn't call me?"

"You wouldn't have wanted to be at this party, trust me. I got wasted here, all by myself, and cried into my hatbox. Oh, and I called things off with Colt."

"The hot cop?" Eve asked, sitting beside me on the bed. "Why? Oh wait, because of your ex flame from back home?" I'd filled in Beth and Eve all about my predicament the night we'd gone out drinking and I'd ended up at Colt's. The girls had been less than helpful, and had laughed off my problem of having two good-looking men scrambling for my attention.

I lifted my arm and peered at her. "Why don't you sound

260

surprised about that?"

Eve laughed. "Is that a joke? A choice between a blue-collared cop or a wealthy, good-looking dude who already has pre-approval from your grandparents—no contest."

Pushing myself up onto one elbow, I said, "Did you ever think I'd get serious about Colt?"

"Not really," Eve said, pulling a face. "We all expected you to fool around with him. But you got more serious than we figured. To be honest, me and Beth have been expecting news of your engagement to Alex for a few weeks now."

I eased myself back down. "Because he's rich?"

"No. Because he's your type." Eve lay down beside me. "What's really going on, Hayley?"

"What do you mean?" I asked, turning my head to look at her.

"You already like Alex—you dated him for a while back home. You know your super-strict grandparents approve. Didn't you say your parents knew him and his family too? So you know your parents would approve, too. And he's good-looking, and rich to boot. Alex is everything you've ever wanted. But…you sort of look like you got stuck with the consolation prize instead."

"Do you really think that?" I whispered. "That Alex is everything I've ever wanted?"

Eve laughed. "And then some. But trust me—he's the best you've picked so far. Some of the other guys you dated were total jerks. You just didn't want to see it."

I nodded, my eyes stinging.

"You look like crap, babe. Why don't you take a shower and try to get some more sleep? I'll call you later, okay?" Eve leaned over and kissed my cheek. Before I knew it, she was gone.

I lay there for a while, her words turning over in my mind. Maybe she was right. A shower would make me feel more human, I guess. When I felt better, everything would look better.

But as I stood under the shower spray, pieces of me

crumbled.

Was I really so shallow that my friends didn't expect me to choose someone as wonderful and real as Colt, in favor of someone wealthy? I sank to the bottom of the tub as my heart fractured into a thousand pieces. The shower pelted my back while I sobbed and mourned the loss of something I wasn't sure I ever really could call mine.

I didn't deserve him anyway.

I was worthless to a man like him.

Susan was right—someone would get hurt.

It just wasn't Colt.

* * * *

Once I'd forced water and food into my body, I started to feel better. By dinnertime I was moderately okay. When it was time for drinks with Alex, I was fine. So I dressed in one of my favorite outfits—a black knit Stella McCartney figure-hugging dress with a crazy bold zipper feature, black pumps and teal pea coat. Whenever I wore that dress, I felt incredible. Powerful. Feminine.

Tonight, its magic didn't work. The last thing in the world I felt like doing was drinking. Or leaving the house. Or seeing another living person.

But because I was still too coward to turn my phone on, I couldn't call Alex and cancel.

I was standing in front of the mirror by the front door putting in my earrings when there was a soft knock. Alex was twenty minutes early. Usually he arrived on the nose, but maybe he was going to invite himself in first.

As I swung the door open, my breath caught in my throat.

It wasn't Alex.

"Colt," I whispered.

"Hey, St. Clair. Can I come in?" Colt asked. His usual playful blue eyes were flat, the humorous quirk to his mouth gone. He looked tired.

I was sorely tempted to tell him no. But he deserved better

than that. He deserved more than my chicken-shit self. So I nodded once and moved aside for him to come into the apartment.

He leaned against the back of the couch and folded his arms across his chest. "What's going on?"

"Nothing. What's going on with you?"

"Don't give me that crap," Colt said, anger rising in his tone. He stabbed a finger at me. "You send me that text in the middle of the goddamn night, then turn your phone off? That's all I get? No conversation, no explanation?"

"My battery is dead and I can't find the charger," I said, crossing my own arms across my chest. His anger brought out my prickly side, and I had to use that. Otherwise I'd dissolve into a girlish mess and be at his mercy.

"Oh, really?" he asked in a flat voice. "Did you forget to plug the phone line in, too?" Colt nodded to the left, where the cable lay on the floor. Clearly not connected.

I blew out a breath. "Do we really have to do this?"

His eyebrows shot up into his hairline. "Do we really have to do this? Are you serious right now?"

"Come on, Colt. I said what I needed to. Why drag this out? What's the point?"

Colt muttered something. "I can't believe this, I really can't." He pushed off the couch and took a step toward me. "I need to stop seeing you." Another step. "I'm sorry." And another. "Bye." We were toe to toe and I tipped my head back to look into his achingly familiar blue eyes, now flooded with hurt and anger. "XO. XO."

"I know what it said, I sent it, didn't I?" I asked, swallowing. "And why come here now? You've had around, oh, eighteen hours? Surely it couldn't have stung that badly."

He narrowed his eyes. "I have a job, remember? I can't just not show up. Lives are on the line. Victims deserve my time. But trust me, had I not been working, I would have been over here at the ass crack of dawn."

I wilted. "Please, Colt, we don't have to do this."

"You know —" Colt chuckled. "I actually thought you were messing with me for a second. But when I tried to call you and got your voicemail, and tried another hundred goddamn times, I knew you were serious. Breaking up with me in a text? I expected better. I really did."

I turned away from him. "We were never really together. You can hardly call it a breakup."

"You came in my bed a few days ago — you said you wanted it to be *your* bed."

"I was drunk, Colt."

He caught my arm and spun me around to face me. "Bullshit," he breathed. Colt searched my eyes, his gaze frantic. "What about Faith, Hayley? What the hell do I tell her? 'Sorry, baby, she doesn't want to see us anymore. Get over it.'"

My throat tightened. "Not my problem."

Colt reared back as though I'd struck him. I wanted to snatch the words and stuff them back in my mouth where they couldn't hurt him anymore. But...maybe this was the easiest way. If he hated me, he wouldn't contest this.

"I told you in the beginning what I wanted, Colt. A man who will treat me like a princess." I met his eyes unflinchingly, though inside I was crumbling. "And a city cop with an ex-wife and a child who he would always put before me isn't that man."

Colt shook his head. "You're going to regret this, Hayley. I swear to God, you are going to regret this."

"Is that a threat, Detective? I know your badge number, remember." The coldness in my voice surprised even me.

He flashed me a disgusted look. "No. You're going to regret it because whenever you make peace with whatever is screwing with your head, you are going to hate yourself. And this time I won't be around to pick you back up again."

"Why are you blowing this so out of proportion?" I cried, flinging my hands out. "Christ, Colt, we weren't even seriously dating! We weren't anything to each other!"

"Don't you dare say that to me!" Colt roared as he closed

the distance between us. "Don't you dare presume to tell me what you mean to me. I let you into my life. I let you into my *daughter's* life. You met my family because I wanted *you* to be a part of my family."

I opened my mouth to answer but was stopped by a knock on the door. *Jesus, it's like Grand Central around here today.*

Colt stepped away and looked me up and down, as though only just now noticing what I was wearing. "I guess that's your date." He marched to the front door and opened it, revealing Alex. "You the new guy?" Colt looked over his shoulder at me and back to Alex. "Good luck. I hope your wallet is big enough. Mine sure as hell wasn't. Maybe that was the problem, huh, Hayley?"

"What's going on here?" Alex asked, straightening his back as though trying to match Colt in height. It wouldn't happen. Colt was bigger than Alex in every way, even in warmth and personality. Alex could never hope to match up to him.

"Absolutely nothing, isn't that right?" Colt asked. "I'd say see you around, but that won't happen." Colt pushed past Alex and disappeared down the hall.

"What did I just walk in on?" Alex asked as he hurried to close the door, as if afraid Colt would return.

"Nothing. Someone I used to know. Could you excuse me for a moment?" I hurried into the bathroom and clutched the edge of the sink. My breath came in gasps. I was on the verge of hyperventilating.

What the hell had I done?

* * * *

I had no idea how Alex talked me into still going out with him. I'd suggested ordering in, but he'd insisted on getting me out into the real world. We went to a small bar a few blocks away and sat in a booth.

Tracing the rim of my cocktail glass, I struggled to concentrate on what Alex was saying. He was talking about his office...I think. But Colt's voice drowned his out so completely he might as well have been sitting right beside me.

I fidgeted in my seat as my own irritation rose. *I hope your wallet is big enough, mine sure as hell wasn't...* That was a low blow. I hadn't deserved that. And neither had Alex. Colt didn't know him from Adam. Did he really think so poorly of me that he thought that was the only reason I was with Alex? Didn't he realize the pressure I was under from other people?

Jesus, he was a—

"I have something for you," Alex said, interrupting my angry train of thought.

I smiled and lifted my eyebrows, hoping my interest was believable enough.

Alex slid the Tiffany-blue jewelry box across the table. "I saw it while I was out this afternoon and could think of no better neck than yours to wear this."

Lifting the lid, I saw a subtle silver pendant, with Xs and Os. It was beautiful and understated, and so not me. Or maybe it was, because it reminded me of how I'd thoughtlessly signed off from the text to Colt.

This was exactly why Colt thought I'd chosen Alex over him. Because of this. Gifts that only proved how little the giver really knew me.

I shoved up from the table and grabbed my purse. "I'm sorry, I have to go."

"What?" Alex asked, shock filling his tone. "Go where?"

"I have to go see someone. And give him a piece of my goddamn mind, the asshole." Without looking back, I left Alex and his pendant in the bar as I rushed outside and hailed a cab. "Brooklyn. And step on it."

I stewed the entire time it took for the cabbie to drive me to Brooklyn. By the time we pulled up in front of Colt's town house, I had ruined my manicure. I paid the driver and climbed out of the cab. Marched up his stoop and hammered on his front door before my anger could fade and I talked myself out of it.

Colt swung open his door, irritation pulling his eyebrows together. At the sight of me, his features smoothed out, leaving only a blank look. "What are you doing here?"

"I came to tell you something," I said, pushing past him before he could slam the door in my face.

"Of course you did," he muttered. "I thought there was nothing left to talk about?"

"Yeah, well, I decided that I had to tell you something anyway." I stabbed a finger at him. "You are an asshole, Colton Deluca."

His eyes widened and he pointed his finger at his chest. "*I'm* an asshole? How in the hell did you come to that conclusion?"

"Because of what you said to Alex!" I cried. "Is that really what you think of me? That I'm a gold-digging whore?"

He held his steady gaze and said, unflinching, "If the black Amex fits."

If I were a cartoon, that would have been the point where my face turned beet-red and steam blew out of my ears. I stormed across the foyer and slapped him clear across the face. "How dare you," I croaked. "You don't know the first fucking thing about me."

"What do you expect?" he roared, getting in my face. "You pull me in, whisper all this stuff in my ear, then turn around and rip it all out from under me. That girl who told me all those months ago that she wanted to be treated like a princess and have expensive crap bought for her—I thought that girl was gone. And yet here she stands in front of me. Pissed because I'm calling her out."

"You don't understand." I shoved my hair out of my face. My entire axle was off balance. My world spun and I didn't know how to make it stop.

"Then why don't you make me understand?" he asked, his tone softening a degree. "Because all I can see is you breaking things off with me so you can be with that douche who doesn't get you, St. Clair."

I turned away from him, not wanting him to see my resolve break.

"Make me understand. Make me understand why he is more worthy of your time. Is it where he comes from? He's not some city cop from Brooklyn with a loud and crass family and a kid of his own to raise. He buys you shit. He'll set you up with a penthouse on Park — is that it?"

"You're saying that we meant more than we did," I said, my voice level despite the racing of my heart. "We were friends, Colt. And we were attracted to each other. That's all there really was."

"Friends who were attracted to each other," he repeated. "Do you even hear yourself? That kind of thing doesn't happen very often. Being with someone who is like your best friend but that you want to rip the clothes off of every minute of the day is a precious thing."

"Jesus, it's an attraction — that's it. I am more than capable of controlling myself around you."

I sensed more than felt him behind me. When he spoke, his breath tickled my ear. "I don't believe you."

I covered my face with my hands. "Stop it."

"You can stop it." Colt moved to stand in front of me. He gently clasped my wrists and lowered my hands from my face. "You can stop it by making me believe you truly think I'm talking garbage."

I lifted my eyes and peered up at him. There was a challenge in his gaze, and a determination that I was so, so familiar with.

"Kiss me and prove you're capable of controlling yourself. Maybe then I'll believe all the other crap you're trying to sell me."

He couldn't be serious…after everything we'd both said, how could he want my mouth anywhere near his?

"What's it going to be, St. Clair?" he taunted. "In or out?"

One kiss…I could do one kiss. One kiss to prove to him that I could control myself, and then maybe he would back off and believe everything else I'd told him, even though a part of me, somewhere deep, deep down, hoped to God he wouldn't. A kiss for closure. A kiss goodbye.

I clasped his cheeks and rose up onto my tiptoes to slant my mouth over his. If I thought he would let me get away with a brief, dry kiss, then I had another think coming. The moment my lips touched his, Colt banded his arms around me and lifted me clear off the ground.

My back hit the wall and instinctively my legs went around his waist. He cupped my throat, tipping my head back so he could pillage my mouth.

I cried out and he kissed me harder. I knotted my hands in his hair, tugging at the roots and trying to convey some kind of animalistic, raw need.

Colt slid his hand up my leg and it disappeared under the hem of my dress. He cupped my ass in his large palm, squeezing the flesh in a way that made me tighten my hold on him with my legs.

I rubbed against him, creating delicious friction that only made me desperate for more.

He broke the kiss and ground his hips into me, making me gasp. "Tell me what you want, St. Clair. Do you want this? Me?"

I sank into him, and mumbled against his lips, "Take me upstairs."

Colt didn't have to be told twice. He carried me up the stairs, never breaking our kiss. He kicked open his bedroom door and instead of flinging me on his bed and having his wicked way with me, Colt guided me to my feet.

He pulled away from me, and mingled with the heat of his lust in his eyes was something I couldn't name. After the frenzy of our kiss downstairs, I expected Colt to rip me out of my clothes and be inside me within a heartbeat.

Instead he gazed down at me, as though waiting to follow my lead.

Things were too far gone for me to back out now.

I'd craved this with Colt for months, and I was finally hanging over the precipice of getting it. He was waiting for me to change my mind, to cry off, if that was what I wanted. Even now, when this was about proving a point, Colt was taking care of me.

Holding his gaze, I undid his belt and unfastened the buttons on his jeans. Colt visibly swallowed as I pushed them over his narrow hips. He helped me lift the T-shirt over his head. I kissed his beautifully formed pecs, skimmed my finger over the flat disc of his nipple then trailed kisses down his rigid abdomen until I met the line of hair that started at his belly button and disappeared into his boxer briefs.

I straightened and stepped out of my heels, putting me even shorter than him. Colt caught my hip and slowly turned me so I showed him my back. He gathered my hair up in his hand and draped it over one shoulder. Slowly, he lowered the zipper of my dress and pushed it down over my hips. The material puddled at my feet and I kicked it away. Colt pressed a delicate kiss to my bare shoulder and slid his fingertips down my side, making me breakout in goosebumps.

He palmed one breast, teasing the nipple until I gasped. I arched into his touch, silently begging for more.

Colt spun me back around to face him. He crouched in front of me and eased my lace panties down my legs. Colt kissed my thighs, my lower stomach, my sternum. His hot breath rippled against my flesh and for a moment he stayed there, his hands clasped on my hips, his lips barely resting on my skin. It was as though he was savoring the moment, was trying his best to commit every feeling, every scent and every sound to memory.

When he rose to full height, I wasted no time in ushering him out of his boxer briefs and getting him as naked as I was.

And…*Holy Moses.*

Colt nude was a sight to behold.

All that rippling muscle, barely contained strength, the dips and planes, broad shoulders and narrow waist, corded forearms and muscular thighs…but his dick. His straining and impressive erection made him irrevocably virile and male. Just looking at him naked would be enough to get half a dozen eager women pregnant.

Colt scooped me up into his arms and laid me down on his bed like I was the most precious thing in the world to him. He pressed feather-light kisses down my body, working me up until I was so tightly wound I could combust.

I threw my leg over his hip and urged him onto his back while I straddled him.

A low laugh rumbled in his chest. "Impatient, St. Clair?"

"Yes. And curious." I'd waited forever for this. I licked his nipple and worked my way down the length of him, exploring him as he had me. Every muscle captured my attention. Every ridge and every bump.

I loved how strong he was, how carefully he maintained his body. It was quite literally a temple and I was so down with worshiping it. When I reached his thick erection, I trailed one fingertip over the head. His cock twitched and Colt moved on the bed.

I took him in my hand, easing up and down the hard, silken length. Colt arched into me and whispered my name.

"You feel incredible, Colt," I said throatily, increasing the speed of my hand.

He groaned and uttered something low and guttural that I didn't catch. His muscles rippled as he strained his back up and off the bed. I watched him react to what I was doing to him.

Colt caught my wrist, pulled my hand free from him and flipped me onto my back. "Babe," he said breathily, "when I come, it's going to be inside you."

I shivered at his words. "I'm ready, Colt."

A cocky grin spread across his face. "I bet you are. But I'm not done with you yet." Colt shuffled back on the bed and parted my knees, completely exposing me to him. I was laid bare under his hot gaze…and I had never felt more beautiful. He lowered his head and ran his nose along the crease of my thigh. "You smell gorgeous. Just like I knew you would."

He then tasted me with a long, slow lick that had my toes curling and my back arching off the bed. Colt dipped his tongue inside me and I about came apart at the seams. He worked me with his expert mouth so thoroughly it was as though he wanted to wring every last feeling from every last nerve in my wretched body.

My orgasm tore through me, but Colt didn't let up as he took me to the brink of madness. My breath left me in pants and I swear I saw stars.

"That was beautiful," Colt murmured, settling himself above me.

"Hmm," I murmured, still coming back down to planet Earth. I dragged my gaze over his face and halted at the conflicted look in his eyes. "What's wrong?"

"I want more than anything to be buried deep inside you. It feels like I've waited forever for tonight. And I can't help but feel like I'm blowing it. Or that it's just tonight – like I'm trying to grab on to thin air and you're going to disappear on me."

"Do you think I would really do that?" I frowned. "Do *this* with you, and just disappear? I'm not... I wouldn't do that to you, Colt. I'm here. Really here."

"I'm going to keep you forever, St. Clair. And whatever comes after that," Colt vowed.

My eyes pricked with emotion as my heart swelled. Why had I denied this? Why had I tried to convince myself that he was worth giving up?

He dipped his head and covered my mouth with his – sealing in his declaration with his kiss. I wanted to swallow the words and keep them inside me always. I wrapped my arms around his shoulders and tried to pour everything I felt in that moment into it. Wanted to tell him how this – how *he* – made me feel. It was something I couldn't articulate, something mere words couldn't do justice to.

So I would show him just what he meant to me. Explain

with my body how he made me feel. I broke the kiss and stroked a finger over his lips. "I want you inside me, Colt. Right now."

Colt released a breath and studied my face for a long moment before reaching over to his beside drawer and removing a condom. He made fast work of rolling it on, and a heartbeat later he was poised at my entrance.

Colt held my gaze as he slowly pushed inside me. I'd never been with a man like Colt before. Someone so raw with masculinity, someone so heavily built with muscles, someone so…big as him. I bit my lip and sucked in a breath at how completely he filled me. Colt hit that sweet spot inside me and I was ready to come undone before he had even really moved.

"Jesus, St. Clair," Colt breathed. He burrowed his face in my neck as he pulled back and slowly pushed in again.

I moaned and writhed beneath him, seeking the release that was only just out of reach.

He whispered my name again as he thrust inside me, saying it like a prayer, like I truly was something to revere. Colt worshipped me, pushed my body to the brink and held me there until I thought I would die.

"Come with me," he groaned, nipping at the flesh where my neck met my shoulder.

"I'm there," I breathed. I gripped his ass, my world spiraling out of control. My orgasm shuddered through my body, hard and consuming.

Colt gritted his teeth and came with a roar, his body tight, each and every muscle flexed. I trembled beneath him, aftershocks still sparking. He pressed his forehead to mine, no words needed, not now.

We lay like that for the longest time—our breaths mingling, our bodies still fused as one.

* * * *

I lay on my front, my body sated and boneless. My head

273

rested on my folded arms and my eyes were heavy and starting to droop.

"Have I exhausted you?" Colt asked and chuckled as he returned to the room. He placed two glasses of water on the nightstand and climbed back into bed beside me. He brushed the hair from my face and dipped to kiss my cheek.

"Completely and utterly. I wasn't this tired after I finished the color run Marley talked me into doing with her last spring."

"I have trouble believing you did any kind of running. Unless it was to a sample sale or something."

I huffed and pushed up onto one elbow. "I'll have you know I kicked ass in that run."

"I bet," he said, an amused quirk to his mouth. "Apart from being tired…are you okay?"

"Are you asking if you broke my vagina?" I asked, lifting one eyebrow.

"No, you smartass. It was a roundabout way of asking where your head is at."

"Oh," I said softly. I rolled onto my back and settled against the plump pillows. In truth, my head was clearer and quieter than it had been in forever. Or maybe I was still in a sex haze and wasn't capable of conscious thought yet. "I-I'm not sure. It's quiet…my head, I mean."

Colt paused before speaking. "I'll take that as a win. So. That must have been the shortest date known to mankind."

I frowned as I turned his words over in my mind. When I finally caught his meaning, I bolted upright. "Oh my gosh, Alex. I totally bailed on him. Wow. I bet he thinks I'm a fruit loop."

Colt snorted. "You mean he didn't before?"

I shot him a withering look.

"You ran out on him? Why?" he asked, stroking my elbow.

Sighing, I shoved my messy hair over to one side. "Because I couldn't stop thinking about what you said. It pissed me off so much I had to come and tell you off."

"Man, I'm sorry, St. Clair. What I said…I shouldn't have."

"But you were right," I said with a sad smile. "And deep down, that's why it upset me so much." And now, with nothing left to lose, I had to tell him the truth. I had to explain to him what made Hayley St. Clair tick. The good, the bad and the downright awful. "You were right. I was breaking things off with you to be with Alex."

Colt scrubbed a hand over his jaw. He sat up and leaned back against the headboard. "Okay. Can't say I'm thrilled to hear you admit it. Can I ask why?"

"Better yet, I'm going to tell you anyway. Your opinion of me can't be any worse than it already is, so I may as well, right?"

"St. Clair…my opinion of you is the same as it's been from the night I met you."

"A spoiled little girl with a clothing obsession?" I joked, though there was no humor left in my body. Not even a drop.

"A remarkable, sparkling woman with drive and passion. Who I want to have hard and dirty sex with whenever possible." Colt stroked my back. "You can tell me anything."

I pulled my knees up to my chest and wrapped my arms around them. "I wasn't lying to you before. I really was breaking up with you to be with Alex. The night I texted you, I'd been out to dinner with my grandparents, Alex, and his parents. All night all I heard was how we were perfect for each other, how our future was practically all laid out. The perfect little Stepford dress, just waiting to stitch me into it so I couldn't ever escape. I'm used to it from my grandparents, they shove it down my throat whenever I see them that they want me married off into a good family. Someone who can further their connections. But that night… Alex's mother told me how proud my mom would be of me."

A tear slid down my cheek. "I miss my mom and dad so much, Colt. I miss them every single day. All I want, all I've ever wanted, is to know that they were proud of me. You grew up in a house with so much warmth and love that it's ingrained in the walls. I spent my teen years in a house where I had to work for every kind word tossed my way. And you want to know something? They always followed a date with Alex, or an invitation extended from his parents to my grandparents."

"St. Clair," Colt said quietly. "You know as well as I do that your folks would want you to be happy. Whatever that meant and whoever it was with."

"I know that, I do know that," I said as more tears fell. "But it all gets messed up in my head sometimes. The memories of my parents aren't as strong as they used to be. I feel like I'm losing pieces all the time and all I really know is that I'd do anything to make them proud of me. And having Mrs. Yates, Alex's mother, tell me that they would be proud… because I was with their son…really, really screwed with my head.

"It's like there are two of me. There's Hayley, the good girl who does as she's told. The girl who dates men her grandparents approve of, who is happy to do charity work because it keeps her out of her husband's hair and pretends he isn't just giving her something to do. She rarely leaves New Hampshire, and is probably an alcoholic by forty.

"Then there's St. Clair. New Yorker. Fun-loving party girl. Has three of the best friends a girl could ask for. Owner of Back in Time, and has opened another four stores across the city with plans for a country-wide expansion in the next few years. She has a smoking hot detective boyfriend and couldn't give a rat's ass what anyone else thinks."

"Call me biased, but I like the second girl." Colt kissed my shoulder. "But I understand where you're coming from. I really do."

"I got so drunk after dinner the other night. I was already feeling pretty raw after what Mrs. Yates said, and I went home and drank way too much and pored over the only things I have left of my parents. Everything is so mixed up in my head, Colt. I don't know which way is up anymore."

"I think… I think you have to do what makes the most sense to you. I can sit here and tell you what you already know — that one path would make you miserable, and the other is the life you really want for yourself but are too afraid to grab. You look at both options and you make the choice you can live with. Can you risk feeling for the rest of your life that you disappointed your parents? Can you defy your grandparents? Can you walk away from a pretty incredible life that you already love? What can you live with, St. Clair?"

Could I live without Marley? If I went down the route of marrying Alex, I'd lose touch with her eventually. She'd have her life in Vegas and I'd have mine in Connecticut. Could I live without my independence? Could I live without Colt?

I squeezed my eyes shut as my heart tripped over itself.

No. I couldn't.

Make the choice you can live with. I couldn't live without him.

"There's no time limit on this," Colt said. "I'm not the guy who is going to give you an ultimatum and demand an answer. You take all the time you need. I'm going to shower, okay? I think you need some space for a few minutes."

I nodded as he climbed out of bed and padded into his bathroom. When the door closed with a soft click, I blew out a huge breath and collapsed against the pillows. The quiet of my head was obliterated. Now there were a thousand thoughts careening around again.

I wanted to be brave. I wanted the courage to tell Colt that my heart lay with him and couldn't possibly belong to anyone else on this earth. I wanted to tell my grandparents to shove it and I wanted to tell Fiona that I was going to kick ass at running her baby.

But I was as cowardly as an ostrich sticking its head in the dirt.

I scooted to Colt's side of the bed and reached for the glass of water on the nightstand. Gulping most of it down,

I wished it was something stronger. I wiped my mouth with the back of my hand and went to place it back on the nightstand.

But a velvet jewelry box made me pause.

Why did Colt have a jewelry box? Had it been a gift for me before things had gone sideways? Something for Faith? Someone else?

I glanced at the bathroom door, the sound of the shower still present.

It wouldn't hurt to peek, right?

Curious is as curious does, so before I could tell myself what a colossally bad idea it was, I grabbed the box and flipped it open.

At first, I didn't trust what I saw.

Because how could it be what it plainly was?

How could it be my locket? The locket that had been taken from me at gunpoint months and months ago?

It had to be a copy. Colt remembered it well enough to describe it to a jewelry maker and had had a serious good copy made.

My hands shook as I lifted the locket out of the box. The smoothness of it against my palm, the weight of it, all these things were as familiar to me as my own face.

I opened the locket, fully prepared to be met with emptiness.

Instead, I was met with the realization that this was no copy.

Something in me cracked.

Maybe it was the last of the walls I'd hidden behind all this time with Colt. Maybe it was the plaster coming off my broken heart, that hadn't healed since the death of my parents.

Whatever it was, something in me had changed. Had healed. Had awoken.

I opened the bathroom door and stepped inside.

"St. Clair? You okay?" Colt asked from behind the shower curtain. When I didn't answer, he poked his wet head around to see me. "What's...?" His voice trailed off as he saw what I held in my shaking hand. "I was going to tell you—"

"Don't say anything," I said. I turned away from him and laid the locket on the counter by the sink. Then I stepped inside the tub, clasped Colt's face and pulled him down for the most intense kiss of my life.

He lifted me clean off my feet. I wrapped my legs around his waist and he shoved me against the cold tiled wall. Colt's erection pushed at my entrance and I arched my hips, eager for him to be inside me.

"I'm covered, Colt. I trust you," I breathed.

With a groan, Colt sheathed himself in me. I gasped at the raw feeling of no barriers between us. He pulled back then shoved himself in to the hilt. I gripped his shoulders and claimed his mouth as he pounded me into the wall.

He filled me perfectly. I stretched to accommodate him and I doubted two people had ever been so connected as we were in that moment.

Colt came quickly and so did I. There was no patience this time. It was a need greater than pleasure, to lose ourselves in one another, to commit an act that couldn't be articulated. To speak a language impossible to translate.

Afterward, Colt set me on my feet and went about cleaning me up. He stroked a washcloth over every inch of me, tending to my body as though it was a priceless piece of art. When he was done, I lathered up my palms with his soap and I ran my hands over every inch of that Adonis frame.

Twice.

Chapter Nineteen

There was a familiar weight against my chest. A comfort made of bronze and chain. I touched the locket where it had settled at my collarbone, hardly able to believe it was really there.

"You've no idea what you've given me back, Colt," I whispered in the darkness.

Colt slid his hand up my body to cover my own. His enveloped mine so completely. I never felt more petite or feminine than when I was with Colt. It was hard to picture anything ever hurting me, or fear ever finding me, when he was around. "I do. I saw it in your eyes when you told me about it that night. You told me how important it was to you and I could see how much it gutted you to lose it."

"Have you been looking for it all this time? Or did you hold on to it as some sort of sex bargaining chip?" I asked, flashing him a suspicious look.

Colt snorted a laugh. "If that was my sinister plan, I'd have cashed in a hell of a long time ago, trust me." He cleared his throat. "I've been checking pawnshops for a while, hoping to get lucky. Then a few days ago, I was in this low-rent place in the Bronx...and it was just sitting there in a glass cabinet along with a dozen other hot pieces."

"Why didn't you tell me?" I asked quietly.

Colt paused for a moment before answering me. "I had it all planned, you know? How I was going to give it to you. I know you're big on anniversaries, and Valentine's Day lands on the nine-month anniversary of the night we met. I was going to take you to Industry and surprise you with it."

At first I was confused. Why did he say it in the past tense, and why did he sound almost regretful? Then it hit me. "But instead I sent you that horrible text and broke things off."

"I was always going to give it to you, St. Clair, even after all that went down. Even if I had to mail you the damn thing. But yeah, you sort of threw a wrench into the works."

"I'm sorry," I said quietly.

Colt rose up onto one elbow. He cupped my cheek and turned my face toward him. "Stop apologizing to me. You told me your reasons behind what you did, and even if I can't understand most of it, I understand you did what you believed your parents would have wanted."

"I feel like I screwed everything up. Not just with you — with Fiona, with my friends, who I hardly ever see anymore, with Alex. Did I lead him on?"

"Probably," Colt admitted.

I huffed and smacked his chest. "Thanks a lot."

Colt laughed and dipped his head to kiss me quickly. "Babe, you could lead a blind man on. You just have this...draw about you. Like your own gravitational pull or something. Why do you think I'm so damn crazy about you?"

"I thought it was my sass."

"Your sass. Right."

I laughed quietly. "Do you want to see it?"

"Your sass? Always."

"My locket, you idiot. Or have you looked already?"

Colt's face sobered. "No, I haven't. It's yours. Only you could show it to me."

The fact that he hadn't looked, hadn't even been tempted, spoke more volumes about the kind of man Colt was than anything else he'd done before. He was strong and solid, so...honest. He was like no one else I'd ever known in my life.

I sat up and folded my legs beneath me. A strong ache grasped my heart, not just because I was showing someone the inside of my locket, but because I was finally listening to what that blood-pumping muscle had been saying for months. My hands trembled as I popped the clasp and opened the locket.

There we were — my mother, with her long golden hair and blue eyes, just like mine. My father, who'd given me his stubborn chin and fiery temperament. And me — a wildly grinning six-year-old with a missing front tooth and unruly hair. We stood in front of the huge oak tree in our backyard that I'd spent so much time climbing…and falling out of.

I couldn't remember the day the picture was taken.

But I remember seeing it every time my father had opened his wallet.

I remember when he'd given my mom the locket for their wedding anniversary the year they'd died.

I remember her wearing it with no picture inside because none had ever seemed good enough.

I remember her telling me that it had to be perfect, because she would never change it.

I remember taking it from her jewelry box before my grandmother had started taking over, and I remember stealing my dad's wallet from the box of things returned to us after the accident.

"I've never shown anyone except Marley before," I said, my voice thicker than I'd expected it to be.

"You were a goofy-looking kid," Colt said. "Thank you for showing me."

"Thank you for giving it back to me." A single tear streaked down my cheek.

Colt brushed it away and sealed his mouth over mine. It wasn't a sexual kiss, it was reassuring and a comfort. And with so much more intimacy than if it had been sexual. "Are you tired? It's late."

It was so late it was practically early. "No. I don't think I've ever been more awake."

* * * *

282

"I'm going to go see Fiona," I said as Colt drove me back home so I could change.

When we'd finally rolled out of bed late the next morning, we'd feasted on toaster waffles and fresh coffee. He had let me talk and talk, going over every foreseeable problem or hiccup I could encounter by taking over the store. Colt had given his input, but like everything else, he hadn't tried to sway me one way or the other. But he'd sworn that no matter what decision I came to, he would be there to support me.

I could have happily stayed cooped up in Colt's home — which had started to feel like my home — but I needed fresh clothes. And now that I'd made my decision, I had to speak to Fiona.

He glanced at me. "Have you decided what you're going to do?"

I sighed. "I'm going to take her up on her offer. I'm going to take over Back in Time."

Colt grinned. "I think that's a pretty great idea."

"Really?" I asked as I chewed on my fingernail. "You don't think I'll run the place into the ground within a week?"

"No," he said with a laugh. "I think you'll kick ass. Just like always."

"I'll guess we'll see."

He reached over and threaded his fingers with mine. "Believe in yourself. Everyone else does."

My heart swelled with both affection and pride. I didn't deserve his blind faith, was barely worthy of it...and yet I was glad to have it all the same.

When we reached my building, Colt found a parking spot and turned off the engine. "I'll walk you up."

"You're not staying?" I asked, my eyebrows shooting up.

He smirked. "Not this time. I have stuff to do, and so do you."

"I bet I could change your mind." I grabbed his chin and planted my mouth over his, claiming him in a sudden, hot kiss.

"You, woman, are a hellion," Colt said when I released him. "And I have no doubt that you could change my mind."

A laugh rose in my throat. "Come on, I'll behave myself."

Colt muttered something that I didn't catch and I got the distinct impression that I had the ability to affect him even more than I knew.

We took our time heading up to my apartment, strolling up the stairs like we had all the time in the world. At my door, I leaned against the doorframe, arching my back and staring up into Colt's expressive icy blue eyes that stripped me bare and left me so vulnerable...and so protected.

Something in his gaze relented.

This thread, this pull we felt to each other — neither of us could fight it any longer, wanted to deny it any longer. And whatever plans Colt had for the rest of the day, I had the impression that he'd just thrown them right out of the window.

"Okay," he said, his low voice rough and gravelly, so much so that it sent shivers down my spine. "I'll stay."

A smile pulled at my lips. I hooked my fingers into his belt and drew him closer. "For how long?"

Colt swallowed. He dipped his head and pressed his forehead to mine. "As long as you'll have me."

Forever, I almost whispered. I wanted to keep Colt forever. I wanted him in my home, in my bed, in my heart...forever.

The words pooled on my tongue, itching to be spoken aloud, to light up the world with their sounds. But I swallowed them, holding them back. We'd only spent one night together — hadn't even decided if this thing between us had a name. I couldn't very well start sharing the secrets of my heart, even though it about killed me not to.

I bit my lip and turned around, fussing with my keys.

Colt brushed my hair from my shoulder and kissed my throat.

A sigh left me and all I wanted to do was melt into his touch.

One minute, I told myself. One minute and we'd be inside and I could do whatever the hell I wanted with Colt, and not have to worry about giving one of my neighbors a free show.

I got the door unlocked and we stumbled inside. I laughed and spun around to press myself against him like a second skin.

The predatory smile on Colt's face faltered as he looked at something over my shoulder.

I turned, my own smile falling completely off my face.

Because there, beside my old orange couch, stood my grandmother, her face pinched, the lines of her mouth set in familiar disappointment and irritation.

"What—?" I started. I cleared my throat and took a step away from Colt. "What are you doing in here?"

"I have a key. Or don't you remember?"

Of course I remembered. I remembered with perfect clarity the day she'd claimed my spare key, the one I'd had laid out on the kitchen counter to give to one of my friends for safe keeping. But she had never used it.

Until now.

Her cool, calculating eyes slid to Colt. "I don't believe we've met."

"No, we haven't." There was no tension or apprehension in Colt's tone. I couldn't tell if it was because he was as relaxed as he seemed about meeting my grandmother, or if his police training had kicked in to neutralize a threat. Colt stepped around me and extended his hand to my grandmother. "I'm Colton Deluca, ma'am. It's a pleasure to meet you."

I cringed at his use of ma'am, and, sure enough, my grandmother's mouth tightened almost imperceptibly. There was nothing she loathed more than being addressed as ma'am.

She looked down at Colt's outstretched hand and took the barest of steps back, as though seeing some dirt or germs the rest of us couldn't. She flicked her gaze to me and

285

I could see the questions there. The demand for answers.

"Colt is my...Colt's my...friend. He's a police detective. He helped me a few months ago when I got into some trouble."

My grandmother folded her arms across her chest. "And what trouble might that be? Why is this the first I'm hearing about it?"

My heart thudded. I should have stopped after detective.

"It wasn't her fault, ma'am. She was the victim of a mugging, and she was left alone by her date."

"And if she hadn't been roaming the streets at all hours like a glorified prostitute, then it wouldn't have happened."

Her words hit me right between the eyes. She'd never missed her target, not once in my entire life. She went for the kill shot every time.

Of course Grandmother dearest wouldn't feel bad for her only grandchild being the victim of a mugging. Of course she saw it as my fault for daring to have a life.

But if I was married with children then I would have been home. Not roaming the streets like a glorified prostitute.

"Well, I don't think she's in danger of *me* mugging her. So your services won't be required while I talk to my granddaughter." She didn't even look at Colt as she dismissed him as though he was nothing more than an annoyance she'd been forced to deal with.

Colt turned to me, his face an unreadable mask.

I opened my mouth but no words would come. My stomach bottomed out. Colt... I knew he was waiting for me to stand up to my grandmother, to tell her that he was important to me, that he wasn't someone to dismiss.

But no words would come.

Something settled on his face then, some base understanding that cleaved my heart in two.

"Then I guess I'll be going." There was a hardness in his tone that I'd never heard before. Colt wore what I assumed was his cop face, the mask he donned when he didn't want to give any hint of what was racing through his mind while interrogating suspects.

And I'd put it there.

He strode past me, taking care that no part of us touched. The door didn't slam. Instead, Colt closed it carefully, softly.

I would have rather he'd slammed it. An argument, even a future one, meant we had something to talk about. Something to fight about.

Instead, his departure felt like goodbye.

After everything that had happened with us over the last week — my thoughtless breakup, the hurtful things I'd said, and now my inability to claim him, it was little wonder he'd left. Little wonder he'd left *me*.

I stared at my grandmother. Searched her face for... something. Anything. "Why did you do that?" I whispered.

She frowned. "Do what?"

"Colt is a good man. Why did you treat him like that?"

"He is a city cop. I'm sure he's got a thick skin."

"That's not the point—" Why was I standing here defending him, when I hadn't a moment ago? I had let Colt leave... What in the hell was wrong with me?

I turned on my heel and rushed out of the apartment. There was no sign of Colt in the hallway, so I sprinted down the stairs. "Colt!" I bellowed, my voice reverberating in the stairwell.

Footsteps below me paused, before continuing.

I hurried as fast as I could, almost breaking my neck as I jumped a few.

Then he was there, his wide shoulders hunched. Not stopping, even though he had to have heard me.

"Colt," I said, barely above a whisper.

Colt's spine straightened as though I'd run him through with a cattle prod.

When he didn't stop, I grabbed the sleeves of his jacket. "Please—"

"I have to go, Hayley."

Hayley. Not St. Clair. "No, please, let me explain—"

Colt slowly turned to face me. "There isn't anything left to explain. I get what you've been trying to tell me all this time. I just saw it firsthand." He shook his head. "I'm not putting myself through this anymore. It took a long time to convince you that I was good enough. But she will remind you that I'm not every time you see her. I'm sorry. I'm not sticking around for the day you believe her again."

My throat seized up and a fierce pain stabbed my heart. But how could I deny what he'd said when it was more truthful than anything I'd heard in my life?

"That's what I thought," he said quietly. Colt hesitated for a moment, then he pressed a soft kiss to my cheek. "Goodbye."

* * * *

My grandmother still stood in the same spot when I returned to the apartment. That word, that *goodbye*, had echoed in my head the whole way back up the stairs. After all the fights, after all the denial, it was done. Colt was done with me.

I couldn't blame him. I'd pushed him away for so long, told him often enough that he wasn't my type. Now he finally believed me. Now he knew all those awful things he thought about me were really, completely true.

Her face didn't move, though the demand for an explanation poured out of her gaze.

It was though I'd been hollowed out. The usual tension, the gut-gnawing unease that spread through me in the presence of my grandmother was absent. The aching loss of Colt didn't press down on me, didn't threaten to tip me over the edge. Instead I felt...nothing.

"I would like you to leave now," I said, my voice as empty and devoid of emotion as the rest of me.

And finally, that icy exterior cracked. My grandmother adjusted her stance, a frown deepening on her forehead. "I beg your pardon?"

"This is my home and I will no longer tolerate you inside it."

"Hayley, I have no idea what has gotten into you, but you had better lose this—"

"No, you don't get to tell me what to do anymore," I said, cutting her off. I had never, not in my whole entire life, interrupted her. "I'm sick of not being good enough, of turning myself into someone that I'm not just to please you. I won't let you push me around or dictate who I should spend the rest of my life with. So yeah, we're done here."

Grandmother straightened her spine and took a step toward me. "You had better remember who you are talking to. Who paid for this home in the first place?"

"And there it is—the money threat. My parents. *That's* who paid for this home. Why do you think I wouldn't let you force me into a Park Avenue prison? Because it would be *yours*. This is my home. Mine. I own every inch of it, and everything in it. You want to cut me off? Write me out of your will? Go right ahead. I don't need you. In fact, I'd go so far as to say I'd be better off without you."

She stared me down.

I stared right back.

No longer afraid, no longer willing to be oppressed anymore.

She cleared her throat and moved past me to the door. "I can only assume after ending the dalliance with that cop that you aren't thinking clearly. I'll expect your apology once you have calmed down."

I bit my tongue as she slipped out of the apartment. Anything else I said would just be cruel and vicious. Not that she didn't necessarily deserve it, but I wasn't that girl. I wasn't someone who hurt another person just because they hurt me first.

For a full minute, I didn't move a muscle.

The air seemed to vibrate around me, a quiet hum that rose in volume with each passing second.

I'd wanted her out of my apartment, but now that I was

alone, everything threatened to collapse on top of me. If Marley had still lived in the city, I'd have gone straight to her.

Instead I went to the next place that felt like home.

Chapter Twenty

Fiona had dressed a mannequin in a gorgeous blue shift dress and pea-green military coat. She herself was a stark contrast to the stylish mannequin. She wore orange tights, a yellow dress and a red furry cardigan.

"You look like a sunset," I mused as I closed the door behind me.

"Well, you know—" Fiona paused when she turned and saw me. "Sweetheart, what happened?"

And just like that, my world fell apart.

I told her everything—*everything*.

My promise to my parents. My denial of Colt. The subsequent arguments, the makeups and the last, final break. The separation from my grandparents, which, unless they learned to accept me, would be a permanent one.

Fiona had locked the store the moment after she'd asked me what happened. I'd then followed her into the back where she'd busted open a bottle of tequila she'd had stashed inside a shoebox.

"What?" she'd asked at my questioning look. "It makes the accounting more tolerable."

She'd listened to every word I'd said, never once interrupting me. Her face had remained open, despite the horrors that had come out of my mouth.

The Hayley she knew was vastly different from the one that other people did. To her, I was the clothes-obsessed party girl. To my grandparents, I was the poor replacement for their daughter who, despite their best efforts, couldn't be molded into what they wanted. And to Colt...to Colt I was the narcissistic, selfish little rich bitch who didn't have a smidgen of integrity in her whole entire body.

And yet there was no judgment, no disappointment in her face.

When I finished, I threw back the rest of my tequila and wiped my mouth with the back of my hand.

"Another?" Fiona asked, already pouring more of the amber liquid into my glass.

"Don't you have anything you want to say?" I asked her, sipping the drink in a more dignified manner than the party girl-esque way I'd just displayed.

"What would you like me to say?" she asked.

I shrugged. "Whatever you're thinking. How I'm a worthless idiot who threw away the one good man I've ever met. How I'm a disappointment to my parents. How you wouldn't trust me with your store if I was the last person on the planet."

"Well, if you were the last person on the planet, then there wouldn't be much call for a clothing store. But it would make a lovely closet for you."

Despite my low mood, a laugh bubbled out of me.

"But I don't want to say any of those things. Because I don't think a single one of them." Fiona placed her glass down and took mine from my grasp. She covered my hands with hers and leaned forward, meeting my gaze with startling intensity. "I want you to listen to me very carefully. Okay?"

I nodded, something trembling inside my body.

"You are not worthless, Hayley St. Clair. You have the biggest heart of anyone I've ever met. You've spent all this time trying to uphold a promise made to your parents, but oh, darling, it would kill them to think you were jeopardizing your happiness to fulfill it."

"Marry a man who will treat you like a princess, baby. Marry a man who will give you the world." I echoed the words my daddy had told me a thousand times. "That should make me happy, shouldn't it?"

"Have you ever wondered what he meant by that? Marry

a man who will treat you like a princess? Does it mean that he wanted you to have a man who would shower you with gifts, set you up in a castle-like house and make sure you never had to work a day in your life?" Fiona asked. Her expression hardened, though not from anger. From trying to get through to me. "In every corny movie, in every Disney musical, the princesses all have a man willing to stand by their side and do whatever they had to, to make them happy. Being treated like a princess has nothing to do with money. And everything to do with giving you the world."

"I'm such an idiot," I whispered for fear of my voice breaking. How had I gotten it so wrong all these years?

"I think your daddy would have wanted you to marry a man just like Colt. Because he is a man who will give you everything you really need. He is a man who will protect and treasure you, just like a princess." Fiona's eyes misted and she squeezed my hands. "And as for your grandparents, if they can't see how extraordinary you are, then it's their loss. And I'm so damn proud of you for telling that awful woman off."

I flung my arms around her then, and cried and cried. I burrowed my face into that hideous cardigan and cried for Colt. Cried for my parents and cried for everything I had lost.

"He'll never forgive me. I think I broke something that can't be fixed."

"Nothing is unfixable." Fiona stroked her hand down my hair and I melted into her touch.

"This might be," I whispered. "I should have claimed him in front of my grandmother. Should have told her what he meant to me, consequences be damned."

"You're human, Hayley. You're allowed to screw up every once in a while. You have two choices here—you can go to that boy and make him listen to what you have to say. Or you can walk away. You've nothing to lose in walking— from the sounds of it, he was pretty final with you. So now, it's up to you. What are you going to do?"

It sounded so easy.

To walk away.

I wouldn't even be the one doing the walking—Colt had already done that. With a hefty shove from me, of course. I would just be…keeping away. I could leave him in peace, not torment him any further, and I would move on from all this. Forge my path from here on out. Hold my head up high for once with my decisions. Keep being firm with my grandparents, do Fiona proud with the store. And I knew what to really look for when a man came along who—

Oh, who the hell was I kidding?

Imagining a future without Colt ripped me apart from the inside out. I couldn't bear a day without him, let alone a lifetime.

He had ended things. Firmly, efficiently ended things.

But I had to make him listen to me. He had to hear what was truly in my head and in my heart.

He might not want to hear. He very well might tell me to go to hell afterward. It may not make a damn bit of difference.

I wouldn't be able to live with myself if I didn't at least try. And, I had been so wrong in assuming that Fiona believed me to be nothing more than a clothes-obsessed party girl. Maybe Colt's opinion of me wasn't as terrible as I imagined, either. Or maybe it was worse. Either way, I was about to find out.

Fiona smiled. "There's my girl. My beautiful girl with fire in her soul."

"Thank you for everything, Fi. I'd be lost without you."

"No, you wouldn't. And when you heal that heart of yours, you'll see it, too." Fiona stood and pulled me up with her. "Now go get that gorgeous man before I try my luck with him."

A startled laugh burst from me and I hugged her close once again. "I love you, you crazy old bat."

She cackled a laugh. "Watch it, or I'll find someone else

to leave my legacy to." Fiona leaned back and kissed my cheek. "Call me tomorrow. I want to hear all about it."

"I will. But, just in case, make sure you've got a truckload of chocolate stashed beside that tequila."

Fiona shook her head. "I have a good feeling about this. Now go, before I have to lock you out."

With another laugh, I darted out of the door and hunted down a cab. It was time to tell Colt the truth. Then if he still didn't want me, I could live with the fact that I had tried.

* * * *

There was just one kink in my master plan.

Colt wasn't home.

I pounded on his door for so long and hard one of his neighbors threatened to call the cops on me. The irony wasn't lost.

For about five minutes, I slumped on his stoop and felt sorry for myself. Then I remembered Colt telling me earlier in the day, before everything had gone to hell and back, that he had plans. Of course, he hadn't told me *where* he had plans. There was one place I could try. If he wasn't there, then I'd come right back here, plant my ass on this stoop and not budge until he came home.

* * * *

Jessie's house looked like a home even when I wasn't sure if I would still be welcome in it. For a moment, I just waited in front of her door, nerves biting at me. There was still time to turn around and get the hell out of there.

But I wouldn't.

I pressed the doorbell and waited as my heart threatened to go into cardiac arrest.

A few moments later, someone flung the door open and Tess stood on the threshold. Colt's sister was every bit as good looking as her older brother. Dark blonde hair tumbled past her shoulders and blue eyes a shade darker than Colt's peered at me.

She broke into a wide smile and stepped aside, motioning for me to go into the house. "Thank God you're here. He's been in a pissy mood since he got here."

Noise filtered into the hallway, the collective sound of a lot of voices all trying to be heard. A child shrieked, followed by infectious giggles that I would know anywhere.

"Just to warn you—Uncle Sal told Colt he wanted a birthday kiss from you. He sort of snarled. Like an animal, can you believe it?" Tess laughed and headed down the hall to the family room.

"Wait—" I called after her. "Is there...? Who's all here?"

"Oh." Tess frowned. "All of us, I guess. My brother is home on leave and Sara's here with her family, too. And Susan and Kent."

"Full house, then," I murmured.

Tess chuckled. "Yup. Come on, maybe now my big brother will actually crack a smile."

Oh, I wouldn't bet on it, kid.

Well, I'd found him, at least.

It just sucked that now I had to do this in front of his entire family.

Woohoo.

Tess, a few steps ahead of me, stepped into the family room.

"Who was at the door?" Jessie asked.

I turned into the room and squared my shoulders, forcing my spine to remain iron-straight. I would not slink in like a coward. I was a fierce warrior. I was a woman, dammit. Hear me roar.

The room was packed. Like, *packed*. Grandpa Joe and Uncle Sal were in their usual chairs, a card table between them. Sophie, Jessie and Faith were crowded around it, all holding a hand of cards.

A woman I didn't recognize, but knew she had to be Sara just because of that shade of blonde, sat on the floor with her back against the couch, three little boys sprawled across her as they stared at the movie playing quietly on the TV.

The man behind Sara on the couch toyed with her hair, almost absentmindedly, as he stared at the movie he had probably already seen a hundred times.

Tess plopped down in the middle of the couch, between Sara's husband and a man who had to be the eldest of the Deluca siblings — Josh. Even if his military cropped hair didn't give him away, the tense lines of his handsome face would have.

And the man I'd come to see — the only man who had ever truly taken my heart — was leaning his shoulder against the wall by the front window. He stared out onto the street and had most likely seen me arrive and pause for a few moments on the stoop.

Oh yeah, he'd totally seen me...and made me walk into this anyway.

I couldn't decide if that was a good thing or not.

"Hi," I said, my voice timid and not at all the warrior tone I'd been going for.

All eyes — almost — swung toward me and I fidgeted with my hands.

"Hey, beautiful girl!" Uncle Sal cried. "Get over here and give me my birthday kiss!"

Sophie groaned and rolled her eyes, while Jessie smacked his arm.

"Hey, that's called abusing the elderly," Uncle Sal protested as he rubbed the spot.

"Hi, honey." Jessie rose to her feet. "Can I get you anything? The food isn't quite done, but we'll be sitting down soon."

"No, thank you," I said.

And still he wouldn't look at me.

Faith slammed her cards on the table and hopped up and down with barely contained excitement. "Snap! I win again!"

"Surprise," Sophie mumbled as she tossed her cards onto the table and fished her phone out of her jeans pocket.

Faith scrambled out of her chair and rushed over to me, throwing her arms around my waist. "I lost my tooth— see?" She gave me a wide grin, and sure enough, one of her bottom teeth was missing.

"Nice. I hope the tooth fairy left you something good," I said. A lump formed in my throat. What if this was the last time I would ever see this girl? What if, after I spilled my guts to Colt, he still didn't want me?

Faith nodded. "Two quarters. Pretty neat, huh?"

"Totally. She only ever used to leave me pennies."

She giggled. "That's because you're super old."

I pretended to huff, and ruffled her hair for the insolence.

"Come play with me—I'm playing cards with Grandpa Joe and Uncle Sal, but Uncle Sal says I'm just hustling them." Faith released her hold on my waist and tugged on my hand.

"I need to talk to your daddy first, okay?" I ran my hand over her hair.

Faith peered up at me with those huge blue eyes of hers. "And then you'll play?"

"If there's time." I crouched down and tapped her nose. "You're an excellent manipulator. Did anyone ever tell you that?"

She giggled. "Daddy, all the time."

"I can see why," I murmured.

"I'm happy to see you." Faith stepped forward and wrapped her thin arms around my neck, holding on as though I was precious to her.

I held her back just as fiercely, knowing full well I could walk out of here and never see her again.

When she pulled back and skipped over to the card table, I rose and crossed the room to where Colt still stared out of the window. I placed my hand on his forearm and tried to ignore the way he tensed under my touch.

"Will you come talk with me, Colt? Please? Just for a minute," I said, lowering my voice so no one else could hear me. The last thing I wanted was to have this conversation in front of his entire family. But I would. If he made me, I absolutely would. I was not leaving this house until he knew.

He nodded once and strode out of the room, leaving me to follow in his wake. Everyone was quiet and hushed as they watched us, and the moment I'd cleared the family room, the murmuring began.

I wonder what they thought was happening.

My phone rang in my bag as I followed Colt all the way through the house and out of the back door. Whoever it was, it could wait. He jogged down the steps until he reached the grass that needed mowing. A few toys littered the yard — playhouses and summer toys that had faded from the sun and exposure.

Colt folded his large arms and turned to face me. His expression was unreadable. For once I had no idea what was going through his head. No clue as to how this conversation could go. He wore that same mask I'd seen before. I could only hope today would be the last day he ever had to wear it in my presence.

"I'm so sorry, Colt," I whispered, taking a step toward him.

Colt held up a hand, halting me in my tracks. "Don't. If you only came here to apologize, to try to make yourself feel better, then save it. There's no point in doing this, Hayley. What's done is done."

His words and his empty, hollow tone hit me square in the face. What if it wasn't anger that made him less than happy to see me? What if it was...pain? "You're right. What's done is done." I ignored the thump of my heart, the racing of my pulse. "I can't change what happened. I won't insult you by asking you to forget about it. But I can tell you that nothing like that will ever happen ever again."

Colt sighed. He turned away from me and rubbed the back of his neck. "What do you want from me here, Hayley?"

"I want you to believe me." My voice broke. "I want you to look at me and see that I have never been more honest in my life than right now. I'm done trying to be someone that I'm not. I'm done trying to please people who don't know how to love the real me."

"This doesn't change anything." Colt's said, his voice ragged, as though I was hurting him more when all I wanted was to make it better.

"I'm sorry, I'm not trying to upset you. But that's all I seem capable of doing." The first tear slipped down my cheek. I swiped it away, not wanting him to see me cry. Not because I was afraid of appearing vulnerable, but because I didn't want him to think it was a pathetic female trick. "When I got back upstairs, I threw her out, Colt. I told her to get out—out of my apartment and out of my life. All these years I've held on to the scrap of family that I had left, but it's not worth it anymore. Trying to keep the pieces of my parents has made me lose the one thing I've cared about as much as them. I can't lose you, Colt. I can't."

He turned then, his face just as agonized as I felt. "I want to tell you it's okay, but it's not. Too much has happened now. And call me a romantic idiot, but I want someone who would shout it to the world that she's with me—that I belong to her. I can't be with someone who would rather hide me away."

Denying Colt had cut him even deeper than I had realized. I tried to imagine how it would have felt if the roles were reversed. If, when meeting his family, Colt had tried to pass me off as no one.

I took a step closer, and when he didn't move or push me away, I took another and another until I was right in front of him. Placing my hands on his shoulders, I pushed up onto my tiptoes and pressed my lips to his ear. "You belong to me."

When I pulled away, Colt's eyebrows had drawn together in confusion.

"I don't need to shout it, because you are my world. *You* are my whole world, Colt. I don't care if no one else knows it, so long as you do. If you want me to, I'll write it in lights on a billboard in Times Square. But you're the only one I need to believe it. No one else matters except for you and me. I swear to you, that I will never, *ever*, deny you again like I did today. My grandparents are out of my life, but if they decide to try to reenter it, they will do so on the understanding that we're a package deal. If they don't like it then they can kiss my ass."

I sucked in a deep breath. "For years, all I've wanted is someone who would treat me like a princess. I never knew how wrong I had it until I met you. My dream of a white picket fence in the suburbs has been replaced by a brownstone in Brooklyn. You make me want to lock the door to your home and never, ever leave. And I didn't just fall in love with you, Colt. I've fallen in love with all of you."

I gestured to the house behind me, and all the love and warmth it held. "I love your mom's place, the madness inside and your insane, loud family. And, oh my God, Colt, I love your crazy, strong-willed daughter. I want her to have a dozen brothers and sisters, and watch her corral them and trick them into doing her bidding."

Colt remained silent during my speech. He didn't move. My phone buzzed in my bag, but I kept on ignoring it.

Stepping to him once again, I covered his heart with my palm. "I'm so in love with you, Colt. I have been for months now. I'm not afraid anymore. I'm not afraid to tell you, to tell myself, that I'm in love with you."

His Adam's apple bobbed. "I don't know what to tell you."

So he hadn't fallen at my feet. So he hadn't swept me into his arms. So he hadn't pinned me up against the wall of his mother's house and kissed me until he robbed me of every breath.

He looked just as hurt, just as broken, as before I'd bared my soul.

Maybe he was done with me. Maybe I was too late.

"You don't have to say anything," I croaked. My eyes blurred and the tears streaked down my face. "I didn't come here expecting to change things. I hoped… I hoped I could, but I knew it was a long shot. I came so you could know that none of this was your fault. It was all me. Me and my stupid beliefs and misguided attempts to make two dead people proud. So don't you dare beat yourself up over this, Colton Deluca. You're going to meet a woman who knows exactly what she has when she's with you, and she won't be afraid to admit it."

"Hayley," he whispered, covering my hand with his.

"You knew me before I knew myself." I smiled despite my breaking heart. "Thank you for showing me that she was someone worth loving."

He opened his mouth to say something, but the buzzing of my phone pierced the silence of the yard. "Whoever it is sounds pretty insistent. You'd better answer it."

I dropped my hand from his chest and fished my phone out of my bag. Blake's name was on the caller ID, but he hung up before I could answer. A moment later, a text message from him came through.

All the blood drained from my face. "It's Marley."

Chapter Twenty-One

The halls of the hospital bustled with activity. All around me, people rushed here and there, conversations mingled, phones at the nurses' station rang. The place was so full of life and energy, but I found myself moving as though in a trance.

I stopped at the nurses' station, about to ask where to go, when someone called my name.

Seth stood down the hall, his eyes tired. He jerked his head and I followed him down the hallway. He stopped outside of a room. "They're in there."

"Is it—?" I started, a lump forming in my throat. "Can I go in?"

He nodded.

Releasing a breath, I slowly pushed open the door and stepped inside.

Blake turned at the sound, and moved to the side.

Her hair was a mess, her skin was pale and she looked exhausted. But she was as beautiful as any goddess.

For a long second, I couldn't say anything. I don't think I even drew breath. But then everything I'd been feeling for the past few hours bubbled to the surface and poured out. "You scared the shit out of me." My voice burst out of me, the tears I'd kept at bay no longer held back.

"This is the first time you're meeting my son, and *that*'s what you go with?" Marley asked, rolling her eyes. "Classy."

"Oh, shut up, you bitch," I mumbled through the torrent of tears.

Blake chuckled and came over to me, wrapping his arms

around me and squeezing me tight. "I know exactly how you feel." He pulled back and hitched his thumb to the door. "I'm going to get some coffee, leave you three alone for a few minutes."

"Get over here, you big baby," Marley said. Her own eyes filled with tears as I rushed to her. She scooted over and I climbed into bed with her, leaning my head on her shoulder.

"What happened?"

"Severe blood loss," Marley said quietly. "Everything was fine—no problem with the delivery. But then I wouldn't stop bleeding. They took me to surgery and fixed the problem. It's fine, *I'm* fine. I promise."

"When Blake texted me…I have never been more terrified in my whole life." I scrubbed my eyes and breathed in the scent of my best friend. "I thought I was going to lose you."

"You think Blake would let that happen? No way. He'd totally hunt my ghostly ass down and force it back into my body."

I laughed weakly. "That sounds like a good movie."

"Maybe with Anne Hathaway playing me?"

"Only if I get Margot Robbie."

"Deal."

"You're really okay?" I whispered.

"Thanks to three blood transfusions, a whole lot of medication and bed rest, I am." Marley sat up a little and peered out of the window to the hallway beyond. "I can't say the same for my poor brother-in-law."

"He took it hard?"

Marley nodded. "Harder than you, I think. Cassidy decided she was ready to meet her son. She and Seth have met him a few times now, and I think seeing me so fat and pregnant had Seth considering them having kids of their own in the future. Then I go and almost bleed to death… He's dealing, but it's shaken him up."

"Has Cassidy been to see you?"

"No. Just my mom and you. Mom just left to go grab a

nap. She'd been staying with us for a few weeks when I went into labor."

"Man, she must have been terrified."

"She kept it together." Marley wiped the last of my tears away. "So do you want to meet your godson, or what?"

I bolted upright. "My *what*?"

She grinned and motioned for me to go around to the tiny crib beside her bed. "Meet Austin Hamilton. Your godson, if you want the job."

"Hell yes, I want the job!" I cried, rushing to see him. He lay there, his face all pink and squished. "Aw, he has your scowl."

Marley laughed, and the sound roused him.

"Can I?" I asked, gesturing to the baby.

"Of course you can," she said softly.

I carefully lifted him and cradled him in my arms. Oh man, he was perfect. So tiny and warm and just... Okay, I totally got it when people said they want to eat babies. I perched on the edge of Marley's bed as Austin yawned and drifted back off to sleep. "He's perfect, Marley."

"Hamilton genes, I told you," she joked.

"I'm so proud of you. I really am."

She looked beyond me. I followed her gaze to where Colt stood beside Blake in the hallway, sipping the coffee Blake had just handed him. "I have a feeling there's a damn good story to all this." Marley settled back against her pillows and patted the spot beside her.

I eased myself round, and lounged beside her while still cradling Austin. And I told her everything. Every part I'd previously left out, and the most recent heartache. She snarled a little at the confrontation with my grandmother, but more or less let me talk uninterrupted.

She squeezed my hand as I told her the baring of my soul at Jessie's house, and the fear that I would walk out of there and never see any of them again. I told her how, when I got Blake's message, Colt had rushed me straight inside and got us flights to Vegas. I told her how he'd never let go of my hand the whole way here.

"You know," Marley said, squeezing my hand again. "All that matters is that you're happy. Just be happy. It doesn't matter if you're rich or broke, unemployed or successful. Just be happy. Everything else will take care of itself."

"I don't know what's going to happen when we get home. I don't know if he's here because he knows I'd crumble without him. I don't know if he's here because he wants to be. But, no matter what happens, I know who I am now. I won't apologize to anyone for it."

"Good girl." Marley smiled.

There was a knock on the door and Seth poked his head into the room. "Hey, Cass is here—can she come in, or do you guys want more time alone?"

Marley glanced at me.

"No, tell her to come on in," I said, shuffling off the bed.

The door opened wider and Cassidy came into the room carrying a huge bouquet of flowers. I hadn't brought flowers. *Why didn't I think to bring flowers?* She glanced between us, her eyes filling with tears.

Blake and Seth followed behind her. Blake relieved her of the flowers and set them by the window.

I approached Cassidy. "Do you want to hold him?"

She nodded and let out a soft laugh.

I passed the tiny bundle over to her and flashed Seth a wink. He grinned back and squeezed Cassidy's shoulder. Seth dipped to whisper something in her ear.

"Okay, I'm going to get some coffee since I raced like a bat out of hell to get here. Evil people." I smiled at Marley and dipped out of the room to give them all some space.

"How is she?" Colt asked the moment I was outside.

"She's fine. She's fine." The smile I wore slipped and Colt rushed to me just as I crumbled. Tears—of relief, of joy, of pride—all poured out of me like I was a freaking water fountain.

Colt held me tightly, tucking my face into his strong chest. I would never have made it without him. He'd been my rock, the one thing to keep me moving.

"Sorry," I said as I pulled back. "My emotions are going haywire."

"You have nothing to apologize for," he murmured.

"I'm going to grab a coffee, do you want one?"

"No, have mine. Come sit down." Colt tugged on my hand and I collapsed onto the chair beside him.

"Thank you for everything, Colt," I said after a few moments. "You stepped up."

He nodded once.

"But you don't have to stay, you know. I'm fine now. Marley is fine, Blake is fine, the baby is fine. I know you have a lot to get back home to."

"What you said, before everything went to hell," Colt said as he drummed his fingers on the arm of the chair. "Did you mean it?"

I swallowed. "I meant every single word. And I had a whole bunch more, but Marley sort of stole my thunder."

Colt turned his head to look at me. "Okay."

Okay? Okay? What in the hell did okay mean? Okay, that's great, let's go home and make a lot of babies? Or okay, that's nice, now kindly get out of my life. "Okay?"

Colt nodded again. "Okay."

I huffed out an irritated breath. "What does *okay* mean?"

"It means, okay. Let's do this."

"Let's do this?" I repeated, my eyebrows shooting up.

"Is there an echo in here?" Colt asked, amusement flickering in his pale blue eyes.

I mumbled something exceptionally unladylike.

He laughed and caught my hand. Colt pressed his mouth to the back of my hand and my heart fluttered. "I'm crazy about you, St. Clair. You know I've been in love with you since the start of this thing. So let's do it. For real this time. You and me. For as long as you want me."

My pulse raced. "Forever?"

"And whatever comes after that."

A giddy, breathy little laugh escaped me. "Okay."

Colt's lips twitched. "Okay."

"Okay."

Secrets, Lies & Imperfections

Excerpt

Chapter One

The streets teemed with people. Bodies spilled out of the bars, singing and laughing. Music pulsed in the air — different songs, different beats that couldn't be discerned unless you were in the actual bar. Promoters armed with fliers stopped people, giving away tickets for free shots and insisting their club had all the best action.

It was spring break. And I was in fucking heaven.

"So what brings you girls to Spain?" I asked no one in particular. The group of five girls had giggled and glanced in my direction for so long I took pity on them and invited myself to join them — bringing a cocktail jug with me.

"We're on holiday from uni," the brunette of the group answered. She rested her elbow on the table and pushed her tits so far out I was surprised they didn't burst free from her shirt. "We just got here."

These Brit girls were my favorite kind of tourists—beautiful, flirty and clearly out for a good time. I placed a hand over my heart. "And the first thing you did was come see me? Aw, I'm touched, girls—really."

Cue collective giggling.

First-nighters fell into one of two categories—the *'play it safe, it's only the first night and I don't even know this guy'* and the *'fucking-A I'm on vacation, bring on the cocks and cocktails, what happens in Spain, stays in Spain'*. The brunette was definitely in the fucking-A category...maybe her red-headed friend too.

She smiled as she lifted her cocktail glass, her eyes full of promise. "Well, we heard a good-looking Yank was chatting up all the girls, so we didn't want to feel left out."

Oh yeah, the redhead was definitely down.

An ice cube smacked off the back of my head, making me start. Scooping a handful of ice cubes out of the cocktail jug, I turned around and threw them back at Jesse behind the bar.

He ducked before they hit him and flipped me off. "Come on, Seth. We're busy, in case you hadn't noticed!"

"Hey, I'm making new friends over here!" I called back with a grin.

A chorus of giggles broke out around me.

"He finishes at two, ladies!" Jesse shouted before giving me a pointed look. Usually we were good with covering for each other while in pursuit of a new lay...but yeah, the crowd was thickening around the bar, and if the owner caught me slacking off, I'd be looking for a new job. And this was one sweet gig.

Vardis was one of many bars along the main drag in the tourist town. Decent in size, it pulled in the crowds. I'd worked for the owner there last summer and when I'd returned last month, he'd hired me back as manager, along with Jesse. It wasn't often we were front of house like this, but two bartenders were out—with those dreaded hangovers that seemed to be catching—and being spring break, it was crazy busy.

So there I was, playing the part of a loveable American rake, charming and memorable, but never permanent. And man, did the girls just love the part I played.

The brunette threw her arm around the redhead's shoulders and pressed their heads together, sending a silent, but very well-heard message. "You'll have forgotten about us by then."

"Sweetheart, you ladies are anything but forgettable," I said with a wink as I rose out of my seat. "Enjoy the drinks — and welcome to Spain."

The group of girls stayed for another hour but the bar was too slammed for me to get away again. They filed out of the door, my two sure things bringing up the rear. They waggled their fingers in my direction and I would swear down dead that I'd be seeing them again before the night was over.

"Your dick's going to fall off if you keep this up," Jesse said, shaking his head. "I can't decide if I should be concerned or impressed."

"Hey, I have a lot of love to give," I said as though offended.

Jesse barked a laugh and reached for a fresh glass to mix the drink ordered by his customer. "Yeah, well, some of them might have a lot of the clap to give."

I grinned and shook my head. "I have no idea what that is."

He snorted his derision and slid the drink toward the customer. "Trust me. If you get it, you'll know about it."

"I might like to be generous with myself but I'm not stupid. No glove, no love, my brother. No glove, no love." I winked at the girl waiting at the bar who was taking a keen interest in our conversation. "Isn't that right, gorgeous? You practice safe sex, don't you?"

"Of course," she purred, lifting her glass to her lips. "I like to get in as much practice as possible."

I held a hand out to her as I looked at Jesse. "You see?

We're all safe around here."

Jesse lifted his eyes to the ceiling. "Yes, yes, what perfectly respectable sex fiends you all are."

When my shift finished, I felt like an ass for leaving Jesse. There were ten other members of staff, but he and I both knew we were faster and more efficient and drew in the serious tips. But when the two girls from earlier showed up at the end of the bar, he knew I wasn't going to stay to help him out.

* * * *

I was nestled in a warm cocoon of flesh when a persistently ringing phone rudely awakened me. Rolling over, I face-planted on a boob. We were a tangle of limbs and body parts, and extracting myself took more effort than I had, especially after an all-night threesome with two girls who tried to outdo each other.

Talk about exhausting.

I spanked a butt to get her to move and eventually I disentangled myself from the human knot. I found my phone in my jeans where I'd ditched them the night before. Glancing at my watch, I saw it was only eight a.m. I guessed I'd had around two hours sleep.

The name on the phone display had me groaning for very different reasons. Throwing my head back, I summoned up the energy to answer. "Hey, Dad, what's happening?"

"Seth. You sound cheerier than I expected." Dad betrayed nothing in his tone as to what he might want—or why he felt it necessary to wake his darling child when he no doubt suspected I'd only just made it to bed.

"Well, that's probably because I'm still drunk." Anthony Hamilton was an intimidating man to many. To me, he was the guy I knew how to antagonize like no other.

He didn't rise to my bait. "Make sure you sober up before checking your bank account. I wouldn't want you to forget, or think you were so drunk you hadn't read the figure right."

Whatever cocky retort I'd been about to reply with, died on my tongue. "What are you talking about?"

"I'm done bankrolling your excuse to fornicate around Europe. There's enough left to get a plane ticket home—which I expect you to purchase today."

Ah, hell. Dad had made this same threat for months. But now...he actually sounded serious. "Sure thing, Dad. I'll see you in a few." What he kept forgetting was I was his son. I knew my way out of a bind.

"You should also know I've canceled all your credit cards."

Crafty old bastard.

The second he hung up, I logged on to my online bank account and there was indeed enough for a plane ticket, and a quick check of flight prices confirmed my guess. He'd left enough for first class.

So for the next two weeks I lived off meager funds, crashed with friends and enjoyed all the delights Spain had to offer before boarding my economy-class flight back to my shackles.

* * * *

Full dark had just settled across the sky as the plane landed, which meant I got picture-perfect views of the illuminated city as we began the descent. The second I stepped off the plane it was as if I'd never left. It'd been two years since I'd left her, but Vegas was still as bold and flashy as I remembered.

Slinging my battered canvas backpack over my shoulder and hauling an overstuffed gym bag behind me, I headed outside to find a cab. The line was huge. If I really wanted to, I could call Dad and have him send a car or—yeah, right—pick me up himself. But the thought of heading to his McMansion any sooner than I had to was not an appealing idea.

Pulling my phone out of my pocket, I scrolled through the contacts, searching for my brother. Instead I got sidetracked when my friend Hank's number popped up. The bum had to be partying somewhere. Always was...and some things never changed.

I dialed his number and rocked back on my heels as I waited for him to answer.

"Hey, Hamilton! How's it going?" Hank asked as he answered, a blast of music coming through the phone.

"Good, man, good. What are you up to?" I asked, smiling.

"I'm down at the Treasure Chest with Jimmy for Mike's birthday. It's fucking good here tonight, Hamilton. It's a damn shame you aren't here!" Hank shouted over the music.

I laughed and thought for a second about how he had worded his sentence. "You're at a strip club for Mike's birthday, but Mike's not there? What an asshole."

"It's old news, Hamilton. Mike is as whipped as they come now. But we still love the guy, so we're celebrating whether he's here or not," Hank said. He had always been considerate like that. "We went to OG's for your birthday."

"How sweet. Get me a drink. I'm on my way," I said, finally next in line for a cab.

"Are you shitting me? You in town?"

A new cab pulled up and the driver got out to put my bag in the trunk. I threw my backpack across the back seat and climbed in. "And on my way."

More books from
Pamela L. Todd

Book one in the Beautiful Sinners series

All she wanted was one night. One night to feel something.
She would never see him again. No one had to know.

The world is at war, but can their love survive?

No one sees her.
No one knows her.
Until him.

Now You See Me

PAMELA
L. TODD

Part of the What's Her Secret? collection

Invisible. A ghost. No one sees her. No one knows her.
Until him.

About the Author

Pamela L. Todd

Armed with scraps of paper and a lot of tape, I sat down to create my first work of fiction aged six. Since then I have been honing my skill and have moved on to computers and have found them to be a lot less sticky.

A voracious reader, I devour as many books a year as I can get my hands on and when I'm not falling head first into other worlds, I am creating my own.

As well as erotic fiction, I also write Young Adult and historical romances.

I live in Scotland with my husband and two children. We also share our home with a bonkers cat who makes life interesting at the very least.

Pamela L. Todd loves to hear from readers. You can find contact information, website details and an author profile page at https://www.totallybound.com/

TOTALLY
BOUND

Home of Erotic Romance